COMET DIS'ASTER

COMET DIS'ASTER

(Latin, *"Dis,"* Evil. Greek, *"Astron,"* Star)

A Novel by L. Eduardo Vega

REGENT PRESS
2000

IV   L . E . V E G A

DEDICATION

To my family, Pat, Eddy, Maria, Jennifer and Becky

ACKNOWLEDGMENTS

The cover illustration is by Ignacio Cisneros; the others are by Patrick Ziercker, Ruben Moreno, Patrick Bowers and Jerry Rockwell (Skidd), all from Tucson, Arizona, and to whom I am most grateful. My special thanks go to my wife, Patricia, Jerry Grace and Richard West, who assisted in research. For copy editing, I thank Kathyrn Lance, Kenneth White and my children, Eddy and Jenny Vega. Finally, I offer my thanks to Pat Phillips, Marlen Jimerson, Ruth Flanagan and Hadith Harper for transcription of the manuscript.

L. E. Vega

TABLE OF CONTENTS

FOREWORD

by David H. Levy

As a pathologist, Dr. Ed Vega has spent his professional career confronting the stark evidence of illness and passing. As an amateur astronomer, he has spent many years observing the night sky through his several telescopes, appreciating its ethereal beauty and significance, and gathering a great deal of knowledge about cosmic impacts. In this book, Vega combines his two loves to produce a riveting story about an episode that, we hope, will never again take place on Earth.

Never AGAIN -- yes, because some scientists believe that an episode like the one Dr. Vega builds at the start of his tale actually took place in our solar system some 3.9 billion years ago. It's a period called the "Late Heavy Bombardment". It might have been triggered when a rogue planet entered the solar system, broke apart by passing close to one of the larger planets, and sent its debris hurtling into all the inner planets. Many craters we see on the moon, including the great plains that form the face of the Man in the Moon, come from that terrible era in which the Moon and inner planets got their stuffing knocked out. Although the Earth was hit many times since, including the great impact of a 10 mile wide comet or asteroid that destroyed the dinosaurs 65 million years ago, those events don't match the incredible destruction the Earth must have seen in that primordial era.

In Vega's remarkable book, a similar threat faces Earth, and the author brings his experience and knowledge to bear as he weaves his most intriguing story of the trauma Earth would face if such an episode were to occur again. The tale is riveting. Since Gene and Carolyn

Shoemaker and I discovered a comet that collided with Jupiter in 1994, we have understood that the people of Earth are, in a sense, living on borrowed time. We often spent evenings in the dome, waiting for the sky to clear, wondering what would happen if a comet like Shoemaker-Levy 9 were to strike the Earth. Vega's story ups the ante: what if the Earth were to be struck by virtually everything the solar system had to toss at it?

Read this book on cloudy nights, and save the clear nights to share its author's passion of observing the sky. Between the book and the night, you're in for quite an experience.

PROPHECY

PROPHECY OF MAASAW, THE HOPI GOD OF DEATH

"Near the day of purification, there will be cobwebs spun back and forth against the sky... The stars will fall down on the ocean,... The Being who gave us breath will hurl from the sky his container of ashes... It will burn the land and boil the oceans,... Our hair and our clothing will be scattered over the Earth,... Nature will cry out with a mighty breath of wind,... The waters will be set on fire,... The conflagration will consume everything,... Then there will be earthquakes, floods and changes in the seasons,... The sun won't be as hot anymore,... snow will fall at the planting season and all the grasses across the land will not grow,... The animals will suffer great hardships,... The plants and everything will freeze,... Then you will come to a time of great famine. Even though only one jar of ashes will be dropped, it will kill us all."

The boundaries of the Hopi's present land reservation are situated only 31 miles from Arizona's Great Meteor Crater. Did the ancestors of the Hopi suffer the horrors of a comet impact? Could this prophecy refer to a comet shower ("cobwebs in the sky") and the disastrous effects of a great comet or asteroid impact?

INTRODUCTION

As you are reading this, the days of the planet Earth and its peoples are numbered, for history must repeat itself.

One hundred million years ago, the Earth was a bountiful planet full of amazing varieties of animals and plants. They filled every ecological niche of the globe. Amongst them, the mighty dinosaurs stood out as the zenith of evolution.

The varied animals and plants of the time were no freaks of nature. Evolution had taken over two billion years to reach this impressive culmination. Dinosaurs are the most successful large-bodied animals in the entire bio-history of the planet. They reigned undisputed for 140 million years. The era of mammals, now only 55 million years old, and the era of humans, a mere 100,000 years, are minor chapters in the history of our bio-system when compared to the biological accomplishments of prior eras.

But the dinosaurs all disappeared suddenly and forever 65 million years ago. They simply vanished. Just as suddenly, 75% of all animal and plant species living at the time also became extinct.

Studying the history frozen in rocks, scientists have discovered that many other sudden major extinctions occurred during the life of our planet. Many present-day scholars argue convincingly that the cataclysms that account for these extinctions occur every few million years, and are due to collisions between the Earth and pieces of rock, metal and ice from outer space — asteroids and comets (planetesimals) smashing into our fragile planet. These scientists also insist that it must happen again. In fact, it could happen in the next few days, months or years. And when it does, the chances of another mass extinction are inevitable. Planetesimals travel at immense speed, on average 65,000 miles per hour, some even faster. Some are quite large, the size of whole mountains. (Comet Halley's solid core is seven miles in diameter). An impact between such a cosmic interloper and our planet would result in an explosion that releases millions upon millions of megatons of fiery energy, like a million nuclear warheads detonating all at the same instant and place. The results would be unimaginably destructive.

Such a massive explosion would be followed by a superheated shock wave that rushes outward and incinerates everything it touches for hundreds or thousands of miles around the point of impact. The searing, white-hot debris flung above the atmosphere by the impact would circulate over the entire planet and then plunge back down as brimstone, setting everything everywhere on fire and scouring the surface of the globe. The Earth would quiver as massive earthquakes add their destructive forces. The coastal areas of the globe would be wiped clean with monstrous tsunami waves, each a few miles high and reaching far into the coastal lands of all continents.

A similar catastrophe could be produced by a nuclear war. A nuclear holocaust would also mortally wound the Earth with hundreds, maybe thousands of nuclear explosions, each detonation releasing massive amounts of deadly energy. There would be no large tsunamis and no earthquakes, but the deliberate detonation of such bombs over areas of high population density and the radiation that followed would also effect massive extinction of life on the planet.

In both scenarios, the real death blow would come through the release of billions of tons of black dust, dirt and ash into the atmosphere — from the direct effects of the explosions, and also from the fires of cities, grasslands and forests that would inevitably follow. The skies would be darkened in a long, continuous night that could last many months, even years. The subsequent long winter, nuclear winter in one case, meteoritic winter in the other, would crush the little remaining life out of the Earth. During such a winter, massive snowfalls would layer tons upon tons of ice over almost every acre of land. Not even the tropics would be spared. The transfer into ice of this unimaginable amount of water would decrease sea levels by 100 or more feet, transforming the shape of our continents and creating havoc with weather patterns. The Earth, once blue and vibrant with life, would become black and cold as death. Evolution would be thrown back 300 million years. New species arising from those few organisms not totally wiped out — cockroaches, worms, rats — would take millions of years to repopulate the planet's continents and seas.

Nuclear war is preventable. But the geological record indicates massive extinctions every few million years, each time Earth is impacted by a large comet or asteroid. With each episode, the planet loses 5% to 85% of its animal and plant species.

Massive comet impacts are more prone to occur whenever our solar system is flooded by large numbers of comets. Some scientists suggest that these comet showers occur on a regular basis, every 26 million years or so. It has been many millions of years since the last massive extinction. In all likelihood, our heavens will once again be filled with thousands of comets criss-crossing the skies. The Hopi Indian prophecies will then have come true. Like a cobweb spun back and forth across the sky, the seemingly beautiful spectacle will be a harbinger of destruction.

This unpalatable reality is inescapable. It *shall* happen again. Will our generation witness this disaster? Will it happen this decade, in a few hundred years — or not for a few thousand or a few million? What can we do to prepare for the next impact? Will humans become extinct under the unavoidable devastation of such a calamity, or will our cunning and will to survive save us against these overwhelming odds?

CHAPTER 1

COMET DISCOVERY
2040 A.D.

It was with innocent joy that astronomers stationed on the moon had discovered what they thought was a new planet or a very small star orbiting our sun, billions of miles beyond the orbits of Neptune and Pluto. They would never have guessed that the year of their discovery, 2040 A.D., would herald the beginning of a new era in world history.

The word spread quickly through the scientific community. Was this the famous and elusive Planet X, finally discovered after a hundred years of search? Or was this "Nemesis," the long-searched-for companion star to our sun?

But it only took a few weeks for scientists on and around Earth to realize that this was no planet or mini star. It was a Mars-sized body of solid matter and frozen gases, not in orbit around the sun, but approaching it almost straight on. If it stayed on its present trajectory, its path would bring it moderately close to the center of our solar system. Then, the gravity of our mother star would throw it back to outer space, never to return.

* * *

As more astronomical instruments were directed to study this interloper from space, new and unexpected data was continuously being announced. Weeks and months of intense scrutiny revealed not a single solid body, but what appeared to be a group of asteroid-like aggregates in a relatively compact group. One central massive body, hundreds of miles in diameter, was surrounded by smaller bodies, gravitationally bound in a relatively stable formation. Each body was covered by thick layers of ice and frozen gases. Never had such a celestial entity been seen or even dreamed. Now it was rapidly approaching our solar system.

* * *

The subject of the televised science news forum was the new planetesimal, as the scientists called it; what everyone else called "the new comet."

One scientist stressed how shocked she and her colleagues were when they learned just a few weeks prior, that the new comet would be torn apart by the gravitational pull of Saturn, and fragment into many pieces. Spectrographic analysis had revealed a great deal of ice around the central cohesive mass of rock and metal. It would have been the most gigantic comet Earthlings had ever seen. On reaching the inner solar system, the comet's coma would have appeared to be two or three times the size of the moon. The tail trailing behind it would have extended from horizon to horizon. Initial data had shown that the large space interloper was coming toward the sun in a hyperbolic path; it would fly by the sun and be only slightly deflected by the sun's gravity. Since it would not be caught in an elliptical orbit, it would leave the solar system forever, continuing its travels through the galaxy undisturbed until it once again encountered a mighty sun. All these predictions had changed when the newer calculations showed that a close approach to Saturn would tear the structure apart. Luckily, Earth was out of the calculated orbits of the cometary fragments so there was no cause for major concern; the pieces were predicted to fly by the sun in a spectacular myriad of comets to be hurled in parabolic trajectories back into deep space, never to be seen again.

"A year from now the skies of our planet will be a spectacle," said the chief astronomer. "Many large comets will be seen at the same time as they glide in formation towards our sun. They will disappear behind it, and will again be seen a few days later as they emerge from behind our mighty Sol. During this last appearance, the entourage of comets will brighten for a few weeks. They will then slowly dim as they leave the inner solar system."

It was at this moment that a young man approached the senior scientist and inexplicably interrupted her. This was obviously not part of the program. "Excuse me," the young man said quietly, "but I have been instructed to give you this message immediately. The Board of Directors of the Science Council has specifically asked you to read it before the end of this program." While all members of the panel stared in disbelief, the young man handed the spokeswoman a folded piece of paper, then departed in haste.

Visibly caught off guard, the speaker opened the paper and rapidly read it to herself. The message was obviously short, but its contents must have been alarming. The color drained from the middle-aged woman's face. Her eyes widened and her lips parted slightly. She glanced nervously at the others in the room, then, composing herself, she stood and addressed them and the unseen audience.

"Ladies and gentlemen, I have important and grave news. Our most sophisticated computers have been asked to replot exactly down to a fraction of a kilometer, the path of the planetesimal. According to this emergency communique, soon after fragmenting, the largest pieces and the remnants of the core of the comet will not continue towards the sun as first thought, but will veer toward a close encounter with the planet Jupiter."

Her words were briefly interrupted by members of the panel, who excitedly exchanged ideas about the news. Some started to ask questions.

"Please let me finish. After the encounter with Saturn, the largest residual central fragments will fly very close to Jupiter, and we can only conclude that they too will fragment, turning into a thousand or more comets. A small amount of this material may be brought very close to Jupiter, even circulating around it, producing a huge new ring around the giant planet. The new rings of Jupiter will make those of Saturn appear tiny and uninteresting."

Many more comments and questions arose noisily from the members of the panel as they interrupted her again.

They again became silent on her insistence. "I'm afraid there is grave news," she repeated, this time with more urgency in her tone. She slowly moved toward the holographic representation of the solar system which floated calmly off to her left, and pointed towards it as she continued.

"As this large body rushes by Jupiter and disintegrates, the new, large comets will further be redirected." Clearing her throat nervously, she continued, "They will be flung out in *all* directions."

"Instead of a harmless swarm of comets screeching around the sun, far from our planet Earth, the likely result will be a chaotic disbursement of thousands of projectiles, many a few miles wide, strewn over all of the solar system. Many of the fragments of the planetesimal will be flung into outer space after their first encounter with the sun. Others will be thrown into long orbits around the sun to return every few hundred or thousand years. We and contemporary generations will never see those again. But others will be entrapped by the combined gravitational effects of the sun and the larger planets into short-period orbits returning to the inner solar system every few months, years, or decades. Wild and unpredictable, these are the real threat. Our skies will be full of comets for many years after the first passage. Ladies and gentlemen, we are in for a formidable comet shower, and yes, the Earth, our own moon, and all the other planets and moons will be bombarded. It is inevitable. It is most probable that some fragments will impact our planet, producing significant destruction and death. Let us hope that none of these pieces of debris that strike the Earth is larger than a mile or so, for if any are, the entire population of the Earth may be in danger. We and many other animal and plant species could be in danger of extinction. We need to brace ourselves for a display of galactic violence that could last for decades, maybe centuries. The peace and quiet of interplanetary space that humankind has enjoyed for so many thousands of years is about to be shattered."

* * *

The people of Earth took the news lightly, at least initially. "So what if we have a comet shower?" pundits asked. So what if, for years, our nice, quiet skies are transformed into awesome displays of comets and meteorites? It would, in fact, be exciting and beautiful. So what if *maybe* we get hit by a few of these comets?

The voices of those who advocated preparedness were ignored except by those who would profit from the comets. "Shelter your loved ones. Buy *Comet Shield* for your roof and vehicles. For free estimates, call . . ." Commercialization of human fear has always been a successful business.

The casual attitude toward the comets changed when the true magnitude of the danger became clear. We could be destroyed, our species extinguished entirely, as had happened long before with the dinosaurs. Some experts pointed out that the original monstrous flying planetesimal was possibly only one of many intruders, each with its own potential dangers. Those experts also theorized that the sun could be approaching an area of increased density within the galaxy: an area of space filled with unimaginable amounts of dangerous debris. If so, this might merely be the *first* encounter of many to come.

A few weeks later there would be more bad news.

* * *

"Holy Mother, this is really incredible! You guys, come see!"

The young astronomer called the attention of the others in the observatory's main control room. They closed in around him as he fiddled with the controls that governed the information coming from a monstrous telescope in the adjoining dome.

The main screen displayed a myriad of usual stars. Then the screen changed, as on command it switched to an enhanced mode at a much higher magnification. Many more points of light appeared. The enhancement resulted in some loss of contrast and detail, but there was no doubt that there were many other, fainter sources of light in the background.

A whistle escaped one of those who had joined them. "Label them," he said.

At another command, most of the points of light on the screen were suddenly accompanied by sets of letters and numbers identifying them as catalogued stars and distant galaxies. Another hundred, most of them fainter, showed no data. The computer was unable to identify them.

The controller issued a request. "Isolate unidentified objects."

A circle appeared around each of the one hundred or so unnumbered dots of light. At another command, six of the objects were enlarged and isolated into cubicles, each one with its celestial coordinates. Each with a central, fuzzy ball of light.

"Is this some kind of joke?" asked one of the observers. "It's got to be a glitch," said another. "I can't believe it! They're all in the same area — way beyond the orbit of Pluto — and . . . they look almost like comets . . . but they're nowhere near where the new planetesimal is located!"

After a few more were isolated and enlarged by the computer, the main operator spoke again. "They *are* comets. I've been looking at this particular small part of the sky for hours. I've checked every system. I've even used some orbiting telescopes to double check. Look." The young man keyed in another command, and his colleagues' eyes widened in disbelief as the computer started identifying each point of light with the most probable label: "Comet . . . comet . . . comet . . . ." Dozens of them. The screen display was then changed to lower power to encompass a larger area of the sky. "Comet . . . comet . . . ."

"It's hundreds — no — thousands of comets out there! They're all coming in from the same direction! We're in for a great show." And then he added, as an afterthought, "And we're in for great trouble."

One of the younger astronomers muttered, "I don't understand. This doesn't make any sense."

"Damn!" said the older of the female astronomers standing behind them. "Don't you see? The planetesimal has perturbed the Oort cloud of comets that surrounds our solar system. It's being followed by an entourage of comets. Not only will the intruder fragment into hundreds of comets, but now it's being followed by many other thousands. We're in for a double whammy, my friends. There may be thousands of comets on their way."

"It's even worse than that," interrupted another astronomer. "It's a triple whammy. The fragmented planetesimal and the thousands of diverted comets will undoubtedly disturb the members of our own asteroid belt and send them out of their present well-behaved orbits. Only a miracle will save the Earth from a major collision." After a few seconds, he spoke again. "We're suddenly going to be a very, very busy profession."

* * *

Scientists predicted that the comet shower would last eight to ten years, and the chances of the Earth colliding with a planetesimal would increase rapidly during the first three years, and slowly decrease after that.

Very many small meteorites in the inches-to-yards size would survive atmospheric penetration and produce limited, yet significant, local damage, especially to agriculture. As an example, experts cited the small, 300-foot diameter comet that hit Tunguska in northern Russia in 1908. Its 10-megaton blast devastated 830 square kilometers of forest, even though it didn't leave a crater. It exploded and was completely vaporized before impacting the ground.

The effects of a major comet shower on the ozone and other atmospheric layers that control our planet's climate, together with the sudden possibly significant increase in water content of the atmosphere, were less predictable, but would probably also be of major consequence.

Another possible problem of a cometary shower was the fact that the increase in atmospheric water and dust could produce a greenhouse effect. The denser layers of clouds would not allow the planet's sun-derived heat to radiate back out. The worldwide effects of increased temperature would be disastrous, especially to the agriculture of the tropical and subtropical regions. The polar caps would start to melt; an increase in sea level of only a few inches would inundate and destroy many of the populated land areas by the seas. Many islands would shrink; others would disappear.

* * *

The bad news was exploited by a number of religious groups. People of all nations and religions sought a meaning behind the horrible fate that awaited them: It was "the final sign of the Apocalypse"; "the end of the world"; "the promised day of salvation"; "the resurrection of the dead."

Some said that the human race was due for extinction anyway, since all species eventually become extinct. The majority of species exist for only three or four million years. *Homo sapiens* appeared at about the same time as our now-extinct cousin Neanderthal man, only 100 to 200 thousand years ago or so. Would our species live its expected life span of a couple of million years, or would our existence be cut short? Humankind had failed so far in exterminating themselves with nuclear weapons and toxic wastes, and were now on the road to repairing most of the damage caused by industrialization and deforestation. Would a comet now succeed where humans had failed?

* * *

As soon as the consequences of the impending comet shower or "comet storm," as some called it, had sunk in, the scientific and political leaders of the world, together with the United Nations, mandated the immediate construction of fifteen strategically situated giant Survival Capsules. Each contained a reservoir of seeds, freeze-dried embryos and eggs, and genetically engineered biological material and data. Included also were abstracted libraries of human culture, literature and art, as well as the scientific data necessary to repopulate the Earth and rebuild a technologically advanced civilization.

Each hermetically sealed Survival Capsule was built deep within the ground. Some used existing mine shafts. Each capsule contained a few floors for human habitation and the rest was for storage. The fifteen capsules were distributed throughout the planet to ensure that in the event of one major impact, at least two or three capsules, with their occupants and stored treasures, would make it through the ordeal. Four capsules were constructed in the northern latitudes: Alaska, Greenland, Sweden, and Eastern Siberia; four in the mid-northern latitudes: Kansas, Spain, Tibet and Northern China; and seven in the mid to southern parts of the globe: Venezuela, Zaire, India, Cambodia, Australia, Argentina, and the Kalahari desert in Botswana. In addition, each country was encouraged and assisted to make its own preparation for survival.

During the early years of the comet shower, the heavens turned into a wonder of light and beauty. Throughout all of humankind's written history up to this point, fewer than one thousand comets that could be seen with the naked eye had been recorded. Now, each night, there were countless comets of all imaginable sizes and shapes.

In their initial passages by the sun, the new comets were loaded with dust, gases and soft ice. These sublimated exuberantly during this first close encounter with a warm star. The tails of these brilliant comets fanned out for millions of miles, filling the skies. Each night brought a different pattern of lights etching the sky.

But the display was not limited to comets. Since interplanetary space was now full of debris, Earth was constantly bombarded by millions of tiny particles, mostly gravel size. The result was a nightly display of continual meteor showers, highlighted regularly by one or more fireballs streaking and further illuminating the night. A typical night brought a few hundred bright meteors an hour. A "good" night would be dazzling, with a few thousand per hour. Not infrequently, Earthlings would witness a meteor storm, an exhilarating display of over 100,000 meteors per hour! The sky would light up whenever a storm raged on for hours. Meteors and bolides seeming to radiate from a particular part of the sky, as that area of the atmosphere collided head-on with a stream of debris suspended in space, left behind by a large fresh comet.

Some fireballs were so bright that they could be seen even in bright daylight. Many would leave behind them trains of glowing gas hundreds of miles long. The jet-like trails in the sky would slowly be deformed by the action of the winds in the higher atmosphere, creating undulating, eerie snakes of luminescent gas.

Astronomers and other scientists learned all there was to know about comets — their composition, diversity and behavior. Like giant vacuum cleaners, the sun and the great outer planets, especially Jupiter and Saturn, gobbled them up by the thousands. Space probes had explored and sampled them. The Earth had been hit by many small comets. Millions of people had died, but the world and its civilization continued.

After the wonder of the first years had faded, people tended to ignore the continual fireworks display. But when the Earth passed through an unusually rich comet tail, the thousands of bright meteors and fireballs tracking through the heavens were enough to elicit expressions of wonderment even from the most jaded.

Three other fascinating events added to the wonder and terror. One was the capture of new satellites by our planet. At any given time, besides its usual large, single moon, the Earth boasted one to two dozen tiny new moonlets. Varying in size from one to 200 yards, the small asteroids, captured by Earth's gravitational pull, added a new dimension to the night sky. Most had unstable orbits, and after months or years, they were either flung out into space or dragged down into the atmosphere, where they burned up or fell onto the planet.

The moon, too, now had its entourage of tiny satellites, but most could not be seen from Earth except with modest-sized telescopes.

The second startling celestial event was the transformation of Earth to a ringed planet. It was not an impressive and brilliant ring, like that of Saturn, but rather a very thin, and, in fact, barely perceivable structure, made mostly of dust particles, that sometimes intensified sufficiently as to be discernible without difficulty. Of course, all the other planets and large moons had either enlarged their prior ringed systems or obtained new ones.

The third, and probably most noticeable, phenomenon was the enlargement and enhancement of the zodiacal light. The zodiacal light, prior to the comet era, was an almost imperceptible band of light that could be seen only on very dark nights when there was no moon, and from locations far from the light pollution of any city. It could be seen under those ideal conditions extending upward from the horizon soon after sunset and prior to sunrise. This light represents the reflection of the sun's light on a band of tiny dust particles suspended at the equator of the entire solar system — the ecliptic. In the best of circumstances, the zodiacal light extended 45° above the horizon. During the comet era, the zodiacal light expanded and intensified a thousandfold due to the new and constant influx of meteoritic dust into the immediate perisolar space. The new zodiacal light extended now like a thick band of light from horizon to horizon and it intersected, at an angle, the faint band of light from the planet's new ring.

Even though most people eventually tended to ignore the continual downpour of tiny meteorites, they did need to take protection from them. Glass windows had to be covered with thick plastic or plywood sheets. Heavy clothing and specially reinforced umbrellas were used whenever it was necessary to venture outside. People were forced to maintain constant awareness of the new 'meteoritic' weather forecasts that tried to predict, day by day and hour by hour, the location and intensity of the bombardment.

Humans learned to keep their eyes open; any meteor that left a nice trail of light behind it could be ignored. But if the meteor had no visible trail of light and was becoming brighter, this meant that it was coming straight toward you and it was urgent to run for cover as quickly as possible. A scream of "straight on!" meant imminent danger.

Meteorites that fell vertically, down from the zenith, were among the most dangerous. Not only were they "straight on," but they were practically never detected, since most people do not go about their business looking upwards, especially when carrying a protective umbrella. In addition, meteorites coming straight down had much less atmosphere to go through, and lost much less of their bulk as a result of friction with air molecules.

When large meteorites struck a lake or river, the bodies of water overran their banks, washed away their surroundings, broke away dams and invaded the countryside and cities. The frail dams of the hundreds of thousands of man-made lakes on the globe were never meant to withstand the destructive strength of massive wave movements. Although millions drowned each year, a "Tsunami Alert" public network that was set in action in the earliest days of the shower saved many millions more. Direct hits to areas of high population density — Los Angeles, Calcutta, Moscow, Buenos Aires, Las Vegas — resulted in millions more lost.

A profitable new business emerged to help the reinforcement of buildings, homes and vehicles: the installation of "meteoritic-proof sheet metal," a heavy armor, which could protect a structure from a meteorite under five inches in diameter. Nothing could stop the larger ones. Plain glass windows were no longer practical unless they had been reinforced or covered. Yet larger meteorites could shatter the thickest panes of reinforced glass. It was calculated during the worst years that walking outdoors carried a 10% risk per day of getting hit by at least one tiny meteorite. Such an impact could result in a painful sting or small bruise, but one could just as easily lose an eye or some teeth. Walkways had to be protected. Reinforced umbrellas and clothing created a new fashion market.

By the seventh year of the comet shower, the largest body to impact the Earth had been only just under a quarter mile wide. Luckily, it had landed on Antarctica, directly killing only a couple of million humans, though indirectly causing extensive damage to the agriculture of the more southerly countries.

The Earth's oceans, lakes and lands were enriched with amino acids and other organic molecules of great complexity, some of which had once been very rare, some totally new. The interloper from space had brought with it the building blocks for a new evolutionary generation. Our ecosystem was revitalized by an influx of water, minerals and chemicals rich in organic compounds from the deepest parts of our galaxy. This input of water and biologically rich material would have enhanced agricultural production the world over, had other less desirable effects of the shower not interfered.

The comet shower brought with it not only a new way of life and death but also new diseases. During the new comet shower, iridium, which is highly concentrated in comets, was absorbed into every form of plant life, so if not properly shielded and grown on purified soil, many vegetables were toxic when consumed. Likewise, cattle meat that was not chelated of the new substances prior to eating could contain dangerous amounts of new poisons. *Iridium neurotoxicity*, a new disease, affected many species of animals. Most humans had access to neutralizing medications to avoid the worst of it, but a new plague, "iridium madness," devastated many.

The modest depletion of ozone from our upper atmosphere by the constant influx of meteoritic dust increased the amount of ultraviolet light reaching the Earth's biomass, producing an increase in tumors, eye cataracts, a myriad of other maladies and mutations. Many of the new experiments of nature, grotesque monsters and useless attachments, were of course doomed to failure. But, some argued, this new diversification would hasten and enrich evolution, even increasing the numbers of potential survivors if the Earth were to be devastated by a major extinction. It was as if nature was preparing the living creatures of our planet to better survive the inevitable devastation that was to come.

CHAPTER 2

SYRACUSE STATE 2048 A.D. APOCALYPSE

Critias, Egyptian priest, to the Athenian Solon:
"You have no knowledge of ancient age... you remember only one deluge, though there have been many.... Your own story of how Phaethon, child of the sun, harnessed his father's chariot, but was unable to guide it along his Father's course and so burnt up things on earth (being destroyed in the process), is a mythical version of the truth that there is, at long intervals, a variation in the course of the heavenly bodies and a consequent widespread destruction by fire of things on the earth."

Plato (427-347 B.C.), in Timaeus

ess *than one percent human survivors. If we are lucky — possi-bly less.* The phrase echoed in Paul's mind, leaving a vast painful emptiness in the center of his chest. That's only ten humans out of every one hundred thousand, he thought. One hundred people out of each million *may* make it. The Earth's population was going to be reduced to a mere one million people. The human race would be thrown back to prehistoric times.

Paul Lopez had been listening to a news update on his communicator. This latest report made it clear that Impact Day, or as some called it, Apocalypse Day, was only three weeks away. On that day, the Earth would feel the impact of a huge comet. For the most part, the ice surrounding the comet would disintegrate on contact with the planet's atmosphere. But its solid metal and stone core, eight miles in diameter, would strike the planet. Would the wound be fatal? Would the Earth be destroyed? Would all humans perish?

"Impact!" the newsman on the communicator said loudly. "There is no way to avoid it. Scientists have predicted that the huge comet-asteroid will hit the Earth at a speed of seventeen miles per second at approximately 5:17 P.M. local impact time on November 2nd, 2048. The point of collision will be somewhere along the coastal areas of northwestern Africa, possibly even hitting the adjoining area of the Atlantic or southwestern Europe. The European impact, however, is considered less likely."

"As it pierces the atmosphere, it will shed its lighter ice covering, like a dandelion losing its seeds to the wind, and the central stone and metal core will plunge through and smash into the Earth. At that moment of instant deceleration, the core will *explode*, releasing one hundred and fifty *million* megatons of energy!"

Paul commanded the briefcase-sized communicator into silence, while the screen still showed the nearby wheat fields and, in an inset, the now-mute commentator.

* * *

It had been a quiet, early fall afternoon in the northern farm lands of Syracuse State. This beautiful area had been known as Upstate New York prior to the redivision of the United States into 85 smaller, more efficient states. The Lopez-LeBlanc family, Paul and his wife, Trisha, sat at a picnic table beneath a large red canopy, gazing at the undulating grain fields so well known in this part of the country. Their remote-controlled combine worked busily on the field; deer jumped out of its way as it moved forward. Jenny, their four-year-old daughter, played beside her parents with her doll, oblivious to the commentator's excited and explicit warnings.

As the sky darkened, light from the three brightest comets sharpened the shadows cast by the weakening rays of the setting sun. As the sun set, the comet-dust laden atmosphere brilliantly dispersed its dwindling light into deep reds and distant oranges. Delicate shades of magnificent beauty that belied the horrors of the approaching doomsday. In the Era of Comets, brilliant comets filled every arc of sky, many visible even in daylight. During the peak of the Great Comet Shower of the twenty-first century A.D., moonless nights were occasionally so bright that fine print was easy to read; nights on the planet Earth had not been dark for most of the last decade.

The comet shower was finally slowing. Initially, it had produced great excitement, but soon the people of Earth had longed for the return of night darkness and the splendorous view of the Milky Way with its countless stars.

Paul Lopez looked down at his little girl as she played with her Raggedy Ann doll under the canopy. His expression of concern accentuated his strong features. Though only one-fourth Hispanic, the tall, thin 34 year old crop engineer's skin had a touch of light brown. His jet black hair contrasted with his blue eyes, so light they looked almost grey.

"One hundred fifty million megatons. Hiroshima was less than one hundredth of a megaton!" he muttered as he stood overlooking the four hundred acre wheat field he had supervised for the last few years. Paul loved Syracuse State. Thoughts of doom disappeared momentarily as he stopped to savor his love for the life and beauty of the country. Just as suddenly, reality drove away all blissful feelings. "Why even bother finishing this job?" he sighed.

"On the contrary, love," his wife said softly. Sitting under the canopy, she too had seemed lost in thought. She knew that the idea of impending death was on the minds of every single human on the planet. Trisha's personality and appearance formed a pleasing contrast to her husband's. Younger than Paul, she was 26, with reddish hair, very light skin, a few faint freckles, and a trim figure; she was almost plain by comparison. Yet on meeting her, others could sense the goodness in her. Next to her, people felt safe and at ease. She sat somewhat awkwardly, due to her late pregnancy. In spite of the cruel reality of the impending impact, her disposition remained clear and untroubled. She refused to accept the idea of the end of the world, especially when she was soon to deliver.

A crop geneticist, Trisha had met Paul in agricultural college. She had been a student and he the most popular among the young professors. They had fallen in love instantly on her first day of class.

"Since Impact Day has been definitely established, the real panic and chaos should start soon," she continued. "The wheat will be worth so much to those who hope to survive in shelters. If the end of the world is really so close, we are free to do whatever we want with it. Let's harvest it and give it away."

Paul didn't respond, but continued to gaze out beyond the fields. For a moment, he reflected on their business. His job had been a comfortable one, though the small company of which he was co-owner could not withstand any major loss in a world of fierce commercial competition. He had inherited this land, which was situated sufficiently north to escape most of the devastating agricultural greenhouse concerns that the comet shower had delivered. Luckily, the field had not received any damaging impacts from the continual downpour of comet debris that had rained upon the planet for so many years.

"Paul?" Trisha's voice brought him out of his reverie. "If you don't want to give the wheat away, I'm sure we could actually sell it just by ourselves. We could be rich!"

"Rich?" Paul laughed. "It's all over, love, don't you understand? Money means absolutely nothing. The rich will be those who live — if anyone lives!" Like a litany, Paul repeated the statistics. "One to 10 million survivors, at the most, on the entire globe!"

Trisha dismissed the prediction as so much pessimism. "Many scientists disagree," she insisted. "Some say 100 or 200 million will make it. Some say it may totally miss or just graze the upper atmosphere. And if it does hit, it will land in Africa, three or four thousand miles away from here. We'll make it; I know we will," she added with conviction.

"I wish I could believe that, love." After a few seconds he added, "Impact Day is approaching fast. We should pack and join your mom and dad at their cabin in Quebec."

"Daddy," Jenny interrupted. Fair like her mother, Jenny was a bright little girl. She had decided to change an uncomfortable situation to what she considered a more familiar and less threatening subject, one she could understand and in which she could participate. "Which is the bad one?" she asked, squinting at the sky.

Paul picked her up by the waist and held her facing him, at arm's reach high above him. His eyes started to tear, and he felt a tight knot in his throat. Was she, like them, already dead? He stood motionless for a few seconds, then he brought her down and cradled her on his left arm. With his right, he pointed to where a huge ball of white light dominated the sky.

Jenny had been born during the comet era and was well familiarized with them. Comets and meteorites and their consequences were part of her normal life. She had never looked at a cloudless sky without seeing many of them, night or day.

The comet coma, a large, irregular central mass of bright light, though rushing at incredible speed in a collision course with the Earth, appeared immobile. Halfway up the western sky, it grew in brightness every minute as the evening sky darkened. Surrounded by a huge haze of less intense light, like a halo, the comet's two large tails appeared to envelop it. It seemed to resemble the face of a maddened lion, with a monstrous mane of gray and silver hair stretching around its massive head.

As it got darker, the splendor of the comet shower became more evident. There were so many comets and so many meteors! The Milky

Way could not be made out since it blended with the diffuse light of dense interplanetary dust.

"Is that the one that's called Disaster, Daddy? Why do they call it that?"

Paul thought for a few seconds, then tried to explain in terms she could understand. "Well, dear, thousands of years ago, even before Grandma and Grandpa were born, people were very afraid of comets. They called them comets, which means hair, because their tails look like long hair falling behind a star. We call this particular one Dis'Aster because that word means 'evil star.' Evil means bad. Very, very bad. Long ago people thought that comets brought bad luck, that many bad things happened when a star with hair behind it appeared in the sky."

"They were right, Daddy, weren't they?" the little girl interrupted. Without waiting for an answer, she continued. She was in safe territory now. "The spots on it are changing, Daddy. It looks different from last night. Why is that?"

Almost by rote, he explained that the huge mass of rock, metal and ice in the center of the comet's solid core was tumbling as it plunged toward them. Then he tried to reassure her: "Dis'Aster really isn't a bad comet. It's just bad luck that our paths have to meet. The comet will explode when that happens. It will die." He paused. "The Earth, on the other hand, will survive, but many, many people will die because of this crash."

"Are we going to Grandma's?" Jenny asked somewhat shyly.

"Yes, darling." answered her father, gazing too intensely into her eyes and causing the little girl to look away in embarrassment.

"Are we going to build the time capsule?" she asked after a moment. "I want to put my toys in it."

"No, Jenny, I don't think we need to anymore," he replied. "There's no time. Besides," he added under his breath, "who knows if anyone will be around to open our little capsule ten thousand years from now."

Jenny looked at her mother with confusion and a little fear in her eyes. "What does he mean, Mommy?"

"Nothing, dear." Trisha said calmly as she started to pick things up from the table. "Let's get ready."

Paul continued to gaze at the sky. A few very bright meteors suddenly shot by. The darkening night allowed the many comets to display their magnificence. They seemed to bow their heads in unison, as if in reverence, toward the mighty gravity of the sun.

A sudden sprinkling of tiny, sand-grain-sized meteorites struck their protective canopy, abruptly bringing Paul back to more practical matters. He spoke briefly into his communicator, and the combine whined to a sudden stop, its lights obediently switching off. "Come on," he said. "Let's go home and pack. It's going to get very nasty."

"Can we call Grandma and Grandpa now?" begged Jenny, wanting so badly to change the mood of the conversation. She loved to use the communicator. Paul recalled how, before the comet shower, orbiting antenna-satellites had allowed easy communication. But the shower had destroyed all of Earth's artificial satellites. Communications had been set back to the older time when modular units were used for communicating among people in different cellular geographic areas as determined by land-based antennas.

With Jenny still on his left arm, Paul peered upward. "No, Jenny, not right now. The skies are going to get very crowded; shuttling may soon become impossible. We have to avoid the air jams. We better get home first."

With a sigh of resignation, Trisha unsteadily got to her feet. She often caught herself wishing to have delivered already. But now, in the face of a major and hasty move, she was glad that the baby was not due for another six weeks. A newborn would only slow them down, especially if premature.

Trisha put one arm around both her loves, and with the other snapped open a large, reinforced anti-meteorite umbrella. She led as they left the safety of the canopied farm control-center for that of their vehicle. The mood was so gloomy it brought an urgent sense of danger to all of them.

"I'm frightened," Trisha admitted.

"So am I, love. I'm scared for all of us." As the electric vehicle took off, the moon, almost full, rose above the eastern hills. Its surface, deep red for years now, just another sign of Apocalypse.

* * *

In every city, in every town, and in the hearts of every human being, chaos reigned. Pilfering, rape, murder. Horror and man-made death spread across the entire globe. Law ceased to exist in many communities. Law enforcement agencies were faced with the dilemma as to what to do with those in jail. Some prison managers had prepared for this eventuality and had built large gas chambers for their inmates. Others simply shot those they considered most dangerous. Others just opened their doors completely and let loose even the most violent criminals.

The coastal areas of southern Europe and the entire Mediterranean basin, together with all of northwestern Africa, had to be hastily evacuated. The destruction and the heat shock wave would reach these areas with enough force to incinerate everything it touched. Tsunami waves, whether the comet impacted on land or sea, could be one or two miles high and would reach hundreds of miles inland. All ships and every kind of water vessel in the Mediterranean Sea and the Atlantic Ocean had to leave for safer waters. They had to find refuge in the Indian or Pacific Oceans.

Even those parts of Europe, Africa and the Middle East not immediately threatened by the sea required stringent protection of their inhabitants, since the fallout of hot ashes would set most of that part of the planet on fire. Not enough shelters could be improvised, yet a mandate from the United Nations required that on Impact Day, or ID, as it was known, all inhabitants of the entire world remain indoors. Subways, caves, the great basements of large buildings and the many underground shopping malls were to be used as shelter for as many as possible. By Impact Hour, all humans were to be sheltered.

CHAPTER 3

THE LAST SPACE MISSION 2048 A.D.

"And I saw a star that fell from heaven which had fallen to Earth and... it opened a bottomless pit, and smoke ascended out of the pit, like the smoke of a great furnace and the sun and the air were darkened and... they tormented for five months... and in those days men would seek death and would not find it, and... long to die and death flees from them."

John: Book of Revelation 9:1,2,5,6 (Apocalypse),
Holy Bible

aptain Kenichi Nakamura felt extremely tired; he seemed to have lost his sense of time. The graying Japanese commander's joints and muscles ached. Not only had he not slept well in the last few days, but the cramped quarters made it almost impossible to find a comfortable resting position even in the absence of gravity.

He gazed pensively at his small crew: Jon Smithson, the handsome middle-aged African-American had piercing black eyes. He was an excellent co-pilot — the best there ever was; and Natasha Petrof, a beautiful young space engineer from Kiev. His heart broke for them. They weren't taking it as they should. They had seemed so strong, so honored to be chosen among the hundreds of volunteers from the Interplanetary Space Agency. Now their inner strength seemed to be weakening, but he was still confident that they would prevail in the end.

The Interplanetary Agency had been near-dormant for almost a decade; space travel had become nearly impossible in the dangerous, murky spies of the comet era. Now, these three humans were Earth's last hope.

* * *

Jon looked absentmindedly at the control panels. He had grown to hate them. He, like the others in the spacecraft, hadn't looked directly at the outside world since they left Earth.

The whole voyage seemed like a dream to him. He thought briefly of his wife, who had begged him not to go.

Like the other astronauts, he had spoken of a sacrifice for the people of Earth, but now knew it had been plain selfishness and greed for glory that had caused him to volunteer. All glory vanished when the comet shower grounded space flight, reducing him to pencil pushing instead of soaring through space. Then this mission: One last chance for the thrill of lift-off. *I should be at home embracing my wife and children,* he thought, *helping them prepare for the inevitable. I've abandoned them when they needed me most. Oh God, please don't let them suffer.*

Jon suddenly felt the stare. He slowly turned his head toward his captain. *Ken's been watching me again,* he thought. *Can he see the moisture in my eyes? He can read us so well. Why is he so much stronger? Or is he just better at hiding?*

He nodded at Nakamura's frigid face. "I'm okay, Captain," he murmured. "Don't worry." He didn't even care that Natasha could hear him.

* * *

Natasha left her seat and floated over to Jon. She put her arms around his broad shoulders, hugging him. "I wish we could look back at Earth," she said in her accented but steady voice. "I'm so tired of the images on the screen. They look so much like simulations that it doesn't seem real."

The spacecraft was, by necessity, totally sealed; no place for a claustrophobic. There were no ports to look out, not that there was much to see anyway. As they traveled through the comet's coma, space around the ship was a haze of white light. And now that they were approaching the comet's nucleus, they had to protect their precious cargo even more carefully. The heavy metal coating of the spacecraft was by now dull gray. The approach to the comet had sandblasted it for days. This, the most formidable spaceship ever built, could repel direct encounters with meteorite fragments measuring a few inches. Only one hundred by fifteen feet, the featureless armored space-tank was so heavy that to launch it from the surface of the Earth had required the use of launch vehicles used by the type retired many decades earlier. Luckily, the murderous comet was within the confines of the ecliptic, thus an easy target.

Since no antennas could withstand the barrage of debris in space and the even higher concentrations of rocks near the comet's nucleus, there was no way to control the rocket from Earth. Even the best computer could not be programed to respond appropriately to all eventualities. The search and destroy mission had to be manned.

* * *

Like a thick cucumber, the spaceship showed no features. A simple ugly, gray cylinder. On its integrity, fifteen hydrogen bombs, three people, and luck, rested the fate of the entire human race.

* * *

At a sudden beep, Natasha immediately returned to her module.

"Grid one hundred and eighty-nine." The computer's voice carried no expression as it reported another routine pick-up on the intensified radar image.

"Roger," Jon said, confirming the sighting.

"How big?" Nakamura asked automatically.

There was no need for the question. The information had just appeared on the screens and was verbalized by the computer in its hollow and vaguely female voice.

"Two point seven meters. Distance: one hundred, sixteen point three kilometers."

Natasha then spoke slowly and distinctly to ensure that the Artificial Intelligence computer would not ask for a repeat of the order.

"Artin — locate object on grid one, eight, nine and aim lithotriptors at object. Then lock. When object is seven kilometers from craft, activate lithotriptors and destroy to fine powder. Out."

"Lithotriptors, object centered grid one, eight, nine, at seven kilometers — dust."

The firm, controlled response from the computer was ignored, since it never required changing the order. If Artin (short for Artificial Intelligence systems computer Series IQ^3) had a doubt as to the appropriateness of the order, it would sternly let them all know.

Without changing direction or speed, the long, cigar-shaped spacecraft rotated slightly. Nobody noticed or cared.

A few seconds later, two separate, heavy three-by-three foot panels of thick metal slid away within the eighteen-inch thick metal skin of the ship. Three seconds later, the lithotriptors had armed, fired their beams of hyperconcentrated ultrasonic waves, and pulverized the rock. The armament retracted and the protective doors immediately closed so as not to expose the weaker parts of the craft to the hostile environment.

* * *

Natasha didn't like the way Nakamura had looked at Jon. Was her fear also showing, she wondered? She knew she was exhausted, although the pills kept her alert and in control. But she was still disgusted with herself. She was afraid. *There is nothing to be afraid of,* she told herself again. *I know what I am doing.* She had wanted it so much. She had felt, as she knew she should, so sure and secure. Yet now, as contact time approached, she was afraid. Was Nakamura afraid?

A simple transformation, instantaneous in this case. She had always accepted that. Thirty-six years of being sure of each and every one of her decisions. The world had never scared her. Why should death?

Does this mean I have a doubt as to what's going to happen? she wondered. *There is nothing afterwards. Nothing. Or is there?*

She was disgusted at her thoughts. She glided toward Jon.

"Captain, may I?" Without waiting for an answer from Nakamura, she grabbed Jon's collar, and with the other hand skillfully tripped his seat belt release, and pulled him straight up and out of his chair. Smiling, she wrapped her arms around the confused American, placed her feet on the back of his seat, and with a strong kick flung them both toward the back of the long corridor that stretched behind the command room. As they floated slowly away from the control area, she kissed him. Holding on to each other, rotating slowly, they drifted until they softly hit the back of the corridor. By that time, Jon's hands had managed to creep up her blouse to the warmth of her breasts. Her hands were working on his belt.

* * *

"Artin, take command. Keep us safe and intact," Nakamura said only an hour later. "We are going to activate the bombs. Out."

"Yes, sir." The hollow voice was the only one that didn't seem to mind what was happening. It knew its mission. It had been programed to accept it as an inconsequential fact.

Jon was the first to glide down the long, thin corridor. He would activate the five units in the back. He felt a knot in his throat. His heart skipped a few beats.

"It's okay," he reassured himself aloud. "It has to be done. It's that simple." Then he lied: "Just another mission."

As the others did the same, he activated his bombs, one by one, each one a sphere eighteen inches in diameter, each one suspended in a large, cubical metal frame. They lined the entire inner portions of the spacecraft, leaving little room for the tiny control center in front and the tiny space toilet facility. Apart from the scanty store of food for the one-way trip, every other cubic inch was an arsenal.

Once he finished activating the last unit, Jon felt frozen, as if all had ceased to exist around him. The image in his brain was that of his wife and two babies. "You should be proud," he had told her. "Damn you, Jon!" she had responded, painful tears in her eyes. "Don't you see we will be alone?"

Artin's voice interrupted his pain. "All fifteen units activated. Thirty-five minutes to impact. All is under control." Natasha looked at Jon and smiled. "See?" she said. "Artin thinks all is well." They both tried to fake a laugh.

A loud knock shook the craft, and then another. Jon and Natasha looked at Ken, startled. "The lithotriptors can't keep up with the particles out there," he said. "Don't worry. We'll make it through."

Of course we'll make it! Nakamura thought bitterly to himself. *We damned well better. This mission must succeed.*

* * *

Nakamura, Natasha and Jon were loosely strapped to their seats. A roaring hiss was all that could be heard as the spacecraft plunged through the particle-rich coma, approaching its target. The sense of expectation had become unbearable.

To the surprise of the others, it was Nakamura who spoke first. "Artin! Damn it, any fractures?"

"No, Captain. No fractures. No areas of weakness identified. We have no more time for maneuvering, anyway. As you should know, the options now do not include a choice of impact point." And then, almost as an afterthought: "There are, in fact, no options."

The screens showed hues of white and gray, speckled here and there by the jets of sublimating gases that spewed from the solid blackened face of the comet.

At exactly one-hundredth of a second before impact, the nuclear bombs detonated simultaneously, each one releasing two megatons of destructive energy. The three astronauts never perceived the initiation of the explosion. They were instantly turned into atoms and subatomic particles, which mixed chaotically with the atoms and particles and a few intact molecules of the spaceship and the adjoining parts of the huge comet.

CHAPTER 4

CHICAGO I.
IN PREPARATION

"Earthquakes and tidal waves will befall us as a result of the tremendous impact of this heavenly body in one of our oceans."

Jeane Dixon (1917-1997 A.D.)

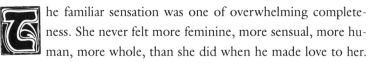he familiar sensation was one of overwhelming complete-
ness. She never felt more feminine, more sensual, more hu-
man, more whole, than she did when he made love to her.
Their dark naked bodies wrapped around each other. Their movements were slow and purposeful to enhance every sensation. His strong
arms were not just around her, they held her into him. The tension in
his arms never yielded, always holding her firm.

As the waves of pleasure receded within her, her feelings of happiness and self-satisfaction were replaced by overwhelming peace as
she felt his body, in turn, shudder with waves of pleasure.

* * *

Julia reflected on those happier moments that morning as she
stood looking pensively through the large windows at the late afternoon Chicago landscape. They had just finished supper, the most
solemn meal they had ever had together. She was normally not a
pessimistic person, but somehow, as she dined with her family, she
had sensed that she was sharing with them a last supper of sorts. She
especially worried about her children. She was now more glad than
ever that she and Robert had intentionally limited themselves to two.

She had only recently taken a vaccine booster that would extend
her infertile period for at least two more years. At the end of that
time she would have her blood tested for the antibody level that would
indicate when she needed the next shot. Family planning had become easy since the advent of long-term fertility vaccines, whose effects could be reversed at will. When pregnancy was desired, the
anti-pregnancy antibody could be easily neutralized by taking a daily
nullifier pill until pregnancy was confirmed.

Sundays had always been special to Robert and Julia: a day they
had sworn to dedicate to themselves and their children. A day of
hiking, fishing, exploring, or just resting. Julie wished now she could
be out in what used to be a beautiful and carefree world. Or if only
they could immerse themselves in the ecstasies of love forever. Instead, she was back to the bitter reality of the present.

She glanced at her husband, then at her children. Again, she
looked out through the window at the Chicago landscape. It took a

superhuman effort to hold back the tears that wanted to burst from her soul. From their apartment eighty stories above the streets of Chicago she could see part of the metropolis and the beautiful lake. The scenery was breathtaking. But she perceived no beauty. Her heart was breaking.

* * *

Robert Horton rested in an armchair in the other part of the living room. Robert was a tall, strong man. Built like a fortress, his physical strength contrasted with his simple and easy-going personality. His curly hair, dark eyes and black skin were a source of great pride, especially since there existed fewer and fewer Americans of pure African heritage in a world where interracial marriage had become the rule, not the exception.

Robert intensely and proudly watched as his daughter, Tammy, played happily with her little stuffed animals, oblivious to her surroundings.

"What a treasure," he said aloud, trying to catch Tammy's attention. "You're not really a little girl anymore. Eight years old. Growing fast, and so smart." She pretended not to have heard the compliment.

Sensing Julia's pain, he looked at his wife, feeling remorse at his inability to comfort her. He was so much in love with his wife, and so proud of her also. His very own Dr. Julia Horton, as he called her. Not only was Julia an intelligent, hard-working and loving person, but she was beautiful, stunning, and as pure African-American as he was. Even though she was his own age, 28, he always felt somewhat strange when they were together in social gatherings. He was an ordinary man; somewhat diffident. She, on the other hand, attracted people like iron to magnet. And she was a medical doctor; he was only a cook, a graduate of culinary arts. Yet, as she often reminded him, he was a *master* in a rare form of art.

* * *

Julia continued to gaze through the balcony windows toward the network of modern buildings and, in the distance, the great lake she loved so much.

In 2048, Chicago was at the forefront of the architectural revolution wrought by the breakthroughs that had created new forms of building materials. "Plasto-steel" and light-weight "Trabecular cement" had revolutionized construction and given the word "skyscraper" a new meaning. The unbelievably strong, yet light, new construction materials could be made cheaply; their density and flexibility customized for every need and situation without jeopardizing their strength.

Buildings by the hundreds rose like crystal needles, each over one hundred stories high, making Chicago a very striking city. Interconnected by a complex network of bridges and transport conduits, the three-dimensional effect was startling. The delicate-looking bridges and conduits easily withstood the continual traffic of transporters heavily laden with people and supplies. They exceeded the wildest dreams of any engineer. As in the past, Chicago continued to boast the tallest buildings in the world, thanks to its base of thick and firm limestone bedrock. Deposited prior to the massive global extinction of the Devonian Era, 365 million years ago, the calcareous remnants of trillions upon trillions of minute planktonic creatures enabled Chicagoans to build the largest and most grandiose examples of the builder's art.

The magnificent structures were a tribute to the ingenuity of the human mind. IQ Sensitive materials and Shape-Memory Alloys served as internal self-monitoring systems that not only detected any changes in a building's integrity, but actually prevented deterioration, making corrections and mending faults as necessary. These "intelligent" materials were in a sense animated; moving and molding under the stress produced by shifting weights and pressures. Earthquakes and great winds were seldom noticed by the residents of the planet's imposing new cities.

Huge panels of diamonized glass enveloped most of the buildings. These immense sheets of glass were covered by a microscopic layer of synthesized pure carbon that had turned glass into an almost indestructible material while still retaining its full transparency. The comet shower had changed most of the world. Shattered windows were initially replaced with wood or plastic. But as the meteorite shower decreased, they were being replaced with double diamonized glass.

A cylindrical transport conduit could be made to span a thousand yards between two buildings without any supports. Trains and buses rushed through conduit systems suspended by magnetolevitation. The Maglevs were extremely fast and silent, due to the absence of friction. Transportation had become efficient, safe and inexpensive.

Robert gazed past Julia, looking at the marvels of the Chicago skyline, with its delicate spires. But the beauty of the scene didn't register. All he could think of was his wife, and how she had changed in the last few days. She was so withdrawn. He knew they would make it through. It would be rough for the next few days and, yes, the entire world would change greatly over the next few months, but he was confident that at least for them, things would work out in the long run. They always had in the past.

Jeffrey, their four-year-old boy, was asleep on the couch amid a jumble of partially packed camping equipment. The large, lightweight backpacks stood in silence as if waiting expectantly for another exciting outdoor excursion.

Julia had made fun of him when he included the small tent. "We won't need tents in the underground transit tunnels," she had laughed. Tammy agreed, "Yeah, Daddy," she trilled. "It won't rain in there you know."

He had explained to them that the tent was for privacy. He didn't want anyone looking at his girls when they had to change clothes. They all seemed so fragile to him in this great city of so many millions.

"I wish we didn't have to go to these damn shelters," Robert muttered as he returned to the packing. But he knew they had no alternative. The kamikaze space mission had failed. The explosion of the spaceship had decreased the mass of the comet by less than ten percent, and had not sufficiently diverted its course. Even worse, astronomers had recently indicated that the comet was coming at a modest angle from east to west. Scientists had warned that because of this angle of impact, the central solid core, or parts of it, could bounce westward as it impacted north-western Africa. Fragments could then land on any part of the North American continent. Cities as far west as the Rocky Mountains, including Chicago, had to be prepared for the worst. The population of Chicago had been ordered to shelter in the many miles of underground transit tunnels and in the basements and underground parking lots of the tall buildings.

* * *

As Julia continued to gaze through the wide windows, she found herself staring at Dis'Aster. She realized then that she had never before sensed true fear. Always secure in her own intelligence and her ability to reason things out, she now felt defeated. There was nothing she could do about the inevitably bleak future and the many years it would take to recover from the damage of the comet-Earth collision.

Mixed with her fear was the realization that modern medicine would suddenly be returned to the comparative dark ages of the twentieth century. Many medical computers would not survive the catastrophe. Most of those that did would soon run out of power, as technology gave way under the effects of the comet's collision. Any remaining energy sources would be ruined in the deep freeze that would follow. Civilization would be on its knees. The catastrophe would create millions of injuries, while the ice age would reduce medical supplies. With limited tools and no proper facilities, the practice of medicine would be difficult, if not impossible. A part of her looked forward to the challenges, but she was not certain she would be able to handle the new, complex reality with competence. With the advent of the comet shower, she had been trained on the Theory of Healing Under Primitive Conditions. But the lessons were all theoretical. She felt totally unprepared for the frustrating reality that was soon to be upon them.

The other unknown, how she and her family would survive with any degree of comfort the next few months, was even more frightening. Julia feared her new duties as an old-style doctor would pull her away from her loved ones; maybe for days or weeks at a time. There was no question that Robert could take care of the children, but the thought of being away from them terrified her.

She looked briefly toward Robert with a hint of moisture in her eyes. His skills as a food preparation specialist would not be required in the underground shelter. All food had been prepared, preserved and ready to eat — no need for embellishments or fancy seasonings.

Robert glanced over at his wife once more, then walked slowly toward the window and put his arms gently around her slender waist. Julia felt his presence but did not stir. He increased the pressure of his grip, reassuring her of his understanding. She moved one hand to cover one of his in a gesture of gratitude. She looked at him briefly, her eyes now running with tears. She turned her face once more to face her adversary. The enemy of all humankind and all that was alive on the planet: a simple comet.

Robert stepped in front of her, as if to protect her from her foe. Lovingly, he took her face in both of his hands, turning it slowly to face his own. The warmth of his caring flowed into her from the tender hand-to-face touch. "I love you," he murmured. What else could he say or do? He, like the rest of mankind, was helpless in the face of this certain calamity.

"We will be okay," he went on. "We're far from the impact point. Don't worry so much."

She thrust her arms around his neck, crying softly. "Not far enough," she cried. "Three and a half thousand miles is not far enough."

Robert suddenly flushed, noticing that their children had been listening with concern. He quickly changed the subject. "We have to finish packing," he said, turning back toward the living room. "I want us to be there at least one full day ahead of our scheduled time so we can organize our area and take full possession of it."

Julia knew what he really meant. He was reaffirming to her that the family came first; that she must be there with them, even if it meant forsaking for one day the scheduled preparations set out by the hospital. She didn't like it, but she knew he was right. She was with him and she would be there. The possibility of not being able to find her family later, during the last-hour rush, was unthinkable.

CHAPTER 5

TUCSON I. RETURN TO THE CAVES

"And there was a great earthquake and the sun became as black as hair, and the moon as red as blood.
And the stars of heaven fell upon the Earth, like figs
shaken by a great wind. The sky vanished, as a scroll
that is rolled up; and every mountain and the islands
were moved out of their places.... Everyone, kings
and slaves, hid themselves in the caves and the rocks
of the mountains."

John: Book of Revelation, 6:12-15 (Apocalypse),
Holy Bible

avid McGuire, his wife, Maggie, their son, Terry, eight, and their daughter, Teresa, five, had been assigned compartment 10D5, the fifth compartment from the left, on the fourth level of the cave's tenth room, in the large natural cave.

Large natural caverns are ideally suited for humans to survive months or years of absolute confinement. Many caves have a continual supply of filtered and purified water, and large cave systems maintain a constant, moderate temperature throughout the year, independent of the seasons.

During the long, deep winter that would be initiated by the Earth-comet collision, the temperature in large caves might drop only a few degrees. A typical cavern's temperature is around 50° to 60° F. Even at 40° or 45° F., people can survive in caves as long as they have supplies of food and dry clothing.

The McGuires had been assigned to share their compartment with five thousand pounds of rice in one hundred-pound bags, to be guarded and distributed only as rationed by the National Guard. At first the living quarters would be very crowded, but as the months went by and more of the material in their cubicle was used up, more elbow room would become available.

While the McGuires stocked and organized their area, they met those assigned to be their new neighbors: families with whom they would share the area for a few months or even years. On one side of their cubicle was the Ziegler family: Bill, Lara and their two young girls. The Zieglers were in charge of four thousand pounds of ground chocolate. Once turned into hot chocolate drink, theirs would be a coveted treasure. On the other side of the McGuires, the Lee family was responsible for hundreds of small cylinders of natural gas, which would be needed for cooking when and if the generators failed. Or if the larger gas cylinders situated outside the cave ran out of their precious fuel or were destroyed by ice or stolen by vandals.

In Tucson, the Arizona National Guard helped organize the habitation of Colossal Cave for this selected group of over two thousand Tucson families. Engineers partitioned the different cave rooms and corridors with metal shelving into multi-tiered, closet-like compartments. The lightweight metal construction, like a child's Erector set, was stark and uncomfortable, yet strong and efficient. Most compartments were rectangular. The smaller ones, to be used mainly for storage, were only four feet wide by six feet deep. Others, to be used by people and for storage, were six feet wide and near ten feet deep, with a height from seven to ten feet.

To the surprise of many, the caves also stocked inflatable rafts and boats. Scientists had pointed out that the debris thrown into the upper atmosphere by the impact's explosion and the resulting fires would gradually, over a period of months or years, fall to the ground. The skies would lighten until warmth began to filter through. The warmth would then be trapped under the relatively thick, higher clouds, while at the same time the atmosphere would be laden with carbon dioxide and other greenhouse gases. Thus, heat would not be released back into space, but would become concentrated under the clouds. Once this crucial state was reached, a dramatic greenhouse effect would thaw the Earth in just a few months. Scientists warned that this great thaw was very dangerous: in a short period of time, great floods would occur throughout the planet, and constant rain could possibly last many months before the climate stabilized.

Less optimistic scientists warned of a longer deep freeze, followed by years of devastating floods. The organizers of Colossal Cave had prepared for an in-between scenario.

Bill had joked to David that they had better build their own large boat and keep it tied down in the desert by the cave for when the climate change occurred. The cave had stocked few of them, for when they emerged to face the floods, there would be no time or materials available to build any additional ones.

* * *

Franklin and Liza Lee, an older Chinese-American couple with no children, shared one four-foot-wide bunk. The Zieglers and McGuires had larger quarters with three bunk beds each. Still larger habitation compartments on the ground floor accommodated bigger families and groups.

Camaraderie and a jovial atmosphere prevailed during the final days of preparation. Strong friendships developed among the new neighbors as they prepared for a cold, boring hibernation that they thought would last a few months, maybe a year. The inhabitants of the cave would need to know and trust each other to survive. Only by working together could they withstand the ordeal. They would all have to become cooks, cleaners, laborers, teachers, nurses and whatever else was required of them.

In other areas of the cave, organizing and stocking the medical emergency room and surgery departments required collaboration among numerous physicians and paramedical personnel. Kitchen areas needed to be engineered so that fumes would not contaminate the air. Some of the stored food would not require cooking, but it was inevitable that much would have to be prepared prior to distribution.

Waste disposal systems, communications networks, air circulation ducts, toxin-absorbing filters and the like required constant maintenance to ensure they functioned properly. Sufficient oxygen had to be available to all, and, even more important, all noxious gases, especially deadly carbon dioxide, had to be effectively removed. Plants were strategically located to help in this endeavor. The main electrical and heating systems were to be powered by a bus-sized mini-nuclear fusion plant outside the cave. It too had to be maintained and protected from thieves.

Unlike coal and gasoline, with their pollution and limited supply, and unlike nuclear power, with its dangerous radioactivity and nuclear waste, fusion energy was clean and waste-free. Prior to the comet era, the world had relied on it and on super-efficient solar power systems to produce the energy needed to fill humankind's insatiable needs. The main material needed for nuclear fusion was salt water, a cheap and abundant fuel.

While preparations continued in and around the caves, the rest of the population of Tucson, as well as the populations of other cities throughout the globe, prepared for the inevitable as best they could. Underground parking areas and malls, the lower floors of large buildings; subway tunnels, and the like, all were filling with the frightened people of Earth.

Tucson was nearly five thousand miles from the comet's estimated impact point, and was not expected to experience the direct effects of the impact-blast: the scorching heat wave, or the hurricane winds. Sheltering of everyone was nevertheless necessary in case the comet fragmented.

* * *

"I just don't understand it," David McGuire said with concern. "The Zieglers were supposed to be here last night at the latest. They knew how important it was to get here ahead of traffic and avoid the panic of the last hours."

Maggie, his wife, shrugged. "You know they're always late for everything."

"This is no time for being late, and they know it. They also know that nobody will be allowed in after closing time."

"I know," Maggie sighed. "They're probably stuck in the traffic. Most of their stuff is here, so all they need to do is carry their girls in. Don't worry, they'll be here soon."

But their concern grew as the hours went by and the last of the cells were filled by latecomers. As the closing hour approached, the cave inhabitants were settling down. There was little talking and activity as everyone prepared for the first night of sleep.

* * *

From the distant corridors came a rush of feet, some stern voices and the cries of toddlers. David, Maggie and the Lees relaxed as they felt the unmistakable vibrations and voices of a family, with some little girls, rushing toward their area and climbing up the metal ladders toward the only still-empty compartment on their floor. They rushed out and looked down the ladder to give their friends a helping hand. But they were met with complete strangers.

"Excuse me, sir," said David. "This is the Zieglers' chamber."

But, David was silenced by the large, panting man as he reached the top platform. Pushing David aside, the stranger snarled, "This is Ten D Four!, isn't it?"

"Yes, but — "

"Well, here are my papers, see? Ten D Four!"

"But you don't understand," David protested. "The Zieglers have had this chamber assigned to them for years; they should be here any minute. They are the ones that have prepared this compartment. This is a mistake. You must have been assigned to a different — "

"Hold it!" the angry man cried. Pointing his large left index finger at David's face, almost touching him, he added, "You are the one that doesn't understand. These are *our* papers, and this is *our* chamber! And let me tell you — "

"Hush, up there!" came the stern command from an officer at the bottom of the ladder. "Public arguments and fights will not be tolerated!"

Only then did David and the stranger realize that they had aroused the attention of the entire large cavern room. Everyone was trying to figure out what was happening. What could already have disturbed what was hoped to be a civilized encampment?

In a harsh whisper, the heavy man, again pointing at David, continued, "We have been assigned to this chamber. Your friends must have been reassigned to another room."

David realized that arguing was futile. The stranger, his wife, and the two little girls were obviously not going to leave.

Fear crept through David's heart as he studied the newcomers. Unkempt and dirty, they all were obviously frightened. Even the angry man, who appeared to be in his late thirties, was trying to hide his fear behind the appearance of anger.

"There's nothing more to say. This is our chamber," the stranger concluded abruptly, as he pushed his way into the compartment. He looked somewhat foolish as he tried to squeeze his sweaty and oversized body into the space between the bunk and the storage.

The McGuires, the Lees and the other members of the immediately adjoining chambers stood in silent shock. Indicating the plastic bags in which the newcomers had brought their possessions, Maggie whispered, "These people aren't even prepared for the interment. Let's go and talk with the officers."

"You stay with the kids," David said. "Franklin and I will go." They descended to the cave floor and made their way to the main entrance of the cave. There, a security officer was contemplating both the large herd of cattle, penned and unwittingly waiting to be deep frozen by nature, and the beautiful cactus-laden landscape expanding beyond him.

On seeing them approach, the officer said sadly, "Take one last look at the saguaros. Taller ones must be two hundred to three hundred years old; they're about to become extinct. All the beautiful plants and animals of this desert will soon freeze into oblivion. And the sunset," he paused dramatically, "there won't be any more sunsets or sunrises for years, probably. Only perpetual night. What a horrible, cold kind of hell our planet will soon turn into."

David and Franklin were not in the mood for philosophy. Ignoring the officer's remarks, they quickly explained what they had just witnessed.

The response was not what they were looking for. "I understand your concerns," the officer said. "I was somewhat surprised, too, when they came in. But he does have all the papers in order, and 10D4 is the chamber that they had obviously been assigned."

But the Zieglers' friends could not accept this. The conversation soon turned into an argument.

"No, I'm sorry, Mr. McGuire," insisted the officer, "there has not been a single case of double assignment. The fact that your friends are not here seems to confirm that in fact there might have been a last moment rearrangement. The doors close in a few minutes, and you are supposed to be in your assigned areas."

"But don't you see," David said, keeping his voice even, "we would have known of a change. They're our closest friends."

"Sorry. I have to get back to my position. This is a critical time, and we're not going to allow any trouble. I order you both to get back to your compartments! Now!"

The officer left David and Franklin standing in bewilderment. The truth of the situation was becoming chillingly clear.

Could it be that the newcomers had stolen or falsified the papers? If so, the Zieglers could be outside the fences now, demanding to be allowed in. There had been no sign or communication from them.

Had they been forcibly detained somewhere? Had they been killed and robbed of their papers? Could it be that, as the hour approached, those who suddenly found themselves unprepared for the inevitable would kill those that had for so long made proper preparations?

Defeated, David and Franklin walked slowly toward the ladder. Briefly they glanced in horror at each other, not daring to speak the fear within their hearts.

CHAPTER 6

QUEBEC I.
THE SHELTER

"Fire from heaven... when the light of Mars fails... white coal will be driven from black; plague, blood, famine, iron and pestilence, in the sky fire will be seen, long running spark."

Nostradamus (1503-1566 A.D.)

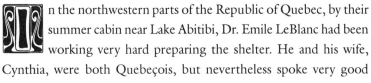n the northwestern parts of the Republic of Quebec, by their summer cabin near Lake Abitibi, Dr. Emile LeBlanc had been working very hard preparing the shelter. He and his wife, Cynthia, were both Quebeçois, but nevertheless spoke very good English with only the hint of a French accent.

Dr. LeBlanc, a biochemist, had patented quite a few chemical innovations, allowing him the luxury of a second home away from the city. He was 50 years old. Of medium height and build, he carried an aura of knowledge and respect. Still good looking, with abundant light brown hair showing only a hint of gray, he now seemed preoccupied and distant. Working intensely for so many weeks had physically exhausted him. It had required great physical effort to empty the underground shelter, clean it and refurbish it.

At times, Dr. LeBlanc had almost stopped working on the shelter. The thought of subjecting himself and his wife to the rigors of survival under terrible conditions for possibly years seemed futile, considering their age and the increasingly pessimistic prognoses put out by some of the scientific community.

A burst of energy and optimism had enabled him to finish, however, when his daughter, Trisha, had called from the States with the news of her family's intention to join them in an effort to survive.

* * *

Only with great difficulty had his daughter and son-in-law, Paul, and their treasured daughter, Jenny, made it past the border. They arrived at the cabin just in time to help in the final stocking of the underground shelter. Hope and love flowed again within the scientist, masking his exhaustion and depression, and, though he knew it was irrational, his anger at the injustice of the situation.

"This is totally illogical," he had told Cynthia so many times recently. "My mind just can't grasp it. After all these thousands of years of civilization, it's all going to go 'poof' and turn into nothing. Why?"

"There doesn't need to be a reason," his wife had replied. Cynthia, also 50 years of age, was a tall, elegant, silver-haired woman. She looked slightly older than her husband. Always meticulous in her dress and appearance, she possessed an aura of dignity an intelligence.

"Why must there be an explanation?" Cynthia went on. "You're driving me crazy with your ponderings about fate, God, evolution, philosophy and all that. Things are as they are, and if you try to rationalize them, you'll be the one to go insane."

Emile sighed. "I would rather we had a nuclear winter. At least then I wouldn't have God to blame!"

"Now, now, dear," Cynthia said gently. "This is definitely not a good time for blasphemy."

Cynthia LeBlanc was, and always had been, a very practical person. She felt there was no need to fight the system or try to change things, since it probably all didn't matter anyway. Her way was to go along and make the best of everything. Getting ready for the greatest holocaust of all time was just another chore that had to be done. And, as such, had to be done correctly. Cynthia had inventoried every single item and its location in the shelter. All the data was neatly stored in her small computer. If all the different sources of power failed, she had enough batteries to keep the computer going for months.

"I'm ready for the end of the world," she laughed.

* * *

The comet's huge outer coma, over two hundred thousand miles wide and composed of gases and fine particles of dust, had made first contact with the Earth's atmosphere. It slowly enveloped the entire planet in an incessant shower of minute meteorites. The sky became a diffuse bright haze, with a continual deluge of dust and sand-grain-sized particles that obliterated the heavens. The downpour of larger fragments of dirt, metal and stone increased dramatically with each hour, as all of Earth was slowly engulfed by the comet's coma.

The relentless meteor shower increased in intensity until the crescendoing downpour made outdoor life almost impossible. Massive extinction began with the thunderous roar of a global sandstorm from the heavens.

The sky became a homogeneous haze of blinding light, as the particles dispersed the sun's light in all directions. For a few days there was no day or night, only hazy brightness accompanied by the constant din of the fine-particle storm, punctuated occasionally by explosions as projectiles landed. The crops of the world, doomed to freeze, were first sandblasted and crushed.

* * *

The tall, narrow, two-story wooden cabin was of a classical style for northern Quebec. The relaxing, light blue color of its outer walls contrasted with the bright red of the window frames and the central door. The roof, also red, curved as it sloped down. This steepness, and the absence of balconies or any other flat-roofed adjoining structures, was a necessity in a latitude of extreme snow falls.

The woods around the LeBlancs' cabin were typical of the area. A blend of evergreen pines and tall, deciduous white-barked trees, the forest provided a haven for birds, bear, foxes, wolves, deer, moose and many smaller mammals. Environmental laws had allowed nature to return to the balance set out so efficiently by the planet before the advent of nonmuscular hunting weapons. Hunting and fishing were permitted, but carefully monitored. Only bow and arrow and non-electronically enhanced fishing gear were allowed.

The residents of the area were mostly outdoor adventurers used to the rigors of the climate. With daily temperatures below the freezing point for over six months of the year, the area of Canada and Quebec close to the Arctic Circle was a haven for that part of the human population that still loved the challenge of survival under adverse conditions. As such, many of these hardy adventurers were not overly concerned about the imminent meteoritic winter. They were well-prepared to survive a deep winter that they expected could last 10 or even 18 months. Of some concern, though, was the proximity of the expected impact. Morocco was only three thousand, four hundred miles away.

* * *

The LeBlancs' underground shelter was situated a few hundred feet from their cabin and was built like a small house dug into the ground. The top part lay hidden under a pile of dirt. It had been built as soon as the comet shower was announced. Made of poured concrete, the forty by twenty foot super-insulated structure had three stories and contained sixteen hundred square feet of living and storage

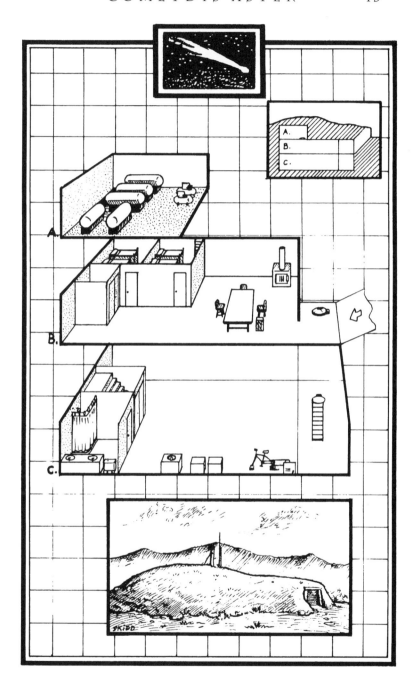

space. Another four hundred square feet on the top floor housed the generators and the water and gas storage tanks.

The shelter's two main floors were both below ground level and very well insulated. The large entrance to the first floor was through a spacious, slowly deepening ramp, wide enough to accommodate cabinets and supplies. The last of the supplies were to be placed against one of the walls of the ramp, leaving space for only one person to pass by. This corridor was separated from the outside by an insulated metal door that was secured by special locks. If the emergency exit and lock system failed, exit through this door would require dynamite.

No one could violate the sanctuary through this opening. Nobody would be allowed to join them, since supplies were calculated for a limited number of inhabitants. They were well armed and could fend off any intruder.

The ramp led down to the main room, a spacious, twenty by twenty foot all-purpose living room. The normally roomy living-kitchen-dining room space now looked crowded and uncomfortable with the heavy stores of supplies that had not all fit into the lower level storage area.

Next to the living room were two small bedrooms, each with three bunk beds. From this floor a steep stairway led down to the basement, where a small, full bathroom occupied one corner. A sealed latrine was next to it in case the plumbing broke down. Also in the basement were a washer and dryer, a large sink, and a small, bicycle-driven mini-generator and air-exchanger. This system was installed in case both the county electricity and the shelter's gas-driven generator system failed. Without energy, the shelter's air could not be circulated or exchanged. Most of the remaining basement was open space for storage.

A second large insulated door separated the living room from the ramp corridor that led to the outside. The ramp corridor itself was not insulated so that it could serve as a large frozen food storage area.

The LeBlancs had prepared for what they considered the worst scenario. Like most Canadians and Quebeçois, they were accustomed to very long and frigid winters. They had always enjoyed the northern outdoors, and were well versed in fishing and hunting even during the worst of winters. The prospect of a continual winter lasting a year or more was a source of concern, but didn't frighten them. They had enough food, supplies, energy sources, water and medicine, to allow them to live comfortably for one or even two years. They also had plenty of powdered milk for all of them, and over two hundred pounds of baby formula and food for the child that was soon to be born. With the effects of isolation in mind, the shelter was also well stocked with exercise equipment, music discs, videos, games, puzzles and books.

The utility floor, above the bedrooms and corridor, consisted of a very well insulated twenty by twenty foot room containing three one thousand-gallon natural gas cylinders and two one thousand-gallon water containers. In case all water was consumed, they had an ice melter consisting of a metal tank with gas burners under it. A heavy-duty gas generator and a smaller auxiliary generator occupied the rest of this floor. The generators would supply the electricity and heat needed. The entire shelter was covered by a mound of insulating dirt that was now overgrown with natural vegetation. The tons of dirt would protect against brimstone and acid rain.

In anticipation of many feet of snow, air ducts reached 30 feet into the air. Braced with steel wires, they looked like tall masts on a grub-shaped green sailboat.

Another heavy combination-locked door linked the utility room with the outside. After the gas and water cylinders had been filled, this door had been barricaded with dirt and concealed.

* * *

The final preparations before sealing the shelter's main door were under way.

The cabin and its clearing amidst the pines of the Quebec forest was flooded with extreme brightness. Colors were mostly lost in the white glare. A continual shower of tiny cometary debris shattered the silence of the area. Every few minutes a sharp tap, or a crack was heard.

In the first days of November, the fall weather had been pleasantly mild. There was no snow on the ground, and a few leaves still remained attached to branches. The many evergreens at the perimeter of the clearing added body and some color to the forest.

The Lopezes and LeBlancs wore clothes and hats made of hard, leathery material, and very dark sunglasses. Little Jenny was attempting to fasten a pair of sunglasses to the face of the LeBlancs' dog with surgical tape. Samantha, a white, shaggy Samoyed, contentedly accepted the affection and the contraption, even though she was already burdened with a padded body suit. "Now, don't lose these again," Jenny scolded the dog cheerily. "You don't want to go blind, do you?"

The family was unloading large containers from a tractor-like loader by the entrance. Working under strong canopies and heavy-duty umbrellas, and wearing protective hats, they looked as if they were ready for a stiff boxing match.

Emile grumbled about the comet as his daughter and son-in-law disappeared into the shelter with arms full of boxes. Jenny, sheltered beneath her colorful umbrella, also shuttled back and forth, bringing supplies and toys from the nearby cabin.

The large, thick metal door of the shelter was wide open, exposing a ramp that dropped slowly downward. A short, robust robot had picked up one of the last of the large boxes from the tractor, and was rolling toward the ramp. The four-foot-tall mechanized computer had been constructed to look somewhat humanoid. A thin metallic sound reminded all present to keep their padded overclothes and hats on, and to use their umbrellas. The robot, unprogrammed for this kind of outdoor problem, looked all around, bewildered by the impacts and sounds of the tiny meteorites. As it cocked its head upward toward the bright sky, camera sensors brought its mechanized metal pupils to a pinpoint. It hesitated another second before continuing its march toward the shelter.

"James, stop!" Dr. LeBlanc commanded. The robot immediately came to a standstill.

"Yes, sir?" the tin voice inquired.

"James, I changed my mind. That box goes in area 17, snug against the wall. End James." The robot immediately resumed its fixed path down the ramp, adding matter-of-factly, "Of course, sir," its programmed response echoing through the shelter. When the robot returned, Emile commanded it to magnetically attach itself to the tractor. He then pressed some keys on a small console, and the tractor responded, returning dutifully toward the cabin, where the last of the supplies waited.

Cynthia glanced up from the list she had been checking and laughed, seeing the bespectacled dog jump onto the tractor's empty driver's seat. "It is so good to laugh," she said aloud. "Everyone around here has been in such a poor mood!"

"We really need all of this?" Dr. LeBlanc interrupted, pointing at a large box of preserved macaroni and cheese, one of his least favorite dishes. "This comet isn't as big as the one that killed the dinosaurs and 95% of the species at the end of the Cretaceous. We surely don't need that gooey stuff to survive."

Without any change in expression, Cynthia replied in a deadpan, "I would like to remind you, dear, that during the K-T extinction, only seventy to seventy-five percent of all species died, not ninety-five percent. It was at the end of the *Permian*, two hundred and forty million years ago, that there was ninety-five percent extinction." Throwing his arms to the sky in surrender, Emile looked at her with fake disgust, while Trisha laughed quietly at the exchange.

A few minutes later, the tractor and robot returned, and again all were busy by the entrance to the shelter.

As Paul moved outward through the shelter corridor, he suddenly stopped and looked in bewilderment at a box sitting unlabeled on top of a pile of other numbered and well-catalogued boxes. Suspicious, he cut open the strings with his pocket knife and looked inside. His suspicions were confirmed. Some totally non-essential items were stacked inside: many rows of beautifully decorated and intricate multicolored wax candles.

"Cynthia!" he called out. His mother-in-law immediately blushed when she saw her box discovered.

"Why do you have your collection of antique candles from the 1990's?" he demanded. "You know antiques aren't needed for survival."

"But they're my favorites," Cynthia pleaded. "They're irreplaceable. They might even be useful. Please let me keep them. They're the only things from all my antiques I've brought in, I swear."

Paul looked at her with amusement. *Candles*, he thought, *what a waste of space.*

"Sure, Grandma," he said aloud. "What other cute little collectibles have you stashed away on the pretense that they might be of use?"

"None! I told you, I swear."

With a roll of his eyes, and now smiling in disbelief, Paul retied the box and was moving down the corridor when outside, a small red light on James' head suddenly lit up, and a short buzzing sound came from within its innards.

"Quiet!" said Paul as he rushed from the ramp. They all grouped together by the entrance and looked around to see where the strangers might be coming from. Paul put his right hand behind his back and pulled a laser handgun from under his jacket.

"I was afraid of this," he said, as he adjusted his sunglasses with his other hand to allow for infrared vision. He immediately saw the two strangers among the trees and bushes by the perimeter of the clearing. Without hesitation, he walked in their direction and placed himself between them and his family.

"This is private land. You have no right to be here. Leave immediately." Paul's loud and stern voice left no doubt that he was very serious. "We are armed," he continued, to make sure the strangers understood what he had in his hand.

In the meantime, Dr. LeBlanc had retrieved a rifle from the entrance to the shelter's tunnel and was pointing it at the uninvited guests, while he scanned the perimeter of the clearing in search of others.

"Please, we are unarmed," responded a young man with a strong French accent. He put down a few bags of belongings and raised one hand. With the other, he still held a protective umbrella high above himself and his companion.

The man, probably in his mid-twenties, was accompanied by a

er woman, almost a girl, who was clutching a small baby in her arms. The infant, partially hidden by her blouse, was breast-feeding, oblivious to the tragedy that was unfolding around it. The strangers' bleached figures looked pale and distant, their faces accented only by dark regulation sunglasses. A bright yellow bandana covering the woman's hair was the only color apparent through the bright haze.

"Our vehicle broke down not too far from here and we can't make it to our assigned civil shelter," said the young woman, also in very accented English. "All we need is shelter for a day or two, till the danger is over. We will leave then. We have our own food."

Paul looked at Dr. LeBlanc. His father-in-law slowly moved his head from side to side.

"I said go!" Paul repeated. "We'll shoot if necessary!"

Cynthia LeBlanc didn't seem to understand the situation. "Emile, Paul — don't you think that maybe we should . . ." She trailed off in confusion.

"No!" Paul said in a low voice intended only for his mother-in-law. His pulse was rushing and his voice shook with anger.

Mrs. LeBlanc started to speak again. "We have so much . . ." she said, but Paul cut her off.

"No!" he repeated. "We made a decision, remember? Nobody, we said." He walked a few yards closer to the strangers. The man was still holding one hand in the air, while the young woman, very frightened now, had tears running from under her dark eyeglasses.

"There is a large farmhouse about four or five miles from here," said Paul, pointing the barrel of his gun toward the northwest. The strangers looked at each other. The man was about to speak when Paul fired.

The red beam hissed through the air a few feet above the heads of the outsiders. The laser made an arc above them, cutting through the trees. Branches and leaves were sheared and broken off. Startled birds flew off, with cries of panic.

"Please," the young man pleaded again as he picked up the duffle bags.

Paul ignored him. "Take that trail and keep going till you see the big silo of the farm," he said. "It's a shortcut that will get you there faster. Now go!"

As the strangers left, Emile continued surveying the area. He wasn't sure if there were more out there. It could be a trick. Paul turned back to face the still-shocked and now accusing faces of his wife and mother-in-law.

"Their vehicle broke down! Likely story!" Paul said sarcastically, searching for a sign of approval that never appeared.

He put his gun away, and with both hands slightly outstretched, reminded them again of their decision. "We made a commitment, we all agreed. Remember? We can't afford to take any strangers." He avoided their eyes and added, "Back to work. We don't have much time."

Trisha put her hands on her swollen belly. With moist eyes she looked toward the woods where the strangers had disappeared. *This isn't like Paul*, she thought. *The damned comet is changing us already.*

Under the pretext of work, Paul rushed toward the shelter to hide his feelings of guilt. As he entered the corridor, he encountered the robot dutifully returning outdoors. "James, move!" Paul yelled irritably as he stormed toward the robot, which immediately turned ninety degrees and bumped noisily against the wall.

"Yes, sir." The robot's expression sounded muffled, since the loudspeaker on its body had made contact with the wall. Its head turned almost completely around, following Paul, awaiting an order that never came.

"James, come here." The robot joined Trisha, who had been holding Jenny. Putting her arms around both her child and the robot, she began to speak comfortingly. "It's okay. Things are going to be okay."

Emile touched his ID bracelet to the heavy computerized combination door, setting the bolts in motion. The wrist bracelets worn by all family members relayed the owner's identification, allowing for instant recognition by doors, vehicles, luggage, and other objects. Emile had just finished encoding the lock's mechanism.

* * *

A little while later, while preparing to bring the last few items in the shelter, Paul shooed the dog out. "Sorry, Samantha, you can't get used to staying in here. Go to the cabin."

Jenny, who was not supposed to have witnessed this, appeared suddenly. "Daddy! What do you mean? Sammy's staying with us, isn't she?"

"Well, Jenny, I hate to tell you this. This is very, very serious business and we just can't —"

"But Daddy," the child interrupted, "she'll die. You said all people and animals that stayed outside would die." In disbelief, the little girl wrapped her arms around Samantha and started crying loudly.

"I'm sorry, my darling, but we can't share the food and the space with Sammy. She'll be okay," he lied.

"Paul, please," Trisha interrupted, pointing toward one of the huge piles of boxes at the sides of the ramp. "There's so much food here, more than enough for all of us."

"I'm sorry," Paul said firmly. "We discussed this earlier, and we agreed. Please, let's not go over it again."

From the ramp, Jenny's grandmother interrupted with a happier tone of voice. "You don't have to worry, Paul. The dog won't eat any of our food," she said. With a smile, she removed a blanket covering a huge stack of cans, bags and boxes of dog food. "I've even set up a small area of the basement for Sammy's doggie-toilet."

"Hooray, Grandmamma!" Jenny cheered, and without waiting further, rushed to bring in her beloved dog.

Paul was furious at having been forced to give in. They had all agreed on the plan. On the other hand, he was relieved that he wouldn't have to upset Jenny, something he had been dreading. It was so difficult for him to see her sad. She deserved a little happiness. Things were going to be very hard in the near future.

"Oh! I forgot my Raggedy Ann!" The cry from Jenny stopped the closing of the door. They all watched with amusement as she darted out with her umbrella, running toward the cabin. There she hurried upstairs, while unwrapping a chocolate bar she had just re-trieved from one of her pockets. She started to eat it on the way to her room. Upon reaching the room, Jenny grabbed her doll, and was about to leave when, on second thought, she considered the other dolls and stuffed animals. There were so many, and she loved them all. Setting the candy bar down, she grabbed one more doll and two stuffed animals and took off downstairs as fast as she could.

When she returned to the shelter, she was almost invisible, nearly hidden by the colorful dolls and stuffed creatures. The adults laughed and clapped as the little girl rushed proudly into the shelter.

As the ramp door closed, Emile took one last look at the world as he knew it. With a sigh of nostalgia and resignation, and after an approved retinal scan, he closed the door firmly, and set the electric locks. His Earth would never be the same again.

Then suddenly, the silence was violently broken by a muffled roar as the shelter door was buried in a ton of dirt. The remote-controlled tractor dumped its last cargo, hiding and insulating the entrance. The tractor moved obediently to the side and shut its engine off.

* * *

A deep silence descended on the forest. The bright haze and the din of the meteor shower continued to intensify. The birds and animals of the forest remained still, as if holding their breaths, frozen in expectation.

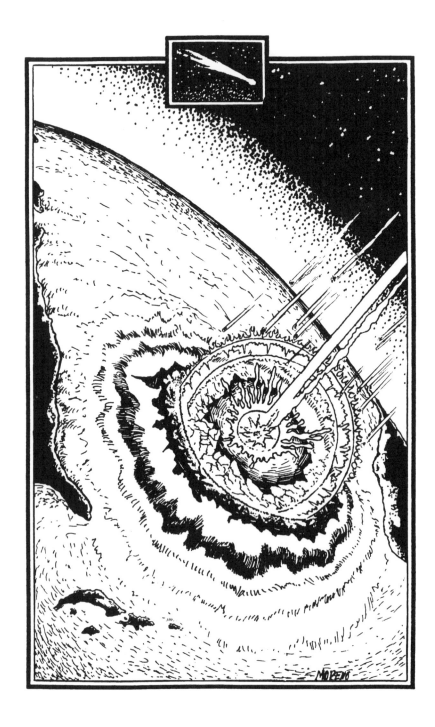

CHAPTER 7

SAN FRANCISCO DATE: 01-01-01 DIS'ASTER'S DAY

"Jesus said to his disciples, *but take ye heed: behold I have foretold you... the sun shall be darkened and the moon shall not give her light and the stars of the heaven shall fall out of the skies... when ye shall see these things come to pass, know that [the end] is near..."*

Matthew 24:29, Holy Bible

n San Francisco, the day had been unusually silent. Practically unnoticed was the change in calendar date. That day, November 2nd, 2048, was now officially called the first day of November, and November became the first month of the year one post-impact (01-01-01 PI). For weeks martial law had been ruthlessly enforced. It had paid off; the city of San Francisco and the entire Bay Area were under effective military control. The Civil Defense Emergency Task Force (CIDETAF) dictated that for two days prior to impact, no one was to leave their home or shelter. CIDETAF estimated that the curfew would last at least three days post-impact. After that, stricter measures would gradually be lifted, but the area would have to remain under military rule for at least a few weeks, maybe months, after the comet had dealt its blow to the planet. Absolute military rule was necessary to deal with the more than tripled population that had resulted when the coastal areas of the eastern states were evacuated.

Emergency vehicles were available to transport sick people to and from hospitals. There was no need to shelter the population underground since it was estimated that if the wind-blast and the shockwave reached San Francisco they would be extremely weak. The worst that was expected on Impact Day in the San Francisco area was strong, hot winds, with damage only to weaker structures, toppled antennas and trees, and possibly some fires. Since no one was allowed outdoors, the total number of injuries was hoped to be minimal. Of more concern was the possibility of losing electric power. Without electricity, water could not be pumped, and doors and windows would not operate. Elevators would not work, and many of the inhabitants of the vertical city would be stranded dozens, even hundreds of floors above the ground.

After the wind storms and shock waves had passed and the damage was repaired, instructions would be given to prepare for the long winter to come. Older homes and buildings that could not withstand the weight of snow would be evacuated and their inhabitants moved to safer shelter. The transition would be smooth. The entire Bay Area was well prepared for survival. The civil and cooperative attitude of its people was an example to the whole world.

* * *

On the 117th floor of a tall and graceful apartment building near downtown San Francisco, Tony and Ann Lambert were gathered with their family around an entertainment center in their spacious living room. They were watching the news on the wall-sized telecommunicator screen. Behind them, large glass doors led to a spacious balcony, beyond which could be seen half of San Francisco and its ocean and bay. The haze from the comet's coma bleached most of the colors from a view that was normally majestic.

Thanks to the many new alloys that had revolutionized construction, the San Francisco Bay Area was studded with beautiful, tall, interconnected buildings that brought most of the habitation well above ground level. The old Trans-American Bank Building, retained as a symbol of an earlier era, was dwarfed by the newer buildings. Transportation conduits stretched gracefully between the buildings and over the large bodies of water.

The Lambert family sat quietly, sipping tea and cold beverages as they watched the newscast. They had all the food, water and medicine they would need for at least a three-week period of seclusion: the worst scenario the citizens of the Bay Area expected. With computerized identification, each member of the family had been allotted a specific amount of supplies, ensuring that no single family hoarded more food than that rationed to them.

The older Lamberts were sitting in a comfortable and colorful couch. In their mid-sixties, they held hands and appeared calm and secure. More tense were their son, Michael, and his wife, Tracy, sitting by a crystal coffee table. The Lamberts' two young grandchildren sat on the soft carpet. A large white angora cat rubbed against the couch, soliciting the rituals of affection it had grown to expect. The cat would have to wait; the family was focused on the latest comet news.

* * *

Tony gazed at his family with pride. His wife, Ann, had been a good companion in both the good and bad times. She had supported him through his drinking bouts and even sat next to him for weeks in the hospital as he recovered from an alcohol-induced pancreatitis that almost took his life. Having faced death so closely, he had sworn never to drink again. It all seemed a distant nightmare now. Had Ann left him, as well she might have given his insensitivity and abuse, he would probably have rotted away in one of the many infirmaries that had been set aside for those with self-inflicted illness. They were places where such patients died quietly and with minimal cost to the community.

Ann sensed him looking at her, the way he did so often lately. She knew his gaze expressed both love and admiration.

Their children were all doing well, and their grandchildren were healthy, radiant with energy. They had little time for mischief, but plenty of time to absorb a well-guided education. Ann remembered how a form of censorship had been dictated a few decades prior, when the world chaos was at its worst. After the crises had finally been somewhat resolved, the centuries-old cry of many psychologists and educators was finally heard: all media, information and entertainment were modified by simple rules of logic to end the negative social attitudes created through the now better understood instinct of mimicry. Voters demanded censorship. The Constitutional Amendments initially were very difficult to structure and impose, but now, almost subconsciously, crime was slowly being tamed.

Ann's reminiscing abruptly ended as the newscaster's voice changed, becoming tense. "Only four minutes, that's two hundred and forty seconds, to impact," he announced. "Our remote-controlled sensors continue to bring you the details of the great comet catastrophe."

"As you have already seen," he went on, "the great cities by the shores of the Atlantic are all empty, or almost empty." The scene changed from the studio to a deserted street in Manhattan. At a distance, a man was seen pushing a shopping cart across an empty street towards the door of a tall building.

"A few last-minute looters are hurrying into buildings. One of our robots interviewed one such person just a few minutes ago. The young man told us that he would seek safety at the top of a building, where the water could not reach him." The commentator laughed and added, "I'm sure this fearless entrepreneur will be getting his justice very soon. Dis'Aster will not be forgiving."

The scene changed to New York's waterfront, where the bay appeared deserted. Not a single watercraft could be seen. With the Statue of Liberty tiny in the background, the remote-sensor moved to a new area and zoomed in on a large group of people. Over two thousand with banners and signs stood on a dock looking out toward the sea. They chanted religious songs, waiting for their final day of liberation. The commentator was silent, allowing the image to speak for itself.

"The impact has been recalculated to occur in the Eastern Atlantic Ocean," he resumed. "It will miss North Africa completely. As you all know, the impact of the one-trillion-ton comet cannot be shown, not even from space, because all that would be visible is the white haze of the comet's coma, thousands of miles wide, obscuring the central asteroid and the actual impact. Most of the ice covering the comet will be vaporized or fragmented on contact with our atmosphere. This will interfere even further with any visual perception of the impact. And of course, once the multi-megaton explosion starts, all nearby sensors will be pulverized. Radar imaging will give scientists the best understanding of the event."

"As millions of tons of ice and ocean water vaporize, the water content of our atmosphere will almost double. All the water and all the debris and dust from the explosion will become part of our atmosphere. In a few hours the Earth's rotation will distribute it, along with billions of tons of soot from worldwide firestorms, throughout the atmosphere. It will become very dark. Earth will plunge into a cold, black night lasting many weeks or months."

"The main crater produced by Dis'Aster should be one hundred miles or more in diameter." The commentator pointed to a large holographic image of the moon. "These two well-known hundred-mile craters, Tycho and Copernicus, were each produced by impacting bodies the same size as Dis'Aster. All of greater San Francisco and the surrounding Bay Area cities could fit easily into one of these crater basins."

The newsman paused, with a brief look of nervousness on his face, and then resumed, his voice as smooth and dispassionate as if he'd been announcing the winning numbers of a lottery.

"And now, my friends, KDUC K3, your complete home station, brings you, the fortunate citizens of the Bay, Impact! As it happens!"

The display changed to animation. A vivid image showed the planet Earth against a black background, with a large, white, shiny comet, its two huge tails falling majestically behind it, suspended near it. The Atlantic Ocean faced the screen. The coasts of Africa and Europe were in the distance.

"Cool!" twelve-year-old Matthew exclaimed.

"Matt, this is *real*, not a movie!" his grandfather admonished. "This is actually very sad."

Suzi, Matthew's ten-year-old sister, glanced at him briefly and smiled with satisfaction. The screen now showed a close-up of the North Atlantic, northwestern Africa, Spain and Portugal.

"The comet," the news commentator resumed, "will land in the Atlantic Ocean. The threat to our Atlantic Coast cities is therefore extremely serious. Tsunamis will devastate all the cities along the Atlantic Coast of North America, North Africa and Europe. Southern Africa and all of eastern South America are also in danger. It is expected that many islands will vanish completely."

He paused to let the gravity of his comments sink in, then continued. "The comet will make its way through our atmosphere in only a few seconds and plunge through the seven miles of ocean in just under one second. The animation you will witness will slow all this down so that we can see and understand what is actually happening.

"When it hits the water and the solid sea floor, Dis'Aster will decelerate in a fraction of a second, from a speed of nineteen miles per second, to a complete standstill. Since our planet is traveling toward the comet at its own speed of nineteen miles per second, the actual speed of impact will be thirty-six miles per second, or one hundred and thirty thousand miles per hour!"

Again he paused, then continued in his warm, professional voice. "The resulting explosion will be equivalent to the simultaneous detonation of over one hundred and fifty million hydrogen bombs. The entire comet will pulverize instantly. White-hot debris from the comet and the ocean floor will be flung into the atmosphere to rain over most of the world. A large portion of the planet, in the few-thousand-mile zone called the 'lethal area' by scientists, will go up in flames." The scene switched back to the animation, which showed the comet approaching the atmosphere.

The announcer began to count. "Forty, thirty-nine, thirty-eight, thirty-seven. My friends, millions of our fellow men, women and children will die in less than a minute as the comet strikes the Earth, sending out waves of hurricane winds and scorching heat. Earthquakes will riddle half of the world and extraordinary tsunamis of unbelievable height will rush out from the impact point. Massive devastation throughout the coastal region of the Atlantic is about to occur."

The image of the comet moved closer and closer to the Earth's atmosphere. The black pocked, potato-shaped monolith slowly tumbled; a huge halo of dust and gases trailed behind it, with geysers of gas hissing out from pockets of sublimating ice.

"As you say a prayer for all those unfortunate to be caught in this tragedy, thank your god or gods for sparing our part of the world," the announcer said somberly. "Here in beautiful San Francisco and the Bay Area, since our latitude is much higher than that of the impact, we are safe, we are alive, and we will remain so.

"Three — two — one . . ."

The animation focused on the rushing comet. In slow motion, it penetrated the light blue layers of the planet's atmosphere.

On first contact with the atmosphere, the comet lost its thick ice shield. Chunks of ice and rock lagged behind the heavier, speeding central core.

In an instant, the intruder traversed the entire two hundred-mile-thick atmosphere and impacted the surface of the ocean.

Even though impact had already occurred in real time, and its detonation and destructive forces were well under way; in San Francisco the animation slowed to demonstrate the details of the catastrophe. Data began to be displayed rapidly on a side of the screen, indicating post-impact seconds, temperature, winds and air pressure.

As the image of Dis'Aster penetrated the ocean, the displayed data indicated what was occurring in real time around the globe. The exact coordinates of impact point became confirmed and ceased to change.

An animated wall of water rushed outward from impact point, exposing the brown sea floor with its mountains and valleys, and, just west of it, parts of the long, rippled mid-Atlantic rift that extends from Iceland to the mid-South Atlantic.

As the walls of water, like an expanding inverted cone (some ten miles high,) started to fall back onto the planet, tsunami waves (many five to seven miles high) raced out from the point of impact in concentric rings.

The Lamberts were suddenly startled by a much-too-realistic explosion coming from the surround-sound loudspeakers. At the same instant the animation showed a flash of bright white and orange light arising from the image of the asteroid, then replaced it completely as the core cracked and then exploded on its contact with the Earth's hard crust. Simultaneously, an animated dome of heat and energy expanded outward at fifteen-hundred miles per hour, overtaking the collapsing wall of boiling ocean water and raced past the huge circle of tsunamis, which by now stretched out for hundreds of miles.

Hundreds of detached pieces of ice which had covered the solid parts of the comet, many of them hundreds to thousands of yards wide, had become separate lethal missiles. Like flying icebergs of colossal dimensions, some exploded in mid-air due to the friction and pressures generated by the resisting atmosphere. Others landed, creating their own craters in northern Africa and on the Iberian peninsula. Many landed in the ocean, producing additional impacts and new concentric rings of deadly tsunami waves, which collided with the others, sending the entire North Atlantic Ocean into a turbulence of unimaginable destructive force.

As it penetrated the atmosphere, the huge central solid core, a mountain of mostly iron, nickel and rock, compressed the atmosphere under it. The planet's air, unable to move out of the way quickly enough, in just three seconds transformed from a gas to a super-heated compressed plasma of chaotic atoms and electrons. This exploding plasma in turn impacted the waters of the ocean. The gigantic comet carried so much inertia that its speed was not affected by the Earth's atmosphere or ocean.

Fractions of a second before the comet actually made contact with the Earth's solid surface there was already in effect a monstrous release of energy as the plasmafied air and water under the comet exploded with an energy equivalent to that of millions of hydrogen bombs.

Then, as deceleration changed from nineteen to zero miles per second, the front portions of Dis'Aster made impact with the solid surface of the planet. In that instant, its metal and rock components simultaneously exploded along with the solid underlying portions of the Earth's delicate crust. As this instantaneous transformation, from solid metal and rock, to an explosive energetic plasma, was occurring at the ocean floor, the rest of the comet, a few more miles of it, was proceeding at incredible speed toward this center of doom, bringing with it more and more kinetic energy and solids, which in their turn would vaporize, adding more and more fuel to the largest explosion in the solar system since that one which accompanied the planetesimal impact that extinguished the dinosaurs.

The computerized animation continued in vivid colors, depicting the most important events as more data came in from remote robot-sensors in the real world.

Made to withstand extremes of temperature and pressure, these robots, whether on land, air, or water, performed exceedingly well during those early seconds and minutes, communicating vital information on the direct effects of the impact. One by one, the robot stations were destroyed, but not before computers were able to reconstruct the exact direction and angle of impact of the comet- asteroid: its exact landing point and the statistical details of the expanding shock wave, winds, tsunamis and additional impacts from the smaller fragments.

These calculations pinpointed the impact at exactly 29.95°N latitude and 28.78°W longitude, or five hundred, ninety miles south of the Azores, six hundred, four miles west of the Canary Islands, and nine hundred, thirty-two miles directly west of the Moroccan coast of Africa.

The animation now showed a huge crater being carved into the Earth's crust. Letters and numbers appeared, indicating a maximum main crater diameter of one hundred and fifty miles, the distance from Washington, D.C. to Philadelphia. The crater's walls reached up to eight miles from the sea floor.

The data displayed gave instantaneous and accurate information relating to all aspects of the disaster. The Canaries, Azores, Cape Verde and Madeira Islands vanished as the shock wave and the boiling sea surge overwhelmed them.

The simulation then emphasized the reddish-white heat wave, 900° F., that hugged the planet's waters and solid surfaces, expanding like fire outward at fifteen-hundred miles per hour, reaching first Africa and then Europe. The announcer reminded those watching that the worst hurricanes produced winds with a maximum speed of only two hundred and thirty miles per hour. Every city by the shores of northwest Africa and those of the west coasts of Portugal and Spain were leveled by the yet unweakened shock wave.

The news commentator alerted his audience that evacuation of northwestern Africa had been only partially successful; to evacuate so many millions of people had been an impossible task. Some remained, choosing not to believe that the planet would really be hit by a comet. Some believed it was all a cynical political maneuver to displace them and take over their lands. Others stayed put, in the religious conviction that if God wanted this to happen, then it should happen. They stood firm and waited for their day of transformation. For many others, evacuation was impossible. Millions of these people were now dead or dying.

"My God!" the commentator suddenly interjected, his voice no longer smooth and professional. "It's much worse than expected! The heat wave is much hotter and the winds much stronger than anticipated. Millions must be dying as you witness this right now."

Then trying to calm down, he continued, "But here in the great Bay Area, we will be safe!"

As the animation continued to show the effects of Dis'Aster, the shock wave crossed over the lands of western Europe and Africa, leaving behind a burning, smoldering countryside.

The commentator's voice shook again as he read reports from sensors in the real world: "Casablanca, Lisbon, Madrid, Barcelona, Paris, London, Dublin — they're all in flames! But Paris wasn't supposed to burn!"

As the shock wave traveled farther, the intensity of its heat slowly dissipated. Its deep orange and white color changed to a lighter and more transparent hue. Only 400° F. now, the wave slowed to six-hundred miles per hour as it reached middle Africa and Eastern Europe. Then its northern and western front almost simultaneously hit Iceland, the Atlantic coast of North America, and the northern countries of South America.

By this time, all the major cities of middle and eastern Europe, as far north and east as Warsaw and Stockholm, were in flames. Then Newfoundland and eastern Canada, the Bermudas, and the eastern islands of the Caribbean were hit by the shock wave.

The intensity and velocity of the heat wave continued to diminish. Now, without a trail of flames and smoke behind it, the dome of death spread more slowly in a circle of intense hot winds.

"Dead! Billions are dead!" cried the commentator, no longer attempting to sound calm. "The simulation we are seeing now is absolutely accurate! It's much, much worse than ever expected."

His voice trembling with both excitement and fear, he continued to comment on the horrifying computer-driven images. "It's unbelievable! The central parts of Europe weren't evacuated! Look! There is no more Spain or France. The British Isles is in flames. So are Rome, Budapest and Berlin!"

The animation displayed another phenomenon. While the huge asteroid-comet disintegrated, much of its matter was thrown upwards, together with many thousands of cubic acres of pulverized sea floor. Millions of tons of white-hot debris that had flown into the upper atmosphere now started to fall back upon the planet. The fire from the sky fell all over the Atlantic, over northern Africa, over the countries of the Mediterranean basin, and the entire Middle East.

The computer placed single zeros over all of these areas, indicating no survivors for millions of square miles.

The commentator, speaking more slowly now, sounded bewildered. "Jesus — look at that! — nobody can survive this." Then, with sudden realization of the dangers close to home, he switched his attention to the changes appearing over eastern North America.

"Oh, my God," he gasped. "Boston — Washington! Washington and Baltimore and Philadelphia! Montreal! Richmond! They weren't completely evacuated either! The computer tells us that they too must be in flames! They are all within the eighty to ninety percent fatality zone!"

"And the tsunamis, they've come a hundred miles or more inland in some areas! Richmond, Raleigh, Columbia, even Atlanta! They're all being washed away!"

He fell silent as many other western Atlantic cities — San Juan, Santo Domingo, Havana and Caracas — were portrayed as cities engulfed in flames.

A second and then a third wave of tumultuous blue waters covered the coastal regions of the entire Atlantic, reaching in some areas over two hundred miles inland. The tsunamis rushed into the Amazon River, reaching inland a thousand miles. The eastern United States and easternmost Canada were also gone.

The commentator faltered. "My parents and my sister," he whispered. And then he started to weep.

The Lambert family continued to listen in mute horror, hugging each other in fear and grief. All the people they knew and loved that lived in those areas of the United States were dead, instantly broiled alive or drowned. Evacuation had been limited to only the first five to ten miles of the coastlines.

The simulation continued, but the commentator remained silent. The circular line of fires devouring cities had ceased to expand beyond Washington, Montreal and Warsaw. The screen now changed to show, without the benefit of the commentator's explanations, the coastal areas of the entire North Atlantic being washed away by giant tsunami waves.

The commentator began to speak again, but his voice was interrupted by static. "Earthquake" was his last word, as the studio's ceiling fixtures and the furniture around him started to fall in disarray. Studio hands appeared, fleeing towards the exits. Just as suddenly, the screen went blank.

* * *

In their beautiful and comfortable apartment one hundred and seventeen floors above ground level, the Lambert family stared mutely at one another. Ten seconds later their apartment started to tremble. Very slowly at first, the teacups and silverware started to rattle. The fine tinkling sounds were soon joined by a distant faint rumble as a thin veil of dust rose from the surface of the city and the surrounding lands.

They all tried to stand as the quake increased in intensity. Never had an earthquake of this magnitude been witnessed by humankind. The strong and flexible building began to sway. Would their supermodern building withstand such a violation of the seismic scales?

In the next few seconds, the Lamberts were all thrown to the floor. Attempting to embrace each other, they screamed in terror. The large glass balcony doors and windows shattered. The cat was the first to understand. Hair on end, it jumped, flying through the balcony, preferring the two-thousand-foot abyss to the imminent danger it sensed.

In the next few seconds the Lamberts' bodies were pulped as the building they had known as home gave way to the relentless shaking and swaying. The majestic buildings of the entire Bay Area disintegrated and fell in unison, burying under billions of tons of rubble an entire civilization.

* * *

Dis'Aster had exploded instantaneously on contact with the Earth's solid crust. The explosion was three million times more powerful than the eruption of the volcano Krakatoa in 1883, and seven-hundred and fifty million times stronger than the atom bomb dropped on Hiroshima in 1945.

The shock wave first hit the Azores and the Canary Islands, incinerating them. It then blasted away the coast of northwestern Africa with temperatures above 800° F. A few minutes later it fell with merciless force on the European continent, striking at Portugal with an overt pressure of eight atmospheres and a wind velocity of 1000-plus miles per hour.

With winds down to four hundred miles per hour and temperatures around 200° F., it was soon upon the British Isles, Iceland, France, Germany and Italy, New York, Boston and Montreal, Washington, D.C. and Caracas. By this time, life on the Bermudas, Bahamas and most of the once-beautiful and radiant islands of the Caribbean had ceased to exist.

The front of the incinerating blast measured in the thousands of miles. Its merciless effects left behind a partial vacuum of smoldering, hot and dry nothingness.

The death blast slowed and cooled as it expanded and raged over the oceans and lands. As it grew more distant from the epicenter, it lost heat and strength but became much wider. At thirty-six-hundred miles from the impact point (Cairo, Moscow, Oslo, Chicago, Memphis, New Orleans, Panama, Rio de Janeiro) it had cooled to a temperature of 140° F., but the winds were still merciless, rushing over the land for close to an hour at one hundred and thirty miles per hour.

Having cooled down to 85° F. at sixty-two hundred miles from the impact point (halfway across the world), the winds at sixty-two miles per hour still produced great damage. For fifteen hours they rushed over the distant lands and continents, finally reaching the islands of the Pacific and Indian oceans, opposite the impact point.

Following the shock-heat wave came a base surge of superheated molten and pulverized mixture of asteroid and Earth crust. This lethal sludge, much heavier than water, rushed out in all directions from the impact point, reaching a few hundred miles before settling down into the depths of the now-boiling ocean and leaving a star-shaped scar with hundreds of spokes around the crater.

Immediately following the impact, ground shockwaves traveled outward; like a ringing bell, the entire planet resounded. This wave propagated at fantastic speed, traversing the entire thickness of the globe, setting off earthquakes and landslides, snapping dams like fragile wafers, and adding enormous destructive forces to those of the heat wave and the tsunamis that followed. The worst earthquake traversed directly through the planet and destroyed the Earth's crust exactly opposite impact point.

From the gaping crater at impact point, a huge cloud of steam and gases spread upward, mixed with the pulverized remnants of the comet's solid core and additional cubic miles of pulverized ocean floor. The superheated mass of chemicals, gases, dust and fragments formed a mushroom-shaped cloud that extended well into the stratosphere. The deadly cloud exploded eastward and westward. Then, as it started to lose momentum, the white-hot grains of pulverized rock started to rain back on the atmosphere, at a rate of many tons per acre. Their friction with the molecules of the upper atmosphere generated such heat that a large layer of superheated vapor broiled the portions of the world beneath the cloud. Atmospheric temperatures there reached over 1800° F., forcing nitrogen and oxygen from the atmosphere to combine, producing nitric acid. The ensuing rain was of unimaginable acidity, poisoning land masses, lakes, rivers, and many parts of the oceans.

Almost the entire Earth was set on fire by raining ashes. The global holocaust spared only the most northern and southern latitudes. The global dust and soot eventually expanded to cover most of the planet, totally blocking out sunlight.

A huge new geographic feature appeared on the eastern Atlantic Ocean: Dis'Aster had left a circular crater one hundred and fifty miles in diameter. The jagged, sharp walls settled two to three miles above sea level. Streaks of ejecta radiated from the crater, some stretching hundreds of miles before disappearing beneath the ocean's surface.

Forests and cities were all set ablaze as hell fell from the sky. Lightning produced by an atmosphere boiling with turbulence, new volcanos, and streams of lava that flowed like rivers, ignited anything. Brimstone and tektites rained once again on the planet. Earthquakes ravaged the entire globe as the molten innards of Earth were thrown into accelerated movement; a phenomenon which hadn't occurred for millions of years.

Oil tankers and fuel reserve tanks exploded like popcorn. Each minute saw a few million more humans die catastrophic deaths.

Fire-storms raged through all the continents, consuming forests, grasslands and cities, creating their own winds that expanded in all directions. These self-perpetuating storms remained unchecked, dying out only when they ran out of fuel. They too added millions of tons of soot to the debris that was already burdening the skies.

The new atmospheric bands of different shades transformed Earth into a small, dark Jupiter.

Our shiny blue planet was no more.

CHAPTER 8

QUEBEC II.
DATE: 01-01-01
THE BIRTH OF HOPE

"And the angel took the incense burner and filled it with fire... and threw it to the Earth; and there followed peals of thunder and sound and flashes of lightning and an earthquake... and there came hail and fire... thrown to Earth; and a third of the Earth was burned up, and a third of the trees and all of the green grasses were burned up."

John: Book of Revelation, 8:5,7 (Apocalypse),
Holy Bible

lthough Trisha LeBlanc Lopez was due to deliver three weeks after Impact Day, she worked as hard as the others, helping to prepare their shelter for the expected long confinement.

"Love, I've told you to call me if you need something moved," her husband admonished as she rearranged some large boxes.

"I know, I'm sorry," she replied. "But we need to get everything in here organized as soon as possible. I just hope we have enough."

"Don't worry, love, we have supplies for at least a year. We could even stretch it to two years if needed. We have nothing to worry about."

"Nothing to worry about?" interrupted Emile. "Let's not kid ourselves." He glanced sideways at Jenny, who was pretending not to be listening. He suddenly felt embarrassed. He had promised himself to spare the others his pessimism.

The physical work, together with the fear and stress, proved to be too much for Trisha. She went into premature labor soon after the shelter had been securely sealed. Her membranes ruptured only an hour and a half prior to the expected impact time, and preparations had to be hastily made for delivering a baby.

* * *

"Well, Grandpapá, it's a good thing you're a doctor so you can help Mommy with her baby," said Jenny excitedly.

"Great help a biochemist is going to be," joked the expectant mother as she braced for the next contraction.

"Don't worry, I've read enough medical books lately to turn me into a great old-style family practice doctor," Emile replied.

The labor progressed rapidly, temporarily distracting the family from the calamity about to reach their part of the planet.

On the only available table, wrapped in sheets and blankets, Trisha pushed hard one more time. *If only it would end soon*, she thought. The baby would be premature. Would it be healthy? *Damn!* she thought to herself over and over again. *They were right. I shouldn't have been carrying and pushing those heavy boxes!* Her desperate thoughts were interrupted once more by the pain of a strong contraction.

"The baby's head is starting to show — don't let go — keep pushing." Her father's voice was well-controlled. He was ready. With one hand he pushed down on her upper abdomen, forcing the baby a few more inches in its progress.

Trisha felt a chill of fear. Something was suddenly very wrong. She felt a tiny tremor and a sudden feeling of entrapment and doom. Her baby was being born. Just a few yards away, the animal world was going mad. Snakes scurried from their hiding holes. Even blind moles and gophers suddenly preferred the certain doom of the Earth's surface. Their homes were safe no more. They could feel the underground terror reaching towards them and the radon gas seeping through the Earth. They could sense imminent death.

Deer, moose and bears stood with erect ears, their hearts pounding. Then they began to dash at full speed toward nowhere. They knew that safety had ceased to exist.

Trisha knew it too. Why was it, that of those in the room only she could sense it? The horror of death was being born with her own child. To the shock of all present, Trisha screamed out, "No, no! Don't let it be born!" Bewildered, the rest present couldn't understand. Had she suddenly gone mad?

The wolves of Quebec howled and scrambled away, crying like puppies. Birds screeched and flew blindly, somehow knowing that in just a few seconds their carbonized bodies would be carried miles away.

The baby's head emerged fully.

At the same moment, the shelter shook violently. The lights flickered and dimmed. The inhabitants of the shelter looked at each other in fear. "Oh, my God! It's here, impact is here!" Cynthia cried as the underground shock wave reached them. A few seconds later they were all thrown to the floor, screaming. Trisha somehow managed to remain on the kitchen table by gripping its edges.

The baby, with only its head out of the vaginal canal, cried out. It was not the usual cry of a newborn's first breath, but a scream of fear, a primeval shriek of horror as the tiny being sensed the calamity all around it.

The shocks continued. The lights flickered once more and went out. The baby's screams mixed with those of the others. After a few moments, someone found a flashlight. Trisha had fallen to the floor, where the baby's body had been born with no one to hold it. Emile was now on his knee, covered in blood. He found the baby and had it in his arms now, the bloody cord still dangling, still attached to the unborn placenta. The child continued to scream, as did the others, while the shaking continued relentlessly. Jenny's screeching was ear-piercing, nearly as merciless as the crescendoing roar of the earth-quake. Trisha finally cried out coherent words. "My baby! My baby! Give me my baby!" The Earth shook even harder.

"Oh God, we're doomed!" Emile exclaimed.

"No, no, we must have hope!" Cynthia cried. But the shaking persisted, transforming the once-organized room into a chaos of boxes, furniture, blood and fumbling bodies.

After several more very long moments, the quaking slowed to a bare trembling. One of the lights came back on. The Earth stood still once more.

"Hope! Yes, Hope. That's what we'll name my new baby. Hope — we must have hope!" sobbed the new mother as she reached out, hugging her bloody and screaming infant.

"But it's not a girl, it's a boy, a beautiful boy!" Emile protested.

"I don't care," Trisha cried, tears still flowing down her cheeks. "His name must be Hope! And Hope must live. As long as we have Hope, we will also live."

The room suddenly became very silent as the family noticed a new distant rumbling. It grew rapidly louder and soon overtook the shelter. The howling noise was deafening. What was it? Then the room started to grow warm, then hot, and drier and hotter, till they could hardly breath. They held on to their throats, gasping for air. The noise from outside was horrifying as the heat-shock wave screeched over the buried shelter. Inside, the baby and Jenny screamed louder than ever. The heat in the room became unbear-able. A new screeching sound nearly deafened them, as trees and parts of the roof of the nearby cabin blew away. The light went out again and the shaking resumed. Air was sucked out of their lungs as the temperature in the room rose out of control. Jenny became silent, as did the others, one by one. Even the baby was now silent in horrified expectation.

"Oh my God, we forgot!" screamed Emile over the roaring din. "Everyone get their oxygen masks on! Where are the scuba tanks?" But it was too late. At one hundred and forty degrees, little Jenny was the first to lose consciousness.

CHAPTER 9

CHICAGO II.
DATE: 01-01-01
AGONY IN THE
SUBWAY

"Before the comet comes, many nations will be scourged by want and famine. A powerful wind will rise... carrying heavy fog and the densest of dust... the great nation(s) by the ocean... will be devastated by earthquakes, storm and tidal wave... they will be divided and, in great part, submerged. The comet will force much out of the ocean and flood many countries, causing much want and many plagues. All coastal cities will live in fear, and many of them will be destroyed by tidal waves, and most living creatures will be killed, and even those who escape will die..."

Saint Hildegard (1098-1179 A.D.)

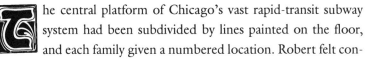he central platform of Chicago's vast rapid-transit subway system had been subdivided by lines painted on the floor, and each family given a numbered location. Robert felt content despite the gloomy circumstances. In the deep underground tunnel, the corner assigned to the Horton family was just right, he thought. He noticed with satisfaction that their designated area, though small, was no doubt better than most. It even contained the wall of an escalator to lean against. Since Julia was a physician, their area was close to the main corridors and elevators, as well as to the main food and supply areas.

They had settled in early, and were now amazed as thousands of people went by, heading deeper into the more distant portions of the tunnels. Nobody would be allowed above this level, the deepest in the system, until after Impact Day. If all was well twenty-four hours later, the crowding would be eased by allowing many millions into the other underground floors and the adjacent underground shopping malls situated above the transit level. The walkways and stores on those floors would be cleared only when the damage and resulting weather conditions could be better assessed and dates for returning home could be determined.

Robert and Julia and their two small children grew increasingly tense as the hour approached for the shelter to close. It was becoming obvious that maybe thousands would not reach their assigned areas because they were late. Many had refused to follow through or could not find their final assigned destinations. Stubborn and frightened groups of people had settled in passageways and taken over areas assigned to others.

Arguing, fighting, pushing and panic were becoming common. The Hortons' feeling of safety changed to anxiety and fear. The noise and confusion grew as civil leaders, National Guard workers, military and police were pushed aside by hordes of latecomers shoving their way through. One of the two transit rail passageways had been reserved for emergency transportation and medical help, yet now some people were settling in that area, while others were being pushed and falling into it.

"You're not supposed to have animals here!" an angered man yelled at a frail old woman with a frightened poodle in her arms. She looked in panic at his glaring eyes, fearing he would tear the helpless creature from her arms. "Can't they understand?" she murmured as she tried to cover the dog with her coat. She hadn't been able to put down her dear animal to sleep, as ordered by the civil defense initiative, nor could she leave it in her apartment. It would die of loneliness. Couldn't they understand? Her frightened glance seemed to cry for compassion, as she and her dog were literally carried away by the mass of people.

The panic that was never supposed to occur was now unavoidable. The Hortons' little sanctuary soon ceased to exist. The small tent was crushed, and they were pushed against the walls of the escalator. Julia, holding the baby boy in her arms, looked about despairingly as people wedged themselves between her and Robert.

Tammy was crying as she held onto her father. Fearing that she would be separated from him, he picked her up and held her close to his chest. She wrapped her legs around his waist and held onto his neck, crying fearfully. He zipped his large sports jacket around her, leaving her head free, then tried to maneuver his way back to Julia. Jeffrey had started to whimper and cry.

The loudspeakers blasted through the corridors, carrying the message that nobody really wanted to hear. "The doors must close now. Please move away, there is no more room in this area. Please move deeper into the tunnels. There is a lot more space further down. You must reach your assigned partitions."

"We are sorry. The doors must close now."

The large, mechanized metal doors slid shut. They slowly came together, crushing those that were trying frantically to get through. Screams of terror filled the corridors as arms and legs were caught and crushed. As planned, the doors opened a few inches for five seconds to permit the mangled to pull away their torn limbs, then closed in a complete seal, oiled now with human blood.

Corridors and stairways leading to the refuge buzzed like beehives as people banged on the doors trying to get in. But it was too late. Those left out had to back away, retreating to the outside, which suddenly appeared to be a very unsafe place. Only the sealed train tunnels would be safe. All other underground areas could flood if Lake Michigan were hit by a fragment of Dis'Aster.

* * *

Within the tunnels, the lights began to dim until they stabilized to a dull, diffuse yellow. Then, in an instant, most of them went off. Only the emergency lights remained, as all the power plants of the great metropolis were turned off. Gas lines were also shut off. If the shock wave reached the area or if earthquakes followed this far, electrical and gas fires could become rampant. Any town or city, no matter how far from impact point, could suffer a flaming death.

Robert and Julia looked at each other. Impact was very close now. Robert reached between two people and grasped the extended hand of his beloved wife as the noise inside the tunnel lessened. The latecomers, realizing they had nowhere to go, stopped and stood, confused, angry, and afraid.

Julia's heart was beating much too fast. This was not supposed to happen. It had been carefully planned for so long, and the instructions carefully explained over and over again for weeks. The computers had analyzed and assigned each square foot of the shelters. Each person, each item had been carefully allotted a certain defined space. She was furious. If only people had listened. If only they had been concerned and responsible, as she and her husband had been.

Robert concentrated on the familiar warmth of Julia's hand. He could feel love and security flowing between them. He was about to tell her that he loved her when a sudden, sharp shock hit the underground shelter.

The entire shelter shook violently for three brief seconds, as if the massive building over them had been hit neatly and clearly with a large mallet. The structure rang like a bell, but its massive strength tamped it back to a standstill almost instantaneously.

Impact? Here, already? Robert wondered. A buzz of voices swelled as others came to the same realization.

"Impact," Robert tried to explain to Julia over the noise, as if she or anybody needed any explanation. He tried to remain calm. "It's on time," he added, trying to be humorous. A small tremor, lasting eight or ten seconds, shook the ground. When it had died out, Robert exclaimed aloud to no one in particular, "That wasn't so bad."

In this moment of calm Robert tried once again to squeeze his way toward Julia, but before he could reach her, the Earth started to tremble again, this time violently. The shaking increased in intensity. A growl from deep within the depths of the Earth filled the tunnels. A fine veil of dust arose from the floor, and dust particles rained down silently from the ceiling. Screaming and pushing, the crowd dissolved into panic.

Outside, more than three-thousand miles from the impact point, the great metropolis of Chicago received the effects of the impact. The entire city started to shake violently. Some tall buildings, mostly the older, less flexible structures, tumbled to the ground. Massive clouds of dust darkened the Chicago skies.

The shaking, rolling and rumbling continued for a long time. Finally it subsided to an almost imperceptible tremor.

The dust-ridden air above the city was suddenly wiped clean as the atmospheric shock wave reached the area. By the time it rushed through Chicago, the shock wave's temperature had dropped to only 140° F., yet the wave still desiccated and crushed all that stood in its way. Most of the city's strongest buildings remained erect, resisting the earthquakes and the one hundred, sixty mile per hour winds. Other buildings fell like sticks.

As the main force of the blast wave passed overhead, air in the darkened tunnels was violently sucked to the surface. The remaining air in the tunnels was instantly transformed to an almost unbreathable, thin and hot gas, practically devoid of oxygen. The decrease in atmospheric pressure acted like a vacuum, leaving behind it a dry, almost airless city.

The Earth continued to shake. Those humans remaining on the streets were flung by the winds to fall as fine fertilizer on fields miles away. Every few minutes, the death count over the world increased by many millions.

* * *

The emergency lights in the tunnel flickered violently, causing more terror, more confusion, and more screaming. The sealed tunnels mercifully retained some breathable air. The human roar increased until the noise was almost palpable. Every child was crying, every adult either screaming in terror or yelling for others to calm down. The tunnel was now a chaotic mass of panicked humanity.

The shaking finally ebbed, the lights stopped flickering, and slowly order emerged from the chaos. People began to help each other and to apologize in embarrassment as they recalled their panicked behavior. The crying of children subsided to a dull whimpering, as their bodies ran out of strength.

* * *

"My husband is hurt, is there a doctor here? Is there a medic?" The distress call barely reached Julia's ears. She was needed. It was only a few yards away. There must be hundreds of wounded around here. Many were dead or dying.

"Yes, here," she called. But nobody could hear her. Still pinned to the wall, she tried to push through and make her presence known. "Here! Let me through, please, I'm a doctor. I need my first aid kit!" This last statement, shouted, was finally noticed by those around her.

"Sorry, lady, we can't move either! Everybody move! Let the doctor through." With Jeffrey still hanging on to her, she managed to wiggle a yard forward when she lost her footing and realized she was being held in suspension by the mass of bodies around her. Now she grew angry again. She had to reach those in need. But suddenly the ground under them rocked again, this time with such a furor that it left no one standing. Again the tunnel filled with terrible cries of pain and horror.

As new earthquakes shook Chicago, the crashing buildings added their own tremors. In the ravaged underground city, many of the emergency lights were now off. Water and sewage started to fall from the ceiling. Robert wondered if all the pipelines above them had broken.

People were on top of one another, suffocating, screaming, falling into the dark transit passageways — gasping for air and grasping for life.

How long did it last? Ten minutes? An hour or two? To the survivors it seemed forever. Even shadows could scarcely be seen as masses of people died. The Earth shook again and again. Brief minutes of relief only accentuated the horror, giving survivors only enough time to fear more.

Pieces of cement, plastic, steel, and piping rained on them as the overhanging maze of utility systems collapsed, killing and maiming thousands more. Yet the falling water and sewage brought a slight but welcomed reprieve from the dry heat.

At last the ground under them quieted. The tunnels were filled with a thick dusty mist and the sounds of suffering. The floors were slippery with human fluids. The crying out for loved ones, for lost ones, for the dead and dying, sounded like the tormented cries from deep within the worst of imaginable hells.

Julia struggled to her feet. At least she had a solid wall to hold on to. Jeffrey was also standing, still glued to her; his arms were crushed around her thighs. He was bleeding from a cut on his forehead. With all the dust in the air, the emergency light barely cast shadows, but she could see Robert with Tammy. She could hardly breathe, but it heartened her to realize that somehow they were alive. They had minor cuts and were badly bruised, but had not succumbed. She reached over to Robert. Still in a daze, they hugged and cried tears of joy at the realization that they were still alive and together.

Their attention was diverted as a radio's volume suddenly increased. An officer was screaming for all to shut up and listen. They heard the broadcaster's excited voice explaining how half of the world, including half of the USA, was destroyed. Locally, Lake Michigan had turned into a violent sea, which sent huge tsunami waves deep into the land. Though all of the underground systems had apparently held well, 90% of Chicagoans sheltered outside of the tunnels were probably dead, either from collapsed buildings or the repeated and destructive tsunami waves. The earthquakes had subsided, and most of the water had retreated back into the lake. Apparently, the comet had not significantly fragmented, and so the Midwest region of the

United States was safe from secondary impacts. All inhabitants should remain in the tunnels. Hot ashes would probably still fall over Chicago and could set much of it on fire. More radio announcements were to follow every hour.

As the radio was turned down, the tunnel exploded with applause and screams of jubilation, in spite of the horrifying news that most of Chicago and much of the world was destroyed. At least most of those here were alive.

Until this moment, Robert had never even contemplated the use of the word "miracle." Yet it *was* a miracle that they had survived. Impact had dealt Chicago a much higher level of destruction than anyone had imagined. And they were so many thousands of miles from impact point! *But, yes,* he thought, *let's be thankful. We are alive.*

"I love you, love you," he cried as he hugged Julia, trying to ignore the bleeding mass of dying and dead around them, the poorly lit, dust-filled corridors, the screaming and crying. A brief minor earthquake shook them, then the Earth became calm again.

"How am I going to help all of these people?" Julia exclaimed. "We need a hundred more doctors, a thousand medics, just for this area alone. My God, where do I start?"

She did not have long to ponder. Everyone in the tunnel fell suddenly silent, as they sensed a new menace approaching. A fine hum began to build in the transit tunnel. Distant now, but getting louder. Gradually the hum became a rumble. Whatever it was that was causing the sound, was rapidly closing in on them.

Julia gripped Robert's hand, burying her nails deep in his flesh. With all the others, she gasped in horror as she realized that a mass of water, human bodies and debris was rushing mercilessly toward them.

Chicago had cracked and fissured. The recent, small tremor had been the last straw. Lake Michigan, one of the largest lakes in the world, was now pushing its way through the broken underground systems of the once great city. Like storm water flooding the chambers of an anthill, the water rushed forth with the strength of a rolling mountain, filling every branch of the tunnel and its passageways.

A mass of water, bodies, and debris filled the entire diameter of the tunnel. When it hit them, they were instantly separated from each other.

Robert felt his body twisting and turning, bumping into objects in the black underwater hell, and he knew he was dead. He tried to send a last thought toward his wife and children — a last thought of love. He could feel his heart in his throat. His tears mixed with the water. Somehow, he sensed that Chicago would not have a single survivor.

The tumbling and pain continued, then suddenly his body and mind came to a stop, stunned by overwhelming pain — a pain that came from both within and without. Was he still alive? Or was this the feeling of death already accomplished?

Then he knew nothing else, only cold blackness.

CHAPTER 10

CHICAGO III.
THE AGONY OF LIFE

"Fire and smoke will fall from the heaven and waters from the ocean will become vapors... millions and
millions of men will perish and those that survive will
envy the dead."

Our Lady of Fatima, 1917

obert Horton slowly became aware of his existence. But where? He felt pain and cold, a cold so deep it penetrated every cell in his body. Where was he? Was he dead? Was this the cruel existence of hell?

Yet, he could feel his surroundings. He opened one eye for a brief moment; total blackness surrounded him. But he *had* opened an eye! He had felt it move. He could definitely feel — *something*. His chest was compressed, his body felt contorted, like an insect trapped in a web.

It took Robert what seemed an eternity to piece it all together. He had been with Julia, Jeffrey and Tammy. They had all, by what seemed a miracle to him, somehow survived the crumbling, the horrible shaking, the crushing that had accompanied the Earth's worst earthquake ever. But the end had arrived in the form of a rushing sea. He hadn't even had enough time to realize that the tunnel was being wiped clean by the waters of an adjoining lake when he lost his loved ones.

He was now quite alone and God-only-knew how long he would remain that way. If those he loved, and the other millions in the tunnel, were dead, why should he be alive? No, he must be dead. It would be cruel fate to remain alive.

A rumble, and then another earthquakes that must have lasted three or four minutes shook him fiercely. He hung on for dear life as debris fell upon him.

The quake subsided. He was once again conscious of himself and his surroundings. His lungs were still constricted; his torso was in agony.

But, yes, he was alive. Gradually he became aware of something else, something clinging to his chest. Something alive, wrapped like an octopus around him, killing him, sucking his every breath.

"Where am I?" he called out. And then he knew nothing again.

The next time he was aware, he was crying and he didn't know why. All he knew was that all were dead except for him. His world had ceased to exist. Could it be that everyone on earth was dead save for him, and this new, symbiotic appendage that was wrapped around his chest, digging into his flesh, giving him warmth and yet taking his breath?

His heart hammering, he unwrapped one of his arms from around what seemed to be a large metal pipe. As he moved his arm, pain shot through him, but he had to reach that thing strangling his torso.

It was still there; he could feel it, wrapped in a death grip around his chest and neck. He could concentrate his attention on the situation, and realized this thing was warm; it had to be alive. The grip, the trembling, the chattering of teeth, all reached his awareness.

It was his daughter. They were *both* alive! Alive, but in a black, icy inferno of pain. He finally realized that they had been flung by chance to an air pocket high in the utility sections of the subway tunnel. His body had become entangled in the wires and pipes of the overhanging utilities, and saved somehow from the rushing waters of death beneath him.

"Julia! Jeffrey!" he screamed at the top of his lungs. He waited — waited — but nothing could be heard except the roar of the water, the murderous water rushing beneath him, water solid with bodies.

* * *

Robert Horton and his eight-year-old daughter, Tammy, somehow made it through the first few days after Impact.

The waters receded, leaving behind a grotesquely ruined underground transit tunnel-system. Earthquakes had spilled the lake into the tunnels. Later earthquakes reversed the pattern, cutting off the flow between the lake and tunnels, allowing the water to empty into the distant suburbs. Chicago's underground rapid transit network was now carpeted with three to six feet of mud, debris, and dead people.

Robert, with the aid of a flashlight, managed to cut some wires, and by climbing down on them made his way to the floor with his petrified little girl still within his jacket. Soaked and freezing, they shuddered at the grotesque sights all around them. Bodies piled and entangled with each other, mixed with the debris of the tunnels and millions of supply boxes, backpacks and other items with which the tunnels had been stocked.

Robert scanned the bodies with his flashlight, searching for Julia and Jeffrey. He soon gave up, realizing that their bodies were probably miles away.

Picking his way through the rubble, Robert tried desperately to find a way out. But all the exits he found were clogged with debris. Plenty of preserved food was scattered throughout the litter, so there was no fear of starvation. They kept from freezing by changing into clothes found sealed in plastic bags. But it was hard to stay dry, and they were always cold. The need to escape the tunnel system became more urgent as days went by and the bodies around them started to decay.

At first, they had carefully made their way around the piles of bodies, moving them out of the way if necessary. Later they simply walked or climbed over the mounds of human flesh in their increasingly desperate attempt to find an intact transit station through which they could scramble up to the ground level. Then they would try to find other survivors, if, in fact, there were any.

Unknown to Robert, the early escape that he longed for could have been fatal. As they wandered in the cold, damp tunnel, the streets above remained an inferno for the first week after Impact. A hailstorm of hot ash, soot and red hot gravel fell over the city for days.

Their progress through the tunnel continued slow and arduous due to the mud, puddled water, bodies, and heaps of supplies, cement, pipes, wires and other construction materials that had fallen from the roof and walls of the tunnels. The rushing water had stripped the walls of all signs and other fixtures, so Robert couldn't tell where they were in the system.

"Don't cry, baby," Robert reassured Tammy over and over again. "We'll find a way to climb out of this mess."

But he grew more worried as days went by. He began to fear that all the stations were blocked by the rubble (mostly large cement fragments), that they were buried alive. To have survived this horror, and then simply to die, made no sense to him.

Distance between transit stations was generally about a mile. The newly renovated system had brought the tunnel network completely underground as far inland as the O'Hare Air and Space Center. At their present slow pace, it would take weeks or longer to reach the area where the transit system finally emerged to ground level. And what if that exit too was blocked with debris?

Robert had no resources to help him escape. Except for his own hands and a few minor tools he had picked up, he was without equipment to break out of what was now one of the world's many large underground cemeteries.

There was no alternative but to head toward O'Hare with the help of his camping compass, hoping to find an exit before the odor from the decomposing bodies became deadly. Sometimes he could smell and feel cold air wafting tantalizingly from between the huge chunks of cement obstructing an exit. The air smelled smoky but was not putrid like the air within the tunnel. Freedom was so close and yet so unreachable. If he could only find some dynamite!

Though he kept reassuring Tammy that they would find a way out, Robert found himself growing increasingly pessimistic. Maybe it would have been better if they had also died. Why had they been spared, if all that had been accomplished was a short respite? But he refused to give up. "We will find a way out," he repeated. "We must."

As they wandered in the cold, he filled a large backpack with preserved food, extra flashlights, containers of fresh water, tools, and medicines. But he had not found anything to help them get out of the maze of tunnels. It was growing colder. Their clothes were always damp, and he feared hypothermia.

* * *

Robert verified the date with his watch; only three weeks since Impact. It seemed like years.

As he and Tammy pushed more debris to the side, his flashlight abruptly swung back to throw light on another of the thousands of bodies they had seen that day. Robert shuddered. A cold wave raced down his spine and his heart lurched in his chest. He forcefully pushed more debris out of the way to get to the face-down body clad in familiar clothing.

No! he thought. *It can't be her! God, don't let it be Julia.* But the closer he got, the more he realized it was her. Until this moment he had clung to the hope that his wife and son Jeffrey had somehow also been lucky and had survived.

His worst fears were confirmed when he gently moved the muddied body onto its side and saw the expressionless face of his beloved wife.

"Oh," he murmured, his voice cracking. "Oh, my love —" He embraced the cold, wet body and sobbed away the deepest pain from his chest. He had known that there was no hope of finding her alive, but now the grief and emotion he had held for so many days finally broke forth.

"It's Mommy!" cried Tammy as she realized what was happening. Now she too was sobbing. But she recoiled in shock and horror as her face touched her mother's cheek. The cold, clammy face was not the warm, loving and reassuring one she knew so well. She screamed in fright as the skin of her mother's cheek stuck to her own and peeled off, revealing the swollen, mottled, pink and purple underlying tissue and releasing the unmistakable stench of putrefaction. She screamed louder and tried to run away. Robert grabbed her and held her close to him for several minutes until she finally went limp and stopped fighting, her screams turning to sobs.

At least he knew that Julia was dead and not suffering. A small comfort, perhaps, but still a comfort. He buried her in the muddy floor of the subway passage, the only human given a decent farewell among the millions dead in the underground shelter of the once-great city.

At first Tammy objected to her mother's burial. It was too much of a confrontation with reality for her. Robert tried his best to convince her that this in fact was the loving thing to do, but Tammy wouldn't listen. She was becoming very depressed. She refused to walk forward without Robert having to pull or carry her. "I want to die too," she said. *How could a child say such a terrible thing?* Robert wondered.

"We must make it to the surface and live, my baby," he told her. "We must forget all of this. Our old life is now in the past."

As more days went by, he began to fear they would die of

asphyxiation. The gas-swollen, decomposing cadavers had started to explode. Macabre concussions echoed continuously through the deep tunnels. Robert knew that the toxic gases would kill him and his daughter unless they escaped the catacombs very soon.

* * *

Robert persisted, walking, digging, pushing his way through. Tammy cried most of the time. Nightmares kept her awake. She didn't want to eat anymore. He had to force-feed her, to keep her strong. For the last few days they made little progress. Tammy was so cold and exhausted that she refused to walk or climb anymore. Robert had to carry her most of the time, slowing them further. Even he was having suicidal thoughts.

The only sign of the external world was the occasional rumble of an earth tremor, or the thunderous echoes of another partially-collapsed building letting go of another few floors.

Suddenly Robert's eye caught a glimpse of a small object in the rubble. It was an old-fashioned butane pocket lighter, the type used years before by people addicted to nicotine.

He picked up the contraption and studied it. After fiddling with it for a while, he managed to turn a spark, but no flame appeared. Finally, after trial and error, he was able to simultaneously make sparks and, holding open the release valve, produce a flame.

"Fire is dangerous, Daddy. It's against the law, remember?" Tammy scolded, temporarily drawn from her stupor by the sight of the flame.

"Yes, darling. But it can also bring us warmth!"

In a few minutes, he found a side room and started a small fire. He used bits of plastic to start the fire and dry some scrap paper and wood. The stench from the burning plastic was acrid, yet welcome, as it overpowered the smell of rotting flesh.

Distracted temporarily from the quest for an escape route, the pair sat comfortably together for the first time in many days as they dried their clothing and watched the flickering flames produce dancing shadows and lights on the otherwise gloomy walls. "It's warm, Daddy," Tammy said. "I like it."

"Me too, baby. People used to cook with fire before it became outlawed. I'll open some cans and make us some hot soup." For the next few hours they ate and slept, waiting for their clothes to dry. They drank hot soup and chocolate. What a treat to feel warm again! They rested and talked with renewed eagerness, temporarily forgetting their horrible prison. But in a part of his mind, Robert was puzzled by the sometimes violent flickering of the flames. He was sure that there shouldn't be an air current far from the main corridor and stations.

The death wish of a few hours past was rapidly replaced by a new hope for possible survival. His pulse rushed as he got up and turned the flashlight to the walls around him. There were a few cracks and warps through which air seemed to be flowing. Was there another room on the other side of the wall? Could he break through? The walls seemed so strong and solid.

He searched his memory for clues that would help save them. He thought of the many adventure stories he had read as a youngster. His favorites had been stories about the olden times when men had to fight the elements and wild beasts to survive. Only those with strength, cunning, intelligence and a strong will succeeded.

Almost instinctively, he rushed back to the fire, picked up a piece of wood and began exposing the flames of the torch to the cracks in the wall. As he moved toward a corner, the flame abruptly flickered and bent towards a thin crack in the wall, as if trying to rush into it.

So that was it. Where two panels met, there was a half-inch, irregular crack and then darkness. The flames and smoke disappeared into it. Maybe the crack led toward another room, that in turn led to the outside.

One of the corner panels was solid cement. But the adjoining panel, the size of a large door, was slightly warped and cracked. Robert pulled a pocket knife from his jacket and probed the area.

It was clear now that there was a major difference between the two panels. The harsh rasping noise of the concrete contrasted with the hollow sound of the other. As Robert scraped harder, the paint started to peel and expose the shiny surface of the hardened plastic.

"Move back!" he shouted to Tammy, who was watching silently, not understanding what her father was doing. He excitedly looked around and found a large square piece of sheet metal. With it, he pushed the entire pile of burning material to the wall, then added more fuel. He and Tammy covered their faces against the intense heat and suffocating smoke produced as the large panel finally caught fire, slowly melting and exposing the unknown world beyond.

As the panel was consumed, it left in its place a dark rectangular hole. Robert pushed the smoldering debris to one side and gave Tammy a flashlight. Then, holding her by one hand, he silently led her through. She followed hesitantly as they ventured from the entrails of the tunnels into pitch blackness, their light beams lost in the immensity of a dark and silent place. Robert swung his flashlight upward; the beam first touched a huge chandelier, then Tammy's illuminated a stark stairway. A few paces farther, and the flashlight revealed the broken glass panels of store showcases. The mannequins of the immense underground shopping mall they had evidently ventured into seemed eerily closer to living people than anything they had seen in weeks.

A silent escalator stood amid the debris. There was not a single other person present, dead or alive. Freedom and fresh air had to be only two or three floors up. Robert prayed that the exit to the street level would not be buried in debris.

They ran up escalators that were frozen in time. Pushing debris out of the way, they struggled upward, and finally exited through broken glass doors.

* * *

The outer world was a bitter shock. Robert could not believe his eyes. He and Tammy had emerged in the central portion of what appeared to be a park. The sky was pitch black, but the remnants of a nearby building were still smouldering, providing dim light. The large clearing was surrounded by disintegrated buildings, leaving only the central area of the park untouched. Robert marveled at their luck — the exit from this particular underground mall was in the middle of a park! They stood for a moment in disbelief, inhaling the cold but fresh air, tainted only by the smell of smoke. The temperature had to be below freezing. Robert perceived death but could no longer smell it.

Once they realized that they were truly outside their prison, father and daughter danced in jubilation. Then they cried. They called out for other survivors, but there was no answer. They returned to the subterranean mall and changed into warm, dry clothes taken unapologetically from the desolated shops. They ate quickly and soon fell asleep comfortably on soft, store beds.

The next morning, the city was still dark. From the blackened, overcast skies came a continual fall of light brown snow, mixed with gritty debris. It had been snowing for days, for the rubble was covered with several inches of the cold, soggy material.

A small amount of natural light indicated that it was, in fact, daytime. Robert confirmed the time with his watch. In the dim light, aided by their powerful flashlights and the scattered fires that were still burning, they scanned in horror the reality around them.

Buildings around the park lay in total ruins. Heaps of rubble hundreds of feet high stood amid a few rare buildings that hadn't collapsed completely. Like giants frozen in time, the lower stories of the remaining buildings stood dark and silent, as if they were the ruins of a long-lost civilization that had been dead for centuries. Like the tall rocks of Monument Valley in Utah, each structure was surrounded by a skirt of debris. The sleet and snow gradually filled the insides of those few buildings not totally demolished. Not a single window remained to protect the rooms within them from the influx of snow. The only sounds came from occasional landslides of rubble.

As Robert and Tammy gazed around them, the demolished cityscape suddenly lit up. Tammy screamed as, for a few seconds, the entire area was illuminated by a huge bolide of fire, piercing through the low-hanging black clouds. As suddenly as it had appeared, the fireball disappeared beyond the horizon, trailing behind it a flickering train of smoldering fire and smoke. The sky became silent and dark again for a few more seconds, then a huge explosion illuminated the sky a dozen miles away.

"That, baby, was probably a leftover from the comet. It's probably been in orbit for weeks," Robert explained, trying to calm his frightened daughter.

They continued walking in silence. The remnants of an old red-brick church looked familiar. But it wasn't until he saw the fragments of a toppled pillar along with pieces of a large cement eagle that Robert realized where he was.

"Logan Square," he breathed. "Unbelievable!"

The historical square had been preserved as a clear park area in the reconstructed Chicago. A huge shopping mall had been built under it — one of the many new "Earthscrapers" that were dug deep into the valuable land. Robert had been there a few times before Dis'Aster. But how could they be in Logan Square when he had been walking for weeks in what he thought was the opposite direction? How could he have been so wrong?

"Daddy," Tammy cried, interrupting his thoughts. "I'm so cold."

"Yes, baby, me too. Let's go down again and get more warm clothes, and some hot food. Then we can come up again and try to find other people."

She glanced at him with a non-believing look in her eyes, a look which almost convinced him that what he had said was very unlikely.

"Yeah, sure," she responded sarcastically.

* * *

Robert and Tammy ventured out of the Logan Square Mall several times, never finding anyone. The shopping mall had been their home for weeks. Today they would again go out to look for others.

Progress was slow. It took them more than three hours to search through two blocks. They couldn't keep warm despite multiple layers of heavy clothing. Could it be that they were the only survivors in this city of so many millions?

Suddenly, they were both thrown to the ground as a new tremor shook the Earth. They were barely missed by huge pieces of plaster and cement from the shattered remnants of a skyscraper.

"We have to keep away from these buildings," Robert said. "It would be so stupid to get killed now, after all we've gone through."

But, as usual these days, he received no immediate response from Tammy; she was getting depressed again. He couldn't help worrying about her emotional state. *She WILL live through this,* he promised himself. *There must be others somewhere.*

"Daddy," Tammy said suddenly, "I found a fish in the street."

"Yes, I'm not surprised," Robert said, as she held out the frozen animal. "Remember I told you that the waters of the lake rolled over the entire city. There are probably many fish buried around here." Robert inspected, then sniffed at the fish. "I wonder if it's good to eat," he mused. "Anyway, let's keep moving."

To Robert's surprise, they found very few cadavers during their searches. He had no way of knowing that most of those caught outside had been buried under the buildings, burned to ashes, blown away by the winds, or washed away by the lake's many tsunamis. Most bodies they did find were relatively well-preserved, since they had frozen soon after Impact.

He found an item he had been looking for, on a young man's arm: a well-preserved personal radio communicator in apparently good working condition. Eagerly, he turned it on and moved rapidly from channel to channel. To his consternation, the hand-held device emitted only static.

For days he tried each channel, identifying himself and calling for help, but there was no response. Even the emergency-only station was silent.

He added the device to the other paraphernalia he carried on his belt, and continued to search with Tammy at his side, or more frequently, riding on his shoulders. They trekked northwest, towards what he hoped were more open and safer parts of the city, but always remaining within a day's walk from their new home under Logan Square.

* * *

"Maybe we're the only people left in the world," Tammy told her dad one day as they sat in a street intersection snacking.

Suddenly they were startled by a deafening crackling sound. What was it? Where was it coming from? It took Robert a moment to realize it was the communicator. He turned the volume down just as the emergency band stopped screeching and as a clear feminine voice spoke out firmly.

"To all survivors. We have a new antenna! We should be able to reach more of you now. The rendezvous place for North-Central Chicago has been changed again. Please pay careful attention. There are too many who cannot reach Douglas Park, so we will try for Humboldt Park. We are told that not too much debris covers it, and some of the major streets that lead to it are possible to travel on."

Tammy stared at the communicator, transfixed and managed a big smile. Robert kissed it as if it were human. "Baby, did you hear that?!" he cried in excitement. He fumbled for the controls and turned the volume up as the speaker, an older woman, began again.

"We keep getting incoming calls from people that we haven't been able to make contact with. Charlie, Mary and Shafer, Robert and Tammy, the Smithson family. Please use Channel 38. If your communicator lacks that channel, try to find one that has it. In the meantime, head for Humboldt Park and keep your 'cator on for further instructions. I will be switching off this channel now and will broadcast this message again on all other channels."

Robert fumbled for Channel 38. A young man was speaking. "Again, to all survivors, as you travel toward Humboldt Park, keep your eyes out for good shelters that can accommodate at least a few dozen people. We estimate that less than one thousand people survived in the entire metropolis. In our area we number about one hundred so far. For a shelter to be effective, it must not be under the shadow of any building or portion of building still standing. It must be at least two or three stories underground and must not be open to the subway system, since tunnels could flood again as earthquakes continue . . ."

As the instructions to the survivors continued, Robert's mind raced with excitement at the prospect of joining others. He grasped Tammy's hands and danced with her. They laughed and smiled together for the second time since Impact.

The large mall rooms Robert and Tammy had found under Logan Square could be used by a few hundred people. The panel to the subway he had melted could easily be sealed. The other survivors would be thrilled with their find. He calculated that they were at least three or four miles from Humboldt Park; he hoped they could make it there in one or two days.

"This is Robert Horton — and my daughter, Tammy — so glad to hear another human voice!" Robert's voice broke and tears filled his eyes. "Can you hear me?"

"Tammy and Robert Horton! Finally we can talk to you. Your signals were becoming weaker. We have been afraid you were trekking away from us. We had no idea where you might be." The young man's voice was like a blessing straight from heaven. "Can you make it unaided to Humboldt?"

"God bless you! Yes, we can. We are on our way! We should be at Humboldt Park by tomorrow or so. And we have a great shelter for your group!" Robert felt a great sense of joy as he saw Tammy smiling so brightly. He picked her up and danced until he was dizzy.

"Come on, baby," he said as he switched the 'cator back to standby. Lifting Tammy to his shoulders, he set off with renewed energy to join the other survivors.

CHAPTER 11

TUCSON II. JANUARY, YEAR 3 POST-IMPACT (P.I.) THE GREAT CHILL

"And a great star fell from heaven, burning like a torch, and it fell on a third of the rivers... and many men died from the waters because they were made bitter."

John: Book of Revelation 8:10,11 (Apocalypse), Holy Bible

Bill Ziegler wondered how his friends were holding on in Colossal Cave on the outskirts of his home town, Tucson. He thought of them each time his shoulder ached from the now-healed wound. He wished he were there with them. He assumed that conditions had to be better in a well-organized shelter than they were in the basement he was in. It was just over two years since Impact. The first year had been terrible. But compared to the present, that first one seemed paradise.

Bill was in the basement of the home of the Larkins, his nearest neighbors. The house was on the top of a small hill, so the wind kept some of the snow off the roof. It also had a slanted roof that, with reinforcement, was able to tolerate the weight of snow and ice. If their house had had a flat roof, like most in Tucson, it would have collapsed long ago.

The main room of the basement was only fifteen-by-twenty feet, yet it had been their home for all these months. It had formerly been an entertainment room, but now it looked like a dungeon, lit by a single, small flame from an old-fashioned oil lamp. The room was dark and cold. The sunken spa, now empty of water, was partially filled with torn, dirty blankets and pillows. It was now Bill's bed. The refrigerator's door had been removed and its shelves now held books, tools, and miscellaneous items. Two other "beds" (which were actually heaps of old mattresses and blankets), a single long table, a dilapidated sofa and some chairs were also in the room.

Toward one end of the room a staircase led upward to the ground floor. The stairs were now filled with debris and impassable. Toward the other end of the room was the utility room with a defunct washer and dryer, another old doorless refrigerator and more junk. On one side of the large room was a bathroom. Flowing water had ceased to exist on day one of Impact. The toilet was the only luxury that Dis'Aster had allowed to remain usable. By flushing it with melt water, they could make it work by forcing air down it each time to ensure that the water and waste would not freeze and block the pipes that led to the sewer. Of course, the toilet was seldom needed in these days of famine.

Bill Ziegler looked about him and sighed in depression. Despite the present circumstances, he had been lucky that Larry and Erika Larkin had taken him in and cared for him. Today, like most days, he lay on the blankets that filled the spa, day-dreaming. Isolation, darkness, hunger, emaciation, cold — these had become the constants of his half-life-half-death, energy-saving stupor that somehow kept him alive. It seemed to Bill that Impact had occurred centuries ago. He again remembered that fateful day. The tragedy never left his mind. He wished he could keep it out of his head, but the memories repeated themselves uncontrollably.

* * *

The day before Impact, he, his wife Lara and their two little girls had been ready to leave their home and head for Colossal Cave. With the imminence of Impact, they felt so lucky to be winners of the lottery that allowed them to be among the few Tucson families to be sheltered in the large cavern. Bill recalled how he had stopped to look at himself in the mirror just a few minutes before they were supposed to get into their vehicle and head for the cave. He was then moderately overweight, his heavy blond beard made him look even plumper. In his early thirties, Bill had seen his law practice blossom and his income increase, but the free time he used to have for exercise and sports had disappeared. Food rationing in the cave would force him to lose weight.

"I guess I'll have to lose some weight in that cave," he told Lara.

"Sure," she laughed. "We've all heard that before." She put her arms around him and kissed him deeply. Aroused, he fondled her small buttocks. Her straight blond hair was held back like a child's pony tail. He remembered her so well. His heart ached now just thinking of her. The two little girls, three and four years old, were miniatures of their mother. So fair and slim, their long blond hair, almost white, hung below their shoulders. They looked almost like twins.

"Time for a quickie?" he joked. "We won't have much privacy in the cave."

* * *

"Okay, honey, everything is in the vehicle," Bill said a few minutes later. "Get the girls from the TV room and let's go."

At that moment, the doorbell rang. Through the monitor he recognized one of his neighbors from down the street, the father of a family with two girls, almost the same ages as their own children. He had never very much liked the fat man, but had always been polite to him. Bill opened the door, caution causing him to grip the small gun he had recently kept in his jacket pocket. The news had been full of stories of murder and stealing in these last few days. The fat man looked nervous, and Bill didn't want to take any chances. As he opened the door, he felt the pleasant, barely cool autumn air flow by him. The fat man smiled nervously. "Hi," he said as he stood with both hands in the pockets of his coat, a coat much too heavy for the present weather.

Bill was about to return the greeting when he felt himself thrown back by an invisible force. His whole body twisted around abruptly as if it had been flung. At the same time he heard an overwhelming, thunderous sound, followed by severe pain in his left shoulder. A fraction of a second later Bill recognized the sound and realized the man had shot him with a gun. An instant later he lost consciousness.

When he awoke, all he could feel was the terrible pain in his left shoulder. He was lying on that shoulder, a stroke of luck that prevented him from bleeding to death. It was luck also that the neighbor, in his nervousness, had missed Bill's heart.

Bill's mind took a while to clear. He despaired as he wondered how long he had been there. He looked at his watch — it was November third! He had been unconscious all during Impact day! Now it was 9:21 in the morning, yet it seemed dark, like on a stormy day. Where were his wife and children? Why weren't they there with him, trying to help him? Why wasn't he in a hospital? He already knew the truth, but refused to accept it.

Somehow, Bill managed to crawl toward the living room where he found Lara and his two girls. All dead. Shot, as well. Murdered as they must have hurried in bewilderment and fear toward the source of the first shot. He screamed and sobbed and hugged their bodies — bodies cold as ice and already rigid.

The trembling of the Earth awakened him again many hours

later. When he opened his eyes he realized the tremors must have been going on for a long time, for all around him lay particles of fallen plaster and other debris. The contents of all the shelves had fallen and shattered. He, and the silent bodies of his loved ones, were covered with dust.

Bill managed to stand and, holding onto the walls and furniture, he reached the kitchen. First he tried to use the phone. Of course, it didn't work. He flipped the light switch with his right hand. There was no light. The pain was becoming worse, and he felt feverish. Very thirsty and hungry, he stumbled over to the sink. There was no water.

Of course, I know that, he thought. All utilities, even gas and water, were to be turned off one hour prior to Impact. He found and swallowed some pain killers and some leftover antibiotics from one of the girls' prior illnesses.

Drinks in the refrigerator and food in the cupboards revived him enough to allow him to walk over to his closest neighbors. He knew that Larry and Erika would be in the basement, according to their survival plans. He also knew that the Larkins probably would not hear him, and that even if they did, that they probably wouldn't come to the door. Still, Bill repeatedly hammered on the wooden door with a rock before he finally gave up and slumped down, leaning against the door.

*   *   *

Looking back at the horror of those first days brought tears to Bill's eyes. The Larkins had heard him after all, brought him into the house and helped him recover. As it snowed softly, they had buried his wife and daughters in the back yard among the dying roses his Lara had cared for with so much love.

Today, more than two years later, he still couldn't get over the agony of his loss. At least his body had healed. The antibiotics and other medicines the Larkins had hoarded, saved him.

*   *   *

Bill's thoughts were interrupted when he heard noises from the end of the room. Larry and Erika were taking their slow walk again, back and forth from one end of the cold basement to the other. The once-handsome couple had been the pride of the high school they both worked in. Larry taught computers and geography, while Erika was the most popular physical education and sports instructor the school ever had. Both were, at one time, enthusiastic joggers with strong bodies which were always in a perfect state of health. They were an example to all and the envy of many. Now in her late twenties, Erika still retained the determination and strong will that had always characterized her. Larry, on the other hand, was becoming despondent and suicidal. Only Erika's presence kept him going.

* * *

"If you don't stop, your ratio of calories will soon tip to the deficit side." Bill, in a matter-of-fact tone, was reminding them of the continual need of moderation in exercise, since every calorie spent had to be replaced with food.

Larry, who had once weighed two hundred pounds and gave the impression of being made of pure muscle, was down to one hundred and thirty-two pounds. With his long beard and sunken green eyes, he looked like an ascetic hermit.

"I guess you're right," Larry answered, dropping his wife's hand. They both leaned against the wall, showing the exhaustion brought about by walking almost half a mile without stopping.

Larry sat on the carpet and lifted a glass of water from a small table. He peered at the liquid carefully, then took a small sip. He then placed himself in his meditation position with crossed legs, hands on his knees and fingertips together.

Bill began to read by the light of the oil lamp, as Erika disappeared into the smaller, adjacent room with a similar lamp.

After a few minutes she returned with a small piece of paper in her hand. She blew out her lamp as she approached the men. They never kept more than one lit in any single room.

"Well, we are down to the basic again," Erika announced. "We have food for only one week at the very maximum."

Letting her know by his tone of voice that he did not appreciate being brought back from his trance, Larry shrugged. "We all know that."

"Right." It was Erika's turn to expose her irritation. "But now I have it down to exact figures," she went on. "I've counted every potato chip, weighed every can and dried food package, and have every single calorie accounted for." When she failed to receive a response, she went on. "We have to go out again and get more food. We can't wait or we'll be too weak from hunger. We have to go now, while we still have some strength. So let's get off our asses and make some plans."

After a few seconds, Bill put down his book. Didn't Erika realize how impossible the task was? First they had brought all the food that was in his house, then, as the months went by, they'd ransacked the murderer's home. After that they moved on to all the other abandoned neighborhood homes that hadn't already been gutted by looters. Then they had waited for the old couple down the street to die, though they had left little to eat. Once they were finished with the most distant homes they could reach, they went on to eat all the frozen dogs and cats. And finally, despite Larry's protests, they'd made a long and risky trek to a small grocery store a few miles away.

"We almost didn't make it back from the last trip," Bill said aloud. The store had been ransacked many times before and was all but empty. "We spent two days digging through the ice, remember? And when we finally did find three miserable boxes of junk food, we were held up by that madman. It was only by luck that we managed to kill him before he killed us."

"It was worth it, though," Erika said in a matter-of-fact tone. "We also got those bottles of cooking oil. If we didn't have them, we'd be sitting here in the dark."

"What good is light if we starve to death?" Larry protested. "We're the only ones alive for at least a couple of miles, and there's no more food anywhere around here. The rest of the desert is under ice. Ice that's as hard as steel!"

Larry sighed bitterly. "Who knew, that by moving into a peaceful, low-density neighborhood in the desert, we'd be depriving ourselves of food in the future?"

"That's bullshit!" Erika snapped, "and you know it! If we lived in the city, we'd already be dead from the mobs that sacked the city after Impact."

"Everybody in Tucson is probably dead by now," Larry said.

"Listen to me!" Erika shouted, her voice shaking with anger. "We survived the shock wave and weeks of incessant earthquakes and fire! We survived murdering mobs of thieves. We have survived two years and two months of horrible Ice Age. So now, are we going to just sit around and die? No! We can't let this happen! I refuse to give up! Get off your butts and move! We have to find more food!"

When there was no immediate response from the men, she went on in a conciliatory tone. "Please," she urged, "let's not argue. It'll just take some work. I've been thinking — when Larry and I used to go jogging in the hills south of here, we sometimes passed by a group of small homes centered around a cul-de-sac. It was about four or five miles south of here. Since they're on top of a small, broad hill, it shouldn't be too difficult to dig down through the ice and into the homes."

After a few seconds of silence, Larry nodded. "It's possible we could find them," he said. "But four miles is a long way to walk on ice dunes in sub-zero temperature."

"I remember those homes, too," Bill said. "They were built recently. I guess we could make it there, but we have to be more cautious this time, be on the lookout for others. And we have to take more tools and weapons."

Erika looked at her watch. "It's settled, then. It's almost midnight. Let's get a good night's sleep and pack in the morning. We should leave no later than nine. If we're lucky, maybe there will be a small amount of light by then. We must be back by four or so, before it becomes totally dark."

* * *

It was January 7th, year 3 P.I. Bill Ziegler and his adopted family, Larry and Erika, were ready. They each wore three layers of insulated underwear, as many socks as they could put on without cutting off the circulation to their feet, three layers of pants, shirts and sweaters, scarves and double gloves, knitted head covers and ski masks under the heavy insulated hoods of their jackets.

They also carried many practical survival items purchased during the early years of the comet era. In their pockets each had a meager ration of food: stale potato chips left over from their last foray into the outside world.

On their makeshift sled they tied some tools, including heavy picks and crowbars to dig through the ice, and precious pieces of firewood torn from the furniture and walls of theirs and their neighbors' houses. They would have to build a warming fire as soon as they got into a home.

If they only had dynamite! Erika had cursed her carelessness for not stocking any. The pre-Impact planning she thought she had performed so carefully had turned out to be full of unexpected voids.

They would drink from dirty snow melted along the way. They couldn't bring any of the clearer, clean water they had at home, because any water they carried would freeze within a few minutes, and they wouldn't be able to get it out of the containers.

They hated the taste of the gritty, acidic, charcoal-flavored ice and snow that covered the Tucson valley. For home consumption, they melted ice and let it sit for days before decanting the clear top and filtering it through many layers of cloth. It still tasted bitter, but was at least drinkable compared to pure icemelt water. Even the clearest of the layers of ice around their home was brownish gray.

"Are you ready?" Erika asked as Larry finished zipping his coat.

"God, I hope so," he answered. "And I hope we haven't forgotten something *vital*."

"Let's go, then," Erika said impatiently. "Open up."

They were in the utility room of the basement. Bill, standing on top of the clothes dryer, cleared the top of the refrigerator of some luggage that held a blanket securely against a hole in the ceiling. Then he pushed himself through the now-exposed hole that led to one of the bedrooms on the main floor. With his small oil lamp, he scrutinized the pile of furniture that helped to hold up the ceiling against the weight of the ice sheets covering the house. Linen sheets and pieces of curtains and rugs were hung from the room's walls in an attempt to keep ice and snow out.

When he was sure that there was no immediate need for repairs, Bill next climbed on a chest of drawers and pried away the large piece of plywood that covered an irregular hole in the ceiling. As he pulled the cover away, a scattering of ice and snow fell through the hole. "Looks okay," he called. "Pass me the crowbar."

Larry, who was now on top of the refrigerator with his head in the bedroom, tossed a long crowbar onto the floor, then climbed into the room. He stood and passed the crowbar to Bill, who had by now climbed onto the surface of the roof. A space shaped like an inverted cone surrounded him. Its walls were made of ice, layered in bands of grey, black and rust. The base of the cone, about eight feet in diameter, lay over that part of the roof. The cone rose upward for eight feet, narrowing with height. From the top hung a rope ladder. Bill stood on a chair and climbed onto the ladder, disappearing into the darkness. Larry followed closely behind him. When Bill had stopped climbing, Larry passed him the crowbar. By this time Erika had joined them, bringing with her a couple of heavy backpacks.

Bill took a mallet and began hitting a wooden plug, made from a tabletop nailed to a stool, that stoppered the hole in the ice over the roof. After loosening the plug with a few blows, he pushed it upward and out onto the ice surface. As pieces of ice fell, there was a gush of air, and chunks of gray-brown snow joined the icy debris on the roof. Larry passed Bill a flashlight.

"The snow is turning gray," Bill reported as he widened the hole. "It's not as black."

Erika lifted a pinch of the new snow to her lips. After carefully tasting it, smacking her lips slowly for a few seconds, she took a larger amount, feeling that it was sufficiently safe for analysis. "It's not too bad," she said after a moment. "Not too acrid or bitter. Very few particles."

Through the years they had learned to use taste to determine the safety of ice. Depending on the amount and type of debris falling from the skies, and on the amount of recent volcanic activity in these latitudes, snow and ice could be edible, sickening or poisonous. The deepest layers of ice were poisoned, since they contained the bulk of the acid rain and snow falls that occurred immediately after Impact.

"There's only a little sulfur," Erika went on. She could barely taste the rotten-egg flavor of volcanic emission. "Maybe things are changing." She passed a piece of the hardened snow to Larry, who tasted it too.

"Not bad," he agreed. "But we've seen this before."

"Maybe the atmosphere is finally clearing," Erika said.

"There doesn't seem to be as much vulcanism, either," Bill added. "We're now about three inches above the last severe bout. Maybe it's coming to an end."

"Can you see anything out there?" Erika called to Bill.

"Yes, a little," Bill replied, his words now faint. He was on the last part of the rope ladder with his head outside. He held a thermometer in one hand and was waiting for the mercury to bottom out. "It's still minus 45° Fahrenheit," he said after a moment.

"Damn!" Erika muttered. Larry simply shrugged and remarked, "I told you so."

"Let's go," Erika said brusquely as she blew out the oil lamp and turned on her flashlight. She handed the rope that was tied to their small sled to Larry, who in turn passed it to Bill. Then the three of them heaved the sled up onto the ice.

Panting and out of breath, Erika and Larry climbed onto the ice surface and joined Bill. The very dim light coming through the clouds allowed for about one hundred and fifty feet of visibility.

"Whoa," said Erika. "It hasn't been this clear since Impact Day!"

"Don't get your hopes up, it probably won't stay this way for long," Larry said.

Erika glanced at him in disgust, then looked away. The scene around them was something from a nightmare. Where once there had been the beautiful rolling hills of the Sonoran Desert, covered with mesquite trees, bushes, wild grasses, giant saguaros and other cacti, now only a flat, devastated landscape of dark ice and snow remained. The hollows of the countryside had all filled and grown to meet the tops of the hills, where the ice sheets lay ten to twenty-five feet deep. From where they stood, the only recognizable structures on the ice dunes were the tips of a few tall saguaros and the tops of a few electric utility poles that had somehow managed to stay erect. The recent winds had kept the tops of these lonely landmarks free of snow and ice. The tallest frozen cactus tip stuck out about two feet above the snow, the nearest electric pole almost four feet.

"Well, the pole is still there," Bill remarked.

"Thank God," said Erika. The pole had been their major landmark on their previous expeditions. Erika adjusted her electric Pathfinder. Luckily, their non-satellite-dependent locating device still worked. Relying on predetermined landmarks, the hand-held mini-computer was much more trustworthy than any compass.

Erika carefully placed the wooden plug back into the ice hole, the sole means of exit and entrance into their home. As she plugged it up, Larry tied a scrap of orange rag to the tip of the Pathfinder's antenna, which they were able to telescope up until its tip stood twenty feet high. He then pushed the mast-like structure into a drill hole they had made in the center of the plug.

* * *

Erika, Larry and Bill went over the list of supplies again and again and rehearsed their plans during the night prior to their dangerous exploit. Aided by a Greater Tucson street map, they plotted their path across ice over the homes and streets that (they hoped) would lead them to the cul-de-sac. They would be walking many feet above homes that they knew were devoid of any food. The new housing development they were looking for wasn't marked on the map, but they thought they could find it.

Erika and Larry attached a second homing device to the utility pole farthest from them. With no satellites in orbit, they no longer had workable GPS devices, so they had to rely on less sophisticated positioning methods.

Erika pressed a button on the computer which instantly computed the triangle. From then on, they would know their exact location in relationship to those two poles as long as they stayed within a range of fifteen miles and as long as no high hills obstructed the

Pathfinder's "view" to the antennas.

Following the predetermined coordinates, they set out in single file, Erika in front with the Pathfinder, and Larry behind her. Bill followed both of them, taking the first turn pulling the sled.

* * *

It was past noon. Visibility had increased to about two hundred and fifty feet.

The trek was hard and slow at first, but they were able to pick up the pace on a downhill run of over two miles. They were now finally in view of the rolling uphill incline that they hoped would lead them to the homes they were looking for.

It took them over three hours to get this far. Now they faced a slow half mile uphill, and then, if all went well, they would start digging.

* * *

The three stood panting at the top of the incline. They had pulled and pushed the sled relentlessly up the icy slope for the last thirty minutes. If only she had stocked cleats, Erika thought in disgust. But who needed ice cleats in Tucson? It was very windy on top of the hilly area, and the drift-snow stuck to their goggles, decreasing visibility. They had to brace each other to fight the dry wind. At least it wasn't snowing. They kept walking.

When they were close enough to see the center of the hill, the wind suddenly lessened, allowing for better visibility. They all stopped at the same time, shocked at what they saw. Catching his breath and not knowing what else to say, Larry finally spoke. "I don't believe it. Those house tops are almost totally clear of ice and snow."

"It's the wind," Bill said. "This place is so damn windy." Only Erika remained silent, carefully studying the situation. The first three homes had three to five feet of clear walls and roofs, with the top foot or so of their windows showing above the snow banks.

"Let's go," Larry said impatiently. "Let's get out of the cold and find some food."

"Wait!" Erika said sharply. She was contemplating all the possibilities. She couldn't forget how they had almost been killed at the grocery store. "What if there are people there?" she said. "I mean live people."

"If they're alive, then they must have food," Larry contended.

"We're alive, and we are out of food," she said.

"You mean that if they have food they must have very little," said Bill after a moment. "They probably wouldn't want to share it with us."

"Exactly."

"What if they prepared better than we did and they have plenty of food?" Larry countered.

Erika gave her husband an irritated sidelong glance. The ice hanging from his eyebrows and whiskers made his silly smile look even more ridiculous, she thought. She sometimes felt she hated him now.

Sensing the tension, Bill spoke again. "Well, there's only one way to find out. We've come this far. Let's go and get out of this damn wind before we freeze into statues."

With Erika leading again, they cautiously approached the homes. Abruptly she stopped and held up one hand in warning.

"What is it?" Larry asked almost in a whisper.

She pointed toward the snow around the home. Larry shrugged, but Bill gasped in shock. He too pointed so that Larry could see it. Suddenly, everyone started talking in whispers.

"It's a trail. Someone's been walking on the snow," Erika said as she studied the trail carefully. "It's probably a few days or a week old. It's almost covered but there is definitely something there."

The barely visible winding depression led from the window of one house to the window of another.

As if on cue, the three squatted on the snow to become less visible to anyone looking in their direction. Erika pulled a hand laser gun out of its holster strapped to her right thigh.

"Now what do we do?" Larry whispered. "There are people around here."

"Probably," Bill said.

"Possibly," Erika corrected. "These trails could be months old, or more. In fact, the more I look around, the more I think they are old tracks, partially frozen and covered with snow. Maybe the wind picked up recently. It might have blown away the covering snow."

"Like dinosaur tracks; fossilized and exposed a long time after being buried," Bill said.

"Is that what you think, or is that what you would like to believe?" Larry asked. "We came all the way here. We have to accept the possibility that there are people alive here. Now, let's keep going before we freeze to death."

"He's right," Bill told Erika. "There's nothing we can do. We either go back home, or finish what we set out to do." He stood and started forward again. After a moment, the others followed.

The side of the house that was closest to them had the most exposed walls. The tracks led to a broken window about two feet square. The inside of the house was pitch black. The roof was at waist level, the top of the window by their knees.

"Hello there!" Bill called into the dark void.

There was no answer.

"Well, we won't need our crowbars to get in," Larry said, dropping the rope harness that pulled the sled. He squatted and pointed his flashlight into the house, only to immediately jump back.

The others, startled, looked at him for an explanation, but Larry remained silent and immobile. Finally he spoke. "There's a body on the floor. Look for yourselves." He handed the flashlight to Erika.

Erika and Bill moved up closer to the broken window. The unmistakable smell hit them as the flashlight revealed a spacious and very disorganized room. Furniture, clothing, shoes and miscellaneous household items were strewn all over the bloody floor.

The beam of light rested on the white and red frozen remains of a large adult person. Most of the bones were half-exposed. One arm stretched out toward them as if begging a hand to safety.

Erika closed her eyes for a moment as Bill let the light fall on the corpse's face. The hollow eye sockets of the bloodied skull stared straight at them. Hair was still partially attached to the top of the head, but the skin of the face was mostly gone.

Swatches of clothing covered parts of the shoulders and hips. It was difficult to be sure, but the remnants of cloth suggested that the body had once belonged to a man, not a woman. The contorted and disfigured corpse lay as if it had been thrown to the floor already half stripped of flesh.

"Hello there!" Bill called again.

"He can't hear you, Bill," Larry muttered. "He's dead."

Bill answered, showing his anger. "Just in case someone *else* is in there."

There was no answer, and one by one they descended into the room. Bill was the first down. He jumped into the room and helped Erika and then Larry descend to the floor. There was very little furniture. An unkempt bed stood against one wall.

Erika noted that there were no sharp pieces of glass on the window frames, as if the broken window had been used many times as an entrance. Could it have been used by someone other than the dead person? She shivered at the thought. There might be someone else around...alive...waiting. She took off her right glove and mitten, while making sure her gun was reachable from its holster.

The cadaver lay sprawled in the center of the large room, close to a decorative fireplace. They walked toward it, but couldn't bring themselves to move closer than six or seven feet.

Bill was the first one to speak. "We have to get the body out of here and bury it." He pointed his flashlight all around the room, then at the floor. Its surface was oily and bloody. Pieces of tattered clothing lay scattered all around it. The half-skinned body had obviously been dragged over most of the floor to leave such stains. There seemed to be some kind of tracks across the floor also, but he couldn't tell what sort. There were no well-preserved shoe prints. What had gone on here?

"Cannibalism?" he whispered after a moment.

"Larry, go outside and get a rope from the sled," Erika ordered. "We need to tie the body and pull it through the window."

Larry looked disgusted, but turned and started toward the window. He took only a few steps before he stopped abruptly. Someone — or was it something? — very large stood in the opening they had just come through.

Before a scream of terror could emerge from Larry's throat, a monstrous, hairy creature jumped from the opening, landed on the floor, and with huge teeth exposed, flew directly at him!

The terrified scream finally left Larry's lungs, only to be cut short as strong jaws caught Larry by the neck. The sharp teeth broke through his trachea. Blood from the jugular and carotids smothered his death scream, filling his larynx and lungs.

On the other side of the room, Erika and Bill stood petrified, watching helplessly as Larry's flashlight flew through the air, and both human and monster fell to the floor. Larry's dying moans blended eerily with the growls of the beast.

It took two full seconds before Erika was able to pull herself out of her shock and fumble for her laser gun.

With eyes fixed on both Bill and Erika, the creature dropped Larry's dead body and lunged forward once again, straight toward them. It was upon them in a fraction of a second. Bill screamed, knowing they were surely dead, and tried to fling his body out of the way. The animal flew through the air towards them. Just before the monster reached them, a burst of laser fire slashed through its neck, severing its head and spattering blood everywhere.

Erika and Bill slipped on the sprawled human cadaver behind them, and fell. The head and then the body of what they now recognized as that of an unusually large hybrid wolf-German Shepherd fell over the three of them in a heap of blood, flesh and bones. One arm of the cadaver draped itself over Bill in an uninvited embrace.

With trembling hands, Bill picked the dead dog's head from his chest by its hair, and with horror and disgust flung it as far away as possible. The animal's steaming blood covered his hands and body. More slowly now, Bill removed the dead man's arm from his shoulder and carefully placed it aside, almost vomiting as he did so. He managed somehow to get up and push the dog's bleeding body from Erika, who lay motionless on her back, eyes open and fixed on the ceiling. She began to whimper like a child. It had been so close! Another second and she would have missed the animal. They too would be dead by now.

Bill pulled her to her knees. They looked around. Larry was dead, his throat cut open and his neck broken at its base. The body of the largest dog they had ever seen lay in two portions on the floor. The corpse it had evidently been feeding on lay twisted behind them.

Still kneeling, Erika and Bill held on to each other and sobbed.

* * *

In another room they found the body of the man's wife. Practically nothing remained of her.

They buried Larry and the other bodies in the ice nearby. They did not bury the dog, but flung its body and head as far as possible from the homes.

They explored the other two homes and, with the help of some diaries and farewell notes, pieced together the history of the small community. Three couples, all retirees, had decided to stick it out together through the long winter they thought would last eight or ten months. It gradually became evident that it was much worse and would last much longer. When they began to run out of food they decided to commit communal suicide. But they forgot to kill their dog, or couldn't bring themselves to do so. After a few weeks without food, the dog must have begun eating the exposed flesh. Slowly and instinctively the animal consumed them one by one through the months.

From their notes, these people had been dead for nearly six months. When Bill and the Larkins showed up, the dog had understandably seen them as a threat to its territory and food supply, and had attacked.

* * *

Erika and Bill found only meager supplies of food from among the three homes and a few others they were able to excavate. The rations helped keep them alive for another full year. But the skies grew darker and the freeze even colder. They eventually ate the dog that had killed their husband and friend. But they refused to eat the human flesh that lay buried and frozen all around them.

With no hope for the future, and only bittersweet memories of the past, they died in each other's arms in the mid-part of the year 4 P.I. — a time when most of even the best-prepared humans living at that latitude had run out of all possible sources of food. The terrible, dark winter continued. Most of the once-blue planet was still covered with bands of heavy dark clouds. For all intents and purposes, the Earth was dead.

CHAPTER 12

QUEBEC III.
OCTOBER, YEAR 4 P.I.
THE HUNGER

"When a comet travels north or points south, the country has a major calamity. Western neighbors invade
and later there are floods. When a comet travels east
and points west, the uprisings are in the east. When a
comet appears in the Constellation Virgo, some places
are flooded and there is severe famine. People eat
each other... If a comet appears in the Constellation
Scorpio, there are uprisings and the Emperor in the
palace has many worries. The price of rice goes up.
People migrate. There is a plague..."

Li Ch'un Feng, Record of the World's Change
(602-667 A.D.)

he shelter in western Quebec was covered by many feet of snow, now packed into thick layers of solid ice. This snow and ice were very different from that which had fallen on Quebec in the past. A cut or crack through these layers of ice displayed bands of blacks, browns, reds and grays. The colors were indicative of the density and variety of the precipitating particles. As the ages and climatic conditions of Earth's history are inscribed in the rings of ancient tree trunks, the bands in the ice revealed the horrors of Earth's new history.

Temperatures had remained around minus 50° to 60° F. Venturing outdoors had been impossible for the Lopez-LeBlancs for the last months.

* * *

Paul didn't know why he was waking up again. They had all, long ago, lost any sense of time. Their periods of sleeping and waking had settled into a roughly forty-eight-hour cycle, with twenty-four hours spent sleeping and another twenty-four awake. This pattern had slowly evolved during the early weeks of their entombment, and was well established by the fourth month. Each one developed his or her own cycle, so that rarely were more than two people fully awake at the same time. They had by then stopped using their watches, which were now of no practical use.

Other natural cycles had also gone haywire. Trisha's menses were erratic even while she remained well fed. When rationing of food was initiated, she soon stopped menstruating altogether. But most annoying was the sense of lost time. A span of forty days could seem like fifteen or twenty at the most.

In addition to the hunger, darkness and seclusion, they were tormented by the deep cold that never left them since they had run out of gas. The shelter was buried in snow and ice, and surrounded by a deep layer of permafrost. To think that there was so much wood out there. But there was none that they could use as fuel. They had not the energy to excavate through the yards of dense ice to reach the precious source of warmth. They lived like cave men — always cold, always hungry, always in fear of death.

* * *

Against one wall of the shelter's living room, wrapped in heavy clothing and blankets, Paul, like a bearded ghost, lay immobile on the floor. His sticky, moist eyes opened as he came out of his dream, a dream with feelings so deep they had made him cry. On a couch a few feet away, curled in a fetal position, lay his wife. Not the beautiful woman of his dreams, but, (as he sometimes thought) something that had once been his wife. He glanced toward her. Her frail, thin body was mercifully hidden, covered with layers of dirty blankets. His eyes rested on her face and he began to cry again. Trisha's pale and cadaverous countenance was expressionless. Her dark, sunken eyes were closed and immobile as she slept.

On top of layer upon layer of melted wax, a single candle burned dimly in the center of the table. Scattered on the table were the paraphernalia they had improvised to make crude candles from the burnt and melted leftovers of prior candle generations. Thanks to Cynthia's collection of antique candles they had enjoyed light for the last year.

The flickering of the dim candlelight accentuated Paul's blank expression and scrawny form. A bundle of rags the size of a watermelon lay on top of the cavity where his stomach should have been. Wrapped in the rags was a tiny infant.

Paul's father-in-law, Dr. Emile LeBlanc, had also been reduced to bones covered by sagging skin. He felt filthy, yet he didn't care. They had all long ago lost any interest in cleanliness. Emile sat stuporous, bearded, eyes closed, sunk deep in a large, dilapidated armchair. The chair had been hollowed into a deep cavity by constant use over the years. His head was laid back, his mouth open.

In Emile's arms lay a thin, pale caricature of a child — little Jenny, seven and a half years old. She looked more like a sick spider-monkey than a human. She was emaciated beyond belief, stunted, and dirty. Sharing their body heat, as they had done for so many months, she and her Grampapá were wrapped in a common heavy blanket. With a dirty thumb in her parched mouth, Jenny stared into nothingness.

Paul moved ever so slightly. The entire bundle of rags and blankets that lay upon him shifted as well, releasing its odor of old feces and urine. He shut his eyes again, trying once more to close out reality. In a distant corner of the room a dusty robot stared vacantly at the pitiful scene of dying humans. It would merely take fresh batteries for the robot to become as good as new. The humans, however, would need plentiful food to return to health. But there was no more food, not a single calorie's worth in the shelter. And the outside world was frozen solid, impenetrable.

I have to get up, Paul's thoughts came to him as slowly as endless time.

Why bother? another voice in his maddened mind argued. *We're all going to die soon.*

Years of isolation and months of near-total silence had disordered his mind. He had been living in a world of thoughts, not one of action or even reality. His mind had split into a dozen people: a party of pessimists and optimists, jokers and murderers, maniacs and strangers. Some were already dead.

Get up.

Yes, I will.

Why?

I have to do it, or else we will die.

Shut up, both of you, I want to go to sleep again.

No. It may mean the end.

Laughter. *The end of what?*

Paul briefly opened his eyes, stared at his trembling hands, and brought them to his face. His tongue felt so swollen. Swallowing saliva had become distressing and painful, as had urination, due to the relentless, malnutrition-derived urethritis. His skin was dry and parched, as if sunburned; but he hadn't seen a single ray of sun since Impact Day. His father-in-law, Emile, always the scientist, had explained to them that Paul had a classic case of pellagra, due to niacin deficiency. Why he had a much worse case than the others remained a mystery. His bizarre mental symptoms (the episodes of anxiety, delirium, mania and hallucination) could, in part, be attributed to pellagra. But they were all aware that psychotic patterns were also commonly seen in anyone imprisoned for long periods of time in small, dark, confining spaces.

* * *

Eventually a small sound broke the deadly silence. The feeble cry brought to an end Paul's mental struggle. He managed to open his eyes again; then he moved one arm, partially uncovering the baby's dirty and emaciated face. It cried weakly again. Even though it was almost four years old, the baby looked more like a one-year-old, one that was dying of hunger. Paul couldn't bear the sight of his own baby or that of the skeletonized figure of his daughter. Jenny's hair had lost its curl and color and was now straight, white and brittle. The signs of kwashiorkor and marasmus were obvious. Protein malnutrition had affected her for much too long. Her dry, flaky skin hung loose and wrinkled over her arms and face, making the child look a hundred years old. Anemia was so severe that the pallor made her resemble a miniature ghost. Dr. LeBlanc could not have foreseen the need, nor could they have spared the space, to overstock with even more of the vitamins, proteins and carbohydrate-rich foods he had stored. Only those could save them now.

Paul moved slowly and painfully. He cursed again at the fact that he was actually alive and could purposely move. He propped himself upright against a wall, then laid his bundle on the filthy, cold floor next to him. He felt so weak and so overwhelmingly cold. Would he ever be warm again? he wondered for the millionth time. He looked briefly at the flickering candle, knowing it was a luxury they couldn't afford. A lot of work and effort went into making the wicks for the candles from old clothing and any fabric that the furniture could spare. But light kept them sane. It had been terrible when they had started rationing light to less than six hours per day. They had then become even more depressed and closer to fulfilling their compulsions for suicide. What if they ran out of wax and other burnables? He felt primitive and so restrained, like a prisoner, a criminal. What had been his crime? The guilt was overwhelming, yet he knew, somehow unfounded. The hunger, madness, darkness, and unending cold... Why did he feel it was all his fault? Had they stayed in America would they be better off, or would they be enjoying the peace of death?

Paul cursed his stupidity. During the first year they had wasted so much fuel on videos, music and so much useless light. They had wasted so much gas to maintain the luxury of 60% F. temperature. Now they could barely keep their bodies from freezing. He looked again at the diminutive baby.

Hope, I am going to get you food, he thought. Then, aloud, his words broke the frigid silence: "Emile, get up."

After what seemed a few minutes, Emile, his eyes still shut, sighed deeply. "What?"

After a few more seconds of great effort, Paul finally was fully on his feet, walking, peering at the tiny pitiful child within the bundle on the floor.

"Food, let's get the food," Paul whispered.

"What food? You fool, you have been dreaming again."

"Shhh. Don't wake them. Food for the baby, for all of us." Paul looked over at Trisha. She lay as if in the deep sleep of death. His heart broke for her. She too was but a few hours or at the most a few days from death. He had never known that starvation could last so long. But there was no more time left for any of them.

Unless —

"You know the food I'm talking about," Paul whispered harshly.

"Oh," Emile protested. "I thought we decided —"

"We need it! Get up! It's our only chance."

With his bare hands, Paul cleaned the dirt and moisture off a glass-covered wall panel, and peered into it. "Damn! It's still minus fifty-two out there."

He was about to turn around when his eyes caught a photograph hanging on the wall next to the thermometer. The picture of his mother-in-law had been taken many years before, when she was a beautiful young woman, full of life.

Pour mon bien-aimé. Avec tout mon coeur.

The words of love written on the lower right corner of the photograph left no doubt about the deep love that bound her to the man she would marry soon after the picture was taken.

Sadness crept so painfully in his heart.

Why all this misery? Why this need to survive?

Paul's eyes strayed over to a smaller, more recent picture next to Cynthia's. In it was Trisha, in her twenties, radiant with happiness. Could anyone ever have been so beautiful? he wondered. He looked over to where Trisha lay like a dirty cadaver. How could this have happened?

In the picture, held tightly in Trisha's arms, was little Jenny, just an infant, dressed in warm, colorful tiny baby clothes. The sight brought tears once again to his eyes. Next to Trisha, sitting proudly on her haunches, was Samantha, a then-healthy and beautiful white puppy. The three of them, mother, child and dog, had actually existed. He himself had taken the picture right here in Quebec during a vacation. It seemed like eons ago.

And to think that I actually killed her. He could not restrain the pain in this thought. *I killed her, suffocated her with a pillow and my own hands.* She was so little and had gotten so thin that she didn't even fight. She was gone in but a few minutes. Jenny had cried so. She hardly had the strength to cry; but she cried and cried when she found her little dog dead and cold as ice, its tissue already starting to freeze.

It broke my heart. For months I couldn't get over the remorse of that murder. But the dog was eating food. "Poor Samantha must have had a heart attack." *I lied to all of them. Only Emile's expression let me know that he knew and approved.*

A small earth tremor shook the room slightly. They all ignored it. Paul moved slowly away from the wall. "Let's go."

Emile slowly and silently arose. His every move brought an agony of physical pain. He placed little Jenny, still wrapped in the blanket, in the deep cavity of the arm chair. The child remained in fetal position, barely moving her lips around her bony thumb. She closed her eyes and laid her face on the head of her favorite stuffed animal. The dirty toy was torn, one eye was missing, the other hung pitifully from the stretched out threads that once held it securely to the face.

Paul picked up a makeshift candle, lit it, then tried to lift a heavy crowbar by the wall. It fell through his weak fingers. The metallic noise shattered the silence around him. Trisha stirred and tried to mumble something. The baby whimpered for a moment. Jenny shifted in the chair. Then all returned to their state of stupor.

Paul tried again and hefted the crowbar. Emile took the candle and carried a pick from a far corner of the room, and the two men slowly walked through the shelter toward the stairs that led to the basement.

With much difficulty they climbed down into the lower room, where they walked among debris, empty boxes, empty cans, and the small desiccated turds they had last produced so long ago. Even the latrine was frozen solid. They made their way to one of the distant walls and stopped a couple of feet in front of it. At waist level, part of the wall had been patched with rough cement. A tiny, pencil-drawn cross marked the center of the lumpy cement that covered an irregular area about one and a half feet in diameter. On the ground under the wall lay a heap of settled dirt.

A few feet away was a smaller irregular hole. The wall had been patched there, too. But now it was open, exposing an empty dark cavity. Dirt and broken cement pieces lay in a pile at the foot of the wall. Over this second hole, in a child's handwriting, was the word "Samantha" and another small, poorly-drawn cross.

Paul took the pick from Emile. He hesitated for a few seconds, then slowly lifted it and smashed it into the patched area of concrete. Above the crudely-covered hole were the initials "CLB." A second strike of the pick demolished the thin cement covering. Emile's eyes started to tear. Cynthia, his beloved wife, his intimate companion of so many years — how long she had been dead he could hardly remember. She had been sick for so long, and it was his own fault, his own stupidity. In spite of her strong character, Cynthia had done poorly after the first six months in the shelter. During the second year, on analyzing her urine, he had discovered that she was suffering from diabetes. He should have planned for it, knowing that non-inherited diabetes is relatively common among those over the age of fifty. In his arrogance he had thought that since there was no known diabetes in his or her families, there was no need to stock medicine for it. It had taken Emile a long time to get over her death. He once felt so sure that he stocked all they would ever need. He had sworn to himself that if anyone died it would not be because of poor preparation on his part. Now, he constantly despaired at his many errors of omission. His vanity had led him to overestimate his indirect knowledge of medicine. A single vaccine would have halted the progression of her disease. A few extra pills in his chemistry armamentarium could have saved her so much misery. He had, in a sense, killed her. Could he do this to her now?

Paul took the crowbar and began to break away more of the cement. The dark cold space beyond it became visible, exposing a head of gray hair and the shadows of a cadaverous face. The frozen skin was white, and the sunken eyes were slightly open. Suddenly, a terrifying scream pierced the air.

Dirty long hair streaking behind her, her bulging and dry red eyes standing out in the dim light, Trisha threw herself upon them. "No! No!" she screamed, using up the last of her adrenaline surge as she pounded her husband's chest with her bony fists. He stood immobile as a statue.

"No! No!" she begged, then gradually slumped, exhausted, to the ground by his feet. Crying, she pleaded, "Please, please, don't eat my mother. You can't! I won't let you!"

Paul remained motionless. His face was cold as ice as she wrapped her arms around his knees and laid her head against his thigh, continuing to sob. "Please," she persisted weakly. "You made us eat the dog. Now you want my mother. I won't eat her no matter what. Please don't eat my mother!"

"We have to, love," Paul said gently. "If we don't, we will die."

"Then better we die. She was *my* mother —"

Emile slowly lifted the pick. "And she was *my* wife." Crashing the pick through the wall, he put an end to the argument, tears rolling down his dirty cheeks. "We have to."

CHAPTER 13

CHICAGO IV.
MAY, YEAR 5 P.I.
THE HORROR OF LIFE

"And another sign appeared in heaven; and behold a great fiery dragon having seven heads and ten horns and on his heads were seven diadems. And his tail swept away a third of the stars of heaven, and hurled them down to the Earth... and the great dragon was thrown down... he was thrown down to the Earth."

John: Book of Revelation 12:3,4 (Apocalypse),
Holy Bible

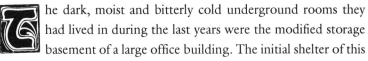he dark, moist and bitterly cold underground rooms they had lived in during the last years were the modified storage basement of a large office building. The initial shelter of this particular Chicago group — the underground malls under Logan Square — had become unlivable after the first few years, due to the accumulation of human waste and the bones of those that had died. The death toll during those first few years was staggering. People died of cold, hunger, untreated diseases, suicide and even murder.

The earth above and around them had frozen so solidly that it had become practically impossible to excavate for food and medical supplies. Many people gave up hope and refused to care for themselves, praying in silence for a death that would bring an end to a life of indescribable misery and suffering.

Almost two years had gone by since they had moved out of their first shelter; four and a half years since the comet had impacted the fragile planet. How they had survived so far, Robert Horton could not understand.

Survivors of the first shelter worked for months on preparing the new one so that it would retain warmth better. Fire was a luxury, as years of scavenging used up most available wood. Since body heat was the main source of warmth, the new shelter had to be small enough to hold that heat within. They tore the insulation from the remains of every building they had access to and packed it under and around the rooms.

The new shelter offered access to other, more remote basements and rooms that were used for waste disposal and storage. One was even allocated as an ossuary for the dead. The new shelter was a long basement, five floors under the remnants of a large office building and next to a parking ramp. It was situated only five blocks from Logan Square. The room could hold up to three hundred people. It was selected because of its low ceiling and unusually thick, insulated walls, to which the additional insulation had been added. The survivors built small cubicles along the wall of the new habitat, each capable of holding two to five people. The cubicles were essentially styrofoam boxes with one open end. They were approximately five feet tall, six feet wide and eight feet deep, affording room only for lying down on the old mattresses and the pieces of cardboard and rug that were layered on the floor.

At one end of the long room, Glord Erickson, the new ruler of the shelter, maintained a large, separate, private chamber for himself and his harem. A few other smaller, lateral rooms were used for storage of the meager medicines and miscellaneous supplies, as well as tools for the repair, insulation and water purification needs of the habitation. Stairs led to an upper floor, which was not insulated and in which were kept any foods that needed to be frozen. The ramp of the adjoining parking lot led to the upper floors. The areas were patrolled twenty-four hours a day by guards who ensured that none from the shelter could steal the allotted rations and that none could escape. The guards were also intended to prevent attacks or looting by other groups of survivors in the vicinity.

Excursions were organized every two or three months to search for food and medicines. These excursions involved weeks of excavating through cement and ice, in the hope of reaching buried stores and restaurants.

* * *

Robert Horton was so depressed that, had it not been for Tammy, he could barely motivate himself to stay alive. His little child was his only love; his strength was his only reason for existence. She was twelve and a half years old now, though she appeared much younger.

Everything had changed. His life, his thoughts, his body; his whole world had changed so! Robert thought a great deal about his planet. The beautiful countryside in which he had loved to hike and explore as the always-curious child he had been, had all turned to ice. Was there any hope? Was there really anything to live for? Looking around him, he sometimes questioned the strength of what he considered the irrational instinct to live. The instinct for survival is so powerful that it allows for immeasurable suffering, even beyond any glimpse of hope or reason.

Each time he thought that they had reached the end, some food was found or some other source of nutrition was miraculously unearthed, allowing them to continue in the agony of existence.

* * *

Robert recalled how, after the first supplies of food had dwindled to practically nothing, they had become like living cadavers. Like those miserable people in the pictures of famine-driven African countries he had once seen in history books. Then, through herculean effort, they managed to break away from death and burrow like rats through the ice, cement and even steel to reach grocery stores and other frozen caches of food. When these were exhausted, and all hope was again lost, the Chicago Council had made the decision to allow for what had now become their living nightmare: cannibalism!

It seemed so long ago. There had been a slight increase in the outside temperature. The survivors speculated that this might be an indication of the beginning of cloud clearing, allowing some of the sun's warmth through. Scientists had said that once that began there would be a rapid reversal of the ice age as the globe went into a momentous greenhouse effect that would warm the planet rapidly.

The Council's reasoning was simple. Since there was now hope of the planet soon being habitable again, it was their responsibility, as perhaps the only people still alive, to ensure that the human species survived. But to do so, the leaders of those days declared, they had to make it through the next few months until the thaw made it possible to again venture outside. To survive those next months, they would have to dig out the frozen cadavers of those buried in the walls and rooms all around them and respectfully, very respectfully, eat their flesh. Otherwise, all might perish before the thaw occurred.

The Council explained that this flesh was preserved frozen for them, as the last gift of those loved ones who had not been as fortunate as they.

"Fortunate?" Robert had laughed. "Who are the fortunate?" he bitterly asked. "Those that are now in the peace of death, or those who continue in the horror of life?"

It had to be done. It was their responsibility as representatives of the only known intelligent beings in the entire galaxy. They had to ensure the survival of *Homo sapiens* at all costs.

* * *

Julia, I miss you so much. I want so much for you to be still alive next to me. But you're probably the lucky one. If you were alive, I would wish that you were dead. Like I wish us dead. Robert's thoughts constantly tortured him. He looked again at his daughter. He frequently conversed with Tammy. At times he caught himself almost believing that he was talking with his Julia — a wife so beloved and now so lost.

* * *

Tammy sensed her father's depression and tried once again to help.

"Daddy, I am praying now like you taught me," Tammy whispered to her father. "The good Lord we love will take care of us. Don't give up. God is waiting for the thaw to start so that we can inherit the Earth as he promised. It will happen soon, I know it will."

Tammy's words continued, unheeded by Robert. He could no longer bear to hear about the *just* God he had once believed in and fervently loved. How futile that belief had been. God had not saved him and Tammy from the horrors after Impact. Robert took some comfort in knowing that his daughter still harbored faith and love, while he felt only emptiness and hatred. No powerful God, he believed, could fail to be moved by so much suffering. No God, no matter how committed to giving humans their own free will, would refuse to intervene and put a stop to so much pain and horror. No God could fail to be moved to some action. No God or even demon could be so cruel as to impose this horror on any living creature, intelligent or not.

"Daddy, Daddy, haven't you been listening?" Tammy was pulling at his clothing. "Why are you crying again, Daddy? Please don't. It makes me cry too." Tears started to well in her own eyes as she embraced her father with her skinny arms.

"We are going to be okay, darling," Robert lied. He had to protect her, he had to keep her safe, safe from the others, safe from the "King."

* * *

Cannibalism permitted them to survive. The great thaw, though, failed to arrive. Consuming the flesh of the dead brought with it a revitalization not only of their bodies but also of their minds. A small minority of the survivors chose to die rather than partake of human flesh. Those that chose to eat, out of duty, plain hunger or just to satisfy the incredible instinct to survive, were shocked by the almost immediate consequences. Having been kept barely alive on meager rations for years, they were not prepared for the feelings of well-being that nourishment suddenly pushed through their veins.

The new protein and vitamin-rich fuel brought long-forgotten sensations of warmth and comfort to their bodies. After just a few days, the survivors found themselves making plans for the future, discussing the construction of a new and better shelter — one that would help them survive the floods that were to come. They spoke of how they would spread out in order to recolonize the planet.

Their bodies and minds were reborn to the notion of hope and strength. Their bodies were again producing endorphins, hormones and hemoglobin. They no longer spoke in whispers. They came out of their deep, lethargic depression to take part in human society.

Dormant for so many years, another of nature's most powerful inner drives was rekindled: libido. The urge for sexual contact had returned. In shock, men saw their erections return. Women felt the warm and vibrant moisture within their loins that they had forgotten once existed. Many younger women marveled as they started to menstruate again after so many dry years. Some even became pregnant, though this was discouraged, because there was barely enough food for the present inhabitants. And who could care for the medical needs of babies?

But as strength and libido were reborn, so was human greed. There were now quarrels and fights over food and sexual partners. There was rape. There were demands for more of the rationed human meat. Some stole human flesh so they could feel sexually stronger and more virile. The assigned peacekeepers had to recondition their weapons as the situation rapidly deteriorated.

A group of men and women organized themselves, first to demand, and then to steal, more of the human meat than was allowed them. Before they were eventually subdued, they had stolen dozens of arms, legs, livers and brains from the dead. One had to be shot dead before the group of newborn barbarians finally realized that they were outnumbered.

The Council's peacekeeping laws were imposed by force to prevent anarchy. Some still complained, arguing that the thaw was in fact starting, and that soon they would be able to explore beyond the present area so confined by ice. But the Council stood firm; however the climatic reaction of the planet to the thinning of the clouds was based only on theories; no one could be sure when the thaw would arrive.

It only took a few months for everyone to realize that the wisdom of the Council was remarkable. In fact, the thaw did not arrive as some had expected, and edible fresh-frozen human flesh was not as abundant as they had once thought.

Once again, jubilation and optimistic feelings of strength and vivacity were replaced by a devastating and depressing air of famine and malnutrition.

* * *

Glord Erickson was very unhappy. A large man of Scandinavian descent, he had had his way as a young man. Tall, red-headed, talented and built like a bull, he had dominated men and women alike since childhood. His impressive physique had been his entree to the world of spectator sports. He had possessed fame, money, and all the power and women that come with it. A very intelligent man, he had exploited both his body and intellect.

But in the deep catacombs of Chicago, Glord had been reduced to the status of a pitiful starving animal. In a semi-stupor, he had lain in his own urine and excrement for several months. At times he was force-fed by those appointed to keep him alive. There were many like Glord, individuals who had become too feeble in body and mind to take care of themselves. Nursemaids had been assigned to keep them alive in an effort to preserve their numbers. The will toward non-extinction had demanded that even the weakest be kept alive until the thaw came, when they might once again become productive humans.

Robert Horton was once assigned to care for Glord. For months he cleaned the filth off him, diapered him, and healed his bedsores. But this was now in the past. Human flesh had revitalized Glord, and his pride demanded that he never return to the humiliating horrors of starvation.

Glord fought for his right to more meat, but he was ignored. He rapidly developed a raging hatred for what he considered discriminating authority. His anger grew to the point of violence. Glord knew what he needed to feel normal. He would not accept the idea of going back to mental and physical weakness. And Glord was not the only one.

Glord organized a group of followers. But in order to ensure success, he would have to take over the entire shelter, subduing the Council. He knew he could do it, but needed more men and women who, like him, were willing to take the necessary risks. Glord plotted for some time, but was unable to rouse the rebel group to sufficient action. At last it was nature that came to his assistance.

During the earlier times of organized cannibalism, to pleasure himself and keep his rebellious group together, Glord demanded and obtained from the Council the right to use one of the larger insulated side rooms for "human satisfaction." This was the what he liked to call the orgies which he had organized.

After episodes of violence, the Council reluctantly allowed these orgies to continue, hoping that the rebel group would satisfy their sexual needs and keep their violent barbarism to themselves, thus not endangering the rest of the survivors. But shortly thereafter, when rationing was reinstituted, weakness and weight-loss returned. It was the return of impotency to some of the men that effected a changing point in their lives.

Glord's hammering of his men was then successful. "In a few more months we won't even have the strength to fight back. We must overthrow the Council now."

Glord told them lies of plentiful cadavers that the Council was hiding. He described the power and glory to come. "It is *our* genes that will repopulate the Earth. *We* will become the fathers of the new planet. Our mission will be to impregnate every surviving woman on the planet so that we and our descendants can rule the entire world."

Glord's well-structured campaign was successful. Once he had enough unconditional followers, he set out his plan. His natural cunning and experience as a leader in sports had made him well aware of the need for swift and flawless execution of a methodically contrived strategy.

In a matter of just a few minutes, the Council's guards were killed and their weapons used to massacre all the top members of the Council. Glord's plans left no room for potentially troublesome prisoners. Besides, they needed to establish a large stock of fresh-frozen food supplies that would ensure their ability to regain and retain their full strength and potency.

As planned, the show of power and absolute mercilessness ensured complete submission and obedience from the remaining survivors in the shelter.

Glord had himself declared King of the new clan, and named his followers dukes and lords. In a continual reign of terror, they ruled in a mockery of government. The new lords assigned working teams for butchering, and for cleaning and rebuilding the shelter. Many inhabitants were made to do slave labor just for the pleasure of the new rulers.

Had this been the only change, it would still have been bearable for many. But the new King and his followers soon craved more excitement. They imposed taxation on their subjects. Since money was of no significance, they took their tribute in the form of clothing, personal possessions, sex and slave labor. Those that complained or would not comply, and even those who could not, due to their lack of strength, were beaten and tortured. Made to stand naked with arms outstretched in the bitter cold until they collapsed, slaves were mocked by their new masters.

The barbarians fattened themselves on the best of the human flesh available. But they made sure that all others were kept fed well enough to perform their tasks, yet weak enough not to be a threat.

All was well for the new rulers until, as the months went by, they too had to start rationing the dwindling supplies of human flesh. Glord sensed unrest among his followers. He had to find more food.

* * *

For Robert, the turning point had been recent — a day when the worst turned into the impossible. He shuddered as he remembered what happened. It was no spur-of-the-moment killing, but a well-planned execution. That they had killed the poor man was bad enough, but then they cooked him!

The body had not been given to the food handlers to be respect-fully dissected, the strips of meat and organs neatly sectioned, freeze-dried and segregated into small rations as was the norm until Glord's reign. Instead, the man's body was dismembered and hacked into large pieces to be roasted on an open fire. The smell of charred hu-man meat added to the horror when the rulers' meal turned into an orgy of gluttony. For their next feasts, the new rulers tried various forms of seasoning and cooking, as if the flesh had come from cattle or pig.

The rest of those in the shelter were forced to eat the leftovers from the cannibalistic orgies of the rulers. Next, they were all forced to participate in the new rites of sacrifice. The new victims, generally those already near death, became "sacrifices to the Gods."

The cannibalistic rites that followed brought out the worst in Glord and his followers. Live sacrifices sometimes included human hearts devoured while still beating — scenes reminiscent of the cruel and bloodthirsty rituals practised by Mayans centuries prior to "civilization."

Most victims didn't even struggle as they were held high up and then butchered alive amongst half-serious chanting and banging of makeshift drums. The "Altar of Death" was used more and more frequently as the rituals became addictive.

But the pleasure, games, power and strength that flowed from each cannibalistic rite was inevitably followed by a deep, oppressive silence. The barbarians could not ignore the fact that these energiz-ing rituals could not be held as frequently as they wished. They knew that if they consumed too many of their human cattle, their fate would be sealed. Some of their subjects had already escaped, and wandered off to die in the frozen outerworld. To keep them alive, Glord had to somehow keep them longing for life. Without any subjects it would be the end of his "kingdom" and death by starvation would inevitably follow.

* * *

This life of famine and horror in the underground of Chicago was being played out in survival communities throughout the world. When such groups reached out beyond their shelters in desperation, they were searching for treasure: not money or emeralds, which were for the most part discarded as useless rubbish, but rather a supermarket or large restaurant full of food preserved frozen through the years. Other valuable finds were drugstores or health food stores containing medicines and vitamins. Other treasures occasionally found were any large groups of animals or people that had frozen on Impact Day or very soon after. Those that had frozen rapidly while still well-nourished could be partitioned and distributed among many.

Less desirable were the emaciated people and animals that had died months or years after Impact Day and had immediately frozen. Their cadaverous bodies provided only a little nourishment. Of even less value, but eaten nevertheless, were frozen pets, mostly cats, dogs, birds, and tiny fish found in demolished apartments and other housing.

Poisonous and inedible were those people and animals that had started to rot before the freezing process preserved them. Opening such a cache released the stench of decayed flesh that not even freezing can surpass.

* * *

Robert began hoping for the announcement of a new search-and-retrieve operation. They had to find some real food, they had to find another restaurant or grocery store. His most fervent wish now was never again to eat human flesh.

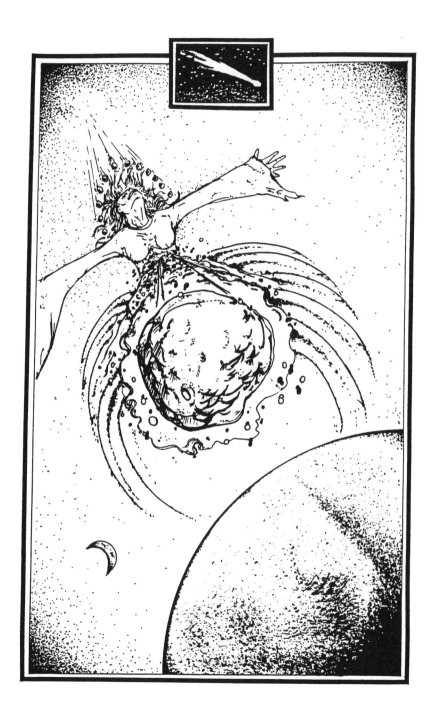

CHAPTER 14

QUEBEC IV.
MAY, YEAR 5 P.I.
LUCK AND DESTINY

"And a great sign appeared in heaven; a woman clothed with the sun and the moon under her feet, and on her head a crown of twelve stars; and she was with child and she cried out being in labor and in the pain of birth."

John: Book of Revelation 12:1,2 (Apocalypse),
Holy Bible

he silence of the dark, frozen forest in northwestern Quebec was broken by loud, piercing hammer-like impacts. Metal rhythmically crashed into ice, slowly fragmenting layer upon layer of ice. Each layer had become as hard as cement and each was banded in many different colors. The packed ice held fast but could not resist the intrusion. Slowly, the layers of ice that covered the escape hatch over the shelter became thinner and weaker.

Finally, with a crash and a gush of air, the seal broke and the crowbar punctured through the last inch of ice. Motionless for a second, the tip of metal pointed toward a black sky.

The piercing now resumed with an almost desperate tempo, its staccato noises mixed with the irregular breathing sounds of heavy labor. The hole in the ice gradually became larger. Again, there was silence.

Paul Lopez poked his head above the newly-formed hole and stared at the desolation around him. As his eyes adapted to the darkness, he perceived the outline of where once, so long ago, had stood a beautiful, wooded vacation haven.

Bearded, pale, and with shrunken cheeks, Paul looked like a skeleton arising from his own grave to look upon his own destination — hell. Not a hell of fire, but of ice, darkness and desolation. It had been many months since they last attempted to venture out. During that time they were forced to make the ultimate decision, to eat Mrs. LeBlanc. Very slowly they consumed her, down to the last tiny cell. They crushed her bones and extracted every drop of marrow. As a result, they underwent an almost miraculous revival. With renewed strength, they were able to ransack the frozen garbage dump next to the basement and extract from it every gram of edible material. Though still very emaciated and weak, Paul, Trisha and Emile now felt they had sufficient energy to explore the outside world and dig through the yards of ice to the nearby cabin till they found something to eat — anything! If they could reach the cabin, they could also find wood and books for fuel.

* * *

In the barely perceivable light of the dark, clouded sky, Paul could only with difficulty make out the remnants of the forest a hundred feet from the top of the shelter. The woods, once so full of life, were now a picture of devastation. The tips of broken tree trunks, stumps and branches stuck out in disarray one to two feet above layers of black ice. Snow drifts and wind had carved the icy landscape into irregular blackened ice dunes.

There was total silence, almost total darkness; the forest was dead. The escape tunnel rose fifteen feet above the cement roof of the shelter. With much difficulty, Paul heaved himself out of the ice hole and squatted next to it. He had on snow boots and pants; but only a dirty sweatshirt covered his malnourished torso.

Despite the cold, he was perspiring, out of breath from the hard labor of excavating through the narrow ice tunnel. Paul passed a finger over the ice, wiping the dirt from the surface and leaving a slightly cleaner line on the cold and shiny ice.

"It hasn't been snowing lately," he muttered aloud. "I wonder if it will last?" He tasted the dirty snow, subconsciously assessing its chemistry.

"Paul, put your jacket and hat on." His wife's voice reminded him of those below. The sunken face of his wife was barely visible in the tunnel of ice under him as she passed him a heavy jacket, gloves, and woolen headcover. "Hurry up, you'll freeze." After he finished dressing, he leaned on the rim of the ice hole. "Guess what," he said, "I can see tree trunks over the ice."

"Take my hand," Paul told his father-in-law, who had just replaced Trisha in the tunnel. Paul helped Emile out. Dr. LeBlanc, also pale and dirty, wore a lot of clothing, with only his gray-bearded face showing. Holding an axe, he stood and looked around him. Just then, Trisha's emaciated face appeared above the hole to peer out at the frightening scene.

"God, it's horrible out there," she said. "Be careful," she added, handing them metal- spiked clamp-on cleats for their boots. "We can't afford either one of you slipping on the ice and breaking something."

"Take care of Hope," said Paul.

"He's fine. Jenny is with him."

"You know," Paul said then, "I think things have been melting here for the last few weeks. I can see some garbage that was still buried under the ice last time we were out."

"God, I pray you're right," cried Trisha. She passed Emile a few pieces of sheet metal and some rocks, then disappeared into the hole. Paul and Emile placed the sheet metal over the hole and weighed it down with the rocks.

Emile stared into darkness toward the buried cabin that was once the beautiful and serene getaway for three generations of LeBlancs.

Paul picked up the crowbar, switched on their only rechargeable flashlight that still worked, and headed towards the cabin. "I can't believe we're actually out!" he exclaimed. "It's been so long. There just has to be something edible in that house."

"Thank God it finally stopped snowing," said Emile. "Look, Paul. You were right. I see some branches sticking out above the ice. We'll have some fuel for a fire. We have to excavate and repair the chimney extension."

They walked slowly toward the area where the cabin should be. Physical weakness combined with extreme caution made the short trek a long adventure. After walking carefully for a few yards, they suddenly stopped. The outline of the cabin was coming into view.

"Look, Emile. The top of the cabin is right above the ice!" They both stood in bewilderment as if a miracle had occurred. The top of the cabin was visible. Partially collapsed, parts of the second floor were exposed, the rest still buried under ice.

"The melting must be happening quickly," said Emile. "And look! Some other tree trunks are showing above the ice. There, to the right of the cabin. Oh, my God, we can get wood from both the house and the trees. We can have a good fire going again after so many years!"

As they reached the remnants of the cabin, both men stopped to admire the rows of huge icicles hanging from the torn roof. The silence was interrupted by the dripping sounds of water falling from the tips of the black shiny icicles.

"Yes!" Emile shouted. "I never thought I would delight so at the sight of melting ice!"

Paul smiled briefly and then in a somber tone added, "This is good;

but remember, melting means the floods will be coming."

They all knew the scientists' prediction, that as soon as thawing started, the forests of the world, containing trillions of tons of frozen dead wood, would start to rot, releasing massive quantities of CO_2 into the atmosphere. The permafrost would melt, releasing methane gas trapped under the thick frozen layers of earth. These gases would join the CO_2 released by the new volcanoes and would set in motion a rapid warming of the atmosphere. As the cycle accelerated, torrential unending rains would pour from the skies and the Earth would be inundated. The great floods would increase sea level high above pre-Impact levels, submerging much of the land of the continents, and making many islands totally disappear.

"Shut up, you damn pessimist, and let's go!" said Emile, as they scrambled to climb into the cabin. The Ice Age had made for a reversal in roles. Paul was constantly depressed and now the most negative of the two.

Using the axe and crowbar, they broke the ice sheets and icicles covering the shattered windows that once stood fifteen feet above ground. They finished breaking what was left of the window itself, then climbed into the second-floor room that had once been a guest room. It had last served as little Jenny's room whenever the Lopezes came to visit.

The flashlight poorly illuminated the room. Jenny's room was a sad sight indeed: dark walls, dilapidated pictures hanging crooked, heavy with dirty icicles. A small bed was encased in ice like a frozen coffin. And the stuffed animals looked cold and tragic, covered with layers of dirty ice.

What was left of the roof had partially collapsed, breaking the window frames. The wind had blown the snow, now ice, into the room, and some of it drifted up against the door leading to the rest of the house. Emile started to hack with his axe at the ice that covered the lower half of the door.

The doctor tried so many times during the last few years to think of what they might have left in the cabin that was edible. He believed they had taken everything into the shelter. Yet he always hoped that they might have forgotten something — perhaps some cans of food, some sugar, a box of cereal, iodine-rich salt, anything!

Paul was helping his father-in-law push away the large chunks of ice when he stopped. His eyes opened wide as he stared in disbelief at an object on top of Jenny's bedstand. It was inclined over a book; the top half was no longer covered by the thick ice that surrounded the rest. Yes, it *was* there! he couldn't believe it, — a chocolate bar! almost whole!

As Emile continued to work, unaware of the find, Paul moved slowly toward the table and passed one hand over the ice, removing some of the soot and dirt. *Yes, chocolate!* He tried to free the piece of chocolate from the ice, but his gloves were too thick. He removed them and scratched uselessly with his nails at the frozen food. He could contain himself no more. He struck the ice with the crowbar so hard that the table top was smashed to pieces. Fumbling, out of control, he found the now-fragmented chocolate pieces and stuffed them in his mouth. The sharp cracking of frozen chocolate and the guttural, frenzied animal sounds punctuated the silence around him.

Paul suddenly became aware of his surroundings. He turned slowly to face the expression of disbelief from his father-in-law. "There's more — here. I, I haven't eaten it all," he stammered as the pain of shame overcame him. He apologetically handed Emile the last small remnant of chocolate. "I'm sorry, Dad."

They both stared at the little piece of chocolate. Reaching out for it, Emile suddenly pulled back his hand. "Save it for Jenny and Hope," he said. He turned, and with one mighty blow broke the door into smithereens. With the help of the flashlight they made their way through, and rushed down the steps, sliding on occasional snow and ice, to the kitchen, the place they hoped would have some stored edibles.

They fumbled through drawers and cabinets, desperately looking, but finding absolutely nothing. Had they been too thorough in taking everything to the shelter? They must have left something. Maybe some flour or sugar. Even a used tea bag would be welcomed.

"Paul." Emile's voice caused the younger man to stop his frantic search. Emile sounded hopeful. Had he found a can of soup, some cereal?

Emile's flashlight was shining feebly on the bottom of a small utility closet. Among the brooms and cleaning rags, and partially concealed by them, was a bag, two to three feet tall and obviously full. Paul held the flashlight while Emile pulled the bag out. He then tore off its top with his hands, and they both dug into it, pulling out handfuls of chunky, dry dog food.

For a few minutes, only the sounds of feverish crunching and swallowing were heard. Like animals they ate until they could no longer move. They looked at each other and laughed.

"Dog food! I never thought it could be this delicious!" exclaimed Emile. Concentrated protein and fat with all the necessary vitamins and minerals any mammal could hope for! Paul rolled on his back, barking repeatedly. They both roared with laughter.

Almost crying, Emile stammered, laughing and crying at the same time. "We are laughing — laughing — oh, I've missed it so much. It's been so many years!" Tears of joy filled their dark, sunken eyes, bringing to them a spark of life that had been absent for so long.

* * *

Upon their return to the shelter, the contrast was striking. Only a few minutes ago, they had barely been able to walk over the ice-covered clearing. Paul was whistling now as he helped Emile with the 50-pound bag of precious nutrients. They joked and skipped on the ice. Nearly drunk under the influence of a sudden dose of protein, they danced all the way to the shelter. They knelt next to the opening and removed the covers they had placed over the hole.

Emile's expression changed to surprise and then amused disgust as his face was bathed in the light and air coming from the escape chute. "Ugh!" he muttered in disbelief.

Paul joined him. "Wow! It sure stinks down there!"

The men broke out again in laughter, and to the bewilderment of Trisha and Jenny, they descended into the shelter — barking.

CHAPTER 15

CHICAGO V.
NOVEMBER, YEAR 6 P.I.
THE UNTHINKABLE

"And something like a great mountain burning with fire was thrown into the sea... and a third of the creatures which were in the sea died..."

John: Book of Revelation 8:8,9 (Apocalypse),
Holy Bible

obert sat silently, stewing in hate yet trembling in fear and anticipation. He was immobile, squatting in his small styrofoam cubicle. The unit was barely large enough for him and his daughter. Their bodies, dirty and covered with as much heavy clothing as possible, were their only possessions. They were looking at the feeble light coming from the other end of the long, corridor-like shelter. At that end, the leaders of the group, Glord and his "court," were gathered in an apparent conference.

"What are they up to today?" Tammy whispered.

Robert looked at her shadowed face before he answered. Everything these days seemed to occur in slow motion; in the frigid darkness, even thinking was an effort. "I never thought that things could be so bad," he said at last. "I don't mean the comet. Nor the cold. It's us humans."

Again it was a few moments before she in turn answered, "Daddy, we have to survive." It was a phrase that they used over and over. She used it in hope. It was also used by others to justify the most unthinkable acts. After another long silence, she spoke again. "They say that the temperature outside has gone up."

It wasn't often that the lords of the New Kingdom used enough light to reach the Hortons' cubicle. Robert could barely see the outline of Tammy's face. She was no longer a child. She was turning into a beautiful woman. She was 13, and her features, even beneath the dirt and despite the cold, were beginning to remind him of her mother.

How he longed for those days of warmth and love! During these years of silence, he relived in his mind every moment of his life with his beloved wife. Every word Julia had ever said, her every expression, their every act of loving, was replayed repeatedly in longing remembrance. Every disagreement, every trivial argument was augmented in self-punishment — as if it should never have occurred; as if it could have been avoided.

The thoughts of his wife and the stir of emotion they created startled him back to the present situation. "It's a couple of degrees warmer, or should I say less cold. We've been close to the freezing point for a few weeks. Maybe there is hope now. If it keeps up, we might be able to go outside in the next few months or so." Then, bitterly, he added, "Or maybe it's just another lie."

"What do you mean?"

"I mean maybe they are just feeding us more lies to keep our hopes up, so that our desire to live is maintained. They don't want us *all* dead."

Though only 13 years old, Tammy understood well what he meant. The horrors of these years had taught her to expect the worst. Unlike Robert, the memories of better times were but a distant fog to her, like vague dreams with poorly-formed images, void of details. She was only a child when the comet destroyed her world. She knew her mother better through him than through her own memory. Her childhood imagination had created a fairy tale of what her early exist- ence must have been like, in what seemed to her the past of a differ- ent and alien planet. The world before Impact Day had become a story to her, an idealized fiction.

Robert suddenly smacked his right cheek with one hand. "Damn it. I hate these bugs," he whispered. He could not get used to the lice and fleas. How they had all managed to get infected in the first place, he could never understand. What he did know was that all it took was one critter. Without medicated shampoos and creams, they had all gradually become heavily infested. He knew they must all reek, yet they never seemed to notice it anymore. They had gotten used to themselves in spite of the years without baths. To make it worse, he had been assigned for years to take care of the sick and those too debilitated to care for themselves. So many times he had to remove their clothing. He still gagged each time. Only Glord and the elite of his court could afford the luxury of hot water and soap. Court mem- bers even carried little bottles of perfume with them to clear the air around them whenever they had to get too close to a "commoner."

Men in the shelter wore heavy beards, adding to the gloominess of the environment. Glord, on the other hand, had access to a cache of old-style razors that required no electricity. Petra, the head mis- tress of the harem, gave him a daily shave while she bathed him and rubbed his muscles. She reveled in her newly acquired glory and power.

Duchess Petra was in her forties, but she possessed an aura of sensuality that was difficult not to notice. She used her body masterfully in her quest for power.

The candles at the end of the corridor were blown out.

* * *

Robert laid his head against the wall in despair. He could not forget the effect that the last cannibalistic orgy had on them. Was it two weeks, or two months ago? He recalled how a recent brief moment of dissent and rebellion by some of the more courageous members of the group had kindled so much hope. But the ruthless barbarian had won one more battle, and made it perfectly clear that the consequences of such action would never be forgotten by the remaining survivors.

Poor Louis, Robert thoughts. A tall, young man in only his thirties, Louis had been a very useful member of the survival group till then. Louis was now dead. It was hard to think of him as a hero.

Louis Guzman had decided that, just as Glord had taken his power by violence, they, too, would organize, and with a well-planned, swift coup, destroy the oppressors. But pressure from Glord's court was too much for some of the rebels. Fear of what would happen if they were caught led to betrayal. Luckily for Robert and other members of the rebellion, Louis held fast under torture.

Glord's rage at the futility of his attempts to extract any information from the brave man was evident. He suspected there were other rebels, but who they were or how many, he was unable to determine. Louis' broken and bloodied body became the center of Glord's rage and would become an everlasting image of terror to the rest of the surviving group. All had been forced to witness the long hours of torture. When he finally died, his battered body was impaled from anus to mouth in front of all of them. He was then slowly roasted in preparation for another cannibalistic ritual.

Standing over the blackened and charred body, Glord screamed to all the members of the group: "Let every one of you scum remember this very clearly. You are nothing but our servants and slaves! If you do not want the same fate, you must follow my rules exactly.

There will be no more dissension; no more laziness; no speaking a single word against me or any other member of my court."

Thrusting his hand down, he snapped off the burnt penis of his victim, took it to his mouth and crushed it between his teeth, smiling with satisfaction at the effect on the audience. He crunched loudly, so that the sounds of his chewing would be heard by all. In the meantime his guards assured that everyone, regardless of age or health, looked straight at the horrid scene.

Glord finished his grisly meal. Once finished, he gave orders to his officers to prepare for a banquet. Louis' charred remains, lifted high by four members of the court, were paraded through the audience, accompanied by chants and a macabre cacophony of drums and bells. They were brought up to the altar, where Glord and the higher members of the court feasted on the most succulent and nourishing parts of the body. Other parts were then eaten by the lesser members of his court. Finally the leftovers, the least desirable portions, were thrown among the audience. As always, eating was a mandate that none dared disobey.

* * *

Robert could not get these thoughts out of his mind. The memories of each horrifying event tormented him over and over. Tammy could feel her father's tension, and it scared her.

Loud laughter broke the silence in the shelter. The light from the candelabra was back on. It seemed the sadists couldn't take anything seriously for very long. Their voices brought Robert back to reality. *What are they scheming?* he wondered. The light and laughter near the sacrificial altar could only mean another sacrifice or Machiavellian plan. But it seemed too soon for another death.

"Let's hope they're not planning another execution," Robert whispered. "There's no one dying or useless now. Maybe they're thinking of another attempt to find a buried store or a group of fresh frozen people."

If they did decide on another search mission, he thought, it would mean a working team and many days of digging and tunneling through rubble and ice-filled basements. Agonizing work, but a relief from the despair of living in the shelter day to day.

Tammy could tell her father's eyes were open by the two tiny reflections of the distant lights in them. The reflections suddenly shifted and became brighter.

A group of lords had started down the long room with a single torch. The light illuminated their barbarian features, deformed by expressions of greed and anticipation.

Robert and Tammy froze as two men and two women stopped by their cubicle. Petra, the "queen bitch" as she was known, was smiling. Their ridiculous regal and militaristic attire, the crowns and medals, brought no laughter. The older man, Harry, the Lord Chamberlain, unrolled a dirty mock scroll and spoke firmly, trying to withhold his snickers. "Robert and Tammy Horton, thou are ordered to respectfully appear before His Royal Majesty, Glord the First, and his just Court." The deadly pantomime was no game to the "commoners", but it brought cheers, laughter and applause from the other members of the court.

Robert felt as if his heart had stopped. The hair on the back of his skull began to stand on end — an evolutionary remnant forecasting imminent death. Unbidden, images of his parents and his wife appeared in his consciousness. A moment later Tammy threw her arms around him. "No!" she cried. "I don't want to die. Daddy! They're going to kill us! They're going to eat us!"

Robert held his daughter tightly. He refused to move, but both were dragged forcibly from their cubicle.

"This can't be!" he cried out in disbelief. "She's much too small. She carries too few calories. I'm still strong and useful and have never made trouble for you! It's a mistake!" he screamed again. He began to struggle, to fight. "It's not our turn," he cried. His words were cut off by a heavy, metal-spiked glove slamming into his face, throwing him into a state of pain and near-unconsciousness. At the second blow he passed out.

* * *

"Well, well, Mr. Horton, are you feeling better now?" A calm, matronly voice awoke him. The true meaning of the apparently reassuring words was soon evident when he realized they came from the lips of Petra. Her tone changed to commanding. "Stand up in front of your KING!"

Robert became more aware of his surroundings as, with the help of his daughter, he stood feebly. Through a haze, he could see that he was standing in front of Glord, seated on his throne.

Tammy held onto him fiercely. Her voice nearly steady, she spoke for both of them, following established rules of protocol. "What does your majesty wish of us?" she asked.

"Robert Horton," Glord said, ignoring her, speaking in a casual, almost intimate tone, "I'm surprised at you. You have never been a problem." He smiled, then turned to his lords and ladies. "We wouldn't harm you, would we?" The laughter from the members of the court ended abruptly when Glord continued, his voice now barely above a whisper. "You are a paramedic and we are proud of you. You have done very well cleaning and taking care of the sick and wounded. You are very useful. Feel assured that we don't want to harm you or your child. We need your help, actually. If it works out, you and your child will have many privileges. Maybe you can even join our court."

Still groggy, Robert didn't know if he understood or believed what was happening. A surge of hope filled his mind as he made an effort to compose himself and comprehend better what was being said.

Glord moved closer to Robert to make sure that all who were not members of the court could not hear. "We may be getting into a crisis here," he continued. "The outside temperature is definitely rising, but not fast enough. We need to devise a way to keep some of the less useful people alive while they consume the least amount of food possible. I thought that with your experience as a paramedic you could help." He paused. When Robert didn't answer right away, Glord continued. "Look at it like a scientific challenge," he said. "A state of suspended animation without loss of tissue mass. We know it's been done in the past, and you're the only one here who can do it."

The reality of what was being asked of him brought waves of nausea to Robert's pained body. They wanted him to help maintain a cattle farm of humans in a state that would reduce energy needs yet maintain body tissue for future consumption. "What?" was the only word he was able to mutter in an attempt to give himself time to adjust to the situation.

"You heard me," Glord said firmly. "If you don't know how to do it, we have all the books you need. As you know, we have found a few large pharmacies and can get all the drugs and chemicals you ask for. As an experienced paramedic, you can help the court." And then, almost as an afterthought, "And help all the survivors in this great shelter."

And if I don't, you'll kill me, Robert thought. "But I'm not a paramedic," he protested. "I'm a food specialist. I've been helping with the sick because someone had to do it." Realizing what he was getting himself into, and sensing the change in expression of the courtiers around him, he tried to salvage the situation. "I've helped since day one," he went on. "I even helped you, Glord — I mean your royal highness. For years, I took care of you and your wounds. I cleaned...."

But he never finished the sentence. A heavy kick from Glord's booted foot caught him at the waist. The second blow, with a fist, hit him on the face, and, in a splash of blood, rendered him nearly unconscious again.

"Nobody takes care of ME!" screamed Glord. "I am KING! And nobody LIES to me! A goddamn cook! Impersonating a healer! We need a goddamn cook and you've been lying to us all this time! I'll have your liver for that!"

Tammy, screaming and crying, was held back by a guard as she tried to reach her father. Two of the lords pulled Robert back to his feet to face their master.

"I'll teach you, you son of a bitch!" Glord cried. He cocked his right arm, preparing to strike Robert again, when Tammy, still screaming, pulled herself away from the guard and thrust herself forward, catching Glord off balance. Before the lords were able to pull her back, she raked Glord's face with her fingernails. "No! No! Don't hurt my Daddy!" she screamed.

Thin streaks of blood appeared on Glord's enraged face, as all around froze in deadly silence. The girl was surely dead. Maybe they were all dead. They had allowed this to happen. Like lightning, Glord slapped her hard, sending the child flying onto Robert, and throwing them both, and those restraining him, into a disarranged heap.

Glord grabbed the large ceremonial sword used in the butchering of sacrificial victims and brought it high overhead, ready to cut Tammy in half, when he suddenly stopped his arms in midair. His eyes widened. Those standing around him noticed too what had caused him to halt his death swing.

Atop the pile of dazed bodies lay little Tammy, whimpering, hugging her father's chest. Her long, heavy skirt was thrown over her back, exposing her dark shiny skin, well-rounded buttocks, and some dirty strings holding a reddened rag to her pubis.

Glord threw the weapon down and swiftly brought his hand between her open legs. In an instant he expertly thrust a finger into the girl's vagina. Tammy screamed.

Robert held her closely and hastily pushed her skirt down. Glord raised his blood-tinged finger to his face. To the shock of all, he sucked the finger clean. "Another goddamn lie!" he screamed, so loud that the building seemed to shake. "It's fucking menstrual blood!" Like a madman, Glord tore Tammy from the arms of her father. Robert screamed as he tried to hold on to her.

In a few swift seconds Glord tore off Tammy's clothes, exposing the tight band of cloth that bound her breasts flat against her chest. He hesitated only for a moment, and then pushed it down to her navel, her beautiful young breasts bouncing into view. "Another fucking lie," he repeated now, his voice thick with lust. "Nine years old, my ass!" He pushed the girl toward the Queen Bitch, who was smiling lasciviously. "Prepare her!" he ordered. "And tie him so he can watch!"

All inhabitants of the shelter were made to witness the violent deflowering. Not even a mattress was laid over the sacrificial table (a block of hard, cold cement.) Tammy's naked body was tied spread-eagled, her hips on the edge of the table. She had been crying for so long she could barely sob any more. To her, the nightmare was not the rape, but the ritualistic death she was sure would follow, and then — she had lived it in her nightmares so many times — her limbs, her breasts, her ribs being eaten until the bones were clean.

"No!" she sobbed, rocking her head from side to side, "No, please don't eat me!" The words were barely audible as she repeated them over and over again.

"In a few weeks, baby, you'll *love* to be eaten," the Queen Bitch replied, smiling. The laughter of the lords went unnoticed by Robert. He tried to conceal his sudden happiness, but let out a quick cry when he realized that his daughter would live. She would be a sex slave; not killed and cannibalized.

"And you, fucking cook!" Petra said, "you will keep her alive, healthy and clean for us to use at our command!"

"Yes, your royal highness, whatever you command will be done," Robert stuttered between sobs. *Thank you, oh, thank you, God,* he thought. *We will somehow live. While she remains alive as their new toy, there is always hope for both of us. I swear somehow we'll get out of here alive and my Tammy will live with me, like a human, not like an animal. There has to be an ending to this madness. I swear we will live.* He cursed the mistakes that had allowed this to happen. He had carefully, and for so long, made sure that she seemed but a child to the court members. When consumption of human flesh allowed better nutrition, her body began to develop. He had bound her budding breasts so that they would never show. Now all had changed in a matter of seconds, and it was all his own fault.

Robert's painful thoughts were soon drowned out by the noise of the ceremonial drums. Glord stood above his victim. The chanting and dancing were interrupted by Tammy's piercing screams as Glord violated her. The screams would never leave Robert's mind for as long as he lived. He cried like a child as he was forced to witness the desecration of the only person who mattered in his life.

Finally Glord himself screamed as, standing tall between her outstretched legs, he orgasmed. With great pride, Glord looked all around. "There will be no more lies!" he shouted triumphantly. "Nothing will be hidden from us!"

Lord Harry, second in command, now approached the table. It was his turn by rights. When Glord moved away, the Duke exposed himself with glee. But the Duke and others would have to wait. Tammy had fainted. Rape was used not only for sadistic pleasure, but also as a threat, and is not effective if it is performed on a body that refuses to react to pain and humiliation.

Tammy was given back to Robert. He was ordered to nurse her and bring her back to them in no more than twenty-four hours. He must bring her to them as a gift, cleansed and adorned with plastic flowers for the others of the court to partake of, and he must show his gratefulness for their benevolence. He must do all of this, and whatever else they demanded, smiling. That was their command. He knew that if he did not cooperate fully, he would be the next to die. And if he died, then who would care for Tammy? He had to live.

* * *

Back in their cubicle, Tammy regained consciousness while Robert and the friend from the next cubicle, Rosemary, cleaned her. Robert continuously hugged and kissed her. He reassured her and covered her with blankets. He gave her a little water — life-sustaining fluid she barely had the strength to swallow.

But they were alive! Tammy was so relieved that they had not been killed and eaten, she could almost forget the deep pain in her lower abdomen. "I'll help you, Daddy," she murmured weakly. "I'll keep us both alive, no matter what. We'll escape." She fell asleep in Robert's arms. Eventually he, too, out of exhaustion, slept.

* * *

Robert knew even before he was fully awake that something terrible had happened. Like the hair-raising howl of a wolf on a dark night, his long, agonized cry brought everyone out of their cubicles. They all looked down the long room and none were surprised when, clutching her cold body, he screamed for his loss.

"She's dead! She's dead!" His sorrowful cries moved even the most cold-hearted members of the court.

Rosemary came rushing to Robert's side. The gentle woman who had frequently helped Robert in his chores as self-taught paramedic, quietly bent over and touched Tammy's face. It was cold as ice. Not the cold skin of starvation and emaciation she had learned to recognize, but the deep, fixed coldness that can only accompany death.

Rosemary gently lifted Tammy's blanket. She wasn't surprised to find blood around the girl's thighs, but by no means could it account for her death. She explored deeper. "Poor child, she is torn inside," she whispered. "My God, I can feel all the way into her abdomen. She bled internally. I'm so sorry, Robert. She bled to death."

Robert knew then that he would one day kill Glord. He would live only for the day he would butcher Glord's body. Nothing would stop him, nothing. His thoughts of revenge mixed with his grief in a confusion of overwhelming feelings. Suddenly he realized he was being beckoned by the members of the court. Could things possibly get worse?

Robert looked up in bewilderment at their faces. They were not laughing. They were not making pretenses of court manners or dictates. They just stood there, some looking very uncomfortable.

"No! No! You can't have her!" Robert screamed as loud as he could. "Nooo!"

The struggle was short and futile. He was tied and tranquilized with intravenous medication. For the next three days, each time he awoke he was tranquilized again, so that he would not hurt himself fighting the restraints.

Finally he realized that to fulfill his vow to kill Glord, he had to rest, had to comply, had to be a good slave. Only then would he have a chance to get his revenge.

CHAPTER 16

QUEBEC V.
LATE NOVEMBER, YEAR 7 P.I.
DESPERATION

"Stars in the sky were seen throughout the world to fall towards Earth, crowded together and dense, like hail or snowflake. A short time later, a fiery way appeared in the heavens; and after another short period half the sky turned the color of blood... [and there were] great earthquakes in diverse places."

Counsel of Carmont, France (1095 A.D.)

I n northern Quebec, the year 7 P.I. began with a clap of thunder heralding an important change in the weather. After a period of relatively dry weather without the continual snow falls of the first few years, there was again a significant increase in precipitation, but this time consisting of soggy sleet, even rain. For the Lopez-LeBlancs, traveling through the woods became extremely slow and laborious. Branches, rocks and tree trunks stood out through the layers of ice and mushy sleet. Overflowing brooks and rivers of freezing waters obstructed headway through areas that previously had been passable.

Paul and Emile dreaded the new outdoors. They were able to move only one mile or so per day. They frequently had to backtrack when they encountered impassable obstacles such as large bodies of semi-frozen water: lakes covered by ice too thin to walk on, ice mountains built up by the wind, cracks and crevices in the ice, or great masses of now-exposed dead tree trunks and branches.

*　*　*

Unlike many places in North America, where temperatures were still subfreezing, Canada and Quebec were further north from the worst, dark-stricken latitudes. Once the skies over these areas started to lighten even to a minor degree, the ice began to melt quickly. Recent months saw a moderate and steady increase in temperature. The warmer temperatures began to thaw the thick ice sheets. But, unlike what many had predicted, the early thaw was slow, and brought increased humidity and cloudiness, lowering temperatures again. This cycle of snow and rain repeated itself over and over.

While Paul and Emile foraged, Trisha usually stayed with the children in the shelter. But occasionally she also had to go and help in the arduous ice excavations in search of dead animals.

As the weather warmed, the landscape became more unpredictable. Excursions became even more dangerous, as tree trunks and branches that had been helpful handles now became unstable hazards.

Within two miles of the LeBlanc's cabin were a handful of similar cabins, mostly old summer getaways for the city folks of Montreal. Paul and Emile took every single ounce of edible matter from these homes, including some frozen pets. In one home, there were human remains, those of an older couple who evidently, on Dis'Aster's approach, had decided it would be easier for them to survive in the woods than in the city. Perhaps they had thought that all would be well after a few months of unusually cold weather. Accustomed to the bitter cold of the area, they had seemingly felt secure in providing themselves with a few more rations than usual. When they later realized survival was impossible, they had opened the windows and sat down in their living room. Holding hands, they quickly froze to death.

Every ounce of meat and blood, marrow, organs and skin from these people, as well as from any others that had frozen to death in the vicinity, was consumed, allowing Emile, Paul, Trisha and Hope to live. Though Emile was now the main proponent of cannibalism, he was worried for his family on two major counts. The most obvious was the potential psychological ill effects of cannibalism (or anthropophagia, as he preferred to refer to the act of humans eating human tissues). His daughter was already having recurrent horrifying nightmares in which she saw herself eating her mother and even her own children. Unlike reality, where small strips of tissue were freeze-dried before consumption, her dreaded nightmares would sometimes find her devouring humans while they were still alive, with both she and the victims screaming in madness, despair and pain.

Paul also admitted to nightmares and, even more frightening, uncontrollable daydreams in which he was a hunter of humans, stalking them like prey, ambushing, killing and eating helpless men and women.

And what about the children? Was their apparent lack of psychological horror a manifestation of a better, but in the long run more damaging repressive mechanism? Emile was very worried about the adults, but tried to convince himself that in the children, the psychological effects would not be so bad. He reasoned that for them cannibalism was simply a normal way of life, a welcomed way to find relief from the pain of hunger. The younger child, Hope, had not known any other way of life, and Emile sensed that for Jenny the years prior to Impact were like a distant dream, a life that she no longer considered real. For her also, cannibalism was a normal and even desirable activity.

Emile's second concern related to disease transmission. He remembered that, in the mid-Twentieth Century, scientists had discovered among some New Guinea tribes a fatal neurological disease, called kuru, transmitted through cannibalism. The Lopez-LeBlancs had chosen not to cook human meat, to mitigate the repulsiveness of the whole activity. In their foraging, the family risked eating the flesh of a person who was the carrier of a deadly virus.

* * *

Emile and Paul were hacking at layers of ice a mile or so from the shelter. A light snow fell as, in the light of a bonfire, they excavated what was left of a very small barn and adjoining shed, both of which were still partially covered with ice. The roofs had been crushed by the weight of overlying ice. The men had searched the buildings when they first found them, but discovered nothing to eat. Now they extended the search around the empty buildings in hope of finding frozen farm animals.

As Dr. LeBlanc's pick hit the ice once more, a large chunk suddenly burst away, exposing the frozen neck and part of the face of a domestic goat. Its desiccated eyes were frozen in a permanent stare. Emile jumped back with a startled exclamation but recovered quickly to bend over and poke the skin with a penknife. He sniffed the exposed flesh. "Hooray!" he exclaimed. "This one is not rotten! It's small and skinny, but enough to keep us all going for a few more weeks!"

"At least we won't be eating cats, rats and skunks for a while," Paul said with relief. "Maybe there are more goats around here. Let's keep digging."

The animals that had managed to stay alive till they froze to death became the life-saving sustenance for millions throughout the world. Cows, sheep, pigs, chickens and horses were the most sought-after, since no one felt uneasy eating every muscle and edible part of their bodies. Bone marrow and organ meats, as in the time of the Neanderthal, were eaten to the last drop for their energy-rich fat, iron and other essential nutrients.

Fish, frozen in small shallow lakes and ponds, were also available but had to be retrieved through much labor. The sealife frozen in tidal pools allowed many otherwise-doomed, to survive the transition years between what became known as the Deep Freeze and the Great Thaw.

A more unusual and varied menu awaited those who eagerly dug through the ice layers into zoos full of exotic birds, mammals, insects and reptiles. Also nourishing were the unusual fish and marine mammals in aquariums.

* * *

Dr. LeBlanc started to exhume the goat. "Excellent," he said, again smelling it. He directed Paul's attention to another slight deformity of the nearby ice. "That may be a good spot, Paul. If we're lucky, it's another goat."

Paul turned and began hacking at the ice, sending chunks and slivers flying in all directions. As a large piece fell by his feet, Paul screamed in horror. He had exposed the disfigured face and upper torso of an emaciated woman clutching a small baby. One of the baby's frozen arms had chipped off and was embedded in the ice. The baby was evidently malnourished, its bones showing under the thin skin. A slab of the woman's cheek was torn off by the ice, exposing the underlying bone.

"Oh, my God!" Paul exclaimed, turning away. "Oh, no! Please don't let it be her!" In anguish, he closed his eyes.

Emile came over and scrutinized the find. He squirmed at the sight but muttered matter-of-factly, "I think you're right." Then, looking at Paul and realizing his pain, he added, "Damn! Why did it have to be them?"

The woman's head was covered by a colorful bandanna. It was the woman and baby they had turned away just before Impact.

Paul began to cry like a child. "I killed them," he stammered as he wept, trying to release the guilt and anger he had held in for so many years. Why should he and his family be alive when most of the world was obviously dead? For a moment he wished again to be dead.

Paul was convinced for a long time that the most pessimistic scientists had been right: over 99% of the human race must be dead by now. Why should his family have to suffer to stay alive?

"They would have died anyway," Emile said. "I wonder if her husband is also around here? Maybe he went for help and never made it back. No wonder the little shed was empty. They must have lived here a few weeks,. maybe even a few months. Maybe the goat was a source of milk for the baby."

"Shut up, please. I can't stand it anymore." Paul couldn't control his crying.

Dr. LeBlanc approached the woman's freshly exposed flesh and took out his penknife.

"No! How could you?" Paul screamed. He grabbed the penknife and threw it far. "I killed them! It was me who sent them away! We are *not* going to eat them!"

"Calm down! Control yourself, you can't let your depression overcome common sense," the older man snapped. "Paul, we had no choice, you know that. Had we taken them in, they would still be dead, and we would be dead too. There wasn't enough food for all. We would not have made it through to this day. At least we still have a chance and —"

"No, no, I can't do it," Paul cried. " I will not be a cannibal again! Never!"

Dr. LeBlanc bowed his head in shame. "We have to be realistic," he said. "You know we've all said that many times before." He put his arm around his son-in-law. "What if we don't find any more goats or skunks or dogs? It's been getting harder and harder to find them, and the shelter is empty again. We can't die now."

Paul fell to his knees. Looking up into the dark sky, he screamed once more for mercy.

* * *

While the goat kept them alive for awhile, many more months went by during which they found little else edible: only a small fox, a few raccoons, and a fawn. It was now October, the last month of the year 7 P.I., and yet the real thaw had not arrived. They were facing death by starvation once more. Emile, always a practical man, pondered how to reach more distant farms and homes. He even wished they could find more frozen humans. Still, he was convinced the great thaw and its greenhouse effect would arrive soon, and with it, their salvation. A few more ounces of food a week was all they needed. He now regretted more than ever the loss of precious nutrients a few months earlier.

Emile was furious at Paul for his inconsiderate and, under the circumstances, inhumane act. "You burned them! You destroyed that woman and her baby! How could you!" Emile almost hit Paul. Trisha had to hold her father back, while Paul remained despondent, slumped in the old armchair. He felt he no longer knew what was right or wrong. He wished he could think no more. "How could you be so damn selfish?" Emile raged. "Don't you realize you may have doomed us all to death? After all we've been through!"

"Leave him alone, Dad! Leave him! He did the right thing." Trisha's words were merciful. She understood her husband, a man so kind, driven to acts beyond reason.

* * *

Paul did not understand why he had done it, but he didn't regret it. He knew those human bodies were next on Emile's menu. Like a madman, he sneaked out of the shelter. Running and tumbling through the chaotic forest, he found them. Hurrying to avoid being caught, he pulled them out of their shallow ice grave and piled the mother and child on a heap of branches and torched it, feeding the fire continuously until there was nothing left but ashes. Like a savage he ran around the fire, screaming, "Free, free! You are free, finally free!"

He lost all control that day, and he was so ashamed. Free of what? Free of death? They had been dead for years!

CHAPTER 17

QUEBEC VI.
EARLY JANUARY, YEAR 8 P.I.
LOST

"There will be let loose, living fire and hidden death, from inside horrible and fearful globes..."

Nostradamus (1503–1566 A.D.)

t was snowing lightly in the dark and frigid woods. With the temperature just above the freezing point, the snow was wet and slushy. It made no sound as it gently fell. Melting icicles clung to dead tree branches. Their dripping joined with the small streams of frigid water to sound their mournful music in the bitter cold.

For Paul and Emile, the sound was like a requiem, presaging their death. The cold had soaked deep into their bones. They were lying on the wet ground, huddled together under an outcrop of icy rock. They didn't have a fire; the snow and drizzle had extinguished all the fires they attempted in the last few days, and they had now run out of matches.

How could it have happened? Paul asked himself over and over. They were only a couple of miles from the shelter when they set out to find the nearby farm. They had hoped to find food to sustain them for months. Instead, they became hopelessly lost.

"We should never have come on this crazy excursion," Paul had accused Emile.

But Emile refused to die with all of the blame. "You agreed. You didn't stop us," he countered. That was over five days ago. They now had run out of energy and hope. Defeated, Paul just lay back, beyond hunger and exhaustion. In spite of the heavy insulating clothes, he shivered. *Hypothermia, exhaustion and no food. What a bad combination,* Paul thought. After surviving seven full years, they were now going to die, lost in the rotting woods of Quebec. Trisha, Jenny and Hope would all be crying with desperation now, wondering what had happened. They too would die soon, of slow starvation; that terrible death that had been haunting them for so many years.

After a few moments of silence, Emile spoke. "Paul, let's go. I think I smell smoke — or something. Maybe we are near that farm."

Paul's slow, weak voice carried no intonation, no accusations, not even sarcasm as he answered. "You're hallucinating. Please leave me alone." The resignation in Paul's words was evident. He closed his eyes one more time and lay back against the cold rocks. He hoped for a quick and merciful death. He could no longer bear the agony of slowly dying of cold and hunger or the excruciating pain of his own thoughts. His eyes watered again as his mind drifted to Trisha's image.

Emile managed to get up. Paul never even noticed, never heard him mumbling. The deep sleep Paul had yearned for finally overtook him.

* * *

After only ten minutes, Paul's mind was brought back from its state of total blankness. "Paul! Paul!" the words came from what seemed to be very far away. Was he dead? Were these words from a speaker in hell? But if he was dead, why did he still feel so cold?

He fell back into unconsciousness.

After what seemed an eternity, he was abruptly brought back again. "Paul! God damn it, get up!" Emile had grabbed him by his jacket and was shaking him.

Paul somehow managed to answer, "Why won't you let me die?" I can't bear to think. I don't want to think."

"Paul, get up! There *is* smoke! This is no illusion. There is definitely smoke in the air. Somebody has a fire nearby. Damn it, get up!"

"Emile, it's useless. It could be miles away," he muttered feebly. Paul laid his head on the dirty ice and hoped again for oblivion. As he drifted into unconsciousness, he murmured his thoughts. "And if we do find somebody out there, we won't find food. We'll become food. We'll be eaten!" Paul's eyes opened again for just a moment as his cheek touched the smeared, checkered, white ice. He closed his eyes, but his mind refused to ignore what it had just perceived. *White ice? Smeared? Checkered white ice?* He could hardly think; but his thoughts persisted.

White, smeared snow can occur only where someone or something has walked. A checkered pattern is a sign of the sole of a shoe or a boot. He opened his eyes again to confirm his findings. Had he dreamed it? The dim light confirmed it. Footprints were all around his face. There were many and in both directions. He had lain down to die on someone's pathway. Paul propped himself up on one arm and beckoned for Emile. "Emile! Look!" he whispered, afraid of being heard by others.

In silence both men studied the poorly-preserved tracks. They were still visible thanks to a long tree trunk that was partially collapsed, producing a high bridge over them, and keeping the path from being covered with new snow or washed away by the sleet and rain. "They're at least a few days old," said Emile.

Sitting on the ground next to the tracks, Paul put his face in his hands and sobbed. "They're going to eat us!" he cried.

"Stop that! Damn it, they are not. They are going to help us!" Emile yelled, and then immediately put a hand over his mouth and looked around the forest in suspicion. Were there really people out there? Emile thought how ironic it was that, having been forced to partake in cannibalism, cannibalism had now become a haunting nightmare.

"Where are we, Emile?"

"You know I don't know where we are," he responded. "My best guess is that we are a few miles north or northwest of the shelter. Somehow we missed the farm altogether in spite of its size and our compass." After a moment he added bitterly, "But you know damn well I've been dead wrong in everything I've done in the last few days."

Emile disappeared into the woods, leaving Paul still sitting with his face in his hands. He was too weak even to cry as he slumped onto the ice once more.

After only a few minutes, Emile again shook Paul back awake. "There are no more footprints, but I'm sure now this is a trail and, I may be wrong, but I think the smoke smell is stronger toward that way." He pointed to an area that looked just like any other. "Let's go, Paul." Somehow Emile was able to pull Paul to his feet. They continued in silence.

They moved slowly, inspecting every torn branch, every depression in the mud and ice. Eventually, they were able to identify an apparent trail. But to where? To salvation? Or to immediate execution and consumption? Paul continued to tremble at his own thoughts. If they found others, would the strangers try to discover the whereabouts of the rest of their family? Would they be eaten, too?

It's a good thing we have no idea where we are, Paul thought. *Even if tortured we couldn't lead them to the shelter.*

* * *

Another hour passed when suddenly Emile, who was leading, stopped in his tracks. "Oh, my God," he muttered. "Oh, God!" he screamed, as loud as his feeble body allowed. He fell to his knees and, for the first time, started crying too. In a few seconds, Paul caught up with him and joined him on the muddy ground. They held on to each other as they sobbed.

There in front of them, barely a hundred feet away, was the source of the smoke. It was a cylindrical, sheet-metal chimney top. It stood out from a mound of dirt covered in part by ice and debris. When Emile was finally able to put his thoughts together, he pulled out his compass, opened it with shaky fingers, pointed it at the shelter and examined it.

"Shit. Paul, it's pointing south, yet we're just south of it. We're on the south side of our shelter!"

"We're home!" sobbed Paul, barely able to speak.

"Damn compass, it's no good! The Earth's magnetic field must have shifted! No wonder we've been lost!" Emile threw the contraption with his feeble strength as far as he could.

The two men scrambled forward. Barely able to walk, they held on to each other. Stumbling, they rushed toward their shelter and into the arms of their loved ones, who all the while waited fearfully, but never gave up hope for their return.

CHAPTER 18
QUEBEC VII.
MAY, YEAR 9 P.I.
THE NEW MONSTER
IN THE SKY

"And I will put your flesh upon the mountains and fill the valleys with the refuse of you... and stream-beds themselves will be filled up from you... I will cover the heavens and darken their stars. As for the sun, with clouds I shall cover it and the moon itself will not let its light shine."

Ezekiel: 32:5-7, Holy Bible

n the dark shadow of the decaying forest in northwestern Quebec, a few figures moved like shadows through a maze of dead trees and branches. The ground, mostly mud, was a soggy mulch studded with puddles. A steady, barely perceptible light rain contributed to the gloominess of the scene. It was mid-day, yet there was barely enough light to see without the help of torches.

Squatted in front of a fallen, rotting tree trunk was a bundle of dirty fur. It looked like a small bear from the back; but there were no living bears or other large wild animals in Quebec anymore. It was a young boy. His breathing movements were practically unnoticeable. The figure moved ever so slightly, as if shaking his head.

The deep acid stench of rotting flesh, wood and leaves pervaded the motionless air. Insects were everywhere. Flies mercilessly bit the small human on the few areas of his face not covered by clothing, yet he dared not move. A dirty rag covered the face from the eyes down. A hood of a mended furry jacket covered the forehead. A fly settled on the inner corner of one eye, sipping warm fluid, while another bit the other eyelid.

Damn! The thought went unperceived by the vermin, but the flies were forced to fly away, startled by a sudden shake of the head. The miniature figure became immobile again, as if frozen. Dwarfed by the dark recess of the adjoining rotting tree, it lay in wait. In its right hand, and partly resting on the right shoulder, was a short laser-Acuzaper rifle held in careful aim against the right mandible. The once deadly and beautifully machined weapon was useless, having been devoid of energy for many years. Its rusted body had been modified into a crude crossbow.

A click; the long dart sprung out, vanishing into the dark hollow of the rotted tree, trailing behind it was an ultrafine fishing line.

"Got it!" cried the boy proudly, pushing the rag from his face. He pulled the string, bringing into the dim light a mouse, impaled through its torso, gasping its last breath. The child, Hope Lopez, was eight and a half years old. He removed the mouse from the dart, then pulled out a pair of rusty scissors and expertly cut off its head, limbs and tail. With a swift stroke of the scissors, he cut open the little animal's abdomen and stripped it of its gut. With one last, dextrous move, he skinned it. Discarding the skin, he dropped the carcass into a plastic bag.

Looking at his grandfather, who was watching close by, Hope said with pride and confidence, "That's five mice so far today, and one rat. We'll eat well tonight — great stew coming up!" Though skinny, pale, and dirty beyond belief, the boy was nevertheless strong. Dressed in heavy clothing, with fingertips protruding from torn gloves, the child knew he had done well. If the hunter is successful, he will be praised and loved.

"I'd say you are a prime candidate for an Olympic medal in marksmanship," said the old man proudly. Emile was glad to see his grandson smile. He glanced at the bag of vermin with disgust, making sure that his expression was not seen by the young boy. The warming weather had at first exposed much frozen food, and allowed the retrieval of food, tools and implements needed for survival. But now the deep caches of frozen foods and goods were all rotting, becoming inedible as water invaded everything. The time of feast was over. Famine was upon this part of the world once more. Emile never thought he would relish the sight of worms and slugs. The children even ate grubs and maggots with glee. They knew no other world but one in which the search for food, any food, was the only drive in life. He wondered with fear if, in other parts of the world, people were killing each other for the precious nutrients that surrounded their own bones.

Bones — his own bones were hurting so! The humidity caused his arthritis to act up. If only they had stocked a few more bottles of aspirin! And he longed for real food, cooked and carefully seasoned. It had been so many years since he had eaten a normal meal, set at a well-presented table, with forks and knives, like humans should.

"What's that, Grandpapá?" the child asked as he rearmed his crossbow.

"What?" the old man replied absently.

"Olin — Olinpek — and medal."

"Oh, just some things of the past. Don't worry, I'll tell you later.

Now let's concentrate on hunting: more mice, maybe even another rat. And we must find some more edible roots and young shoots."

Dr. LeBlanc was still concerned about their diet. The all-protein, no-vegetable diet of cannibalism had kept them alive, but barely so. The lack of grains, starches and certain natural vitamins and minerals had left them undernourished and weak. At least now they felt better as the diet became more varied.

* * *

Dr. Emile LeBlanc was no longer the handsome, strong man of just a few years past. Gone was his respectable intellectual look. Though only fifty-nine years old, his hair and beard were now white. He looked thin, wrinkled, weather-beaten. His movements were slow and awkward, his permanent frown a result of constant worry and pain. The years of confinement, hunger and depression left permanent marks on his once-graceful face. The loss of his wife and the bitter, seemingly everlasting and damp cold had carved their scars into his every cell. He suffered continuously the agonies of arthritis. The pain allowed for little sleep. There were no medicines left, and the hope of finding any was practically nonexistent. Recently a chipped tooth had developed into a nightmare cavity. He dreaded the inevitable — Paul would have to pull that tooth out with their only pair of rusty pliers, and without the benefit of anesthesia!

The pain in his joints was momentarily forgotten as his bearded face broke into a smile. He had a surprise for his grandson. While digging in the mud he had just found an unusually long nightcrawler. He carefully pulled the worm out of the mud, making sure it didn't break. "Come and see, my child," the old man beckoned. "I have a world record beast." He grinned as he pulled the nightcrawler out and then carefully cleaned it in a can of water, expertly squeezing the contents out of its guts.

The 12 inch long worm, wriggling frantically, hung over the old man's face as he slowly inserted it into his mouth. But the worm would not agree to descend into such an unusual cavern. Its antics brought out a mischievous smile from the little boy. "That's a fat and lively one. He's trying to escape!" the boy laughed.

The old man was not going to lose the fight. Cutting it in half with his teeth, he swallowed whole his portion of the morsel and gave the other half to his grandson, who chewed with delight and gulped it down in seconds. They both laughed, then Emile's expression became wistful. With a deep sigh he said, "This was a real treat, but somehow, even though I know it can never happen, I still dream of someday having a hamburger again."

"What's a hamburger?" asked Hope.

"Well, a hamburger is a piece of meat, cooked over a grill. It's beef, from a cow, like a moose but shorter and fatter. It tastes much better than old frozen moose meat. Anyway, the meat is placed in a bun, between two pieces of bread — remember? We've told you about bread. And you add some pieces of tomato and lettuce, onions — those are vegetables. Remember the pictures I showed you of those in a book? You then add some ketchup, that's a soup-like thing made out of tomatoes. Salt and pepper, and voilá, you have a hamburger."

The little boy looked amused but perplexed. "I thought you told me that you called those things between bread a san..., sandwich."

"Forget it," said Emile in frustration. "Our old eating habits were somewhat complex. Maybe in a few years we can grow wheat and make some bread. There won't be any cow meat, but maybe we could try it with rat. You are right though, sandwiches and hamburgers are somewhat alike. It'll be even a few more years before I can make you a peanut butter and jelly sandwich. Now there's something tasty."

"Peanut butter? Mom told me that peanuts are tasty seeds that grow underground, and butter is made from cow's milk. Milk is white liquid that comes out of the ma-, the ma-ma-ry things of many animals. So how can you have peanut butter?"

Emile brushed the child off with a wave of his hand. "I'm sorry," he said. "You're right, I am just dreaming of the impossible, of those many good things that are now gone forever. I'm confusing you with my blathering. Go on. Go hunt for more food. Let's get practical here and be the mighty hunters and gatherers we have learned to be. You are the keenest one of us — don't know what we'd do without you."

The boy beamed a smile of satisfaction, and walked slowly away,

placing a kiss on his crude crossbow. It had stopped raining and a
breeze started to pick up.

The pair turned in different directions to continue their foraging; their footsteps muffled by the soggy ground. Hope grimaced
with disgust as he walked by a rotting deer, dead for many years but
only recently exposed. Its body was blackened by thousands of flies
and roaches. Not as disgusting, but too bitter to be edible except in
desperation, were the legions of ants that covered the rotting land.
Though welcomed because they helped clear the foul-smelling debris that covered the Earth from horizon to horizon, their bites kept
everyone alert as to where they stepped. Luckily for the ecosystem,
ants and earthworms had not been killed by the ice age. Without
them, the soil could not be aerated and the return of plant life would
be practically impossible.

As the thaw began, the Earth spewed forth a pestilence of insects
and rodents. Most other animals in the area had perished. The land
was riddled with decomposing wood, fetid compost and the rotting
flesh of all that had once lived there. Many types of insects now lived
off the decomposed flesh. Without birds, bats, or other natural preda-
tors, most insects proliferated unchecked. But insects that needed
nectar, pollen and fresh leaves no longer existed.

Coming to a clearing in the dilapidated forest, Hope looked
first with curiosity, then with amazement at a faint, unfamiliar flickering on the surface of a puddle that stood alone in the center of the
clearing. Cautiously, he approached the water and squatted a few
feet from it. He could not understand what he saw, nor why everything around him seemed so different. He couldn't understand why
his face was wrinkling on its own, his eyelids narrowing as if in pain.
He shuddered.

Hope sensed danger. There was something alien here. It perme-
ated the atmosphere. He had learned to be suspicious of everything;
in every thing and every place since he had been born there was pain.
Something in his mind told him to look upwards. As he did so, his
expression changed to disbelief and then fear. He abruptly looked
down and covered his head, dropping his crude weapon. Ever so

slowly he looked up again and gazed with wide eyes, trembling at the sight of the monster. With dirty hands, the pale child shielded his face. Peeking through his fingers, he began to whimper and cry. The huge monster looked menacingly down at him, its face constantly changing. He felt the threat of death hanging over him.

Nearby in the forest, Trisha heard her son's cries, dropped her precious bag of vermin, and ran toward him. Pale and beaten, her ragged clothes flying behind her, she looked like the survivor of a medieval plague. Soon, reaching her son, she knelt and took him by the shoulders. "What's the matter, baby?" she asked gently.

The petrified child pointed a shaking finger at the sky. Trisha followed his gaze and gasped. She covered her mouth as if trying to hold back her own screams. "Oh, my God!" she whispered in disbelief. Her eyes started to tear. But these were not the tears of pain that she had lived with for so long. Hope looked at her in astonishment. Her face, her clothes, everything about her was so different. He could make out her features with a clarity he had never seen before. Not finding in her face an answer to calm his fear, he looked up again at the monster as it continued to change its expressions and it silently peered down at them.

Trisha started to sob and then screamed, "Paul, Jenny, Papá! Come! Come quick!"

The rest of the group scrambled through the broken woods, rushing through mud and puddles. Emile was first, followed by Paul, who held Jenny by the hand. Pale, dirty, hair matted around her frightened face, the 13 year old girl could scarcely keep up with her father. Paul stopped and took his thin, frail daughter in his arms, to carry her the last dozen yards.

They reached the clearing and found mother and child huddled together as if hypnotized. Paul and Emile stopped a few feet away from them, unsure of the situation. Paul put Jenny down on the ground. Looking at each other in confusion, they approached the pair.

Trisha was finally able to speak. "Look," she said, pointing up. "The sun, the sun!" she whispered, as if she didn't dare speak the word too loudly, as if she were afraid that the miracle would vanish like a cruel mirage.

For the first time in over eight years, the cloud layers over Quebec had become thin enough to allow such a sight. As if alive, Sol's colors shifted constantly, with hues of gray and brown. The thinning clouds rushed under the barely visible but unmistakable disc.

The entire family stood as if paralyzed. The child, Hope, finally broke the silence. "Mommy, what is it? Will it hurt us?"

"No, baby, it's our friend, it's coming back." Trisha slowly stood up next to her husband. All heads were still angled up in amazement and wonder, almost in adoration. Trisha started to cry again as she threw her arms around Paul. "We *will* be warm again," she sobbed.

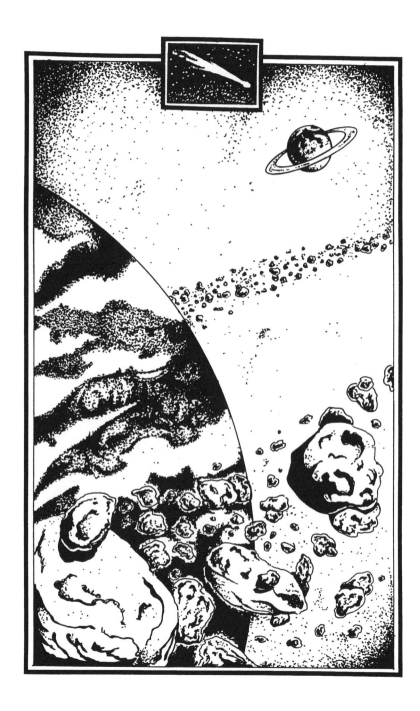

CHAPTER 19

THE NEW SOLAR SYSTEM

"And there will be great earthquakes... and famines, and pestilence and fearful sighs and from the heavens great signs... signs in the sun and moon and stars, and on the Earth anguish of nations, not knowing the way out because of the roaring of the sea and its agitation... when you see these things come to pass know ye that your deliverance is at hand..."

Luke 21:11-28, Holy Bible

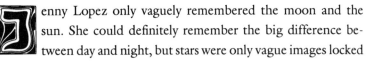

enny Lopez only vaguely remembered the moon and the sun. She could definitely remember the big difference between day and night, but stars were only vague images locked deep in her memory. She did, however, unmistakably remember comets. As a child, she had delighted in their variety, their beautiful shapes in the ever-changing skies of happier, pre-Impact years. Even though she was then just a young child, she could never forget the majesty and mystery of the comets. Or did she remember them so well because she had learned that comets were followed by darkness, cold, hunger, and death?

Hope, on the other hand, like all survivors born around or after Impact, knew of no sky during his first years of life. He lived those years like a rodent, imprisoned in a cold, dark, musty tunnel. Then, once it was possible to venture into the outside world, the only sky he knew was dark.

When the clouds finally cleared enough to let through the image of the sun and the moon, they became a source of wonder to the children of the new world. Adults and older teenagers took upon themselves a great new task, that of educating the younger children, filling their minds with the good and wonderful aspects of nature, helping them forget depression and the pain they had lived with all of their lives. The children's yearning for knowledge came to tax the minds of their parents or adoptive families. How was it that they knew so little? Adults found it hard to believe that all they had assimilated during their childhood was so absent from the minds of the children. It was impossible during the ice age to share knowledge with them. The dark years had dulled the minds of all.

As the thinning clouds began to part, leaving, at times, large gaps in the sky, Venus, Jupiter and Saturn broke through. Uranus and Neptune, with their huge new rings of light, could now be seen easily with the naked eye for the first time in recorded history. And the apparition of the stars! First, all the brighter stars and finally even the Milky Way returned to the wonderment of humankind. Aristotle, thousands of years ago, and others of his time believed that the Milky Way was the "remains of many comets." This concept was possibly

derived from a great comet shower that left interplanetary space pol-
luted with fine particles and made the entire night sky appear as a white
haze. When the spatial debris cleared, after possibly dozens or hundreds of years, only the Milky Way remained: a band of diffused light.

* * *

Jennifer Lopez could barely read. All the books in the shelter
had been burned for fuel, but luckily many were found in nearby
cabins once the ice started to melt. Though 13 years old, she had to
struggle to understand and verbalize what she read out loud to her
little brother. The eight-year-old listened attentively as they sat by a
fire in the early evening, next to the cabin that had become their
home once again.

A brilliant meteor crossed the sky and disappeared behind one of
the clouds. "Wow!" exclaimed Hope. "Did you see that one? It was
so beautiful!"

"Aren't you listening?" asked Jenny. "I've been reading to you,
and all you're doing is looking for silly meteors! Well, you haven't
seen anything! When I was a little girl there were hundreds of those
each hour. Besides, Daddy says that there are very few comets and
meteors left. He says the comet shower is over now. You missed all
the real good ones that I use to see! Anyways, it says here that you
were born under the sign of Scorpio. That is a constellation that is
shaped like a scorpion." Seeing the blank expression on Hope's face,
she explained: "A scorpion is an ugly and nasty insect with big pinch-
ers on it." She made a disgusted expression with her face and pinched
her hands. Hope grimaced at the thought. "It also says here that
people like you — born under that sign — are going to be scientists
and doctors." She laughed. "Dad says that there aren't going to be
any universities for a long, long time, so I guess that takes care of
that." She continued reading, but mostly to herself now, since Hope
had laid his head down and was watching for more meteors.

"It also says that people with your sign have something to do
with the planet Pluto," Jenny went on, "that some great things have
happened to people under this sign, but also that horrible things
have happened." She looked at Hope, but he wasn't reacting. "Pluto,

your planet, and I'm not making this up; it says so right here, is the planet of the underworld, poison and death." She looked at him again, annoyed that he seemed not to be listening. "Maybe it's all your fault," she said. "You were born on the day Dis'Aster landed." Then, yelling, "You killed millions of people and made us all miserable!" Angrily she kicked dirt at him and took off toward the cabin.

A few minutes later Trisha found Hope still lying by the fire. "There you are. What are you doing outside by yourself?" The light of the fire allowed her to see the tears in his eyes. At first he wouldn't tell her the reason for his pain, but after some coaxing he told her what Jenny had said. By that time Paul had joined them.

Trisha comforted her son. "There are many things from the old world that were silly and not true at all," she murmured. "Astrology is one of them. In the olden days some people used astrology just for fun. There is no truth in what Jenny was saying. She was just being mean."

"Kids can be so cruel," added Paul. "You know, Hope, the best thing in the world that ever happened on Impact Day was the fact that you were born. Don't pay attention to the stupid things some people of the old world used to believe in. Can you imagine, that the position of one or more planets in the sky could in any way influence what happens to any one particular person on Earth, so many millions or billions of miles away?" He laughed and tickled his son, who pulled away. "Come on, Hope, you're always the joker these days. Don't let some silly old superstition get to you. You'll hear and read about many silly things like that from the past. Some people even used to say they had seen flying saucers, spaceships from other planets! They would lie, just to call attention to themselves. Hopefully all that ridiculous stuff will not be part of our new culture. Maybe we should burn that book."

"Whoa!" screamed Hope, smiling again as a bolide showed up in the sky. His dad picked him up. Paul was smiling, too. "You know I love you, you little rascal." He tickled his son again. They both laughed.

* * *

Later that night Paul woke up as drops of water fell through their cabin's poorly mended roof and onto their bed. There were more leaks that needed to be repaired. The rain turned into a steady shower that lasted over three hours.

"You think the floods are coming?" asked Trisha with concern in her voice.

"It's been so wonderful the last few months," he replied. "I was hoping that the good weather would last longer for us. Our part of the world is probably one of the first to thaw out, being so far north. If the rest of the world is also starting to thaw, then, as scientists predicted, I'm afraid we are in for months or years of constant rain."

CHAPTER 20

TUCSON III.
SEPTEMBER, YEAR 10 P.I.
THE GREAT THAW

"The temple was filled with smoke... and no one was able to enter it till the seven plagues of the seven angels was finished.... The first angel poured his bowl into the Earth and it became a loathsome and malignant sore... and the second angel poured his bowl into the sea... and every living thing in the sea died... and the third poured his bowl into the rivers and springs and they turned to blood... and the fourth poured his upon the sun and man was scorched with fiery heat... and the fifth angel poured his upon the throne of the beast and his kingdom became darkened... and the sixth poured his upon the great river Euphrates and its waters were dried up... And the seventh angel poured out his bowl upon the air and a loud noise came out... and there were flashes of lightning and sounds and peals of thunder, and there was a great earthquake, such as there had not been since man came to be upon the Earth... and the cities and the nations fell... and every island fled away and mountains were not found..."

John: Book of Revelation (Apocalypse), 15:8 and 16:1–20, Holy Bible n Tucson, Arizona, the horrors of the great floods were threatening the survivors of that area.

When the Great Thaw reached their latitude, and as their shelter slowly flooded, the few survivors of Colossal Cave had to abandon their shelter and settle in the pitiful ruins of what were once impressive buildings of Tucson. From there they foraged for food and supplies buried among the remains of the devastated city.

During pre-Impact days, Tucson was a sprawling, modern community that had refused to grow vertically and persisted in retaining the low southwestern profile of older times. The city, flanked on the north by an impressive chain of mountains, and boasting rolling residential areas and large open expansions toward the south, east and west, had a limitless appearance.

But for those few dozen who emerged from Colossal Cave, the view was one of horror. They looked in amazement at the ruins of their civilization. Gone were all the homes and buildings. Gone were the saguaro cactus. Gone, in fact, was any sign that any vegetation had ever existed. Instead of the beautiful desert city they remembered, all they could see was a never-ending expanse of water, freezing lakes and puddles. Scattered here and there were islands of mud. The city had been crushed into dirt by the weight of a glacier, then washed away in just a few months of precipitous warming. And the survivors saw a foreboding black and white fortress of ice covering the higher parts of the mountains to the north.

The search for food and medicine was difficult and treacherous. Without bulldozers or cranes, rummaging through concrete and the remaining ice pockets was exhausting labor that only occasionally resulted in worthwhile finds.

David and Maggie McGuire and their group of about sixty other survivors had recently settled in the ruins of a building, Once a tall and majestic commercial bank in mid-town Tucson; only the first floor and basement remained. They had managed to seal most of the leaks, and the few habitable rooms were relatively dry. It was a mockery of a shelter, but even so, a welcome haven from the oppressive and continual rains. They considered themselves lucky in spite of the difficulties. At least they were alive.

As the temperature continued to rise, it became evident that their sanctuary would have to be evacuated. The ice on the mountains just north of the city was melting rapidly. Massive flows of water and debris were washing away the entire area. A hasty escape to the less treacherous lands to the east was organized. The long-range plans were to trek farther east, since they knew from the early post-Impact radio reports that California's coastal lands west of the San Andreas Fault had all been submerged, and that the areas near the new shore-line would be uninhabitable for centuries. Since leaving the ruins of the city required leaving behind all major sources of food supplies, they would have to salvage as much as possible before hurrying away.

The McGuires lost their daughter to the famine of the latter part of the New Ice Age. Their surviving son, Terry, now a strong teen-ager, proved to be of great help in finding and retrieving supplies. But Terry suffered a serious leg fracture as, in the haste to retrieve food, most concerns for safety had been put aside. The fracture and open wound were soon infected. As the group embarked on the long and arduous march east, the McGuires were forced to stay in the Tucson ruins for a few more days until Terry's temperature came down. Two other couples stayed with them.

David retained his strength, and Maggie, her beauty; but today they looked haggard. They pondered what to do next. Their only son, their hope for the future, was seriously wounded, and now sep-tic. They had to nurture him back to health at all cost. In order to do so, all they needed was to find some more antibiotics, and a stable shelter that could protect them for just a few months. Then, perhaps their dream could come true — the decade-long dream to settle down and begin a new life. It would be a fresh and productive life in a new world. It would be a harsh world, but one full of promise. They could help it to develop. There were so few survivors, so few good people like themselves whom civilization could count on for a new beginning.

"Let's gather everything and leave as soon as it's light in the morning," David ordered. He was uneasy about the increasing height of the new rivers.

But as the feeble early morning light awoke them, their hearts sank in despair. They were now stranded on an island half a mile or so across that had been created by a sudden change in the icewater rivers raging from the mountains. They hastily tried to build a makeshift raft for themselves and their supplies, but as the water continued to rise, they were cut off from the materials they needed to finish the raft. They took refuge on the highest part of the small isle in the hope that, as had happened before, the torrential waters would shift and allow them to continue on.

Just as they thought that the top of their little hill, growing smaller by the hour, would disappear, the flow of waters shifted and the island stopped shrinking, allowing them to make new plans.

They decided to tie David, the strongest of them, to the end of a strong fishing line. With the aid of a makeshift floating device, he would float down the current and swim away from them until he reached the land across the river. Once on the other side, he would walk uphill until he was opposite them, then pull over a stronger rope that was attached to the fishing line. They could then pull themselves, one at a time, through the one hundred-foot torrent of frigid water to safety and march rapidly away from the flooding valley.

The ordeal was terrible, but David was strong, and when he made it to the other side and walked into sight across from them, they all cheered in jubilation. The heavier rope was pulled over and secured to the remnants of a building.

The first to go across was Maggie. The rope was threaded through a large metal ring to which she was tied. After battling the violent white and brown water for over fifteen minutes, she finally pulled herself to the other side. She was nearly too exhausted to hear the great cheer that was raised as she made it across. But the jubilation came to an abrupt end as a sudden, violent commotion was felt and the earth shook under their feet.

A huge mass of ice had just broken off the south side of the mountain range, releasing with it an avalanche of ice and rock and the contents of an enormous lake that had formed above a dam made of ice, earth and tree trunks. Their expressions of joy were replaced by horror as they, the river separating the group, and the islands around them were dwarfed by an enormous body of water, ice, mud, rock and debris approaching them at unbelievable speed. The surge front was over a hundred feet high. The torrent carried with it hundreds of conifer tree trunks, boulders the size of houses, and immense chunks of blackened ice.

Their terror was short-lived. They were swallowed up by the murderous, semi-solid wave. Two miles wide, the water avalanche carved through the valley, resurfacing everything.

CHAPTER 21

QUEBEC VIII. MARCH, YEAR 11 P.I. THE DROWNING PLANET

"The horizon will burst into flames, 7 to 12 suns will appear in the heavens and they will dry up the seas and burn the earth. The Samvartaka [the Fire of the Cosmic Conflagration] will destroy all. The rain will fall in flood for 12 years and the Earth will be submerged and mankind destroyed."

Vishnu Purana, 24–25, Mahabharata (Hinduism)

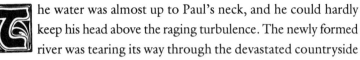he water was almost up to Paul's neck, and he could hardly keep his head above the raging turbulence. The newly formed river was tearing its way through the devastated countryside of what used to be Quebec. Paul tried to keep his feet from being torn from the mud as he attempted to force his way forward while still remaining in control of his own position. They had to reach the other bank of the river soon. The rushing water made it hard to hold onto Hope, who straddled his shoulders. The 10 year old boy was terrified. He didn't swim well, and knew that the turbulent current, full of tree trunks, broken branches and debris, could drown him. The strong rope around Paul's waist tugged violently, almost making him lose his balance. He looked back toward Trisha, but his wife, who was supposed to be only a few feet behind him, had vanished under the surface. The merciless pouring rain kept his eyes so full of water he could hardly see, yet he knew that she had to be close by. A few feet beyond was Emile, also trying to reach the spot where Trisha had submerged. Emile held Jenny on his left arm. The petrified girl was holding onto her grandpapá's forehead, occasionally covering his eyes with her hands as she tried to stay with him. "Mommy!" she screamed. Emile in turn shouted, "Hold your breath!" then ducked under the water. He grabbed Trisha by the hair and then by her backpack, and straightened her as they surfaced. All three gasped for air as Trisha regained her foothold on the mud, and reached for Paul's outstretched hand. He held her firmly as she and Jenny sobbed in terror.

Fire, then ice and then water. A comet's scourge never ceases till it extinguishes you, Paul thought as he struggled to stay put. He shouted over the sound of the rushing waters, "Keep coming! Don't give up!" He continued to pull them along with the rope that held all five of them together. The backpacks were heavy, but their contents were too important to be left behind. The various means for starting fire were the most precious, though some were as primitive as a small bow and string for starting a fire by friction. There were also knives and ropes. The pot they carried was essential for boiling, in order to rid the water of diarrhea-producing bacteria and to cook the little edible material available. His pack also held an old gunpowder rifle and a few hundred bullets, all wrapped in waterproof plastic, carefully preserved for that dreaded first contact, the feared moment when they would meet, if ever, other humans.

It was the middle of the day, yet the downpour was so fierce, and the overlying cloud cover so thick, that they could hardly see each other. Paul's huge backpack made for additional resistance against the water that was trying to tear him away. He knew that if the under-tow pulled him off his feet, his overweight backpack and his own weight would drag them all with him, and in just a minute they would all be drowned.

A tree trunk hit Emile from behind. The thick broken piece of what, ten and a half years earlier, had been a live pine tree, struck the old man square on his back; only the backpack prevented the tree's sharp edges from piercing his skin. Emile held fast in spite of the pain. The tree trunk hovered, then swirled sideways and rushed past them.

"Keep coming!" Paul urged again. Just then a sharp branch stabbed him in the left thigh. The pain was even worse when he pulled it out of his flesh. He almost let Hope drop. The child started to cry, holding on to his daddy's neck for dear life.

"This branch is fixed!" shouted Paul. "We may be near the other side." As he pulled the sharp branch out of his leg, blood mixed rapidly with the dark brown waters. He held the branch with his hand and heaved. It didn't give. He smiled and pulled himself for-ward, shouting again, "Yes! The bank is coming up!" He felt his feet bring his body several inches above the level of the water. After a few more seconds of painful exertion, he was out of the torrent and pull-ing them all up with both arms. Jenny whimpered incessantly, her pale face reflecting the suffering that had been near-continuous for almost her entire life.

As the downpour continued, Paul spoke again, catching his breath between words. "We'll rest only one minute. We must reach higher ground." He set Hope down on the mud. While the other three sat, he remained standing, alert in case the newly formed river suddenly rose. Their goal was to reach the top of the hill next to them; to be safe, they had to be at least fifty feet above the present water level. They learned this deadly lesson over the last few months: the raging new water systems were unpredictable as they formed throughout the countryside, changing courses continuously. Paul hoped that this hill would be high enough, and just as important, wide enough that it wouldn't be washed away in a matter of hours.

"Let's move on," he said. His wife and father-in-law obliged silently, but the children both started to cry again. They were exhausted and couldn't bear the thought of having to climb the slippery and muddy hill. Hope, sobbing, declared that he wasn't moving any more.

"Goddammit, Hope, you can't set us back! Get up!" shouted Paul. Then, they suddenly froze in panic; for the first time in ten years, they heard the voice of another human being.

"Who's down there?" a man's voice thundered above them.

Hope and Jenny screamed. Emile and Trisha tried in vain to cover the mouths of the little ones and at the same time hold onto them, since both children were desperately trying to scurry back down the hill.

The voice in heavily-accented English called again, "Don't move or we'll shoot you dead!"

There was silence as the Lopez-LeBlancs realized they were caught between the torrential water below them and weapons of death above. Paul regretted that his only weapons were buried deep in his backpack. They were defenseless! The children screamed, kicked and fought in a desperate effort to free themselves from the adults and flee at all costs from the most menacing presence they had ever encountered.

"Come up very slowly," another man's voice called down, "with your hands up." After a few seconds of no reply, the voice spoke again, this time inquiringly. "How many of you are there?"

Paul responded, "Only five. There are only five of us, just two children and —" His words were cut off by a command from above.

"Come up slowly, I said, with your hands up! We are heavily armed!"

Jenny and Hope became limp; they could struggle no more. Hope became silent, but Jenny couldn't stop crying. Paul, Trisha and Emile looked at each other as they saw the unmistakable silhouettes of humans lurched above them, barely discernible through the heavy rain. They were indeed heavily armed. Paul could not repress his thoughts: Would they be killed for their flesh? Would they be eaten?

CHAPTER 22

CHICAGO VI. JULY, YEAR 11 P.I. ON THE MOVE

"Once more, after the usual period of years, the torrents of heaven [will sweep] down like a pestilence, leaving only the rude and unlettered among you."

Plato (427–347 B.C.), *Timaeus*: Egyptian Knowledge

t had been raining mercilessly over Chicago for many months. The murky water seeped down, filling every nook and cranny as it washed away the soot and ashes that had accumulated for over ten years.

From the melting ice oozed out a black grime. The foul, poisonous concentrate of chemicals that had been raining down upon the Earth since day one of the post-Impact world now mixed with the remains of humans, animals, plants, chemicals and fuels. Kept frozen for a decade, the city's biomass was now thawed, and the stench was unbearable.

Thick, dark purple slime oozed its way into the shelters where Chicago's few survivors waited for the day they would again be free.

But the air outside the shelters was becoming worse than the stale air they had been forced to inhale for so many years. The open spaces were now infested with flies, mosquitoes and cockroaches. The putrid air was unbreathable and in some areas even poisonous. In fact, the world outside was turning out to be more dangerous than it had been during the worst of the freeze. The dangers of ice and cold were replaced by the perils of disease and uncontrolled floods. During the early thaw, ice expanded and contracted continuously for years, causing the remains of buildings to crumble like termite-ridden timbers. The underground tunnels and basements that had remained dry for so long were now slowly filling with putrid fluids.

The Great Thaw was upon them, and with it the greatest flood that modern humankind had ever witnessed. It brought to the minds of many the proposition by some that Noah's fabled flood had been the result of a massive post-Impact meltdown. For the survivors, it was imperative to escape the brutal new environment or perish.

* * *

Glord's band carefully prepared to escape the ravages of the floods. They would have to leave their underground shelters and find a safe place that would keep them secure until the floods subsided. But to survive, Glord needed enough slaves and food for at least a few more months until the surface of the planet became safe again.

Glord pondered his dilemma over and over again. To be able to live during the next few months, he knew that he would have to kill and eat a few more of the survivors of his clan. He would also need to capture more victims from the other surviving groups that were also being forced to surface. At first these people had been easy prey. But the word was out and capturing or killing others was becoming more and more difficult.

He hoped to continue foraging for frozen bodies, but there were no longer any around him. The temperature continued to climb, and, although some deep tunnels and basements might still contain caches of ice, these were becoming unreachable as the city flooded. Without ice to preserve the bodies of his victims, and with the supplies within the city ruins out of reach because of the flooding, Glord and his barbarians were again in danger of death by starvation.

How could they eat and at the same time preserve the slaves needed to establish the Glord Kingdom? He needed food, supplies, and time to build his empire. He had dreamed of his great empire for years. Nothing would keep him from that goal. He would be Emperor! Not of the mockery of a kingdom he had been forced to establish underground, but of a real empire with political borders, currency, loyal subjects and a police force to enforce his laws. He needed only a decade or so of isolation to establish a firm new nation. Once he had the necessary strength, he would expand its frontiers. He would be feared and respected by all, achieving historical immortality.

As Glord's new army ventured out, their numbers grew. All the misfits, and those full of hate or desiring power, joined Glord. The dictator's reputation for power and rewards had spread through the lands that were once the Midwest portions of the United States and the middle portions of Canada.

Glord eventually found the critical link in the chain of events that would lead him to his goal. He was disappointed in himself in not having thought of it sooner.

The plan was simple: choose the most worthless of slaves or captives, apply a tourniquet, and surgically amputate an arm. The best of the meat would go to him and his court, while nutritious soup would be made from the rest for the others. The marrow and the softer parts of the joints would make a lasting paste that could be preserved for weeks. Meanwhile, the slave could still walk and would not need to be carried. Glord would ensure that these sources of fresh meat would be kept as healthy as possible. When needed, he would take the other arm, then, one at a time, the legs. Other slaves would carry the live, limbless cattle. A surgical technician had joined his ranks who could remove, one by one, a kidney, the spleen, the testicles, uterus, ovaries and other non-vital organs.

Glord would make sure that the victim was force-fed some of his or her own flesh to ensure survival of the rest of the calorie-rich body for as long as possible. Finally, the head would be separated from the torso, and the remains of the victim would all be eaten as quickly as possible before the precious food became rotten.

Glord was very pleased with himself. All he needed now was to escape the flooding cities and set up camp in a safe area not too far from Chicago. In their travels, his lords would raid any bands of survivors they encountered for slaves, tools, flesh and equipment. Above all, he needed scores of children to become loyal subjects and eventually grow up to become powerful soldiers.

He admired his own genius. In the past, the threat of rape and torture had made many subjects submit to his wishes. Later, the threat of death and being eaten in cannibalistic rites effected increased submission to his will. Now, the fear of live cannibalism would make even the strongest of humans bend to his every desire.

CHAPTER 23

QUEBEC IX. (PART 1)
NOVEMBER 1, YEAR 14 P.I.
NEW YEAR'S DAY

"Fire fell from heaven and did not die down until it had burned the whole surface of the island..."

British historians from antiquity referring to an apparent catastrophe that in 441 A.D. left Britain destroyed and depopulated for centuries.

enny very slowly counted each step. "One, two, three, four and five." She bent over and gently pushed one index finger into the mud, and inserted a single blade of grass. Ignoring the hordes of flies, she pulled a handful of smelly compost from the small bucket she carried, and carefully patted some of the compost around the blade of grass. The tiny blade dangled wet and dirty under the gentle rain. Jenny pushed mud around it and stood. She cleared the drops of rain from her face with the back of her hand, smearing mud and compost over her cheeks. One long step over the planted blade and again, very slowly, "One, two, three, four and five." With each step her naked feet half-buried themselves in the sodden ground. The mud rolled between and around her toes. The water-soaked ground and the drops rapidly filled her footprints.

Jenny wore a long, faded dress. At one time it must have displayed brilliantly colored flowers. The dress reached her knees, where another skirting of cloth of a somewhat similar design had been added, bringing the dress down to her ankles. The dress had originally had short sleeves. Additional sleeving covered her arms almost to the wrists. She swatted at the gnats and mosquitoes that mercilessly bit her face and hands. She continued, undisturbed at her task as the rain intensified. She looked back at the long row of blades, now being flattened by the rain. "Don't worry," she said out loud. "When the sun comes out, you will be safe again." With a smile, she continued to talk to herself. "Daddy says that within a year or two we will have a meadow." Just as she said this, she abruptly stopped, her eyes widened and her smile grew bigger. A few yards in front of her, a dandelion sported two tiny yellow flowers. She put the blades of grass in the pocket on the left side of her dress and carefully knelt by the little weed.

Though seventeen years old, Jenny Lopez was small and frail. She gazed intensely at the dandelion flowers and whispered, "It's time for love, but you have to promise to be good." Had there been a stranger to witness her, it would have been difficult for him or her to tell whether Jenny was a young child at play, or a slightly retarded young adult with childish features and a womanly body. The rain intensified. The dress clung to her as the drops of rain poured from the front of her torn straw hat like the curtain of a waterfall. Rivers of water snaked through the holes in her hat and ran down her now almost expressionless face.

Jenny cleaned her hands on her dress, then cupped one hand carefully, almost reverently, around the two tiny yellow flowers, protecting them from the rain. With the other hand she took a plastic bag from a pocket and laid it on the mud next to the weed. Slightly shaking, she removed from the bag another dandelion. Water pouring from her hat cleaned the little weed's dirt from its roots. As if horrified by her mistake, Jenny rapidly covered the roots with more mud, placing the plant in the plastic bag but letting the solitary yellow flower stick out through it. Somewhat embarrassed, she looked around to see if anyone had noticed her carelessness. Ready once more, she again cupped her left hand over the two tiny flowers. She smiled, noticing that the tropical-like rain had diminished to a finer and gentler fall. With her left hand still cupped over the flowers, she took the bagged weed and gently touched its solitary flower to the others. She gazed at the flowers and smiled briefly. Then her eyes glazed, and for what seemed a long time she stared blankly into the distance. Soon little tears joined the drops of rain still clinging to her face.

"Jenny!" The commanding tone of Paul's voice was unmistakable. She stood, but did not turn to face him. Her father had been plowing with a primitive hook-shaped branch a few yards away and had noticed her sadness. Paul was forty-seven years old now. Although almost totally gray, weathered and thin, he looked strong and handsome. He watched his daughter with concern. She had not recuperated from the years of malnourishment, confinement and horror as well as the rest of them. Emile said that she was either mildly retarded or suffering from a bad case of post-traumatic stress syndrome. The doctor worried, as Paul did, that she might never be completely normal again and that she, the fairest of them all, was at greater risk to develop skin cancer. The sun, when it was present, was too strong. They feared that the post-Impact atmosphere was ozone-depleted, allowing greater amounts of harmful ultraviolet radiation to reach them. They had no melanin vaccines to protect them as they had in the past.

Paul shook off his worry, then smiled and said, "My little bee, keep pollinating. You must realize how important your work is."

Without looking at Paul, Jenny placed the plastic bag in her pocket, careful not to damage its precious contents. She squatted again and placed a group of pebbles around the dandelions, marking its fertilized status. Paul watched her walk toward another distant yellow speck in the field. He squinted as the sun appeared and the storm-laden clouds sped away into the distance. Drenched in rain, Paul sweltered in the humid 122° F. heat. He could scarcely remember the bitter cold of the ice age.

And to think that twenty years ago I moved to Syracuse because I couldn't take the heat of Arizona! Paul thought. *Compared to northern Quebec's new weather, the worst Phoenix summer seems like a picnic.*

The sun had come back with a vengeance. Occasionally, for months at a time, the skies would darken again, when a surge of volcanism erupted somewhere on the still-restless planet. But today Sol shone over the Quebec countryside with newfound energy. Clouds, real clouds — the nimbus and cumulus of the older age — were back in all their magnificence. And most miraculously, it seemed to Paul, the landscape was studded with specks of green as grasses, shrubs and even some pine trees were starting to regrow.

The Earth and its inhabitants were extremely lucky that Impact occurred in late fall. The northern latitudes, hit hardest by the effects, would have taken millennia longer to recover had the disaster occurred in early or mid-summer. As it was, the northern temperate deciduous plants and many animals and insects had readied themselves with seeds and eggs for winter.

Squirrels were seen by some, near the now much-enlarged Abitibi Lake. That lake had become steaming hot during the early stages of the ice age due to the new movements of the tectonic plates. The geothermal spot allowed for many a local species to not go extinct. Paul marveled at the miracle that some creatures had somehow survived. He looked at the remnants of the forest around him and thought again about the significance of it all. The rotted trees and grasses created a thick compost, a great fertilizer upon which any surviving seed could grow. But whenever he was outdoors, he always felt a deep strangeness — an emptiness that had taken him a long time to decipher. The new world was greening, but it was mute. Deadly silent. There were no birds to herald the presence of life. Without the songs and endless chatter of birds, the outdoors had lost the sounds that trumpeted creation. Even more frightening, it had dawned on him not long ago that without birds and bats, the distribution of seeds would be a major problem. One more back-breaking chore he and the rest of the surviving humans would have to undertake if the recovery of the planet were to take only a few thousand years instead of millions.

The Lopez-LeBlancs toiled like primitive farmers in the small field near their old cabin and the now-flooded and useless underground shelter. They hated, yet loved the harsh heat. It had brought back life and hope. Even the crushed scenery around them was beautiful to them, but, compared to pre-Impact Quebec, the land was a barely thriving wasteland. Trees and brush were beginning to bud, many even had new branches with vibrant, fresh green leaves. Insects buzzed all around, but they were not the beautiful butterflies or bees of the past. Instead they were mostly flies, gnats and mosquitoes, which made life even more miserable in the unbearably humid heat.

For the Lopez-LeBlancs it was spring. It had taken many years to arrive but it was finally here. In spite of the tribulations it was beautiful and welcomed.

In the very distant north, the thin plume of a small volcano could be seen. The planet's many new volcanoes made for a continual display of incredibly beautiful sunrises and sunsets. Looking toward the south, Paul was startled once again as he gazed at the magnificent bright ring above the scattered clouds. Visible even during the day, a saturnian band of various colorful shades encircled the Earth. It was truly a magnificent spectacle. The original ring had been rough, irregular, dark and foreboding. Now it was composed mostly of dust and fine gravel-sized particles. Most of the larger pieces had fallen back to Earth or been flung out into space. Only a stable, thin ring remained. At night it sparkled with breathtaking colors. It was fascinating to watch the planet's shadow roll over the ring as the night went by. During the day the ring was not as startling, but was complete, uneclipsed, and constantly changing to various shades of silver, depending on the sun's angle. The ring would probably last one or two thousand years before becoming too thin to be seen by human eyes.

For those few survivors near the Earth's equator, the new ring system was a bright line of light crossing the center of the sky and dividing it neatly into northern and southern halves. During the day it was pale gray. At night, it became a bright line of pure white light which crossed the entire firmament from horizon to horizon.

For those few survivors in the southern or northern parts of the globe, in what used to be Canada, Russia, Argentina, and South Africa, the rings were a breathtaking multi-hued series of bright bands. Each one was a different size and color; by night, each was separated from its neighbor by thin, black void-bands, by day, clear blue space. From this angle, the rings were beautiful. But for the survivors living near the planet's equator, the rings above were a scourge of calamity from which some remnants of Dis'Aster still rained.

* * *

Trisha laughed out loud. "You know, it's really funny, " she said as she walked with her family to the small field. Trisha was almost forty, yet she had regained her youthful appearance and composure. Though thin and pale, she still had red hair and her freckles always brightened her smiling face.

"We are so proud of this great cornfield that we have," she said. "But when you really look at it, it's pitiful!" The seeds of corn had been found stashed away in the ruins of a neighboring farm, saved as a treasure until the great floods were over and they could be planted.

Her father and husband joined in the laughter as they scrutinized the shabby cornfield: a few rows of battered, sick and wilted plants, all of different heights. Barely able to hold themselves up, the plants bearing corn had to be braced with sticks. A pathetic sight indeed, but a miracle at this particular point in humanity's history. Emile drew himself very close to the rows of corn and brought his face only a few inches away from one of the ears so he could see it clearly. What he wouldn't give for a pair of glasses! Not only did he suffer the normal changes in vision that come with age, but cataracts had developed quickly. Emile, now sixty-three years old, believed the decreased ozone layer was allowing too much ultraviolet radiation to reach his eyes. He hated the lack of the amenities they grew up with and had taken for granted.

Apart from his eyes, and the arthritis that pained him continually, Emile had managed to bring himself back to relatively good health. Completely gray now, and with weathered facial skin, he looked much older than his sixty-three years.

The children failed to understand what was funny about the cornfield; they were so proud of the wonder they had helped to create. Hope, a strong teenager now, had never tasted a fresh vegetable of the types people had been used to prior to Impact. The only ones Jenny could remember were the long carrots she used to feed the horse she had been allowed to ride at Syracuse State as a small child. She had recently asked her parents about the horse she had loved. "Horses are most likely extinct now," they had sadly informed her. "We may never see one again."

Trisha thought back to the miracle of their rescue only a few years back. How they had been saved by other survivors from torrential rivers in the midst of the worst part of the Great Thaw. How the strangers had become their closest friends, and how they had all struggled together in the never-ending saga of survival. Each day bringing a new menace and a new close call with death.

During those years they had fought against the overwhelming greenhouse climate. Escaping the floods had then been humankind's only concern. But these floods also brought life, for where the rains had not washed it all away, there was a layer of slowly solidifying dirt, many inches thick. The new geological stratum — rich rotted vegetable compost, ashes and the many organic compounds brought into the Earth by the comet shower — provided a rich soil for regrowth of plants and all kinds of microscopic life. The new geological stratum would persist for millions of years, its concentrated iridium a permanent brand pinpointing the date of one more comet-borne extinction.

* * *

Paul lifted his hat and wiped the sweat from his forehead. "Boy!" he exclaimed. "For years we freeze to death — now we're being boiled alive like lobsters at a clam bake."

"What's a clam bake?" asked Hope.

Hope was a strong young boy, tall and handsome. His last few years of freedom and relatively good nutrition were accompanied by a sudden growth surge. Already five-foot, seven inches tall, the resemblance between the thirteen-year-old and his father was striking. Strong and dark, he carried Paul's piercing light blue eyes. He was obviously mature for his age. Having known so much hunger, cold, pain and sadness, he contributed in all the struggles. Always working, always helping, with never a complaint, he lived only for the survival of the group.

Jenny, on the other hand, at age seventeen, was much shorter than her younger brother. The horrors of the first years of confinement apparently arrested her growth. Without the supplements of vitamin C stocked by Emile, they would all have suffered the merciless effects of scurvy. Likewise, stocks of vitamin D prevented rickets in the children and osteomalacia in the adults, which could have been fatal.

"I'll explain to you later about clams, lobster and parties by the sea shore," Paul told his children. Addressing Trisha, he added, "I can't get over how little these kids know!" Then to Emile, with mock solemnity, "Oh great wise man and healer, honorable finder of corn seeds, today is New Year's Day, November first of the year fourteen, and Hope's thirteenth birthday. On this memorable day, thine is the honor to cut the first corn."

"Okay, everybody," Trisha announced with enthusiasm, "We've been waiting for many weeks for this very special occasion. We'll have the honor of being the first on this new world — or at least the first ones on this part of the planet — to eat fresh corn. We will cut the largest ears of ripe corn and divide them among the five of us."

"The six of us," corrected Paul as he gently caressed the bulging abdomen of his wife.

Trisha nodded, smiling, then shushed the others and murmured a prayer: "We thank you, Lord, for this food that is so special to us." She paused briefly, then continued. "And give us this day, and every day, our daily bread." She was embarrassed that she couldn't remember the standard prayers. She was about to continue when Jenny, in her usual low voice, interrupted, thinking that the prayer was over.

"Corn, mother. It's corn, not bread."

"Yes, dear," said Emile, "we're going to have corn, but the prayer uses bread to mean all the edibles that are given to us."

They had long ago given up trying to explain to the children about all the things they had taken for granted prior to Impact. Even now, the children became upset when hearing about this never-ending list of things that they couldn't even begin to imagine. "Anyway, Grampapá," Hope went on, "I agree with Dad. You should be the one to cut the first ears of corn. After all, you *did* find the seeds."

Emile accepted the honor emotionally. There hadn't been much honor to be had in the last few years.

Paul handed Emile a rusty knife.

* * *

In the torn perimeter of the corn field's clearing, behind a thicket of dead or struggling weeds and brush, two menacing faces peered through the branches... watching.

The aging man, dirty and bearded, with black and broken teeth and bloodshot eyes, held his left hand over his lips in a gesture of silence. The woman, even filthier, awaited his command. With greed in her eyes she scrutinized the unsuspecting victims and the corn. She could already taste the corn. Sweet corn. It had been too many years. She brought her finger to the trigger of the rifle.

With a swift move of his hand, the man signaled and they rushed, with weapons trained on the startled family. He shouted, "Stop! Freeze!"

The couple stopped in mid-field, halfway between the brush and the corn. From here they could survey the entire area. The partially reconstructed cabin, smoke rising from its chimney, stood silent a hundred feet away. "I think this is all of them," he said.

"Don't Move! Get away from that corn!" Petra bellowed, her weapon trained on them. "Don't move or you're dead!" Glord taught her well the power that fear of death carries over all humans.

In shock, they stood as if turned to stone. Emile, Paul and Trisha had their hands up. The children looked at the adults in bewilderment. Paul quietly directed Hope and Jenny to raise their arms. They didn't understand, and in the confusion started to talk to each other.

The man shouted at the children, "Hands up, you shitheads! And shut up! Do as they do, you stupid turds!" As the children awkwardly lifted their arms, he added, "Don't know nothing do you? Comet brats!"

Petra laughed nastily. "We'll teach you lots of new things, won't we, Harry?"

"Shut up, bitch!" he snarled. His glance went first to the corn, then to the others one by one, and finally fixed on Jenny. His eyes widened with pleasure as he looked her up and down. Jenny shrank against her father.

"Don't move or you're dead!" screamed the woman again, pointing her rifle directly at Jenny. Petra stumbled and almost fell as her mate viciously elbowed her away. "Don't you dare kill *her*!" he rasped. "She's mine."

Suddenly Hope dashed toward the safety of the cabin.

"No! No!" screamed Trisha. But her warning was too late. The intruders shot at the young boy as he zigzagged, trying to avoid the bullets. He had almost reached safety when his arms thrust into the air, his head fell back and chest forward, and he fell immobile by the side of the cabin.

"Don't move or you'll *all* die!" the man shouted at the rest of the family. They held each other in a desperate embrace. Jenny and Trisha started to cry in despair. Paul and Emile stood motionless, in shock.

Hope dead! Paul thought, stunned. *No! Hope can't die now — without Hope all is lost.*

The barbarian couple could only have survived the great blackness with treachery, murder and deceit, he thought. How could God have allowed such scum to survive? Why should such lowly creatures be permitted to perpetuate the human species? In his daydreams, at the beginning of the Great Thaw, Paul had envisioned a new society composed of honorable citizens like his family and their newfound friends. This new world would be one of unprecedented goodness and justice. How far from the truth he was. What a fool he had been to dream that only those that he considered worthy would make it through!

"Move away from that corn," the woman snarled as she and her mate approached closer.

Petra was once more enjoying the pleasures of power. She would have her way with all of them. She had been the "Queen Bitch" of Glord's early empire. Now, displaced by younger and more beautiful women, she was exiled from the high court and demoted to a lowly Sergeant. Her companion, Duke Harry, also fell into disgrace. Both were sent out ahead of Glord's army as scouts.

With her rifle she gestured the family to move a few yards away from the cornfield. Harry grabbed the largest ear of young corn with his left hand and tore it off, almost destroying the plant. Still holding his rifle, he started to peel the corn with his teeth, enjoying the fresh smell of the moist, precious treasure. The woman continued to guard the horrified prisoners. Harry bit into the raw, soft corn, his blackened teeth desecrating the product of so much love and toil.

But the crunching sounds were interrupted. Hope, unnoticed, moved one hand under the cabin's lower planks, reaching for what he knew was there. Until then, only he was aware that he was never even scratched by the barbarians' bullets. Snatching up the gunpowder rifle that his father had taught him to use so well, he whirled in an instant and, still sitting, fired with deadly accuracy.

Their reactions were too slow. One of Hope's bullets pierced Harry's left cheek, thrusting him into his companion. Petra stumbled, then ran toward the safety of the nearby trees and bushes, trying awkwardly to return fire. The interchange was short, and she fell to the ground in the middle of the clearing, dark blood flowing from her head.

The wars for food had just begun.

On the mud, with his reddened eyes fixed open, Duke Harry clenched the corn between his teeth. The yellow ear was slowly covered by the man's blood as it dripped from his torn skull. This image of terror would become for the Lopez-LeBlancs a grisly symbol of the years to come. After surviving nature's worst disasters, they would now have to struggle against other humans, fighting for food as well as fighting for their own lives. They would now have to fight the warring bands of criminals who pillaged and murdered for food and slaves.

Hope rushed to his family. They hugged and wept with joy. "We thought you were dead," Trisha sobbed.

"Great shooting, Hope! Great shooting, son," Paul said over and over.

The woman lying in the field suddenly stirred. Gripping her automatic rifle, she swiftly aimed it at the young boy. Just as quickly, Hope trained his weapon on her, and frantically pressed the trigger. *Click*. The chamber was empty.

The barbarian woman smiled. She looked indifferently at her dead companion, then with hatred at the boy. "I'll eat *you* alive," she said. She stood, pointing her weapon at the adults. Hope dropped his own to the ground.

Petra took aim. "No!" screamed Hope. Trisha put her hands over her eyes.

The air shook with the deafening roar of high-powered rifle shots. The first bullet hit Petra's right arm, ripping it from the shoulder. Her head and torso were flung upward at the impact. The detached arm flew into the air. The second carefully placed bullet pierced her pubis. Her body bent at the waist as, screaming in agony, she instinctively brought her only remaining hand down to her destroyed vulva. The final two bullets smashed through the former Queen's face and skull, splattering blood onto the field. Her rifle, still clutched in the hand of the severed arm, discharged repeatedly and harmlessly into the air as the fingers gripped in spasmodic reflex.

* * *

Moments ago, they had all been dead. They had seen the dark bore of the rifle and heard the shots. Yet somehow, at this precise instant, they were all still alive. In unison, their eyes all moved to focus on that point in the perimeter of the field from where the shots had rung out.

Out of the crumbled woods walked a tall black man, heavily armed and in full camouflage gear. He stepped cautiously, a large framepack on his back. He was a walking one-man army. He was panting as if he had been running, arriving just in time for the kill.

Hope ran to place himself between the newcomer and his bewildered family, trying frantically to reload his rifle. The black man moved closer, pointing his rifle at the ground in a gesture of peace. He lifted his other hand.

"I come in friendship," he said. "Don't shoot, please, I'm a friend! I've been after these two for months. Harry and Petra, both prominent members of Glord's kingdom. Finally, they're dead!"

"Glord's kingdom?" Emile repeated inquiringly.

"I'll explain later," said Robert Horton. "Right now you should know that others are out there, and they're coming this way. Scouts of a barbarian army are on search-and-destroy missions; they're clearing the way for the rest of their troops."

Reaching the corn field, Robert kicked Harry's body. "I'm sorry, I've just hated them so much." He kicked one more time, flinging Harry's bloody face away from the precious corn. The black man carefully retrieved the ear of corn and cleaned it on his trousers. "We'll save this one for seeds," he said. "No need to waste this treasure!" He stretched out his right hand to Paul. "I'm Robert Horton, and I come —" He whirled suddenly, a finger to his lips, pointing his gun toward the bushes where sounds of movement could be heard.

Paul and Emile quickly grabbed the dead strangers' weapons and, together with Hope and Robert, targeted the bushes, unsure of the exact location of the new enemy.

"Jenny, Trisha. Go to the cabin, get the other weapons and cover us from the windows!" Paul whispered. The women immediately hurried toward the cabin. "Be careful," he added, almost in a prayer.

Abruptly ten heavily armed young men and women emerged from the bushes. "Ne tiré pas!" one nervously called out as he held his hands and weapon in the air. "C'est nous!"

With a sigh of relief, the members of the family recognized their friends.

"Nous avons entenu les coups de feu. Nous sommes venu tout de suite," their leader, Pierre, said.

The band of young men and women were armed with a mixture of new and antiquated weapons: old-style powder rifles, heavy-duty bows and arrows with shiny, steel-glass arrowheads, laser rifles refitted as deadly crossbows capable of hurling a mini-spear through aluminum plate. The ragtag guerrilla army was ready for battle in an age where only ingenuity and intelligent use of available materials could produce effective weapons.

Jenny ran out of the cabin, dropping her crossbow, and flung herself into the arms of the youngest man, Ervi, a teenager like herself. "Thank God, it's you. Thank God," she sobbed. Ervi was a strong young man, brown-skinned, with mixed Asiatic and Caucasian features. The two groups met in the middle of the open field and embraced in joy.

"Sorry," Robert said, "I don't speak French."

"Well," said Pierre in good, (although strongly accented,) English, "guess you really didn't need us after all." He glanced with disgust at the torn bodies of the barbarians. Pierre, at thirty-five, was a thin Caucasian with pale eyes and long blond hair tied behind his neck. A single metal loop earring set off his striking features. After greeting the Lopez-LeBlancs with hugs and kisses, he answered Robert. "I said not to shoot. That after hearing the first shots we came as fast as we could. What happened here?"

Trisha quickly explained the unwelcome excitement of the last few minutes. On hearing the daring finale of the story, Ervi congratulated Hope and slapped his back. Hope could not hide his pride as one by one the other neighbors congratulated him.

Emile started to introduce Robert to the newcomers, but was interrupted by Pierre. "We all know Mr. Horton. He was just in our camp a few hours ago. Great job, Robert."

"Thank you, Pierre, but the praise goes to the boy. If it weren't for him, I would have been too late."

It started to rain again as they continued to talk, oblivious to the drops in the comfort of camaraderie.

"Get the fortification plans out, Paul," said Emile. "We obviously need to build it much sooner than we ever thought, and we have to renew our efforts to find more buried garbage dumps and landfills. They are our only source of supplies."

"While you men work, we'll make the best corn chowder you ever tasted," said Trisha. "At least," she added with a rueful laugh, "the best since Impact."

She and Jenny hurried into the cabin while the men and the younger women began planning for the wars to come.

CHAPTER 24

QUEBEC IX. (PART 2)
NOVEMBER 1, YEAR 14 P.I.
NEW YEAR'S DAY

"When I raised my eyes I saw... a ram... its two horns were tall.... And look!, there was a male goat coming from the sunset upon the surface of the whole Earth... and there was a conspicuous horn between its eyes... and I saw it coming into close touch with the ram... and it struck the ram and broke its two horns, and threw it [the ram] to the earth... and the male goat... for its part... as soon as it became mighty, broke its great horn, which became conspicuously four instead of one, towards the four winds of the heavens. And out of one of them came forth another horn, a small one, and it kept getting much greater towards the south and towards sunrising. And it kept getting greater all the way to the army of the heavens so that it caused some of the army and some of the stars to fall to the earth."

Daniel: 8:3-10, Holy Bible

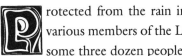rotected from the rain in the partially restored cabin, the various members of the Lopez-LeBlanc family mingled with some three dozen people of all races and ages. Babies suckled from their mothers' breasts, while Trisha looked on, longing for her new baby. Everyone greedily devoured the pieces of corn mixed with other cut-up edibles in a clear, lightly flavored broth. In other times it would have been considered poor man's food, but on this occasion, corn soup was a banquet for celebrating the first harvest of the people of New Quebec.

Plans for the fort lay open on a table. The men and women gathered around it were discussing the need for more tools and materials. The fortification plans closely resembled the forts used by the American pilgrims and, later, the American cavalry to fend off warring Indians: a perimeter of straight pine trunks tied together with rope, with a single large door, in this case a drawbridge, that crossed over a deep brook. Antennas and communication dishes stood out from the lookout posts, since they hoped to build solar-powered generators. The fortification was an almost comical blend of medieval castle, early-American fort, and modern space station.

"Robert says that most of the barbarians will be coming from the west and southwest," interjected Paul. "We may want to have additional lookout posts in this general area." He indicated a hilly and rocky region on the map.

"Good point, Paul," agreed Robert. "But only after you've built enough batteries to ensure constant radio contact with those in the posts. Otherwise it would be too dangerous for those stationed alone. These are brutal and merciless mercenaries. I was lucky to escape them as the band surfaced in Chicago. I know their ways!"

"Tell us, Robert, how many people are coming?" Ervi asked.

"A lot, no doubt about it, maybe a thousand or more," the man answered. "The word is definitely out; the barbarian group from Chicago has migrated toward the northeast. The cities are stinking, uninhabitable ruins — they've been abandoned to the rats and roaches. People are building villages far from the cities, and Glord's horde is be-ing pushed even farther out. This local environment with rapid vegetation regrowth, is ideal for the barbarians," he added. "They know we're defenseless. Their scouts have identified these locations as having small isolated groups of people. Their scouts were already here today; their army can only be a few weeks away." He let these last phrases hang in the air as he waited for more questions.

"But why should they come here?" demanded Ervi, sounding angry. "There's only wood and water out here and the toil of hard work — farming! What do they really want?"

"The most precious loot they seek is women and children." Seeing their reaction, Robert felt his heart ache as he remembered Tammy. "I'm sorry to say it, but that's the truth."

The hum of rain could be heard as Robert narrated his own story. He told of how he had miraculously escaped Glord's group and made it out of Chicago, that dreaded city of darkness; how the city ruins were all deserted now and the barbarians were out en masse looking for food, slaves, women and children — and a place of their own.

Glord's group had previously settled north of Chicago, but their atrocities resulted in their expulsion from the area. Small armies had been organized to destroy the barbarian group, but had succeeded only in forcing the relentless cannibals to leave the vicinity. Glord went farther north, only to be defeated again in Wisconsin by the alerted survivors of that area. He then headed northeast, to get away from large, organized groups, and to take by surprise any small clans of survivors in northern Quebec, which he had decided would be his new "Promised Land." To achieve his final dream and reach this destination, the place where he could build his empire, he needed more slaves and children, and, a very scarce commodity, the women to bear them.

Robert explained that many women had killed themselves rather than be constantly raped and abused. Others had killed themselves so that their flesh could be consumed by the others, the ultimate sacrifice of kindness.

Trisha interrupted Robert to describe her own experience. She related how, when her father and Paul had unearthed her mother from the frozen niche in the wall of their basement, she had refused to be part of the cannibalism. There was no way she could allow herself to eat her own mother's flesh.

"Anyway, as it turned out, it was actually very fortunate that on that day I did not eat of my mother's flesh," Trisha told the listeners. "That very first time, soon after they ate it, Paul, Emile, Jenny and the baby Hope all fell into a deep sleep. I became very concerned when I couldn't arouse them. Their respiration became extremely shallow. They had all drifted into semiconsciousness, a very unnatural sleep. I thought they were all dying. I realized that the food had poisoned them. I finally woke each one and made them throw up. To make a long story short, we eventually discovered that my mother had actually killed herself with an overdose of pills."

Emile interrupted, "I went back and checked the inventory of medicines. A bottle of powerful sedatives was found empty."

"Jenny almost died, since Paul had force-fed her some of Cynthia's liver," Trisha went on. "The liver concentrates these chemicals. We almost lost her. Luckily Hope, on his own, threw up practically all of it. It was too much protein for the poor starved child. Throwing up actually saved his life."

"From that moment on," said Emile, "we carefully rationed her meat and our bodies gradually became used to the narcotic she took."

"I was shocked," said Trisha, "when I realized that my mother killed herself so that there would be more food for the rest of us. She saved our lives — and then, as Paul put it, her frozen body gave us a second chance to live. I was so overwhelmed by that realization, that I couldn't turn her sacrifice down."

"This type of sacrifice was in fact very common and enabled many to survive," Robert said. "To those who sacrificed themselves, the world will always be grateful."

Robert continued his horror stories. Cannibalistic orgies and bloody, pseudo-religious and satanic ceremonies had occurred all over the globe. All present would eventually hear many more of these horrifying stories.

The members of the group settled down to discuss Robert's news. As Robert looked from one worried face to another, he felt bad to have instilled so much fear, but it was necessary if they were to survive. So many good people around him! What a difference from the years of living with barbarians. Most of the women over the age of thirteen were already pregnant or nursing babies. He felt warm in the presence of the family-like gathering.

Paul continued, addressing himself to Robert. "When the Great Floods were finally over and we felt safer, though damn hot in this new greenhouse, we realized that we had in fact survived. The waters were receding; grass was starting to appear; seedlings of trees and shrubs were emerging; even some tree trunks that looked dead were coming back to life. It was finally spring, twelve years late." He paused, then shrugged. "So we said to ourselves, what do we do now?"

"Make babies!" Trisha laughed.

"Even though it may seem that the decision was easy to make, the reality was more complex," Paul went on. "We discussed over and over whether the idea was a sound one. Had the women regained their health sufficiently to ensure healthy babies? We couldn't afford the deaths of any more women. Neither could we care for premature or unhealthy babies. What if the Great Thaw were followed by some other climatic change or other calamity? Babies would slow us down if we had to move again."

Robert nodded; he'd heard these arguments from other groups.

"We also realized," Paul continued, "that pregnant and nursing women wouldn't be much help in building and farming. We needed people power for everything — but above all, we needed more people."

After studying all angles and possibilities, they finally agreed to segregate their society and fashion it on the model of the European settlers who had come to North America centuries past. The women's job would be to have babies and ensure their growth and health. Since this limited their mobility, they would also fabricate, mend and clean clothing. They would become the medics and make and repair tools; they would preserve food supplies, ration them, and cook. They would keep the camps organized, clean, efficient and healthy, and participate as much as possible in any farming activities close to their camps.

The women's seemingly primitive assignments were at first accepted humorously. Only later did they realize the monumental effort required of their every single waking moment. Even cooking was extremely time-consuming. With practically no canned or otherwise preserved food, no usual condiments, and only a few pots and pans that could withstand the fire of a hearth, keeping everyone nourished was a full-time job.

Men would cut the timber for the homes that had to be built. They would forage for tools and food. They would try to build generators for electricity, erect antennas for communication and build primitive radios. They would construct carts, bicycles, and tricycles for transportation until they acquired enough technology to build self-propelled vehicles. Since there were no horses or oxen, they had fewer resources for transportation and farming than did their ancestors five-thousand years ago. And they would also search for and find, at any cost, seeds to be planted in the new fields, which they would till by hand, to ensure crops that would keep them alive once the meager remaining supplies from the buried towns were exhausted. It came as a shock to all when they realized that what they thought was a revolutionary redistribution of labor was in fact the way of life that had existed centuries back, that what they had thought was a male-imposed inequality was instead a very logical division of responsibilities that allowed for a better chance of survival for all.

Finally, men and women would make love. An unofficial rule required that every woman over thirteen who had reached menarche must be pregnant or have recently delivered. She must nurse her baby a minimal amount of time so that she could become pregnant again as soon as possible. The best milk producers would be assigned as nurse mothers, and the others would become pregnant as soon as possible.

"Well, I must admit that I envy you guys," said Robert, half-joking. "It's not every man who is lucky enough to live in a place where the law dictates continual lovemaking. And with such beautiful women!"

The compliments were received with smiles and pride. "Thank you, Robert," said Ervi, who had been listening to the conversation. "You need not be jealous long. I have been given the honor to ask you, plead with you if necessary, to stay here with us. We need more strong people among us. We need your knowledge, your strength, your honesty and leadership. And —"

"And we need your genes!" The sentence was finished by Neida, one of the most stunning of the women present; her beauty accentuated by the drops of perspiration they all wore in the sweltering heat. With an inviting smile, Neida handed Robert another bowl of the corn chowder. He smiled shyly, then changed the subject by looking at the soup with suspicion, for among the corn and dandelion were little pieces of meat, or something resembling it.

"I hope it's mouse or rat, not grubs," Robert said. "I can take roasted crickets because they taste like salted peanuts. Roasted ants I can also eat, they taste like popcorn. But grubs — I hate grubs!"

Everyone laughed, yet nobody disclosed the contents of the soup. The children were especially amused. "Adults are so persnickety about what they eat," said Hope. "Grubs are the best thing around, especially when they're full of that pasty yellow stuff!"

At that remark, Robert grimaced in disgust.

"Don't ask questions, Robert. Just eat your food — it's good for you!" added Hope. Everyone laughed at the reversal of roles.

Robert smiled. "Thanks for the food, whatever's in it. And thanks for the invitation. I was hoping you'd ask me to stay. It's been a long trek since I escaped from Chicago. I came this far to warn people of Glord's approach. From here, I can extend the message to the few camps beyond; probably not many since this area is as close to the Atlantic as survival permits. Glord believes he can conquer this area easily and form his kingdom here. He believes, and he's right, that the groups of people from the Chicago area that organized to destroy him cannot afford to follow him this far.

"I set out with a handful of men and women to alert the survivors of the northeastern countries. My comrades will make contact with me in a few days. We need to get every survivor from this area together. Only with unity can we possibly repel and destroy Glord's army. But I have to be frank. I have a double mission. The first is to save you from the horrors of the cannibals, to ensure that you are not captured. The other is to organize all the communities of this area into an army that can finally destroy that murderous pack. I will gladly join you and help you prepare for battle. I would be honored to become a member of your new nation. I have no desire to ever return to Chicago."

"Then welcome, Robert!" said Emile heartily.

CHAPTER 25

QUEBEC X.
APRIL, YEAR 14 P.I.
THE WAR

"So many floods shall happen that there shall scarcely be any land that shall not be covered by water, and this shall last so long that except for what lives on mountains and in water, all shall perish. Before, and after these floods, however, there shall be... a great deal of fire, and burning stones shall fall from heaven, that nothing unconsumed shall remain. The world shall be so diminished, and so few men will be left on Earth, that not enough will be found to plow the fields..."

Nostradamus (1503–1566 A.D.)

aul, Pierre, and a dozen other leaders of New Quebec's local encampments were busy organizing and hastily trying to finish their fortification. For lack of a better name, it was referred to simply as "The Fort."

During those months, Robert and five other volunteers had set out in pairs to warn other groups of the deadly threat that was on its way. All survivors in the general area would be needed to organize an army of at least equal force to that of Glord's. The Fort's scouts also scavenged the ruins of any farms or towns on their way, always in hope of finding an intact landfill. They were searching for metal, glass, any items that could be used as weapons, radio communicators and other objects that might be useful in the warfare to come.

Glord and his barbarians would not be prepared for an organized defense, much less an attack. The people of The Fort sent a handful of adults with portable communicators toward the west, in the hope of detecting and killing any other of Glord's scouts, and to find Glord's main force and radio back its location.

* * *

Luckily for those at The Fort, Glord and his army were enjoying a reprieve from the harassment of those who had been pursuing them. Now that his enemies from the west had finally given up trying to kill him, Glord took the opportunity to rest, reorganize, and scavenge for additional supplies. Once he felt strong again, he would continue east where he planned to settle his kingdom in what had once been the Republic of Quebec. He swore, however, that he would return one day to Chicago and crush those who had humiliated him. No one would dare oppose his forces, and it would be centuries before the world's population would be big enough to threaten his descendants.

Another indirect benefit to those at The Fort was the barbarians' renewed involvement in cannibalistic and ritualistic orgies, (a pleasure denied them in their haste to flee). Now that they felt at least temporarily safe, they had time to again enjoy the pleasures of totalitarian power. Their trek east was delayed more than originally planned, until Glord got nervous about staying put in one locale for so long. Glord had to show force in order to separate the barbarians from their pleasures and bring them back under his will.

"Our promised land lies east of here," he thundered. "I want everybody off their asses, right now! Vacation is over! We have to finish building larger carts so that our slaves' work can be more efficient, and so we can take our weapons and booty with us. And I want those babies and children well cared for!" Glord paused. "As of today there will be no more killing of slaves unless I personally authorize it. I don't want any more *accidental* deaths, either. If you don't want to become meat for my table, you had better obey."

The message was made perfectly clear the very next day when, with a swift swing of an old-fashioned sabre, Glord decapitated one of his lesser officers. "Laziness, lying and insubordination will not be tolerated," he announced to all. He learned of the young officer's secret attempt to set up a separate group and head elsewhere. Glord didn't trust the man in any case; he was too independently-minded. One of Glord's more subservient subjects had betrayed the young officer's trust; the traitor was amply rewarded with an increase in rank and the associated fringe benefits — more human flesh, more sex.

The delay allowed those at The Fort to build a strong fortification. They cleared a few acres of the mostly dead forest. They would have preferred to burn the area clear, but knew a large fire would attract attention to their location.

Scouts from The Fort had not yet been able to locate Glord's camp, and some suggested that his army had either been destroyed or had set out in another direction.

"Let's not become complacent," Robert had told them after returning from his most recent excursion. "Chances are they *are* on their way. This is a very large country, but they are bound to find us eventually. It is a risk we cannot ignore."

* * *

Glord and his army ventured east again. He no longer sent expeditions of two or three scouts, it had proven ineffective; and too frequently the scouts were never heard from again. He now dispatched larger groups of one to two dozen well-armed men and women.

When these scout groups found an encampment of survivors,

they approached, feigning friendship. They quickly killed the leaders and enslaved the rest. Some of the dead were eaten on the spot to ensure the utmost fear and obedience from the new slaves. Rape was encouraged, but unnecessary deaths were forbidden and such wasteful behavior was severely punished.

Glord's army grew in strength as new slaves enabled the transportation of more supplies and weapons. The children were kept loyal through fear, compliments and rewards. Those who adapted to Glord's ways were given "junior officer" rank and allowed to bully the other children and even adult slaves.

* * *

Robert turned on the communicator strapped to his arm. Since the solar panel on his back didn't generate much power, he used the device as little as possible. He also wasn't as sure as the engineers back at The Fort that the enemy could not detect and decipher his specially coded transcommunication band.

From his post high atop a mountain, and hidden within a rock outcrop, he had followed the progress of Glord's army for the last few days. Powerful binoculars allowed him to keep track of them while still remaining at least three miles ahead of the main group. He could not risk being found by a scout party.

"Looks like they're going to camp for a few days this time," he reported. "The slaves are unloading the main tents from the carts." His voice was calm as he added to himself, "Those poor bastards will get a reprieve from their burden."

Paul's familiar voice came back, short and precise. "Copy. We will go ahead with plan Charlie. Out."

So it's Charlie, Robert thought as he nodded to himself in approval. A slight smile played about his lips. Only a single, swift, surprise attack could result in total victory. They could not afford a long war. They must triumph with the first battle! *We are going to hit them first,* he thought. *No more waiting.*

* * *

In Glord's new encampment, there was much activity as his hordes unpacked and prepared to rest for a few days. They had trekked hard during the last week. The landscape was barren and rose slowly up-hill. Floods had erased all signs of civilization. There were no roads, no maps. Compasses were very difficult to read since they no longer pointed to the north. They had to make travel plans based on the sun and the stars. Clearing a path for the carts and pulling them through the uphill terrain had been extremely demanding of everybody's physical abilities. The present locality was rocky and it slowed their progress considerably. The slaves couldn't keep up for long the backbreaking chores: moving rocks and tree trunks, pulling and pushing the huge wooden carts.

The long lines of slaves, tied together with ropes, chains and plastic lines, were weakening. Glord did not want to drive them to total exhaustion. He wanted no more suicides, no more accidents, and especially, no more fractured bones. He would keep their wills broken, but he needed the strength of their bodies.

* * *

Atop one of the smaller carts, heavily armed and surrounded by a myriad of radios, telecommunications devices, solar power panels and antennas, the Communications Officer called for Glord. The thin man's oriental features were accentuated by small, round gold-rimmed glasses, taped and mended. Under the partially-broken glasses were poorly healed scars and a graying goatee. He kicked the solar panels. "Fuck!" he shouted in frustration. Was it his batteries or was the transmission truly ended?

Packi thought again about what he had heard, how best to deal with it, and especially how to benefit from it. He must tell Glord, of course, but how was a matter of concern. Glord might react with interest and reward him, or with rage and have him beaten. He had requested an important conference with his leader, but Glord had not answered.

"Get up!" Packi shouted, cracking his whip over the eight women lying panting on the ground. "You've rested enough! Move me over to the main headquarters! Now!"

The women assigned to pulling the communications cart quickly restrapped their head and chest harnesses and started pulling without

delay as the man again cracked his long whip. At least they had only a couple of hundred yards to go, and then they could rest for the night. As they headed for Glord's main tent, the slave women braced themselves. The first few feet were always the hardest. The large and wide tires helped roll over the stones, and soon they picked up an efficient pace.

As they moved forward, they passed the children's army of over two hundred boys and girls, ages five to fifteen. The children were divided into groups by age, and, within those age-groups, by rank. Those most unconditionally loyal to Glord were appointed as junior officers and put in charge of the others. Packi licked his lips when they passed the cart with the caged boys. Incorrigible boys were castrated and, as had been customary with the Carib savages that Columbus found in the Lesser Antilles, the capons were then fattened for special feasts in honor of the King and his court. Attached to the cage was a crude sign: "Disobey Glord's law and you too will be a capon."

They reached the tents that made up headquarters, and the Communications Officer silently waited for Glord to redirect his attention from his maps. Glord finally glared at the thin yellow man. "What the hell do you want now?" he bellowed.

"Sorry to disturb your highness, but I've heard it again, sir. No doubt this time, your majesty. Someone is using a communicator in the vicinity, no more than twenty-five miles away. It might even be closer. It's a very unusual band in a totally unidentifiable code. I cannot make out a single word, but it's definitely there."

Glord absorbed the unwelcome news in silence.

"It's a good thing, your majesty, that with my experience and all this equipment I have put together, I have been able to give your majesty such good service. I thought, Sire, that —"

"Shut up and keep your ears open." Glord knew what the man wanted but at the moment he didn't want to be distracted. Either someone was spying on him, or some of his own men were up to no good. Whoever they were, he had to find them and kill them as soon as possible.

Glord turned to one of his nearby lords. "Give Radioman his choice of company for twenty-four hours. I understand he likes young boys!" he chuckled. "But make sure he is on those radios most of the time."

* * *

The attack on Glord's camp was a serious disappointment to all the people of The Fort. Glord appeared to be ready for them. Never before had he set up battle stations all around his encampment. Nor were camouflaged outposts expected. Glord must have suspected that he was in danger of an organized attack.

The first assault took Glord's outposts by surprise, but their preparations for such a possibility had significantly decreased the impact. Paul's group had been modestly successful, but Robert's division produced little damage and itself suffered casualties.

The assault weakened Glord, but since it did not result in total victory, it gave the barbarians time to reorganize. The Fort's people rushed home, where they were now forced to develop new plans — defensive plans.

* * *

What had been planned as the one and only battle was the first of a war that would last for years. Neither side was large enough or strong enough for a decisive victory. A guerrilla warfare of sorts ensued. Small battles resulted in damage and casualties on both sides and required retreat for weeks and months to recuperate.

Glord was continually forced to move his camp farther and farther southwest, not the direction he wanted. The Fort, in turn, was partially burned and had to be rebuilt a mile west of the original.

"Westfort" as it was now called, was no farther from Glord's main camp, but it was constructed in a more strategically placed area. The neighboring hills provided ideal lookout posts, and the larger pine trees of the area made stronger logs for the walls; these walls were now made chemically fire-resistant. Water came from an underground spring, which couldn't be diverted or poisoned by the enemy. The perimeter of the new clearing was farther out, to ensure safety from most weapons. Westfort was large enough to support a small agricultural field within the walls, and there were now sufficient generators to provide energy for most needs, including some small laser weapons and a few primitive gas and steam driven vehicles.

Within Westfort, a few thousand lived at its most populous time. Every survivor from the entire northeast eventually immigrated there to escape Glord. As the years of battle continued, the population on both sides of the war fluctuated continuously. Not only were there casualties, there were also desertions, even on the Westfort side. Some families insisted that the war effort was futile and left in hopes of finding livable lands to the south. But most stayed, knowing that no place on the continent would be truly safe until Glord and his army were defeated.

CHAPTER 26

QUEBEC XI.
SEPTEMBER, YEAR 16 P.I.
TREATY

"And I saw another strong angel descending from heaven, within a cloud and upon his head a rainbow. And his face was as the sun and his feet were as pillars of fire.... And he set his right foot upon the sea and the left one upon the Earth, crying out with a loud voice, as when a lion roars..."

John: Book of Revelation 10:1,2,3, Holy Bible

aul Lopez felt a deep, inner chill. His soul seemed to shrink within him. His shoulders sagged as his strength began to fade.

He had set up this conference with Glord. It had seemed to him, and to some others of his group, that the war had reached a stalemate. Both sides had suffered too many casualties. To this were added casualties from appendicitis, strep throat and other diseases so easily cured prior to Impact.

Morale was at its lowest point. Even Emile had died in a direct mortar hit near the compounds of Westfort. That loss was a major blow to them all. With him, his help, support, work, and love had passed away. Though nearly blind, his knowledge of biochemistry had been vital in agriculture, medicine and many other aspects of the community's needs.

So much material and energy had been wasted on battlefields. And it seemed now that there would never be an end to it. Paul had suggested that if he could negotiate with Glord, he would be able to convince him of the uselessness of the war and the need for a peace treaty. Under Paul's plan, Glord would be allowed to migrate south or southeast without fear of casualties or loss of supplies.

For the treaty to work, there would have to be a freeze on all offensive on both sides, allowing the barbarians time to reorganize, rebuild their vehicles, and move out of the area.

The only logical place for Glord's people to go was to the south or southeast; maybe even beyond the old USA-Quebec borders. Eastern Ontario and the old Syracuse-New York State areas were deserted, and Paul was convinced could support a new country. Westfort's people would ensure Glord safe conduct so that other groups, enemies of Glord, would let them pass through. Westfort would even guarantee that no one would be allowed to follow Glord or attack his kingdom once its new boundaries were delineated far from theirs and separated by a no-man's land at least two hundred miles wide. Paul's optimism mounted when Glord agreed over the radio to meet with him. But he was not prepared for Glord's reaction to his proposal.

Glord and Paul met as planned, unarmed and alone in a deserted clearing. The weather was beautiful and sunny. The climate was finally settling down to the normal rhythms of seasons, though it remained much warmer at that latitude than before Impact. The treaty table was a solitary rock about six feet wide and three feet high. Each man stood alone, separated from the other by the large rock. Paul wore a camouflage guerrilla outfit. Glord, now with head shaven to appear even more menacing, was dressed in his usual outlandish mixture of royal and military clothing.

From the beginning, the meeting did not go as Paul planned. Glord would not buy his ideas. The barbarian exploded with laughter, ridiculing his suggestions. "There's no way you can guarantee the actions of others," he said. "As soon as we're exposed, even your own family will jump at the opportunity to try to exterminate us."

Glord continued to dismiss Paul's other ideas. "There is nowhere for us to go. To the south and southeast, there is nothing but devastation. Impact scorched the northeastern USA much too badly. You think I haven't thought of all this? I have sent scouts there, and there is no hint of vegetation! Nothing has survived! Not even seeds or insect eggs are buried in the dirt. That damned land you talk about is uninhabitable. There isn't even any humus for planting. Do you expect us to walk away from victory and settle to die in that wasteland?"

Some of the land was as Glord described, but other parts could sustain life, with work. But Paul couldn't convince Glord, and the conference deteriorated into a yelling match.

"Paul," Glord said firmly, turning the tables, "the only way you and your group can possibly survive is to join us. The advantage of the war is definitely on our side. We have new recruits coming to join us all the time. Mercenaries bring weapons and supplies. For a woman or a child, they'll get us anything we want! We have tons of gunpowder and can make as many bullets as we want. What do you have to barter with? Love?" He burst out laughing again. "When did you last get new supplies? Or weapons? Admit it, your allies are too worried about their own business to help you any more."

"We don't need their help," said Paul stubbornly.

"Besides," Glord went on, ignoring him. "You cannot withstand any more casualties. We can easily replenish our armies with recruits by offering them food, slaves and power. And we can always catch more slaves." The strategist watched Paul's reactions carefully. "Paul, think seriously about this." Glord's tone of voice now suggested a benevolent attitude. "You and the rest of the Westfort people can end this useless war with simple cooperation. You can all join my people and settle with us in this great new frontier. This is an offer I never thought I would make, but times have changed and I am willing to compromise."

Paul didn't answer.

"I promise to forgive anyone who joins us." Perceiving Paul's building rage, he added, "I know you wouldn't all approve of our way of life, so for a two-year period you could live in a separate area of our city. You wouldn't be harmed unless you attacked us again."

Paul could hold his outrage no longer. "I came here in good faith!" he exclaimed. "How dare you treat me as a defeated enemy, giving us a handout. You're offering a promise that I know you will never keep! If I were to accept your humiliating bid, all of my people would become your slaves!" Paul was ashamed of his naiveté. Horton and the others were right after all. Glord had come to the conference only to demand surrender, and to learn what he could of Paul's and Westfort's weaknesses. *I was 34 years old when Dis'Aster struck Earth,* Paul thought. *I am now 50. Will I ever learn not to trust?*

"Think what you will," said Glord. "If you do not accept my generous offer, the war will go on." Paul felt something snap in him, and he confronted the barbarian with his true feelings. "If we must continue to fight, then, Glord, you can prepare to die! For we are the righteous, and we must be the winners of this war."

"Must?" Glord laughed, as if Paul had made a bad joke.

Paul accused Glord of barbarism and cannibalism, called him an animal, primitive, uncivilized scum. There was no way, he told Glord, that such vermin would live to repopulate the planet. The Westfort group, on the other hand, were civilized people. They were the good, decent people that were needed to rebuild the planet. Evolution demanded *their* survival and not Glord's. The genetic structure of those like Glord would poison the Earth. Only honest, hardworking people should propagate human kind!

"You arrogant fool!" Glord shouted back. "How stupid can you be? How dare you insult me! You have just doomed yourself to death!"

"*Arrogant?* Me doomed to death? You're the one that —"

But Glord's thunderous voice drowned out Paul's anger. "Yes, you arrogant, pitiful parasite! How dare you speak to me like that!" Glord stared into Paul's eyes across the makeshift conference table. "You've talked about good and evil, evolution, genes, the survival of our species, as if it were an old movie divided into the good guys and the bad guys. You conceited worm! How can you suggest that the survival of your group of anemic weaklings would be better for the new world than my people, or others like us all over the world?"

Paul opened his mouth to answer, but Glord went on. "When the Spaniards, the Portuguese and the English first came to America and won these lands through brutal and merciless battle, was that savagery bad for civilization or did it lead to progress and to a stronger human race? When Cro-Magnon man annihilated the Neanderthals and conquered Europe by cruel and ruthless force, was that bad for *Homo sapiens?*

"When Genghis Khan slew hundreds of thousands of men, women and children, to expand his domain, did that set the human race back? Or rather did his strength and cunning allow the expansion of the civilization that eventually turned this damned planet into the technological center of the entire galaxy?"

Paul's face could not conceal his shock as Glord exposed his own philosophy. For the first time he felt fear. As some had suggested, Glord was more than a simple, brutal butcher. This man was also a thinking, articulate and cunning leader.

Could Glord be right? Someone had once said that "war never determined who is right, only who is left." Paul remembered how he had once marveled at the knowledge that history is written only by the victors. He shuddered. Would it be better that barbarians now rule the world as they did for so many millennia during the early history of civilization? Was the survival of the species better ensured through the brutal strength of those like Glord rather than through the almost-religious toil of those he had thought — until this very moment — were on the "proper" side of the human race?

"Might is right" was the motto that King Arthur had unsuccessfully tried to defeat in Camelot. Was the meaning behind that motto what was needed once again? Were the group of men and women he lived with out of touch with what was needed at the present time? Perhaps New Earth would have to wait for brutal force to form a strong, unyielding base before civilization and technology could arise again. Perhaps a dictatorial base was needed before his ideals, his vision of civilized culture, would have the potential to persist and mature. He suddenly felt defeated. His deepest and strongest beliefs had been given a devastating blow. What right *did* he have to divide people into good and bad? The whole idea now seemed so childish and stupid.

Through Paul's mind rushed the inevitable conclusions: Drake, a murderer and thief, a lowly pirate, was now and forever lauded in the western world's history — "Sir Frances Drake," a hero in both history and adventure books. So too were Cortez, and the American cowboys and Cavalry. They conquered only through brutal force, killing millions in their wake.

All over the recovering world, there were hundreds of clans and makeshift armies fighting for survival. Who was to say to whom history would grant its blessings?

"Paul," Glord spoke softly now. "Put yourself in my place. I cannot take my people back west. They are waiting there to imprison and execute us. You may think the Chicagoans and Minnesotans are nice people, but I can tell you they will show no mercy to my people." He paused for a few seconds, then went on, "They are just as ruthless as any of us."

"The West is lost to us forever. They are growing stronger there. We must build our own country or we will be destroyed and our land will be taken from us. To the south and east, Dis'Aster's scourge has left nothing but deserts and stinking, poisonous lakes. Like you, we have little choice for land. Maybe it is destiny that brings us together.

Must one of our peoples die so that the other may have a home? Why can't we share this land?"

"We were here first," interrupted Paul. "You have come hundreds of miles. You have no right to —"

"I understand," Glord interrupted. "I wanted the area north of Chicago for us. That was our land. But we were pushed away. We were pinned between them and the waters of Lake Michigan. But the waters parted for us during an earthquake. You know this. We walked over the beds of sand and then, after we crossed, the lake filled up again. Many of my people actually believe this was an act of God. They'll die for me, Paul. It was not my plan, but I am here now. I am responsible for over two thousand people. This is our only possible sanctuary. Join us and so much bloodshed will be avoided."

"Don't give me that bullshit about the parting waters!" Paul snapped. "That happens a thousand times a year in these areas. I'm not one of your fanatic followers! And you want me to trust you, Glord? You want me to place the fate of my people in your hands? If you betray the treaty, as I think you will, I will be solely responsible for the destruction of our own dream, and the enslavement of my loved ones. Your officers would kill me and all our strong men, and then you would eat us in your celebration of glory. That has been your way of conquest — why should I believe you are going to change? No, Glord. What I came here for was to let you know that you can leave the area in peace. We won't attack. We don't care about your damned promised land. This is *our* land."

Glord straightened and took a deep breath, then smiling said, "Well, Paul, then I will have to kill you."

Paul blanched.

Glord continued to smile. He slowly put his right hand into the sleeve covering his left wrist.

Paul's heart began to race. They both had sworn to be unarmed. What a fool he was to have trusted Glord!

Glord pulled out an ancient, tiny gunpowder revolver and directed the barrel point-blank at Paul's face. The click of the hammer being pulled back rang through the clearing. "You are a great idiot,

Paul," Glord said.

Paul stared at the tip of the barrel.

"You will die, Paul Lopez," Glord said calmly.

Helplessly, Paul thought of his family: his parents, Hope, the dark and cold shelter, beloved Jenny, *so frail*, Trisha. To end this way, to have let his people down — what a shameful way to die. He refused to obey the impulse to scream. He refused to obey the instinct to flee, and held strong in refusing to beg for mercy. He would die as a fool, caught in a desperate act to save his people. But he would not die as a coward.

"Yes, you will die," Glord repeated. "I *will* produce great harm to your longevity. But not now. Later, Paul. Right now, you are more valuable to me as a messenger." Glord again smiled triumphantly as he put the gun away and pulled out a roll of paper from the inside pocket of his ragged, medal-laden jacket. "I want you to take this message to your people. It is *my* message of peace," he ordered. "It is *my* offer of life which I extend to those of your people who are smart enough to join my forces. I promise them not only escape from certain death, but also a solemn pledge of only one year of my benevolent slavery. Then they will have the freedom either to stay with me or leave unharmed. In exchange for them, you and the rest of your officers can go to Minnesota or wherever you wish. But don't *you* decide the destiny of those women and children."

Paul immediately sensed the trickery behind the offer. "You will not weaken my people," he said. "They will not fall for your bribery." His words were cut short as Glord leaped over the rock. In a second, the barrel of the small gun was pressing painfully against Paul's forehead.

"Go! or I'll kill you right now. Take the message to your people and let *them* decide what they want to do with their own damn lives!"

CHAPTER 27

QUEBEC XII.
OCTOBER 20, YEAR 18 P.I.
THE SIEGE

"The day... shall come, a cruel day, and full of indig-
nation and wrath, and fury, to lay the land desolate...
For the stars of heaven and their brightness shall not
display their light: the sun shall be darkened... and
the moon shall not shine with her light..."

Isaiah 13:9-13, *Holy Bible*

he outer walls of Westfort — massive vertical stacks of conifer trunks — were reinforced and the whole fort was expanded. Three layers of pines were strengthened with cables of light steel (the remains of a suspension bridge). When the reinforcement had been completed, Hope Lopez felt his people now had a better chance against the barbarians.

As the Police Chief of his people, Hope felt an overwhelming sense of responsibility. They jokingly called him "Sheriff," a nickname he quietly enjoyed. But it was no picnic for this now-seventeen-year-old to fulfill the roles of both civilian and military ruler. The power that came with the dictatorial privileges granted to him by his people terrified him. He had matured so in this ruthless world, so much responsibility for the lives of the people of Westfort rested on his shoulders.

Was all this power turning him into a ruthless person? All he needed was the vote of three of the twenty members of the Council to imprison or to execute, or to have someone, even a whole family, banished from Westfort. Banishment and exile were feared more than any punishment; it meant slavery, rape and torment at the hands of the barbarian lords that surrounded them.

It was now two years since the failed treaty attempt. Years of relentless warfare had killed and maimed so many. The quality of life in Westfort had slowly deteriorated to the depressive monotony of entrapment and occasional skirmishes of guerrilla warfare. So many of their strong and brave men and women had died. In the meantime Glord was slowly colonizing the area around them, as if it was already his.

Since his election, and thanks to his ruthless tactics, Hope had kept his people alive and together, and for that they were grateful. But the situation was deteriorating, and the enemy grew stronger while Westfort's own forces weakened daily.

There had come a time when Westfort's leaders were so divided that nothing could be accomplished. Fresh new leadership was needed. Another major battle was lost, probably unnecessarily, and in desperation the Council gave Hope the "sheriff plus three" power of vote, stripping itself of power; the Council could no longer rule. Hope had proven to be a merciless leader and warrior. He was selected not for his blood lineage, but for his cunning and survival instincts. His strength had held them together for months.

Finally isolated in a siege, Westfort was now reduced to a purely defensive position. Despite their efforts, some of the walls of their fort were burning again. Help did not arrive from the Minnesotans. The citizens of the Republic of Minnesota had their own wars to fight as they tried to preserve their nation's boundaries. Not even the Lansing encampment, the only one relatively close to Westfort, had sent a rescue mission. Westfort was on its own. The rest of the world was too busy with its own survival to care for the fate of a few desperate hundreds living in the outermost fringes of the New World.

Desperate indeed, their last plan had to succeed.

* * *

By late afternoon, the people of Westfort were ready. Six women and four men, mostly elderly, chronically ill or wounded, had volunteered for the plan, a reach-out-and-destroy mission of unprecedented type. Following a detailed plan, each set of two volunteers would man a war-rover.

Ysela, "the old wise woman" as she had been called, had been one of the first to volunteer. The growing lumps under her arm led her to discover a larger one in her left breast. Cancer, mostly conquered prior to Impact, was making a destructive comeback after almost two decades without vaccines.

Each war-rover was painstakingly assembled from various scraps of vehicles found in the area. Wheels and tires were of different sizes. Seats were put together to be as light as possible. Some of these topless, jeep-like contraptions were powered by makeshift steam engines. Others used small gas engines that were barely strong enough to move the vehicle. When loaded, they could roll at twenty or thirty miles per hour at the most.

With a sense of excitement not felt in years, Ysela scrutinized her life and pondered her death, certain to come in the next few minutes. She wondered how many of the barbarian scum she would ultimately kill. She despised them, for they had distorted life and made war the most important goal of her people. So much wasted energy and life that should have been used in rebuilding her beloved planet.

"Go!" came Hope's stern command through the tiny earphones. Ysela drove her steam- powered rover forward.

Not far away, Trisha sat crying. She knew that this was the last time she would see her husband.

Paul Lopez set his own rover in motion, as did the other three. Two had to be push-started. The crude vehicles were loaded with the fort's last grenade launchers, laser-seekers and machine guns. Ysela's mate, Nita, dear old, black Nita, now too old to really understand or care what was happening around her, lifted up a white flag of peace as all five rovers headed slowly in different directions away from the smoldering fort.

The two people in each rover were dressed in battle uniforms. One drove while the other held high a white flag. Paul stood tall and proud. He had made the radio contact with Glord, and needed to make sure Glord would recognize him.

Glord smiled at the sight of the approaching vehicles. "So they want to beg for mercy," he said. "But there will be no bargaining, absolutely none. They are starving and they have lost the damn war! Only full surrender is acceptable. They won't kill their children, it's against their way. The children and women will finally be all ours — and my kingdom is *here*!"

Glord's coded communicator flashed the final resolution to all his officers throughout the perimeter. "Accept them and take them prisoner, *alive*. But just in case it is a trap, send some well-armed negotiators to meet them far from our main lines."

As the rovers approached the heavily armed groups of negotiators, Hope, from his vantage point atop the only remaining tower of the fort, pushed a button that lit a signal on the dashboards of all five rovers. Their drivers braced themselves, then simultaneously barged forward at full speed, their rockets and grenade launchers spewing fire.

"Ahee!" screamed Ysela. With one fist pointed forward she steered the awkward machine toward the enemy while Nita blasted them with machine gun fire. "Ahee!"

Taken by surprise, the barbarians suffered casualties, both among the negotiators and among their main flanks, now barely within reach.

As the battle raged, a much larger group of Westfort's people, all those capable of running, came rushing forth, mostly on foot but also using all the remaining bicycles and other makeshift vehicles. They pushed out in unison from the smoldering ashes of their burning haven.

"Ahee!" was the battle cry. Screaming and shooting, they rushed forward, even though only a few of their weapons could hope to reach the distant and well-entrenched army.

But the battle was already over, just as it had begun. The five scout vehicles soon lay in pieces, destroyed, and their intrepid crews dead or dying. The human wave that left the relative safety of the smoldering fort retreated as soon as they started receiving casualties. It was the end of a day that would be remembered for millennia.

* * *

"I told you not to trust them!" shouted one of the barbarian officers after seeing so many of his good soldiers dead or wounded. Glord looked back at him sternly, restraining himself from the impulse to jump on this insolent officer and rip his head off.

"I didn't think they were this stupid!" Glord shouted back.

"They weren't stupid, don't you see? They know they have to surrender unarmed, one by one, or lose their chance to pass their genes. Remember that is their only goal in life! This way they knew that they would at least kill a few of us before they finally surrendered. *They* were not stupid!"

Glord stared at his officer. The suggestion that *he* was the one who was in fact stupid was too much for the King. With a swing of his powerful arm, the leader bashed the officer with the side of his hand gun. Only half-conscious, and bleeding from a broken nose and jaw, the impertinent officer fell to the ground. No one dared help him as Glord shot him once through the forehead. As the dead man's body was dragged away, Glord glared at the others, reminding them that he was the only real boss.

The sun set one more time on what was meant to be New Quebec.

* * *

As their evening of triumph settled in, the barbarians laughed at the futile attempt to weaken them. They drank and feasted while they waited for the fire to destroy the remains of the fort. Not even fire-retardant wood could hold back the intense heat of so many embers. In the morning the residents would have to surrender; there was no other way.

The barbarians knew that the world had too few inhabitants for mass suicide to be considered by the people of Westfort. It was just a matter of waiting. They would then divide the strong slaves, the women and the children.

From Westfort, there was only silence.

* * *

Even before the sun was up, Hope and the pitiful remnants of his army stood by the remains of the fort's main entrance. Most of the walls and towers had crumbled. So little was left of the fortification they had so painstakingly built. Behind the warriors were the old, the wounded, and over two hundred children.

As dawn began to lighten the scene, Hope stood with a bazooka-like contraption in one hand. In the other was a white flag, the white flag of surrender he had never dreamed he would have to use. He had always sworn that death would be better than surrender. On his right arm he wore a black band, a sign of mourning. Now even his father was dead. Trisha stood by him, tears still rolling from her eyes.

Waiting for the early morning to brighten, the survivors of the fort stood behind Hope and Robert. Women and children waited in terrible expectation. What would the next few minutes bring? Would it be death? Or, worse still, rape and torture?

Hope gave the bazooka to Robert. It was their only weapon with long-range capabilities. The sun peeked above the horizon. Red, and beautifully framed next to a distant volcano, its rays bathed the battlefield.

A nervous visual exchange among them indicated the uncertainty in their minds. And the fear.

Robert Horton aimed toward the perimeter beyond the desolated field. Any place was as good, or as bad, as any other. The projectile would produce the same effect.

Bahroom!

The grenade shot off in parabolic flight, exploding a few seconds later in a splatter of fire and smoke close to the innermost circle of their enemy's camp.

Trisha gripped Hope's arm. Jenny fell on her knees and prayed.

Would this be their end? A maddened army of a thousand savages rushing toward them, mutilating, piercing, raping, laughing, killing?

In their minds they could sense it —

But there was no response. Hope dropped the white flag.

* * *

In the early dawn of that glorious morning, the leaders and soldiers of the barbarian army were all dead or gasping their last breaths. Dead also were some of the slaves. Only a few lesser soldiers who had by now escaped the horror around them and a few dozen bewildered slaves still lived. The slaves, still chained, looked as if they had witnessed a miracle.

Robert was the first to search through the bodies. He thirsted to find Glord alive. He had sworn personally to kill him so many thousands of times. He could finally avenge Tammy's rape and shameful death.

It didn't take long to find the barbarian leader. Glord's large body lay crumpled, cold as ice, dead. His left hand was clutching his abdomen, his jeweled crown still on his head, his mouth surrounded by bloody foam. His eyes bulged as if in amazement. He had somehow pulled himself back onto the throne. He would not die on the filthy ground. He was King!

Those around Robert were unable to hold him back. He grabbed Glord's torso, and, screaming and cursing, he beat the corpse's face with his fist. Then, like a madman, he took the king's long sword out of its sheath and slashed and slashed until he fell exhausted to the ground.

*   *   *

Hope marveled at the results of their strategy, at the astuteness and intellect behind it all. Robert had been right in his prediction. He had assured them that after each victory, Glord always celebrated by rewarding *all* his officers and soldiers with the meat of the defeated. To ensure that every warrior relished at least one large bit of human flesh, Glord sometimes even killed some of the captives. Each cannibalistic orgy deepened the bonding of his horde.

Hope walked proudly among the dead. What a stroke of genius his grandfather had masterminded and his father had made reality! Emile had long ago devised the plan, because he believed that otherwise this part of the world would become not a bastion of hope, but a center of hate. New Earth, if he could do anything about it, would not be a hell for its people.

Hope abruptly stopped his pacing when he saw a freshly broiled human forearm a few feet away. Most of the flesh was gone, exposing the long, skinny white bones. Yet the hand had not been totally consumed and was still surrounded by nourishing flesh. Its bloodied fingers were still whole. The fist was closed, as if in anger. What a sacrifice his brave people had made to ensure the survival of their group! The remnants of cannibalism lay all around him. The smell and sight brought back deep-rooted feelings. He looked closer at the hand. The impulse was too strong to hold back. Memories rushed through his mind.

Hope knelt and picked up the bloody arm. Without hesitation, he brought the still-intact hand to his mouth. Those around him looked on in horror and disbelief. "No!" screamed one of Hope's officers. She pointed her rifle at her master. "No!"

But instead of biting, Hope tenderly kissed the small ring on his father's hand, then pressing it to his cheek, he began to weep. "Thank you, my dear father," he murmured. "Had you not first volunteered, there would have been no salvation for your descendants. Thank you, Papá. I'm sorry it had to end like this, but again your love has brought us life."

* * *

A few weeks earlier when the defeat of Westfort had become inevitable, Paul had reminded everyone of the availability of the poisoning stratagem devised years prior by Dr. LeBlanc. After much debate, two volunteers, the oldest women of the fort, said that they had already lived long enough. They were not willing to be incarcerated and suffer the rape and other humiliations that Glord would impose upon them in defeat. But just two volunteers were not enough to produce the necessary effect. They needed at least eight or ten volunteers to be able to provide sufficient food for most of Glord's army. The Westfort survivors were markedly outnumbered by now. Glord had not completely destroyed them only because he wanted as many of them alive as possible. An easy, victorious attack had been at Glord's hand for days now. But the value of the human booty was too high for him to waste.

After the old women spoke, Paul made his own decision. He had been toying with the idea for days. He would not surrender; he would rather die. He knew that his son, Hope, and many other men, would also choose death over surrender, and would die in the last battle. So Paul too volunteered for the sacrifice. Many protested that Paul was too valuable, and in immediate response Hope and other young people also volunteered. But after a long discussion, it was decided to accept Paul's offer and that of seven others in addition to the two original women. With Paul as the leader, the negotiation scheme would be believable and the plan's success insured.

The poison had been administered to the volunteers intravenously. Carefully formulated years back by Dr. LeBlanc but only recently concocted, it would remain stable and harmless in the volunteers' blood. Once ingested by the cannibals, it would first be changed into a different chemical by the acid and digestive juices of the stomach and duodenum. This new substance would remain unabsorbed until it reached the distal small intestine and large bowel, one to two hours after consumption. Then, the new chemical would be activated by bacteria in the large bowel to an absorbable form that was lethal even at small concentrations.

It was known that, to avoid poisoning, the barbarians would force-feed some of their less valued slaves and await the results, as Roman Emperors did millennia ago. Since within the first hour or so after consumption there would be no negative results, the barbarians would feel secure and embark on their last orgy of victory and cannibalism. By the time the taster slaves started to show symptoms of envenomation, it would be too late for any that had eaten even the slightest amount of human flesh. The time capsule of death in their digestive systems would be merciless, and they would die a quick, agonizing death.

* * *

The barbarians' nearby stronghold, now devoid of effective leaders and warriors and protected only by a few jailers, was easily conquered. Among the many children, over a hundred were Glord's. His oldest son, his name carefully chosen for its desired effect, Barrabas, was subdued only with great difficulty. The slaves — over a thousand men, women and children — were set free.

CHAPTER 28

QUEBEC XIII.
NOVEMBER 1, YEAR 19 P.I.
DEATH OR SALVATION

"In the year 1999 and seven months, from the sky will descend the great king of terror."

Nostradamus (1503-1566 A.D.)

ope was helping to tear down the remains of the outer walls of the fortification. "I told Robert and his crew to keep the north tower and part of the north wall around it intact," he told his mother as they gazed around at the busy survivors. "They are the only parts not burned. We should keep them as a monument to those who died here. I want something to be left of Westfort," he went on. "Something to remain as a testament to those who helped keep us alive: my father, your father, and the hundreds who gave their lives for freedom and a decent New World."

Moisture appeared in Trisha's eyes as she resumed work. "Gather more of that wood, children, and stack it over by that cart," she instructed the youngsters around her, most frolicking in the pretense of work. "We are going to celebrate New Year's Day tonight, so we need to clean up this place. It is also Hope's birthday."

She gazed with pride at the little boys and girls around her and at her own baby girl, now four years old. Some of the babies were her grandchildren by Hope, and there was even one by Jenny, who had finally achieved fertility. But Trisha also felt a pang of great sadness. Her husband was dead, and it had been so close. They could all be dead now or enslaved. It seemed a miracle that a future actually stretched before them. They now had the daunting task of rebuilding the civilization so abruptly and cruelly lost. It would take many centuries before there existed again the comforts that they had taken for granted only two decades ago. The task was formidable.

* * *

Trisha's thoughts were interrupted by the distant sound of something at first only vaguely familiar, a sound which she couldn't rationalize or identify, but which simultaneously brought upon her a sense of expectation, vulnerability and fear.

She and Hope froze for a second as everyone in the camp stopped their laboring to listen.

From very far away, beyond the clouds, to the southwest, they could hear it. The sound was clearer now. It was coming closer and approaching very fast.

Trisha gasped and covered her mouth with one hand as she recognized the sound. Hope recoiled with horror at the new, unknown threat. Like a child he ran to his mother and put his arm around her. "Mother, what is it?"

The small children, sensing fear in the adults, started to cry, some grabbing onto Trisha's skirt. With the strength that comes along with motherhood, she pulled them towards her like a magnet. "Hush!" she said. "It's an airplane and it's coming this way."

"An airplane?" Hope asked in disbelief. Hope and all the children continued to stare at her in bewilderment.

"Oh, I'm sorry," she said. "None of you have ever heard an airplane. You've never seen a real one!"

The other members of the camp gathered outside by the crumbled remains of the main building. Hope, Trisha, Jenny, Ervi, Pierre and the children joined them. Robert rushed inside a building.

Hope found himself overwhelmed by this new potential enemy. An airplane! He had seen pictures of them. They had transported goods and people high above the clouds, another of the so many things from the past that were incomprehensible to him. He had heard that such machines could travel from Montreal to San Francisco in just a few hours. Some could even fly into space. He had also seen pictures of military airplanes that carried enough armaments to destroy anything and everything for hundreds of miles around them. Why was this airplane coming toward them? Were they to struggle in war all over again?

His shoulders sagged in despair. He and his people had absolutely no hope against an army of airplanes! They were doomed! All had been to no avail. He had been naive to believe in peace. "Mother, I don't think I can fight any more battles," he said. "How can we stand up against this type of enemy?"

The clouds beyond parted, as if being pushed aside. The huge military airplane, over two hundred feet long, appeared suddenly. They all gasped in awe. It slowly descended, approaching the encampment. Its wings rotated, converting the jet into a hovering craft. The engines slowed to a barely audible hum, keeping the craft motionless one hundred feet above the ground and three hundred feet away from their group. Hope feared the intruder but marveled at the immensity of the military transport vehicle. He was awed at how complete it was; how perfect; how powerful.

The children were all crying, shocked at the sight of such an incredible machine, much larger than they could ever have dreamed existed. Only a small percentage of the population of Westfort were old enough to remember airplanes. Even Jenny, twenty-one years old now, was terrified.

Robert darted out of the building with a communicator in his hand. "Identify yourselves," he shouted into the radio.

A few seconds of silence went by before the tension was finally broken. "Well! Thought you'd never ask!" replied a calm man's voice. "We've been trying to communicate with you for a while. You should keep your 'cator bands open, you know."

The voice sounded strange to Hope. There was something different about the voice and accent. He felt even more uneasy.

"Identify yourselves," Robert repeated.

"Sorry, old chap," the voice went on. "You must identify yourselves first."

"I am General Robert Horton," Robert exclaimed, to the surprise of those around him. Granting himself the impressive title, he sounded very much in control, obviously the effect he sought for. "I'm in charge of this fortification." Looking around at the pitiful appearance of the fort and its people, he quickly added, "Don't let our appearance fool you! We are heavily armed and can blow your plane to pieces with the touch of a button."

Laughing, the voice came back. "Unlikely threat, dear chap," it said. "Our scanners show that you have nothing that can harm us."

The bluff hadn't worked. Robert tried to think what to do, when the voice resumed speaking. "Robert Horton, eh? Well, good on you, my friend. We have you on our computer list. From Chicago. An escapee from King Glord's army, I see. Did you know that Glord has a very handsome bounty on your head? Who else is with you?"

Robert stood frozen in disbelief. How could they possibly know of him? What if they found out that his group had killed Glord?

Hope abruptly grabbed the communicator and shouted into it, "Hope Lopez-LeBlanc here! What do you want of us?"

"One moment, young man. Calm down, remain cool," replied the stranger. "We don't have you on our list, but we do have a Paul Lopez and an Emile LeBlanc as positive survivors for these areas."

Positive survivors? What could he mean by that? Trisha wondered as she took the communicator from Hope's hand. "Trisha, that is, Patricia LeBlanc-Lopez. My husband Paul Lopez and father Emile LeBlanc are both dead."

"Patricia. That's right, we have you in our computer files too. What's your citizen's pin number, Trisha?"

My personal identification number? she thought in shock. *My God, why would they want my number?* "Well, I haven't needed to use it since Impact. I know I used it hundreds of times a week prior to Impact, but I really don't remember."

"Please try, and you too, Mr. Horton."

After a few seconds of silence Robert seemed to come back to life. He grabbed the little radio. "082597-381-88-9535," he recited. It had come back so naturally that he wondered in amazement how he could have forgotten it.

"092197-296-40-5260," Trisha slowly pronounced.

The younger people, including Hope, looked on bewildered. What on Earth were citizen's numbers? What did all this mean?

"Very good," the officer's voice came back, "I see the equipment remains of Glord's army all around you. But where are Glord and his people?"

Hope looked around. They were powerless and doomed. It would be useless and stupid to try to fool these people. They would find out soon enough anything they wanted to know. He took the communicator and announced, "They had us totally surrounded." Then almost apologetically, "But we managed to destroy them. They are all dead!"

"Whoa! You'll have to tell us later how you managed that!"

The huge plane came down for a perfect, smooth and controlled landing. The captain's voice spoke again from their communicator:

"The horror stories of Glord and his barbarian court have circled the globe. You seem to have achieved the impossible! We thought we wouldn't make it here in time. You needn't worry any longer, Santa Claus has come! Good on you, my friends."

"Who the hell is Santa Claus?" Hope asked, looking at his mother in bewilderment. Could it be that the tone of voice was now actually friendly? Or was this some kind of cruel joke?

"Sorry, folks, but we had to ensure correct identification and take time for our scanners to survey the entire area," the man went on. Then he added, with amazement, "You really did kill them all! Congratulations!"

The survivors of Westfort looked at each other in bewilderment as the ship's engines were turned off.

"You are the last stop on our trip to make contact with survivors of the North American continent."

"Down under! That's it," Robert exclaimed with sudden recognition. "That accent! They're from Australia."

"Sorry we're so late, but we've been battling our own wars during the last few years. It seems every group of surviving humans in the Pacific basin wanted to conquer Australia and New Zealand."

As a huge ramp opened from the side of the plane, the survivors read the ship's name: *Noah's New Ark — The Confederacy of New Zealand and Australia, Australian Division.*

"They're friends!" Trisha exclaimed as she started forward. The others followed in a rush.

As the plane's huge door opened, the survivors beheld miraculous gifts. Leash-held by smiling, uniformed men and women were sheep, goats, cows, pigs and llamas. Unlike the fabled ark, this ship brought two females of each, each one pregnant, along with freeze-dried semen for artificial insemination. There were also horses! Trisha and the other adults shouted in delight. Finally, a reliable means of transportation in a world without roads, and the help they needed so badly for plowing the fields! The Australians had also brought chickens, ducks and geese, each followed by a line of noisy young. Finally, puppies and kittens. Man's best friends had survived too!

The ambassadors released wild birds and bats to help control insects and distribute the seeds of the woods and grasslands around them, and in plastic containers brought a variety of juvenile fish to restock the many lakes of the area. There were also thousands of pounds of seeds and tree seedlings for reforesting the ravished land.

The captain explained that the seeds they had brought were specifically selected to produce crops of high yield that generated low levels of methane, to reduce as much as possible the greenhouse gases. He also explained that one of the many reasons for their delay in distributing all these gifts had been the need to harvest sufficient volume of seeds and animal stocks for dispersal throughout the world.

The Australians also brought books, pens and paper, and entire encyclopedias on how to rebuild civilization and replenish the planet's soil and waters with a new, balanced ecosystem.

Finally, they released a most precious gift: bees and butterflies! Without them there would be no hope for flowering trees and bushes. Without them there would be no fruiting trees or wildflowers, and Quebec's land would never live as it had once before.

During the next hours, information flowed between the visitors and the New Quebeckers. The ship's captain reported that there were probably fewer than six million humans left alive on the face of the planet, about the same number as had populated the Earth in Neolithic times, nine-thousand years earlier.

He went on to explain how New Zealand and Australia and the rest of the most southern parts of the planet had been the first to emerge into spring, and that of the many underground silos managed by the United Nations, only those in Mongolia, Japan, Antarctica, Argentina, South Africa and New Zealand survived the direct effects of Impact, the ice age, looters, and the great floods. A few other similar but smaller shelters and silos, including two in Australia, had survived also. The crews of these shelters had managed not only to survive throughout all the natural disasters that accompanied Impact, but had fended off all attempted invasions by marauding gangs. Thanks to them, the world now had sufficient plankton, seeds, frozen embryos and eggs to ensure the viability of thousands of species from the vegetable and animal kingdoms, especially most of those that humans needed for survival.

The new Republic of Patagonia was replenishing animals and plant stock to the few survivors of eastern and northern South America. Chile took charge of the countries of western South America and Central America. Amongst all the countries of the world, New Zealand had been affected least by Dis'Aster. Mortality there had been only about eighty-five percent. Australia and New Zealand had formed a confederacy, and while New Zealand and the Japanese helped most of Asia, the Australians had all of North America. The South African countries had the formidable task of restoring the essential living supplies to the few survivors of what was left of Africa and Northeastern Europe. The Mongolians had the rest of the world.

"You are lucky that we have been able to reach you so far away from our homeland," explained the captain. "This area is the farthest habitable zone in what's left of North America. You are also lucky, in that from here west lies the new breadbasket of the world. Scientists have calculated that what used to be Quebec and western Canada will now be the most fertile land for growing wheat and other cereals. You should be proud." And then, looking all around him, he added with a sigh, "What a strong people you must be to have overcome all that you have confronted!"

The children were amazed by all they were seeing and hearing, but were still very afraid. While they watched in awe, Trisha embraced half a dozen puppies and kittens. "Don't be afraid, children, come play with the little animals," she urged.

The puppies and kittens, overcome with happiness at the presence of youngsters, threw themselves into the children's arms. Children and adults all laughed as the most playful of the puppies toppled over one of the younger of the children and licked her face. The child's face lit up with laughter, and the puppy barked with glee as a new friendship was bonded on New Earth.

EPILOGUE

By the end of the First Century P.I., the world was progressing with extraordinary momentum. The first half of that century saw much warfare, but eventually the higher values of humankind prevailed. By the end of that historic century, almost 22 million humans lived on New Earth. This new age saw those inhabitants peacefully working side by side, some exploring and recolonizing, others building towns, cities and countries out of the wasteland. And then there were those who retrieved and rebuilt the technology which had existed prior to Impact. But the most important chore was to restock the lands and oceans with plants, insects, plankton, fish, animals and birds.

Finally, through cunning and preparation, humankind had paid back its debt to Mother Earth. Her skin was pocked once again; but this time, man, the pride of her creation, had the medicine with which to heal her. And most importantly, those children, and the generations that forever followed after...they would see to it that their Mother Earth would never again be forced to spend millions of her precious years recovering from any other Dis'Aster.

AUTHOR'S NOTES

In this novel an attempt is made to fuse fiction and science. While much of the scientific data included in this novel is accurate and as up-to-date as possible, the book is not intended as a scientific treatise. Much scientific license has been used. Readers should realize that even the most current information available on subjects related to comet impacts and mass extinctions are subject to conjecture. Different theories exist regarding the cosmic and planetary issues explored. The author has brought forth in this book only those issues that he finds most appealing. There are, in libraries and book stores, many excellent books which explore these matters more completely; most of them are easy reads even for the non-scientist.

As comets and asteroids travel through space, their trajectories frequently bring them in close proximity to the planets, including Earth. The surfaces of the solid planets: Mercury, Venus, Earth and Mars — and the surfaces of most moons of the solar system, are pocked with craters. Most of these craters are not the result of volcanic activity, but are scars left over from impacts with comets and asteroids (planetesimals).

Over 180 craters on the Earth have been unequivocally identified as being produced by collisions with planetesimals and the geological record indicates that every few million years a catastrophe of immense magnitude affects the thin coating of life that exists on our planet. One such event made for the extinction of the dinosaurs and at the same time extinguished over seventy percent of the species that lived on the Earth at that time. Other similar, but more remote episodes have resulted in over ninety percent extinction rates.

During the last few decades, sporadic near misses have been documented in which small asteroids have flown relatively near our planet. Prior to present time, we did not have the means to identify these potential impactors.

The collision of our planet with a large planetesimal could happen any day. Are the people of Earth ready? A small planetesimal striking the Earth could kill a few million people and leave the rest of the world unharmed. But if the uninvited visitor is big, let's say three to eight miles in diameter, as many of them are, the impact would kill billions and thrust so much dirt and smoke into the atmosphere that the entire globe would be covered with black clouds.

Imagine our planet with clouds totally blocking the sunlight for one or more years. The biomass would freeze. Most of all living creatures would die. Could humans, with all their intelligence and technology, survive several years of global temperatures below the freezing point? a few years without crops, cattle, chicken, fish?, without the ability to farm and produce medicinal herbs, vitamins and other essentials? Cities and towns not destroyed by the initial explosion or tsunamis would be covered for years with many yards of snow and ice. The tropics could suffer almost one hundred percent extinction. Could any human on the planet survive? Are we prepared today, or has our present state of complacency already doomed *Homo sapiens* to extinction?

* * *

On June 30th, 1908, at 7:17 a.m., a small planetesimal, measuring approximately 300 feet and weighing some 100,000 metric tons, devastated a desolate forest area in Siberia. The Tugunska planetesimal exploded in the atmosphere with a force of 10 megatons, destroying all the trees in a region 31 x 24 miles wide. The comet or asteroid never hit the ground, yet its effects were catastrophic. Observers saw a huge fireball with a blazing tail over 500 miles long. A few reindeer herdsmen inhabited the area. Five were killed, as were over one thousand of their reindeer. Had the Tugunska comet arrived only 4 hours, 47 minutes later, its explosion would have leveled

Leningrad, killing most of its inhabitants. How many millions would die if a similar small comet exploded tomorrow over London or San Francisco? Had Tugunska exploded over the Atlantic Ocean just east of New York City, the resulting tsunami waves would have hit a metropolis totally unprepared. Hundred of thousands, maybe even millions would have drowned or been killed by collapsing buildings as the enormous waves bashed the defenseless city.

On October 30, 1937, Hermes, one of the "Apollo" asteroids that routinely approach Earth's orbit, passed by our planet at a distance of 559,000 miles, only about twice the distance to our moon. This is considered a near miss in astronomical terms: a deviation of only a minute angle in trajectory can mean thousands of miles on a long-distance scale. Hermes, a good-sized asteroid of 1 mile in diameter, could one day impact the Earth.

10,000 to 30,000 years ago, and possibly witnessed by the early Indians of the North American Southwest, a solid iron meteorite roughly 50 yards in diameter fell near what is now Flagstaff, Arizona. Traveling at 25,000 miles per hour, the 50,000 ton hunk of metal exploded on impact, leaving a crater almost one mile wide and 984 feet deep. It killed all living creatures for at least 30 miles around its impact point. Any animals or humans looking at the strange apparition from the skies would not have wondered at its meaning for long, as they would have been incinerated only a few seconds after impact.

In June, 1178 A.D., the moon was apparently hit by a one-mile diameter asteroid. The huge explosion from the impact was witnessed by humans as a flaming torch on the upper horn of a thin crescent new moon. Gervase, a monk from Canterbury, recorded his own story of the incident, which he himself had witnessed. At the described location, the moon bares a very recent 13 mile wide crater called Giordano Bruno. Had that asteroid instead hit our planet, the huge fireball would have killed many, and the ensuing mini-ice age, though small in comparison to others of the past, would have set civilization back hundreds of years, delaying the advent of the Renaissance and the Industrial Revolution. We might today still be in the Dark Ages. It doesn't take much to change our climate. The clouds from the volcanic eruption of a single volcano, Krakatoa, in August, 1883, produced "the year without a summer" that resulted in famines and plagues all over the world. Hundred of thousands died.

In the evening of March 31, 1965, a huge explosion occurred over a desolate area of British Columbia. The object, probably an icy comet, flew over that part of Canada and exploded high in the air over the town of Revelstoke with an energy release equivalent to that produced by the Hiroshima bomb. Had its timing been only slightly different, it might have exploded over Washington or Moscow. A nuclear war could easily have been initiated had the explosion been interpreted as the first in a series of incoming nuclear warheads, but all the explosion left was a fine layer of dust over the snow.

On August 10, 1972, a large meteorite weighing a few thousand tons grazed the Earth's upper atmosphere 30 miles above ground level. The huge fireball streaked and skipped through the day skies of Utah, Idaho, Wyoming, Montana and Alberta, a distance of 1000 miles. It was seen and its sonic boom heard by thousands of people in plain daylight before it departed the atmosphere in the skies above western Canada. Had its trajectory been minutely different, it could just as easily have landed on Salt Lake City or disintegrated over mid-town Calgary. The meteorite would have exploded on hitting the ground, releasing a fireball of energy measuring at least one mega-ton. In October 1996, a similar skimming meteorite, heading east over North America, skipped over Artesia, New Mexico, went back into orbit, and re-entered the atmosphere, only to bounce off again over the Pacific Ocean near Los Angeles, California.

At sunset on December 10, 1984, a brilliant fireball was seen over Statesboro, Georgia (USA). Twenty-five miles further south, people were alarmed at a strong whistling sound that reminded a Vietnam veteran of an incoming mortar round. A three-pound mete-orite fell 112 feet away from him, demolishing a mailbox before em-bedding itself 11 inches into the ground.

One of the most spectacular impacts occurred recently. In north central Argentina, some 300 miles from where the Buenos Aires me-tropolis lies today, a group of 10 oblong pits pock the otherwise grain fields. The largest pit measures 3 miles by two-thirds of a mile. Some postulate that the Rio Cuarto depressions represent scars left over from a smallish asteroid or comet that fragmented and struck there only five to eight thousand years ago. Based on research of the crater field, it seems evident that the solid structure, at least 500 feet across, approached from the north on a very shallow glancing angle of only 10 to 15 degrees. It must have been visible to the Indians of South America for thousands of miles before it hit the ground. Coming in at 14 miles per second, the fireball must have been spectacular. If a similar impact were to level Buenos Aires today, two or three million people would die in less than ten seconds.

A one-quarter-mile asteroid (1989-FC) was discovered after it whisked by the Earth in April 1989, at a distance of only 450,000 miles. It has a short orbit and swings by the Earth every 13 months. Scientists have estimated that other objects of about the same size or larger fly by the Earth at least every couple of years. Most are never seen, since astronomers just don't have the time to pick up these brief encounters during their sky surveys. Studies of its orbit show that in some of its next passages, 1989-FC will come even closer to our planet. Probably 1200 feet across, if it hit the Earth it would dig a crater 10 miles wide and one-half mile deep, and explode with a force equivalent to 2,000 one-megaton hydrogen bombs. Everything within a 40-50 mile radius would be incinerated and the changes to our climate and agriculture would be devastating.

On April 6, 1990, a one-pound meteorite crashed through the roof of a house in Glanerburg in Holland, and broke apart. The owners were out at the time and found the hole in the ceiling upon returning home. Calculations of the meteorite's trajectory indicated that it was a fragment of the half-mile-wide asteroid known as Midas 81. If Midas itself had fallen on Holland, it would have destroyed most of that country, killing most, if not all, of its inhabitants.

On May 17, 1990, a fiery bolide plowed into a Russian farmer's recently planted wheat field only 745 miles east of Moscow. The one-yard-diameter, pure iron meteorite excavated a crater 33 feet wide and 13 feet deep. The meteorite, very small as compared to most

Earth-crossing asteroids, weighed 3,000 pounds, and the impact produced an explosion equivalent to that generated by setting off one and a half tons of dynamite. Had it instead crashed into a crowded apartment building or into a train or busload of people, many would have died.

Only during the last few decades has there been enough interest in the dangers of asteroid and comet impacts to search for and document them. One or two small but significant impacts must occur every century; most have gone undocumented. And since the Earth is two-thirds ocean, most fall in the seas and go unnoticed by man.

On the 17th of January, 1991, astronomers discovered a small asteroid, only 30 feet across, as it rushed by the Earth at 25,000 miles per hour. At its closest approach it was only 106,000 miles from our planet, the closest approach of any asteroid discovered to that date. Had the little asteroid crashed into the Earth, it would have exploded with an energy release equivalent to 10 Hiroshima bombs. Had this occurred over the Middle East, the nations at war there at the time would most certainly have interpreted it as a nuclear warhead, and within minutes many real nuclear devices could have been detonating all over the area. More recently, in May 1996, Carl Hergenrother and Tim Spahr, young astronomy students from the University of Arizona, discovered the largest asteroid so far to pass by the Earth at a distance of less than 280,000 miles. The 400 yard planetesimal could one day strike our planet, causing massive local destruction and probably worldwide famine-producing changes in climate that could last a few years.

During July 1994, Comet Shoemaker-Levy 9, the most important comet of the present era, made us aware of a startling reality. The large comet, fragmented by the force of Jupiter's gravity, fell piece by piece onto the giant planet. The spectacular event was awesome and yet also terrifying. Had the same comet fallen instead on Earth, many millions, possibly billions of us, would have died.

Now that we have evidence of the association between massive extinctions and planetesimal impacts, Comet Shoemaker-Levy 9 arrived to warn us of the ever-present danger of incredibly major global disasters.

A mile-wide meteorite-induced crater has been discovered buried under the wheat fields of central Nebraska. Evidence indicates that this impact occurred only 3,000 years ago. A blazing fireball, 50 times brighter than the sun, must have been witnessed by the local Native Americans as it plunged through the atmosphere. If a similar small impact were to occur today over any highly populated area, the human death toll could exceed 25 million.

* * *

Luckily for us, the Earth lately has been at peace with larger celestial bodies. Comets and asteroids — planetesimals in the range of hundreds of feet in diameter — only hit the Earth every few thousand years. Those measured in miles seem to strike the Earth every few million years.

The Earth carries only some of the scars from the more recent large cometary encounters. Unlike the other solid planets and most moons of the solar system, the Earth is a dynamic planet, still evolving. Tectonic activity moves the continents very slowly, continuously changing and remodeling the planet's surface. This, together with our rains and winds, has erased most of the craters that were created by planetesimal collisions.

* * *

The worldwide fear of comets among primitive peoples, as harbingers of death, bad luck, famine and wars, suggest that the Earth has suffered relatively major meteoritic impacts during much of humanity's past. Our vocabulary still carries the scars: *Disaster*, from "Dis," Latin for the god of the underworld of death, disease, misfortune and everything that is evil, and "Aster," Greek for star. *Catastrophe* comes from "kata," Greek for downward, something dropping, falling down, and "Astron," star. *Cataclysm* originates from "kata" and "clyzen," Greek words meaning "to fall and wash away." These examples, along with the many prophecies that allude to "stars" falling upon the Earth, indicate an obvious association between human terror and stellular phenomenon (comets and asteroids.) The conclusion is unavoidable; prehistoric humans probably witnessed the holocaust of at least one, and possibly more than one, cometary impacts. Those impacts probably didn't occur within the last 4,000 years, or the writings of the Sumarians, Greeks, and Egyptians would have documented them in detail. Yet they probably could not have occurred more than 12,000 years ago, or comets would not be so prevalent in our existing vocabulary and superstitions. Therefore, a large impact, or impacts, probably occurred between 4,000 and 10,000 years before the present.

In order for the fear of comets to be worldwide, all or most areas of the planet must have been affected by the impacts. If only a single comet collided with the Earth, then only those survivors from a few hundred miles surrounding the impact point would have made the association between comet, death, famine and disease; this is not the case. Instead, quite a few comets must have been identified in the sky ("like cobwebs," as the Hopi prophesy suggests). Our early ancestors must have witnessed many impacts across the globe. For they understood that comets can and do fall from the heavens; and they knew that when they do fall, they are accompanied not only by explosive, destructive consequences, but also by long-term calamitous effects on the weather.

In this book I quote a variety of "prophesies" and historical documents, many from the Bible. They suggest the origin of humanity's fear of comets. John's Book of Revelation, written nearly 2,000 years ago, can be interpreted as an account of events of the distant past dealing with major cataclysms. Most of these disasters arriving as fire from the sky at times when "stars" are falling from the heavens. What did John know that we don't? What had he heard from word of mouth or read in now long lost historical scrolls? What did the scholars of that time teach in *their* history of antiquity?

In January, 1996, a new comet, Comet Hyakutake 2, was discovered by a Japanese amateur astronomer. The huge ball of ice, metal and rock, two miles wide, rushed only 15 million miles by Earth on March 25 of the same year. Had its trajectory been only slightly different, we would have had only three months of warning on the inevitable impact and possible human extinction.

As you read these words, an asteroid or comet may be heading for an collision with our planet. Modern astronomers have only recently begun to devote some of their attention to identifying small asteroids whose orbits cross that of the Earth. With modern computerized telescopes, these astronomers are shocking the scientific community by finding one or more such potential "Dis'Asters" per month, many more than anyone ever expected. The chances of the Earth being hit by one of these bodies increases with time; thus the chances of a significant impact in our immediate future are quite realistic. If that were to occur, a few different scenarios are possible, depending on how close to impact point you are when it happens.

* * *

A strange noise may envelop you quite suddenly, and before you even have time to get up and go to the window to investigate, a small asteroid the size of a house has landed in your town and instantly vaporized you and all of the other thousands or millions of humans living around you. That would be the end of you, yours, and everything dear to you. This is the most merciful scenario.

If the asteroid landed somewhat further from you, let's say one or two dozen miles away, you would not be as fortunate. In this case, you would have time to get up, go to the window and try to figure out the origin of the approaching strange noise. Suddenly, a large rumbling sonic boom would repeatedly bang and rumble as a 10,000 ton ball of sizzling rock and metal flies overhead. All the windows, mirrors, glasses and cups of your home suddenly shatter into smithereens as the sonic boom intensifies. Having been thrown to the floor and almost deafened, you realize that the infernal noise is lessening and your home is no longer shaking.

You get up, and with great trepidation, look out through the now glassless window. You may see nothing unusual. But you will hear the screaming of your neighbors and the ringing of alarms, as your neighborhood falls into chaos, bewilderment and panic. Many, cut or seriously wounded, will be screaming for help. A few seconds will elapse, during which your mind struggles to assess what has happened. Then, miles away, as the flying chunk of rock and metal hits the ground, you find yourself flung to the floor, tumbling like a rag doll, as your house or apartment shakes. "Earthquake!" The word briefly crosses your mind. But what was that that flew over the house and why was there a flash of blinding light? Was it a nuclear bomb? Before you have time for one more thought, the heat shock wave hits your house, setting it and you on fire. The ten or twenty seconds of horrifying pain leave no time for thoughts, reason or comprehension. You can't even hear the multi-megaton explosion that follows, because your ear drums have exploded and you have started to melt. You die squirming, as your lungs expel steam and your brain cells become poisoned with the circulating deadly debris of boiling skin, tissue and blood.

Had you at first rushed to a different window, you might have seen a huge trail of fire and smoke traversing the sky, and you would then have had a few seconds of time to understand that a large meteorite, asteroid or comet had penetrated the atmosphere, passed over your town, and was now heading away from you. You might even have thought, erroneously, that you were lucky, since the horror was heading away from you. But that misconception would have ended very shortly.

But then, maybe the impact doesn't occur that close to you. Imagine yourself comfortably seated in a farm house, surrounded by miles of placid wheat fields. A one- to two-mile wide asteroid or comet impacts, on land or sea, 300 to 500 miles away from you. If you survive the initial shock, earthquakes, and the 200° F heat wave, the fate that would befall you is much worse than you could ever imagine.

A few minutes after the shock wave passed over your home, the skies would abruptly darken. You stagger out of your partially crumbled home and watch in horror as a boiling cloud of blacks and browns rapidly enfolds one of your horizons. This bore front, approaching like a dark hell, is festooned on its perimeter by a medusa of lightning, the likes of which you have never seen or imagined could ever exist. You stare in disbelief at the onrushing monster and notice that the ground under its approaching front is turning into a giant dust storm, laden with destructive tornadoes, which rip the landscape apart and carry with them cars, billboards, humans, cattle and homes.

You might then hasten inside and pray that the strong basement of your masonry home can withstand the onslaught. In the basement you duck under a desk, just before the fury hits your home and levels it. Like a land tsunami, this superheated sludge of dirt and debris rushes over your neighborhood, leaving little standing. As the roar over you diminishes, you feel that you have somehow been spared. The floor above you creaks and starts to crumble. You hurry upwards, climbing over the remains of your home, seeking the safety of the outdoors. You stumble and crash against objects in the midday darkness. *Why is it almost pitch black?* you wonder. You ignore your pain, your cuts and bruises and the bleeding from your wounds, and you scramble outside, where you stand in shock. Your house is gone.

The expanding front of the maddened atmosphere has passed over you. There is almost total darkness. The dry, hot air is filled with dust and smoke. The sky over you is a boiling of dark clouds. All you can see are the fires of a few homes in the distance. You don't hear a human sound. You must be the only one left alive. But now you hear something new, like a developing rain storm approaching. Heavy, thick drops spatter around you. You look forward to the rain water, to cool and cleanse your filthy body and clean your wounds. But when the first drop falls on you, you scream in pain and look straight up toward the source. The blackened sky is shimmering with tiny spots of light that are falling towards you. The white-hot brimstone starts to fall more heavily around you. You scream again, and start running like a maddened animal, as particles of hot ash and white-hot pieces of dirt rain on you till you fall, screaming in agony as each particle burns a hole in your skin, until your whole body is broiling.

But then again, the scenario may be different. A five-mile comet may impact any ocean or landmass, four to six thousand miles away from you. You may think that you are truly lucky to be so far from calamity. Think again. If you are in fact "lucky" enough to live a few thousand miles from impact point, you may be spared the instant death of the impact's crushing earthquakes or scorching shockwave, or the slower death by fire and brimstone; but no one is lucky on a day of cosmic collisions. You will rush not to a window of the office where you work, but instead to the radio or television. In shock, you will learn what has happened far away on another part of the planet. You may have been peacefully at work, but now your life has abruptly changed. Yes, you can understand what is being said over the television, but what it all really means, you cannot yet comprehend. Especially, you cannot grasp the alarm in the voice of the scientist who is trying to explain to the audience the magnitude of the calamity. He is saying that millions are dying due to the disaster, the earthquakes and tsunamis. He is talking about a global ice age, about dying crops, about no food for the cattle and the chickens to eat, which translates to no food for you and yours. He talks about your being forced to stay in your home or in a community shelter for six months or maybe a year or two. Community shelter? Is there one around? He talks about everything you have come to take for granted coming to an abrupt end. This man must be mad! How could he say that transportation for both humans and goods will come to an end in about two to three weeks when the gasoline in all your town's service stations runs out? That there won't be any electricity or running water? No natural gas? What is this about snow falling, even in the tropics? What about the snow not melting for many months or years, turning into yards of solid ice over roads, lakes, even over the streets of your own neighborhood? What is this about acid rain followed by acid snow?

The scientist goes on to talk about the death of most fish and other life forms in the lakes and oceans of the entire world. What? No more trips to the sushi bar? Finally, it would all start to sink in. Suddenly, you realize that you will need food for your family, and extra food for the dog and cat. But wait, the newscaster now lets you know that the Dow has just suffered its worst crash ever, down 97%! You realize that when a major comet or asteroid approaches or lands, the stock market doesn't just crash, it dies! Another newscaster on the television is saying that the tsunami waves are going to be about two miles high and will penetrate and destroy everything 100 miles from much of your country's coastline. Could that really be possible? Could it be true that your mother and father, who reside in a retirement community by the ocean, will be washed away and killed in approximately one-half hour? You rush for a telephone, but, of course, they lines are all taken by others. You try your mobile phone, but all the lines are busy! Without realizing it, you are suddenly rushing to the elevator. You can't understand why none of the elevators are stopping at your floor. You run down seven flights of stairs, and halfway down you finally realize that the chaotic noise around you is coming from hundreds of other people rushing with you down these same stairs.

You start running towards the building where your car is parked. But you see that the supermarket across the street is flooded with people. You hesitate only a second, then rush toward the store, pushing and shoving (so unlike you). You fight with everyone, pushing even little old ladies out of your way, until you can no longer place a single additional item in your cart. You stuff the last ones in your pockets and cradle some in your arms, then try to crash one of the jammed lines. The line is moving unusually fast, you are glad to notice. When you finally get to the counter, you realize what all the yelling is about. The manager is rushing from counter-to-counter, talking secretively with all the cashiers and all the other helpers and handing them something that looks like wads of money and jewelry. You know that all of the employees must also want to go home. Only the promise of something very substantial keeps them there.

The manager shouts, "Only cash; no checks or credit cards! If you don't have cash, then get out and leave your cart right there. Someone else will take it!"

You think how lucky you are that you have just gotten paid, and you went to the bank this very morning. You have $600 cash with you! The basket contents are about $400. The cashier takes one quick look at your cart and says, "One thousand dollars."

"A thousand dollars!" you scream back; "I don't have that much! Listen, this is illegal — you can't — "

The manager appears from nowhere and shouts at you, "Too bad! Next!" You try to reason. "Let me see your wallet!" the manager demands. You hesitate, but take your wallet out. The manager grabs it from you, opens it and removes all of your money. "Six hundred and twenty-one dollars. What else do you have?"

A few minutes later, you cross the street with your cart full of food and not a penny left on you. Also you are minus your gold wedding ring and watch, but you still think you are pretty lucky. You stuff the trunk of your car and start moving out of your parking spot, when you see your best friend from work rushing into the parking area with his own shopping cart full of bags. Suddenly, your friend is on the ground with a crushed skull, as two well-dressed ladies have just hit him on the head with a brick. They take his cart and disappear into the parking area.

You want to help your friend, who is now convulsing in a pool of blood. Nobody else stops to help him. You won't either, because you have to take the food to your home. You drive by his body with tears in your eyes. You are already a savage, fighting for survival.

Life is now back to basics. You realize you have been thrown back 5,000 or even 100,000 years, when survival of the meanest was man's motto.

It takes you more than four hours to get home. "Thank God I had a full tank of gasoline," you mutter. During the worst trip of your life, you saw thousands having to abandon their own vehicles, their cars having run out of gas or overheated in the massive traffic jam. During that unforgettable journey, your radio reported murder and rape, looting and pilferage. Yet impact was so many thousands of miles away. You know now there is no way to control the maddened world around you. Upon comet impact news, law ceases to exist. The police cannot help; they are giving up and rushing home to protect their own loved ones. The National Guard is trying to take over, but the roads are jammed. Helicopters can only carry a few. Only this morning, this was a civil, law-abiding community.

Someone on the radio is talking about blackened skies and no crops for a couple of years. You then realize your foolishness and naivete. How long can you feed your family with this last trip to a supermarket? Four weeks? Can you stretch it to six or eight weeks?

And then what? Without the usual, continual line of trucks and trains bringing hundreds of tons of food daily to your community, and without continually renewed gas supplies for heating and electricity, how long will any of you live? As you near home, you drive by one of the houses of your neighbors and envy them. You know of their survivalist attitudes. You used to make fun of their paranoia. *Would they help me?* you wonder. You consider stopping and begging for a hundred-pound bag of rice. From one of the windows, you notice a rifle barrel sticking out. You realize your mistaken assumption, and wonder instead if everyone in the neighborhood knows how well-prepared they are for this type of an eventuality. But do they have enough weapons? Could they withstand a horde of a few hundred desperadoes?

At home it is all tears and fear. Where is your oldest daughter? Is she alive? If not, was her death merciful? You fear the worst. But you will never, ever know. You start rationing the food, reinforcing the doors and windows. You fill all the bathtubs with water and add a little chlorine to them. No more baths or showers. You hope that between the spa and the bathtubs you have enough water for at least a few months.

And for what? In a few weeks, the many feet of snow covering your home will start turning to ice, crushing it. The darkened skies will not allow the sun to warm the air around you. The spiraling effect of cold turning to colder will bring your community to its knees, then to its death. If you and your family are not killed for your meager rations, or for the flesh on your bones, you will probably all starve or freeze to death in the next four or six months.

* * *

The latest evidence indicates that the comet or asteroid impact that killed the dinosaurs at the Cretaceous-Tertiary border occurred in the Gulf of Mexico. Newly discovered geological formations show that the islands of the Caribbean were walloped by huge tsunami waves, as much as three miles high, 65 million years ago. While elsewhere in the world the deposits of debris from the time of this massive extinction are one to two inches thick, in the Caribbean Islands they are up to 1,500 feet thick. The conglomerated debris is laden with microscopic glassy spheres, shocked quartz (signs of impact) and huge boulders many feet across. The crater from this massive impact is situated at the tip of the Yucatan Peninsula, by Chicxulub, Mexico. It is deeply buried under layers of limestone and measures 186 miles in diameter. It is one of the largest impact craters ever discovered on any solar system body. The intruder must have been truly gigantic, probably a mass of rock, metal and frozen gases measuring 10 miles in diameter.

Whether this behemoth landed on land or the sea, the effects on the world would have been the same: massive extinctions on the land masses and oceans of the entire northern hemisphere, and lesser extinctions in the lands and seas closer to the South Pole. Nevertheless, life on the entire globe was catastrophically diminished.

* * *

Major extinctions wipe out 50% to 90% of families and seem to take place every 26 to 30 million years; minor episodes of extinction, in which only 3% to 20% of species die out, occur every five million years or so. Major extinctions may be produced through impacts with planetesimals five to ten miles in diameter, while lesser extinctions may be associated with impacts due to smaller structures or other causes within the planet, such as vulcanism. Luckily, after each major extinction the survival of some small groups of highly evolved creatures allows the Earth's ecosystem to be replenished in but a few million years. However, if the Earth were to be battered by a truly gigantic asteroid of 25 miles in diameter or larger, the resulting extinction might leave alive only unicellular organisms such as viruses and bacteria. In that case it would take another three billion years for life to once again reach its present form.

* * *

The chances of a planetesimal impacting the Earth are much higher during a comet shower. A sporadic comet like Halley's is unlikely statistically to hit the Earth, just as it is much more likely to hit a flying small bird with a shotgun than with a pistol. Comet showers probably only occur every few million years: either when our solar system approaches a zone of increased planetesimal density in the arms of our Milky Way, or when a star passes close to our own and disturbs the comets of the distant Oort Cloud that encircles us.

The last of the major extinctions occurred in the middle of the Eocene period, roughly 35 million years ago. We are thus at a time in history that is past the 26 to 30 million year periodic extinction cycle that some scientists have proposed. In theory, we should expect another massive extinction soon.

* * *

ARE WE PREPARED FOR THE NEXT IMPACT?

Humans are unique in that we are probably the first species capable of making a difference in the history of a planet such as ours. Like any other life form, humans too can at any time be annihilated by a single planetesimal impact. But if some humans survive, the planet need no longer wait through millions of years of evolution to replenish its lands and waters. For the first time, planet Earth has created a method of self-protection. It has built, within the brain cells of a single marvelous species, the tools for preserving and then transplanting and distributing the most essential plant and animal species, ensuring a much more efficient and rapid recovery period.

Humans can stock deep vaults with seeds, germinating cells, eggs and sperm, and the genetic materials and data of most of the planet's flora and fauna. With the use of cryogenically frozen eggs, and through genetic engineering, the Earth could again be green and teeming with life after a major impact, not in millions of years, but a mere few hundred years. Tons of freeze-dried plankton could be dispersed into the waters. Entire coral reef systems could come alive again. Grasses and selected insects could be distributed in strategically chosen portions of the globe.

* * *

Our fragile planet is always in danger of colliding with a major asteroid or comet. It could happen at any time, maybe even today or tomorrow. Since we never know when the next strike will occur, it is our responsibility to prepare for such a destructive encounter. This can be accomplished by three different modes of planning.

The first is — ANTICIPATION. This requires governments to

direct and support astronomers from all over the world in the search for asteroids and comets in the hope of identifying any Earth-striker years prior to impact. Evacuations and shelters can then significantly reduce the damage to the planet's human population in the event of a known collision. With sufficient time, the threat, may even be averted.

The second is — PRESERVATION. This would ensure for the first time ever in the more than three billion years of Earth's biological history, that disasters of these types would never again obliterate most of the Earth's biological richness. We now have in our hands the tools to ensure that future impacts need not decrease our biological diversity by more than 20% to 30% of important species. We can preserve seeds, eggs and embryos. We are presently in the process of coding the genetic makeup of many species. By these and other methods we can *choose* the species we want to survive, so that logical food chains that take millions of years to evolve can be reinstituted only decades after an impact.

Of course this safeguard can only occur if *Homo sapiens* survive. Therefore, the third necessity is — SHELTER. Deep and large shelters must be built throughout the world. It is our responsibility to preserve ourselves. Not just for our individual self preservation, but also because we may be the only intelligent creature in our galaxy, perhaps the only one in the entire universe!

It is then our responsibility to immediately accelerate research in the sciences that lead toward anticipation, preservation and sheltering.

And the need is urgent. If a major impact occurs in the next few decades, we may already have lost precious time in the quest for non-extinction. It could well be our own fault, if, ten or twenty years from now, the Earth is forced to struggle toward a new biological healing, this time without horses or dogs, cattle or sheep; without salmon, tuna or herring; chickens or ducks, egrets or ostriches. Without wheat, corn, rice, potatoes or squash. Without zebras, llamas, elephants, wildebeests or lions. Without tropical forests or coral reefs.

And what of humans? Could we survive an impact if unprepared? Are we ready for Dis'Aster now? And if some of us do survive, could we live, sharing our planet with only rats, cockroaches, lichen, moss, flies and worms? Could we wait 3 to 10 million years for nature to repopulate the planet? Could we propagate our species and repopulate the planet without wheat, corn or rice, chicken or cattle? How many decades could we survive on old canned food? Maybe we won't deserve to survive, or maybe we won't want to live with the shame of our own stupidity. We could have been ready!

L. Eduardo Vega, M.D. is a pathologist living in Tucson, Arizona. Surrounded by both professional and amateur stargazing astronomer friends and professional world class observatories in the "Astronomical Capital of the World", Ed pursues his life long passion for astronomy. Having obtained his first telescope as a teenager in the Dominican Republic, his interest in astronomy exploded after looking through the magnificent telescopes built for him by Mr. Max Bray of Phoenix. Together, Ed and his wife Patricia conceived the idea of an astronomical observatory dedicated to education, one that would be specifically designed for teaching astronomy and related sciences to the public (especially children). In 1990 the Vegas opened the Vega-Bray Observatory, one of the largest and most complete amateur astronomical observatories in the world. In 1995 they opened Skywatcher's Inn, a first class Bed and Breakfast lodging facility, adjacent to the Observatory. For more information on the Vega-Bray Observatory and Skywatcher's Inn see *Sky and Telescope Magazine* (December 1995 pp.74-76 and August 1999, pp.84-85) or view their web page at: http://www.communiverse.com/skywatcher For more information or reservations for Skywatcher's Inn contact vegasky@azstarnet.com, or call 520-586-7906.